WHISPERS OF THE ELDEROAK

DAUGHTER OF THE EARTH TRILOGY
BOOK 1

K.M. GORDON

K.M. GORDON

MY DEAREST READERS

Writing is often emotional and raw, this book being no exception. Though there are many humorous and cozy moments, this book deals with some challenging topics and hard scenes. I wanted Ava's struggles to be realistic as she tries to navigate and find her place in the world. If you would like a list of content warnings, you can check out my website at www.km-gordon.com on the 'books' page. I decided not to list them here to avoid potential spoilers, but know that this is a fantasy book with a war brewing so it does include violence and other difficult scenes. Please take care of your mental health and take a break should you need to.

I hope you enjoy Ava's journey and thank you from the bottom of my heart for supporting my very first novel. I'm honored to share Whispers of the Elderoak with you.

All my love,

K.M. Gordon

To those of you who are trying to find your place in the world. Just remember if anyone stands in your way, crush them.

WHISPERING BOG
ELDEROAK
MONTERRE
MOSSHAVEN
EMERALD MOUNTAINS
OAKSHIRE
GREYWOOD FOREST
PORTAL FROM AVA'S FARM
DAEMON WA

HAN
BOREALIS
ROSTHAVEN
CAELESTIA
ONDING
IGNEOTHENIA
TORVAK
SAXUMDALE
CHIRNHOLD

1

va Winslow was accustomed to being alone. In fact, she often reveled in it. The tranquility soothed her, allowed ample opportunity to just breathe; to be herself. But true loneliness had crept its way into her life, like she was singing a song but no one was there to listen.

And now she had no one at all.

Hands on her hips, she released a sigh as she stood in the foyer of her late grandfather's farmhouse, surveying the few boxes she had just finished unloading. It had been nearly twenty years since she last saw him, and now she was the unexpected owner of his fifteen-acre flower farm.

She wandered down the hallway, fingers caressing the peeling plaster along the wall as she was flooded with memories. She had always known her mother had magic, had witnessed her speaking to animals and reviving plants with just a wave of her hand. Ava would laugh and beg her to do it again, just to see each brown crunchy leaf unfurl and return to its former verdancy.

The farm was where she had giggled as she chased her mother through the fields, catching her as she feigned defeat.

I

Where they had created daisy crowns and adorned each other's heads, dubbing themselves queen and princess while they pretended her grandfather was an evil sorcerer bent on capturing them.

Ava passed the intricately carved wooden staircase and entered the living room. Tall picture windows were framed by ivory floral curtains that swayed in the breeze, looking over the property where a massive oak tree provided shade—the one she used to swing under while her mother sang songs in a strange, mystical language.

The farm had been a refuge for her and her mother. Where Ava could truly be herself, free from the sneers of other children on the playground; the snide remarks they made when she would rather speak to a bluebird on the fence than play with her peers. Where she didn't have to worry about being cornered behind her school, cowering beneath hateful words. *'Your mom's a witch! Witch! Witch!'* She'd cover her ears with her hands, trying to muffle their chants.

It made sense her family was viewed that way. Her home had been full of dried flowers and herbs and her mother and grandfather worshiped a goddess they called The Earth Mother. While Ava found her family's faith endearing, she learned people didn't like different; they feared what was deemed other. So, she shoved her beliefs into a box and never spoke of it outside of home.

She plopped down on the plush couch, opening the box sitting on the coffee table. As she flipped open the top, her eyes caught on a photo of her as a child with her mother. They were smiling in the kitchen, covered in flour as her mother taught her how to make chocolate chip cookies. The corners of her eyes welled with tears as she stared at the picture, a lump sitting tightly in her throat.

Slamming the box shut, she wiped off the wetness of her cheeks and rose, carrying it to a nearby coat closet in the hallway. Opening the door, she placed the box on the floor and shoved it as far back as possible, as if she could shove her sorrow inside with it and lock it away forever.

SHE DROVE along the dirt road in her run-down SUV, classical music providing tranquility to her commute to town. Though the circumstances were devastating, she found herself glad to be back. She hadn't known her grandfather well—he was a peculiar man with proclivities for secrets—but she remembered the way his eyes crinkled when he smiled. How he'd gasp in amazement when Ava would sprint toward him, little arms full of flowers she had discovered on her self-proclaimed adventures.

One day, Ava and her mother had stopped visiting. She'd been around twelve years old when her mother sat her down over her favorite dinner of homemade ravioli and informed her that Grandpa was too sick, and their visits had started to distress him. It had remained just the two of them until the world stole her mother from her just before her thirtieth birthday. And now, almost three years later, it stole her grandfather too.

The road turned paved and curved through the hills as a sign appeared in the distance, welcoming her to the small town.

Piney Hollow. Population: 1,371

Seeing the sign after so many years rocked her more than she thought it would, reminding her of the trips to town she would take with her mother. After her death, she hadn't really cared to meet new people or forge new friendships. Her mother had been the only person who truly understood her oddities. What hope could she have that someone else would? She had cried and raged, her grief so raw and intense she drowned in it and was only recently pulling herself back out.

Now that she was in a new town, perhaps she could push herself to make a friend or two. She could only hope.

Ava drove around, giving herself a brief tour to re-familiarize herself with the layout and passed by a quaint library, post office, and a couple of charming antique shops. At last, she found the only supermarket in town and pulled into a parking spot just as their lights turned off, closing for the night.

Abandoning her quest for groceries, she pulled back onto the main road and made a U-turn, parking in front of a small diner with a neon sign above the door that read *Mel's*.

She entered the diner, the smell of grease and coffee hovering in the air. Booths of worn maroon and chipped tables lined the densely decorated walls. Old wagon wheels, vintage photos and hub caps took up so much space, the color of the peeling paint was indiscernible. She sighed with relief at the low lighting, making it easier to hide among the shadows.

"Take a seat anywhere you like," announced a middle-aged waitress, moving from table to table with her graying hair and navy polo.

Ava made her way to an empty booth in the back corner and took her seat, hunching down in the dim space. Though she had visited her grandfather's farm as a child, she wasn't sure if the locals remembered her or if they'd heard any rumors regarding her being the new proprietor. Shoulders slumping at the possibility of being judged yet again, she buried her face in the menu as she waited for the waitress.

As she finished scanning the offerings, she was interrupted by a gruff voice. "Hey there. You must be Ava. I'm Mel, the owner. What can I get ya?" said the man, flipping the page of a small note pad and pulling a pencil from behind his ear.

He was tall and wide, his presence taking up ample space. Looking to be in his early sixties, he donned the same polo as the waitress and a dirty black apron that had seen better days.

She returned the greeting with a smile. "Hi. It's nice to meet you. Um—how did you know my name?" She tucked a lock of her strawberry blonde waves behind her ear, then fiddled with the peeling plastic on the menu.

"It's a small town," he chuckled. "Everyone knows everyone. You'll get used to it." He ran his hand through his receding gray hair. "I promise we don't bite."

She laughed, unsure what to say. "Thanks. Um... I'll have a mushroom swiss burger and fries. What beer do you have on tap?"

His booming laugh bounced off the walls. "Tap? Where do you think you are?" he joyfully teased. "We don't have anything on tap here. We can give you a fancy glass though, so you feel like you're back in the big city."

"Oh, sorry. I'll just have a Coors. Thanks." Her cheeks warmed at her faux pas.

Mel wrote down her order and wandered off, chuckling to himself and mumbling something about 'city folk.'

A few minutes later, the waitress arrived with her plate of steaming food, looking mildly inconvenienced by the extra glass she carried for Ava's beer.

"Oh, you didn't need to bring that. Thanks," Ava said with a kind smile, trying to win her over.

"Mmm hmm," the waitress murmured as she set her plate, glass and beer on the table and walked away.

Well, that was a bust, she thought, frustrated she had already irritated people.

Halfway through her meal, she was interrupted by a feminine voice as a woman close to her own age approached her table. "Ava?"

She had mousy brown hair with hazel eyes hiding behind a pair of tortoise shell glasses. She smiled, and her calming presence put Ava at ease.

"Yes?" Ava looked at her, pausing. "Um. I'm sorry but..." She regarded the woman standing before her. "Wait... are you..."

"Eleanor," the woman finished with a nod, smiling warmly.

Ava gasped. "Oh my god! Eleanor!" She popped out of her seat and hugged her childhood friend. "I can't believe it! It's been—what? Like fifteen years?"

"Twenty," she replied.

"Come, sit down. Do you want to eat with me?"

"I'd love to." Eleanor took a seat across from Ava, adjusting her glasses. "I'm sorry about your grandpa. He was always so nice to me."

"Thanks. I hadn't seen him in years. It was kind of a shock when I got the call."

The waitress came back around, and Eleanor ordered a chicken sandwich and iced tea before turning back to Ava. "I heard through the small-town grapevine that he left you the farm."

"Yep."

"Does that mean you live here now?" Eleanor's voice was hopeful.

"Yeah." Ava gave her a half smile. "It's weird, isn't it? I never thought I'd be back."

"What about your mom?"

Ava fidgeted with her hair. "She... she died a few years ago."

"Oh god. I'm so sorry. I didn't know."

"Thanks. I don't really like talking about it," she added, before changing the subject. "So how are *you*? What have you been up to?" She shifted in her seat as David Bowie's voice sounded from the jukebox in the corner.

"Well, I'm the librarian now," she explained as the waitress delivered her food. "I took over for my parents. They retired and moved to New York a few years ago."

"That's wonderful!" Ava took a sip of her beer. "I remember how much we used to love playing hide and seek in between the bookshelves. Being a librarian suits you."

"Thanks," Eleanor said, picking up a fry. "I had forgotten all about that. And remember when your grandpa used to tell us those strange stories..." she trailed off.

Ava nodded. "I do."

What they didn't say was that the most memorable stories Ava's grandfather used to tell happened outside of the library. The two of them would snuggle up under fuzzy blankets on the couch while Grandpa waved his hands and threw himself into his tales.

Tales of mystical realms with princesses and demons, orcs and goblins. A land ruled by the fae who could perform magic such as manipulate gravity or raise lava from the earth. While most of the stories fascinated her, there was one that had terrified her as a child. About a king, longing for power, who was tricked by a demon promising him great wealth. Because of his greed, he let the demon into their world under the guise he would be made emperor over all the kingdoms. But upon arrival, the demon killed the king and brought his demon queen and their armies into the magical realm, starting a great war that lasted over one hundred years.

"Ava?" Eleanor's voice pulled her from her thoughts.

"Sorry." She twirled a lock of hair around her finger. "I was thinking."

Eleanor smiled as if remembering Ava often got distracted and lost in her thoughts, even as a child. A habit she still hadn't rid herself of.

They spent the rest of the evening catching up, reminiscing about gathering acorns and leaves to make their 'witches brew,' and drinking lemonade on the porch in the hot summer sun. Ava told Eleanor about some of her adventures in the field with the animals she researched as a wildlife biologist and Eleanor filled her in on the quirky townsfolk and which ones checked out the smuttiest romance novels from the library.

"It's always the old ladies or the stay-at-home moms," laughed Eleanor.

"Why does that not surprise me?" Ava giggled as she sipped the last of her beer.

As they finished eating and said their goodbyes, they made sure to exchange numbers and Ava invited her over for dinner so they would have even more time to catch up. Back in her car, she smiled to herself as she made her way back home.

Maybe she wouldn't be alone after all.

2

riars ripped at her clothing and tore at her skin as she sprinted through the woods, barely noticing the sting against her flesh. She didn't know where she was or where she was headed; only that she had to escape. She willed herself faster as something drew nearer behind her, lungs burning with every push of her legs. Breaking through the dense trees, she found herself in a clearing scattered with ruins.

A massive tree glowed in the distance, hardly visible through the woven forest. Its ancient and formidable power called to her, urging her toward its ethereal presence.

A creature emerged from the woods behind her. Searching, sniffing and rustling through the trees, it drew closer by the second. Backing away from the sounds, she tripped over a stone and fell backward, flailing. Her arms couldn't find purchase as she was enveloped in total darkness. Her body tingled, pressure causing her ears to pop and as she continued to fall, she barely made out someone calling her name. "Ava!"

Ava woke with a start and sat up in bed, drenched in sweat. She was in her bedroom at her grandfather's farm, not running through the woods from a terrible unknown creature. Heart still racing, she rubbed her face and took several deep breaths, just as her mother had taught her to do when she was scared. In through her nose and out through her mouth.

No dream had ever felt so real. She could still feel that strange tug toward the glowing tree. As if she needed to reach it, touch it. It felt important for some reason; was it part of a memory, twisted with age? And what about that voice? It had been a man's voice, and she couldn't shake the urgency in the way he shouted.

Hands still quivering, she pushed the dream out of her mind and checked the time. 7:02 am. Too worked up to fall back asleep, she slipped on her ivory robe and fuzzy slippers, fighting the morning chill of the house, and made her way to the kitchen on a quest for caffeine from her otherwise empty pantry.

The kitchen was sizable, with a marble topped center island perfect for cooking—one of Ava's favorite past times. The windows overlooked the shaded backyard, a sliver of morning sun peering through the trees brightening the space that was open to the dining and living room.

Her coffee finished brewing and as she poured herself a cup, she mentally reviewed today's tasks. Grocery shopping was her top priority. Afterward, she would explore the land to re-familiarize herself with the layout of the farm.

She headed to the office, the stoneware mug warm in her hands, to look through her grandfather's instructions before she journeyed into town. The room was dusty, with dark wall-to-wall oak bookshelves and an antique desk. Ava opened the window to allow in the morning breeze and bring fresh air to the stale room and turned to the desk. A binder labeled *To the Future Caretaker. Flower Farming 101* had been placed on top.

She sat down and skimmed the pages divided into sections based on the time of year. Each section listed when to plant each flower, what time of year they bloomed, along with their watering and fertilizer requirements. There was even information on troubleshooting pests, diseases, and other unexpected hurdles. Luckily, it was fall so she would have months to learn before she needed to have things up and running again by spring.

Setting the binder aside, she turned her attention to the bookshelves. She skimmed the titles, overwhelmed by the sheer number of volumes. *Peonies: From Seed to Harvest. Soil Health for Beginners. So, You Want to Start a Flower Farm?*

Continuing her exploration, she opened the desk drawers and rummaged through their contents, not quite sure what she was searching for. She pushed the last drawer closed in bored defeat, but it caught on something and jammed halfway. Cursing, she re-opened it and tried to slam it harder. When that didn't work, she yanked it out, rougher than intended and it crashed to the floor, pens and office supplies scattering.

"Shit."

Ava scooped up the supplies and dumped them in the drawer when she paused. There was an imperfection in the wood. Inside the drawer cavity was a small compartment, the lip of a door barely visible.

Curiosity piqued, she felt around the edges, using a pen to pry the door open the rest of the way when her fingers weren't enough. The wood popped out, revealing a small black journal. She ran her fingers along the cover, tracing the edges of the worn leather and remained on the floor, the worn rug soft beneath her as she crossed her legs.

The moment she lifted the cover everything stopped. The curtains stilled as the breeze outside ceased and the hair on the back of her neck stood up. Goosebumps rose along her arms as she looked around for anything out of place, sea glass green eyes scanning the room. Everything appeared the same, but she could still feel it. As if the earth was urging her to pay attention. After a moment, life resumed and the sensation was gone.

Heart still racing, she drew her attention back to the book and read the first page. The entry was dated more than thirty years ago. The day of her birth.

She survived the birth, thank The Mother. Ava is beautiful, the spitting image of her mom. They're going to move to the city, but she promises to visit. I can't wait.

She skimmed through the journal, yearning for more. For some kind of information. Most of the entries were short like the first. Brief snippets about random happenings in her grandfather's life or their visits to the farm. She found another and began to read.

My daughter's magic is waning. We've been in this realm too long, but we must do what we need to in order to protect Ava. Preserve her life until she is ready to go back.

She paused. Go back where? Ava thought back to the strange language her mother would sometimes sing in. They weren't from here originally, she was almost sure of it. And though she knew her mother had magical abilities, she had never been told about other worlds. It sounded like something out of a story book.

Ava flipped through the pages. As if the answers would jump out and announce themselves. Another entry.

My girls must move to a new hiding place. I've made Sarah promise not to tell me where.

Her eyes flicked up to the date at the corner of the page. It was around the time they stopped visiting, when her mother had told her Grandpa was too sick. What were they hiding from? What did Ava need to be ready for? She flipped further and found an entry dated just a few days after her mother's death.

My sweet Sarah passed. Her body couldn't fight the cancer any longer. I will tell everything to Ava soon. Her mother wanted me to wait until she was truly old enough to understand the prophecy and responsibilities she must shoulder. My poor daughter. I will miss her so.

Prophecy? Ava chewed her lip as she wrapped her arms around her knees, still holding the journal in her hands. It sounded like her grandfather's usual paranoia. Prophecies weren't real... right? She flipped through the rest of the journal, but the remaining pages were empty. As if he had given up and just stopped writing.

Frustration boiled over as she thought about her family; angry that those she trusted most in the world had been so secretive. Ava never knew where they came from, never knew why her mother could perform magic or what was lurking in the forest beyond the flower fields. The forest her grandfather was always watching and warned her never to enter. She wanted answers. Needed them. It was one of the reasons she decided to move out here.

She rubbed her temples. Should she ask Eleanor? She had been around when Ava's mother performed magic and had spent hours playing with her on the farm, aware of her grandfather's oddities. Though it was so long ago, maybe she would remember. Ava hoped Eleanor didn't think she was crazy.

Rising from the floor, she placed the journal on the desk and finished cleaning up the mess. She tried to attribute the strange journal entries to dementia or some form of madness, her mother's death pushing him even further away from sanity.

But she wasn't very successful at convincing herself of this. Something felt off.

She wished her mother were here to comfort her. She always knew the exact thing to say when Ava went too deep within herself, lost in her thoughts and anxiety. Her mother had been tough. The rock on which she stood. An unbreakable force.

Whenever Ava struggled as a child, she could always count on her to be a steady unwavering presence, pushing her to face her challenges head on.

"Crush them," she used to say when her insecurities tried to win. *"All the obstacles that stand in your way. Crush them, Ava."*

She wasn't sure she knew how anymore.

ASTERS, daisies and lobelia swayed beside Ava as she meandered through the fields, their botanical scents floating on the breeze. Honeybees were hard at work inside bright red blooms, gathering the last bit of pollen before the first freeze urged them into hibernation. The conservationist in her warmed at her grandfather's fervor to preserve as much native flora as possible while tilling land for his business. It was something they had all been passionate about, protecting local plants and animals.

She entered the flower fields through a wooden archway covered in climbing red roses and as she walked up and down the neat rows of flowers, she spotted several of her favorites. Dahlias, zinnias, and sunflowers stretched as far as the eye could see in a rainbow of color. She buzzed with excitement as she imagined herself spending time out here, nurturing and harvesting her bounty.

She stood in silence, hands on her hips, appreciating the view. This land, this homestead. It had always felt like home more than anywhere she'd ever lived. It called to her. Whispering her name on a crisp fall breeze, filling her soul with tranquility.

She longed to find peace. Hoped her heart would be healed through this connection with mother earth. After years of uncertainty, of moving around the country and repeatedly starting over, maybe she could settle. Build a life here. She took a deep breath and closed her eyes, taking it all in and letting the subtle gusts of wind caress her very spirit.

She changed course and ventured into the woods. She wasn't a child anymore and she wanted to explore. Needed to. As if it was drawing her in, begging for its secrets to be revealed. Despite the childhood warnings, she pushed on. If her family wanted to keep her out of here, they shouldn't have died and left her all alone.

Ava followed a path which wove through towering pine and fir trees and eventually vanished under the overgrown brush and vines. Leaves crunched beneath her feet as a squirrel chattered overhead. Sunlight waned as the canopy grew denser and she picked her way deeper into the wild, stepping over fallen logs smothered with viridescent mosses.

As she hiked through the grove, she felt as though she was being watched. She paused, muscles tense as she evaluated her surroundings, searching for the source of her unease. Squinting, she peered between the trees, trying to focus her vision in the dim light. She wrapped her arms around herself as she began to wander again, still aware of the mysterious sensation.

Moments later, the feeling intensified and this time she stopped and looked more closely, scanning around her with sharp attention. She inspected the grove, landing on a pair of dark eyes gazing at her from between the shrubs.

It was a doe. With soft brown fur and white spots, its large ears moved about as it listened for predators. It didn't appear scared and drew closer as she spoke with it in hushed tones. She'd always been abnormally gifted with animals and held out her hand as the deer stopped and sniffed her fingers warily.

She stretched her hand out further, but quicker than she was able to make sense of, the deer turned, searching the forest behind it. It bounded off into the woods as if something else was lurking just beyond the shadows, leaving Ava behind. Leaving her alone.

A chill went down Ava's spine.

The forest had gone quiet, no longer chiming with the songs of birds or the squeaks of chipmunks. Even the breeze ceased, as if the forest held its breath, waiting. Ava took a few more uneasy steps when the rustling of leaves sounded behind her. She turned toward the sound, and a flurry of animals flew past. Birds darted through the treetops as rabbits and more deer rushed around her in a frenzy.

The small stampede was gone within seconds, the forest silent yet again. Though she knew it was time to go back to the house, she felt a tug. A thread pulling her further into the woods. Into the dark. She took another step toward it when something moved in the corner of her eye.

Ava whipped around just in time to see a tall shadow disappear behind a tree. Warning bells pealed in her head, and she turned and ran out of the forest, racing the sun as it set behind the trees.

Heart pounding in her ears, she broke into the open field of the farm and doubled over with her hands on her knees, panting. When she checked her phone, she saw that three hours had gone by. Impossible. She had only been in there for an hour at most, she was sure of it.

As she caught her breath, a twig snapped from just beyond the tree line and she could have sworn she heard breathing behind her. Taking no chances, she took off in a run all the way back to the house, not even sparing the forest a second glance.

3

va hummed to herself as she cleaned up the flower field, pulling the spent plants and tossing them into her wheelbarrow for composting. Eleanor was coming over for dinner tonight and though it seemed silly, she wanted the farm to look the way Eleanor remembered it from her grandfather's care.

Smiling at the thought of having a close friend, she didn't notice the truck driving down the dirt road until it pulled in front of her house.

Rocks crunched under the tires as it inched up the driveway. Ava shielded her eyes from the morning sun, watching it approach. It was a run-down truck, blue paint flaking along the hood, and the rumbling of the engine ceased as the owner turned it off.

The door opened and out stepped an absurdly handsome man. Tall, with blonde hair and piercing blue eyes, he wore jeans and a red flannel, barely concealing his lithe muscled frame.

"Can I help you?" she asked, shifting on her feet. Who was he and why was he here?

The man brushed his hand through his hair as he strode toward her, leather boots crunching on the gravel. His lightly tanned skin hinted at his time spent outside.

"I'm sorry to alarm you," he said in a low voice that warmed her cheeks. "I used to work for your grandfather, and I just thought I'd swing by and see if you needed any help."

She reached her hand out, scrutinizing the stranger. "I'm Ava."

"Henry," he replied, shaking it.

The moment their hands touched, a tingle worked its way up her arm. She sucked in a breath and looked up at him, but he didn't seem to notice. The sensation spread throughout her body and she cleared her throat, letting go of his hand.

"He didn't mention anyone working on the farm for him," she said, trying to feel him out. He didn't mention anything at all because she hadn't talked to him in years. "What type of work did you do?"

"Mostly odd jobs. Things he was unable to do himself physically." He shoved his sleeves up to his elbows and her eyes caught on his tanned forearms. "Repairs on the buildings. Hauling soil. Stuff like that." He smiled, seemingly friendly, then gestured to a large barn off to the side of the property. "I repainted that for him a couple of years ago."

"I could use the help," she admitted. "It's just..." She sighed, toying with her braid over her shoulder. "It's just that—I don't know you."

"I know. I'm sorry, it's weird. A random man shows up while you're here by yourself. I know how it looks." He winced. "What about a trial run?"

She tilted her head, hands on her hips. "Meaning?"

"Give me a few small jobs and see if you like my work. I promise not to come inside your house or bother you. And if you're satisfied, then I'll do more. If not, I'll leave."

Ava crossed her arms, but knew she was in a bind. "Alright," she said. "I'll make a short list of repairs I need done. Can you start tomorrow?"

"Absolutely." He smiled disarmingly. As if he couldn't get any handsomer, the wide grin transformed his face, his eyes bright. "Is nine o'clock too early?"

"That's fine. I'll see you then," she said as she tried to keep her voice steady.

Henry gave her a broad smile and re-entered his vehicle, waving out the window as he pulled away. The truck disappeared down the road, and as the dust settled, she wondered if she'd made a mistake. Was it rash to allow a strange man access to her property while she was alone?

STRING lights illuminated the porch as Ava and Eleanor ate dinner, their small feast spread across the large outdoor table. Music played from a small speaker sitting on a side table, next to the bottle of wine they had brought outside for refills.

Her favorite thing about this farmhouse was the massive wrap-around porch, front and back connected by verandas on both sides. There was enough room in the back for a large outdoor sectional, a dining table and chairs and a conversation set. There was also a hammock Ava had spent many an evening in, drifting off as she read herself to sleep.

Ava loved to cook for others. It was something that had always brought her joy and she delighted in trying out new recipes on her guests. Tonight, she'd made flatbread pizza with arugula, hot honey and goat cheese accompanied by a large chef's salad and homemade lemonade.

"Middle school was rough," continued Eleanor, about halfway through her favorite stories of childhood mishaps. "One time, I was asked to read aloud in science and instead of saying organism, I accidentally said orgasm. It was so embarrassing."

Tears streamed down Ava's face, and she nearly choked as she took another sip of lemonade. "I'm sure you're not the only one who's done that," she said. "Once, I was walking in the cafeteria with my lunch tray and somehow tripped over my own feet and fell backward. My tray spilled all over me and I was covered in food."

"It seems old habits die hard," Eleanor teased, nodding at Ava's shirt.

Ava looked down at the glob of honey on her white tee. "Well, fuck." She laughed as she dabbed at it with a napkin. "You know," Ava said. "I'm glad to be back here. It's been way too long."

"Me too," Eleanor replied, smiling. "Middle school wouldn't have been so awkward if you hadn't left me!"

"I didn't leave you! I was whisked away to south Texas just before seventh grade. I didn't want to stop visiting..." Ava's tone turned solemn. "I missed you."

Ava didn't realize how much she had missed her friend until she said it out loud. They'd spent every summer together for twelve years. Then it all stopped. She hadn't even gotten to say goodbye.

"I missed you too. So much." Eleanor gave her a sad smile. "What happened? I remember my mom bringing me to the farm and playing with you whenever you were in town. Then you just disappeared one day."

Fidgeting in her seat, Ava took a drink and remained silent a few moments before answering. "I don't know. I just remember my mom saying we had to move and we lived too far away to visit." She paused, deliberating on whether she should show Eleanor her grandfather's journal or not. Though they hadn't seen each other in two decades, Ava trusted her. She had been there when her mother performed magic, when her grandfather told his strange stories. Eleanor wouldn't judge her.

Standing up, she said, "Wait here. I have something to show you."

Ava retrieved the journal, then sat back down at the table and handed it to her friend. "I found this when I moved in."

Eleanor opened it and flipped through the pages, eyes scanning the entries. "This is... what does any of this mean?" she asked.

"I don't know." Ava shook her head and pursed her lips. "Do you remember my mom doing anything weird when we were kids?"

"Um—like what?"

Ava grimaced. "Like... God, it sounds stupid saying it out loud—" She took a breath. "Like witchy stuff..."

"The journal mentioned magic..." Eleanor trailed off. "Actually, I—"

Before she could finish, a scream echoed in the forest beyond.

Ava froze, heart leaping in her throat as her eyes shot to the woods beyond the backyard.

"What was that?" Eleanor whispered, looking around.

"I don't know." Ava's heart raced. "Let's get inside."

They started to gather the dishes as another cry resounded, closer than before. Ava's hair stood on the back of her neck. The scream was not quite animal and yet not human either. Ava searched the yard again, dark save for the faint illumination coming from the porch lights, but saw nothing.

"Forget the dishes," uttered Ava as she pulled Eleanor inside and locked the door behind them.

Ava poured two glasses of wine, handing one to Eleanor as they settled themselves on the couch. All was quiet now and the forest resumed its usual nighttime sounds. An owl hooted in the distance as the women listened for any more sounds indicating danger.

Still on edge, Ava pulled a green throw onto her lap and turned back to Eleanor. "Do you think it's gone?"

"I don't know. What the hell makes a sound like that?" she asked.

"No idea…" Ava couldn't help but glance to the window.

"Do you think that's why your grandpa wouldn't let us go in the woods?"

Ava's eyes snapped to Eleanor. "You remember that?"

She sipped her wine. "I remember a lot of things."

"Like…"

"What you asked me earlier…" Eleanor adjusted her glasses. "I always thought I was imagining this, but one time I swore I saw your mother wave her hand over a dead sunflower." Eleanor lowered her voice. "…and suddenly it was alive again."

"You didn't imagine it," Ava whispered, looking at her hands in her lap.

"Seriously?" Eleanor's eyes widened as Ava met her gaze. "Is magic… real?"

"I—" Ava stuttered. "My mom told me it was," she said, a pang of sadness ringing through her at the thought of her mother. Eleanor studied her silently. "Do you believe me?"

Eleanor's eyes brightened. "Of course I do. I just—it's been so long. It feels weird to talk about…"

"I know."

"Have you ever been able to do anything like that?" Eleanor asked.

Ava shook her head. "No."

"About the journal… Do you think your grandfather was just—" Eleanor began.

"Crazy?"

Eleanor huffed a laugh. "Yes."

"Probably."

They remained silent, a thoughtful expression on Eleanor's face. "Okay." Eleanor sipped her wine. "What do you want to do?"

"What do you mean?"

Leaning forward on the couch, Eleanor scrutinized her. "Let's figure it out."

"How?"

"Let's just say this is real..." She paused. "We search for clues. If we can't find anything then we'll know that your grandfather was senile and maybe your mother was a witch or something."

"And if we do find something?"

Eleanor gave her a half smile. "Then I guess we aren't crazy."

Ava laughed quietly to herself, pondering Eleanor's words. It sounded like a good plan. She just needed to prove or disprove her grandfather's ramblings and then maybe she would have some answers. As the women remained silent, Ava's mind wandered back to this morning.

"Sorry to change the subject but do you know a guy in town named Henry?"

"Cunningham?" Eleanor asked.

Ava took a sip of wine. "I didn't get his last name."

"Tall, blonde... Ridiculously good-looking?"

"Yep. That's the one."

"Yeah, I know him. Not well, but he's nice." Eleanor crossed her legs. "Does odd jobs around town. Why?"

"He showed up at the farm this morning, claiming he used to help and basically asked for work," she answered.

"What did you tell him?" Eleanor took another drink.

Ava scrunched her face. "He starts tomorrow."

Eleanor laughed heartily.

"What?"

"Ava, he's *hot*," she blurted.

Ava bit her lip before replying. "Yeah, I know. I guess now I'll have something even prettier than flowers to look at while I work."

4

___

The wood floors creaked beneath Ava's feet as she plodded to her bedroom after brushing her teeth. Still somewhat tipsy from the wine she and Eleanor had drunk, she was ready to burrow under her down comforter and sleep the night away.

She sat at the edge of her bed and clicked off the vintage Tiffany lamp on her nightstand, shrouding the room in darkness. As she lifted the covers to settle herself, her eyes caught on something outside.

Ava froze as she tried to comprehend what she was seeing. From her second story bedroom window, she had a view of the flower fields at the front of the house and the forest beyond. And right at the edge of the woods, stood a tall shadowy figure. Motionless, it stared directly at her from between the trees.

It was just some local messing around on her property. Right?

She grabbed her robe from the hook on the door and headed down the stairs, fumbling in the dark for the light switch. Making it to the front porch, she prepared to chase them off when she noticed it hadn't moved, still watching her.

26

Her feet froze, a voice in the back of her mind telling her to run. It was taller than she originally thought, at least several feet higher than herself.

Her blood ran cold as she stared at it, unable to pull away her gaze.

Though she sensed trouble, she couldn't resist the tug pulling her toward the forest, closer to the shadowy silhouette, and began to walk forward. As she approached, it reached out its arm, curling its fingers, and beckoned her to follow as it turned away and headed into the woods. She didn't want to, tried to turn around and go back inside but her feet started moving as if they had their own plans.

Her heart raced as she continued after the shadow, still trying to fight against her rebellious body. This was wrong. She had to go back to the house.

Reaching the edge of the woods, the figure turned and looked at something in the distance. Now that Ava was closer, it appeared to be a woman, nude with long hair covering her breasts, though she still couldn't see her face.

Ever so slowly, the woman's head tilted, and her piercing blue eyes settled on Ava. She lazily opened her mouth as if smiling, wider and wider, stretching far and revealing jagged pointy teeth. Claws elongated where fingernails should have been, the trickle of blood falling to the ground. Just as Ava readied herself to turn and run, it screamed.

Ava's breath was knocked out of her as she crashed into a solid surface. Her limbs were trapped in a soft embrace and she thrashed around, trying to free herself. Released from her silky bindings, she sat up and was almost blinded by the sunlight.

She was on the floor in her room, tangled in her sheets.

Birds chirped outside her window as morning welcomed

the day. It wasn't night anymore. What happened? Had that figure been real? Was it a dream?

She didn't remember going back inside or going to sleep.

Taking a deep breath to calm her still racing heart, she climbed off the floor and tossed her bedding back on her bed. It must have been a dream. She drank too much and went to sleep; she just didn't remember. But it hadn't seemed like a dream. It was different from her others.

Something wasn't right. Then, she saw it. Her robe was on the floor, not where she usually hung it up. She truly had...

A knock sounded on her front door.

Nine o'clock already? She had forgotten to set an alarm and must have slept in after all the wine. Normally an early riser, she cursed to herself as she pulled on a pair of jeans and a long-sleeved black t-shirt.

Throwing her frizzy waves into a low ponytail, she bounded down the stairs and ran to the door. When she opened it, Henry was leaning against the front porch post, his arm above him, a wide grin on his face.

Her heart fluttered at the sight of him. "I'm so sorry," she said, out of breath. "I didn't realize what time it was."

"It's alright," he said. "I haven't been waiting long." He looked at her expectantly.

"Oh," she remembered. "The list. I'll be right back."

She rushed to the office and returned, handing him a short list of things to be addressed on the property. There were a few rickety pieces of railing on the porch she wanted him to repair and a pile of wood near the greenhouse she needed moved. She was also hoping he could chop down a small half dead tree near the flower fields, not wanting it to fall over on her during her chores.

He looked it over and nodded. "I can do this," he said, then added as she winced at the sunlight, "Are you alright?"

She rubbed the back of her neck. "Actually... I'm a little hungover."

He chuckled. "I can see that. Well, why don't you get yourself some coffee and rest a bit? I'll knock if I need anything."

"Okay. Thanks."

She closed the door and watched him walk to his truck, opening the tailgate and searching for his tools. The way he had smiled at her twisted her insides like a teenager with a crush. And that laugh. It brushed over her skin and made her shiver with desire. What was wrong with her?

As someone who tended to overthink everything, Ava chastised herself for her instant attraction as she started the coffee pot and waited for it to brew. Though she had been on plenty of dates and even had a couple of serious relationships, she found most men either disregarded her or only wanted one thing. Once they got to know her, they often found her wildlife knowledge or almost obsessive fascination with nature weird. It was like they wanted some vapid giggling trophy wife, and the moment she started talking about her master's thesis on the endangered status of the Northern Leopard Frog, they lost all interest.

She poured herself a mug full of dark roast, adding a splash of cream as she mentally reviewed the list she had given Henry.

Ava felt awkward just sitting while he worked alone outside, so after about an hour, she made her way to finish cleaning up the last of the dead plants in the garden. As she walked toward the greenhouse located on the side of the property to retrieve her gloves, she turned the corner and ran straight into Henry.

"Whoa," he said as he steadied her, grasping her shoulders. "You're on a mission, huh?"

"Sorry, I wasn't paying attention," she said, nervous as she looked up at him.

His blue eyes twinkled as he responded. "Lost in thought?"

Lost in those blue eyes, she mused.

"Something like that," she said, shifting on her feet. "I was headed to the greenhouse."

"Actually, while you're out here. Could you help me with something really quick?"

"Umm... Sure."

Ava tried to calm her nerves at the request as a strange sudden desire to be close to him washed over her. It was like she wouldn't have been able to say no even if she wanted to.

He walked with her, headed toward the broken railing on the porch. "Could you hold these still while I hammer? It'll go much quicker with the two of us."

"Alright," she said as she grabbed one of the balusters and held tight.

Henry pulled the hammer from his tool belt and placed a nail. As he worked, he asked, "How are you liking it out here?"

"It's peaceful. I used to visit when I was a kid and it's nice to be back," she answered as her arms vibrated, trying to keep the railing still. "How long have you lived here?"

"A few years," he replied.

"And do you like it?"

He nodded. "Yep."

They spent the next twenty minutes making their way to each loose railing piece, silent save for random comments about the weather or the upcoming holidays. Though she was still nervous, it was easy being in his company. He had a way about him that somehow drew her in. Made her curious.

Moving to the remaining baluster, she inquired, "So, you knew my grandpa, huh?"

Placing the last nail into the wood, he tapped the hammer against it as he answered. "Kind of. Not well. He was a man of few words. Usually, just handed me a list and that was that."

She sighed. "Yeah. Sounds like him. He was a little strange."

"You don't say," he teased as he smiled up at her. Finished

with the porch, he stood up and regarded her. "I finished your list."

"Already?" She was shocked, but as she glanced around the property, she noticed the tree was down and all the wood was in the preferred location. "Wow, you're fast."

"Maybe. But I'm thorough." He gave her a wink.

She blushed. "Well, thanks for your help today," she said as she dusted her hands on her jeans.

"I can come back tomorrow if you have anything else that needs to be done," he said, voice hopeful.

She couldn't think of anything else off the top of her head, but decided she would find something for him to do because, admittedly, she wanted him to come back. "Sure. Same time?"

"Sounds like a plan," he said as he walked toward his truck. "See you tomorrow, Ava," he added as he got in and drove away, a subtle smile on his face.

As she watched the truck disappear down the gravel road, she realized she was excited to see him again. Wanted to know more about him and be in his presence. Turning around, she made her way to the flower field to finish the last bit of weeding, trying to put those twinkling blue eyes out of her mind.

AFTER ABOUT AN HOUR of work and a pile of dead plants beside her, she stood up and wiped the sweat from her brow. As she prepared to gather the discarded flowers, a strange sound interrupted her from the edge of the forest. Immediately she was brought back to last night's dream as she turned toward the direction of the noise.

It was a faint cry of fear and pain, like an injured animal or a scared child. Comforted by the presence of daylight, she grabbed a shovel and searched the tree line. The cry sounded again. It was much closer this time.

Then, she saw it.

Just at the woods' edge, was what appeared to be a bobcat, though different than the ones she had studied. As she neared, she saw superficial claw marks along its side and it whimpered as it lay still.

"Oh!" she cried out, dropping the shovel and rushing over. "Oh my gosh, you poor thing," she said as she approached it with caution, hands trembling.

As a child, she and her mother often helped injured animals. Creatures never balked at their presence but always remained calm, especially around Ava. It was as if she had the magic touch, able to communicate with them in some silent language.

And now, just like in childhood, the bobcat didn't appear fearful as she knelt to assess its wounds but instead seemed to relax, as if it knew she was there to help. She tentatively reached out, stroking the cat's head and whispering to it, noticing it was now calm.

"I'm going to help you, sweet baby," she whispered.

It looked back at her as if it understood.

She removed her sweatshirt and wrapped the bobcat, minding the injuries while it watched her with curiosity. She carried it back to the house and laid it down on the floor of the kitchen, rushing to the bathroom for her first aid kit.

Ava washed her hands and donned a pair of latex gloves from the kit. She found a bottle of saline solution and flushed out the wounds as she sang. A song her mother used to sing to her when she felt scared.

> *"Hush now, little bird.*
> *Don't be afraid.*
> *All your fears,*
> *Let me unlade.*
> *You're safe with me,*

*Don't you cry.
While I sing to you,
Our lullaby."*

She couldn't keep the tears in as she finished cleaning the wounds and bandaged up the feline. She hadn't thought about the song in years, and it had come to her out of nowhere, the grief raw once more.

Her tears fell as more memories of the farm surfaced. The smell of lavender in the kitchen as her mother brewed tea; the songs of chickadees who nested outside her bedroom window; her mother sewing pretty dresses so she could pretend to be a proper princess; grandfather sitting on the porch with his morning coffee; spending every holiday in the kitchen cooking extravagant meals for just the three of them. Her heart ached as she thought about how much she missed her mother and how desperately she wished she were here to help her.

But she wasn't here anymore, and Ava only had herself to rely on.

She wiped her eyes with the back of her arm and spoke to the animal. "You're safe here with me."

She grabbed some old towels and blankets from the hall closet and piled them in the corner of the living room, creating a temporary bed for the animal until she could get to the store for supplies.

After a moment, the cat got up and padded over to the blankets, looking at Ava as it curled up and breathed a sigh of relief. She walked over to it and reached out her hand as she crouched. Without hesitation, it purred and rubbed against her. Now that she had a chance to look closer, she realized this was not a bobcat.

The fur was lighter, almost white, and had a mix of swirls and stripes in place of the usual bobcat spots. The tail was long, and solid black paws faded into stripes just above the ankles.

She—because Ava had discovered it was a she—still had ear tufts, but they were much longer, more reminiscent of a lynx. Then there were her eyes. They were a lavender color, something she had never seen before in her years of working with wildlife. Perhaps it was some exotic pet that had gotten lost?

Now Ava had a project for Henry. She'd swing by the hardware store and look for a pet door and ask him to install it.

"I'll be back in a little bit," she said to the now sleeping cat, hoping it would be fine alone for a while. She was probably crazy for leaving a feral animal alone in her house, but somehow she knew nothing would happen.

5

"**O**uch!" Ava exclaimed as she smashed her thumb with the hammer for the third time.

Henry chuckled, taking the tool from her. "Here, you hold it again and I'll finish."

They were working on the back porch today after Ava realized they had missed some wobbly pieces and she had insisted she try nailing some of the supports in, irritated no one had ever taught her to use a hammer when she was younger.

"I'm not the most coordinated," she huffed, sucking her throbbing thumb as the chill breeze rustled Henry's hair.

Had she offered to help to be close to him? Maybe. Probably.

Yes.

Henry smiled, his gaze dropping to her thumb in her mouth and his eyes slightly darkened before he turned and began to hammer the railing. "It's cute," he said.

Was he flirting with her?

"I'm glad I'm cute, I guess." She laughed, blushing as she grasped the top rail to hold it still.

"Much cuter than my last employer." He briefly glanced at her.

He was definitely flirting with her.

"My grandpa? I should hope so." She raised an eyebrow, trying to hide her nerves.

Why was she so nervous around him? She didn't tend to get nervous around men. Usually they annoyed her, but there was something different about Henry.

They finished the back porch and Henry stood. "So, you used to do archery?" he questioned.

"Huh?" She looked at him, confused as she leaned against the newly repaired railing.

He gestured to her hoodie displaying the logo of her college archery team.

Glancing down, she replied, "Oh, right. I was on the team in college. I was actually really good."

She was more than good; she was excellent at it. Archery became a way to manage her stress throughout college, a way to escape from the all-nighters and relentless studying she often imposed on herself. Though she had never been very athletic and hated team sports, archery gave her something to focus on, something to provide confidence. She missed it.

"So, you can't hammer a nail straight but you're good with a bow and arrow?" He shook his head.

"I never said it made sense." She laughed. "Sometimes I'm clumsy but for some reason archery came easily for me. No idea why."

He leaned forward and reached around her.

She straightened. "What are you doing?"

Continuing to lean, he extended his arm and grabbed something off the railing behind her, stopping a few inches from her face. "I'm grabbing my tool," he said as he retrieved it and stepped back.

"Oh," she squeaked, face flushing yet again.

Had he done that on purpose just to get closer to her? It sure felt like it. Butterflies erupted in her stomach as she realized she wanted him to get close to her again.

He smirked. "Show me where you want the pet door installed."

Pushing herself off the railing, she led him to the back door. "Here, please."

"I'm going to have to keep the door open while I install this. Is that okay?" He grabbed his toolbox and carried it to the door.

"Yeah," she responded. "I have some work I need to do in the office. Holler if you need anything."

He nodded and she left the backdoor open as she went inside. Entering the office, she found the bobcat, who she had dubbed Luna, asleep on the rug near the desk. She shut the doors, embarrassed Henry might see her and judge her for keeping a wild animal in her house, and sat at the desk. Fortunately, he never asked what the pet door was for and she didn't mention Luna.

After ten minutes of staring at the binder full of information, unable to concentrate due to her stupid brain thinking about when Henry reached for the hammer and what his lips would feel like on hers, she picked up her phone and texted Eleanor.

So I think I'm crushing on the handy-man.

Of course you are. Like I said, he's hot.

He called me cute.

Seriously?

Yea… I feel like a teenage girl. This is so dumb. I'm a 32-year-old grown ass woman. Why am I getting all giddy? I've known him for like two and a half days.

Is he there now?

Yea. He's installing the pet door for that cat I told you about.

Awww. That's sweet. Next time he comes over, you should answer the door naked.

NO. This isn't a porno.

It should be. That would make a good porno. The young single woman running a flower farm is seduced by the hot handyman who always wears flannels.

That's… an interesting visual.

You'd better text me the second he kisses you.

He's not going to kiss me.

Sure. Whatever you say.

Come over for dinner Friday?

Ok!

A knock sounded on the office door and Ava jumped, dropping her phone. Henry was standing outside the doors, waiting. Rising from her chair, she grabbed her phone and slipped out of the office, closing the door behind her so Luna didn't emerge.

"Sorry. I called your name, but you didn't hear me."

Face bright red from her conversation with Eleanor, she replied, "I was… distracted. Lots of paperwork is involved in running a flower farm, you know."

"Uh huh." He looked down at her. "I just needed your help with one last thing, and then I'll be done."

"Alright," she answered as she followed him to the back door.

"Just hold this while I screw it in," he said, sitting on the floor.

She sat down next to him and held the frame of the pet door still as he used his drill.

"I heard some fun stories about your grandfather's farm," he said, concentrating on his task as a lock of blonde hair fell in front of his eyes. She resisted the urge to brush it out of his face.

"Stories? What stories?" She glanced at him.

He shrugged, almost finished with the last screw. "Probably just a bunch of bullshit but people here can be superstitious. Something about spell books and witches. You know, stuff like that."

"I've never heard anyone say that before."

She wasn't surprised people talked in this small town and was used to the accusations of witchcraft and spells following wherever she and her mother had moved. Rumors had likely circulated about her grandfather as well.

"It's why people didn't want to come out here," Henry continued. "Abraham was... weird. It freaked people out."

"But he didn't freak you out?"

He sat up and shook his head, finished installing the door. "I don't believe in that stuff. So, no."

"I don't believe in that stuff either," she said. But she actually did.

FRIDAY MORNING ARRIVED and Ava got dressed in her usual farm uniform of a t-shirt and old jeans. Henry was on his way to help her clean out the greenhouse and she wanted to get it done before Eleanor came over later. He'd been coming every day for almost a week now and she was feeling more comfortable in his presence as time wore on.

Luna had settled in and was going in and out as she

pleased. Her injuries had healed miraculously well, allowing Ava to remove the bandages sooner than expected. She had installed the pet door to let her new companion decide if she wanted to stay or go live in the wild again and so far, she seemed to want to stay. She'd leave for a few hours to hunt or do whatever it was she did, but she always came back. The cat had become a steady presence for her, something comforting as she continued to navigate this new life. She had begun to feel less alone now that she had Eleanor, Luna and Henry, and though she hadn't made any other friends, she promised herself she would go into town and try.

The rumble of Henry's truck sounded outside, and Ava walked downstairs and met him in the driveway. "Good morning." He beamed as he collected his supplies and they headed to the greenhouse.

The greenhouse was large with plenty of room for starting seeds and space for storage. Framed with vintage windows which opened for ventilation, it let the perfect amount of light in for growing plants. Set against a backdrop of old oak trees, the glass on the windows seemed to sparkle as the morning light of the sun bounced off the roof. Excited to get it cleaned and in working order, Ava opened the creaky old door for Henry as he carried his tools inside.

It was full of dust, crumbling seed packets and broken pots. Old bags of soil were piled in the corner, some ripped open and spilling their contents onto the floor. Parts of the shelving were wobbly, and Henry got to work on repairing these while Ava discarded the trash.

"So... are you alone in this town?" Henry asked as he adjusted a loose board before drilling it back in place. "Got any family or friends here?"

"No family. It's just me," she answered, throwing a broken pot into the large trashcan they had brought inside. "Eleanor is a childhood friend, so we've been hanging out... but that's it."

"The librarian?"

"Yeah. We used to play together as kids when I came to visit."

Henry glanced at her. "Wow, that's cool. Was it weird to reconnect with her?"

"Not really." She shrugged. "It's easy. We still have a lot in common even though it's been twenty years."

"Twenty years?" he asked as he turned to work on the next shelf. "Why have you been gone so long?"

Taking a rag, she wiped dust from one of the potting benches as she answered. "My mom and I just moved around a lot."

He stopped and looked at her as something subtle flashed in his eyes but it was gone so fast, she surely imagined it. "That must have been hard."

"Actually... yeah. It was. It was almost impossible to make friends." She fiddled with the rag in her hand. "Umm... what about your family?"

He walked to his toolkit and grabbed more supplies, then stood in front of the shelving right next to where she was standing. Taking a nail and beginning to hammer, he answered over his shoulder. "Kind of the same story. Moved around a lot. Don't have any family left and ended up here. I like the quiet."

That was why he had that look. He'd been through something similar it seemed, though she decided not to ask about it. She didn't feel it was appropriate to push when they barely knew each other.

Ava leaned over, grabbing a bag of soil to move it outside. "I like it here— ahh!"

A mouse darted out from among the soil and Ava shrieked, dropping the bag and quickly backed into Henry. She turned around and faced him, her back now against the potting table behind her.

She looked up at him and laughed. "Sorry. There was a mouse."

"Are you afraid of mice?" he asked.

She shook her head. "No, it just startled me."

Henry was standing close, looking down at her with a hint of mischief in his eyes. He inched even nearer as she pressed into the table behind her, his eyes dipping to her lips. "What *are* you afraid of?" His voice had gone low, sensual.

She cleared her throat. "Don't laugh... horses," she answered.

"Seriously?" He tilted his head.

"Kind of," she rambled as she often did when she was nervous. "I mean I'm not *afraid* of them, but I've never ridden one, and they make me nervous and always freaked me out as a kid and they're big and can stomp—"

Henry interrupted her rambling. "Ava."

"What?"

"Stop talking so I can kiss you."

Her heart leapt in her throat. "Okay."

Henry leaned in, looking deeply into her eyes. She met his gaze, unable to look away as he leaned in further and tilted her chin, lightly kissing her. Their lips met, soft and careful. Cautiously, he parted her lips with his tongue, and they explored each other. Her hands moved to his chest as his went to her hair, fingers intertwined in her soft locks.

It was a delicate kiss full of warmth and she wanted more. She didn't care if they were covered in dirt and sweat or that she barely knew him. She wanted him. Needed him; like she was not in control of her actions. She wouldn't have been able to say no even if she wanted to so she pushed the loss of control from her mind and allowed him to keep going.

As if he read her mind, he increased the intensity, passion building as his body pushed hers into the shelving. Gasping, she moved her hands to his hair and deepened the kiss further, throwing all her qualms away as she was only able to focus on her need. Henry's hands roved over her body and grasped her waist, lifting her to sit on the bench before him. She could feel him hard against her as he stood in between her legs and pressed closer, one arm on her lower back pulling her toward him and the other cupping her breast over her shirt.

He kissed her neck and she threw her head back and moaned, begging for more when his cellphone rang.

Henry backed away and ran his hand through his hair. "Sorry, I have to take this." He walked out of the greenhouse, answering his phone, leaving her there panting.

After adjusting her hair and clothing, Ava exited the greenhouse as Henry was hanging up the phone. "I'm so sorry. One of the businesses has a broken window and wants me to come look at it right away." He didn't appear embarrassed at all about what had occurred.

"Of course," she responded as he approached her.

He lifted his hand to her face and traced his thumb over her bottom lip. "And we can finish what we started another time..." he promised before pulling away and heading back to his truck, toolbox in hand.

She followed and stood on the front porch as he shut the car door. Elbow hanging out the open window, he smiled broadly. "I'll see you soon."

Ava watched his truck disappear down the driveway as she mused on what just happened. She didn't regret making out with the handyman in the greenhouse. Grinning to herself she realized it was sort of exciting, something she needed in life after all the consequential changes she had been through.

Besides, when was the last time she actually had fun?

A THUMP and then the pitter patter of paws sounded as Luna trotted down the stairs, drawn by the noise of plastic as Ava opened the package of raw chicken. Though Luna came and went as she pleased through the new cat door and hunted for most of her own food, Ava had decided to treat her with some meat tonight as she waited for Eleanor to arrive for dinner.

Luna bounded into the kitchen and rubbed against Ava's legs, purring loudly.

She set a plate of chicken next to a bowl of water and Luna ravenously bit into her dinner. Ava wasn't nervous around her, despite her being a wild animal, and smiled to herself as she watched the cat. As she was about to start on tonight's dinner, the doorbell rang.

"That's our guest," Ava told Luna, who ignored her, hunger taking precedence.

She walked down the hall and opened the front door.

"I brought dessert," Eleanor said as she held a tin of home-made brownies.

"My favorite! Thanks," said Ava as they made their way back to the kitchen. "I'm sorry, I haven't started cooking yet. It'll be quick though."

Eleanor took a seat at the kitchen island as Ava filled a pot with water and set it on the stove, a click sounding as she turned on the gas. She poured two glasses of pinot grigio and handed one to Eleanor, who thanked her and took a sip.

"Is this the bobcat you texted me about?"

"Yes! Can you believe it? Isn't she amazing? Just be careful. She's friendly to me, but I don't know how she'll be to strangers."

"She's *definitely* different. You were right," Eleanor replied as she leaned down and allowed the cat to sniff her hand.

Luna seemed to accept Eleanor's offering and rubbed against her, chirruping happily. Ava relaxed as she realized Luna seemed as happy to be with Eleanor as she did with her.

"Did you name her yet?" she asked.

Sheepishly, she looked at Eleanor. "Um... I know I shouldn't have... but yes. Luna."

At the sound of her name, Luna perked up.

Eleanor smiled, hazel eyes sparkling. "I think she likes it."

Ava laughed. "I think so too."

Ava finished dinner and plated their food, suggesting they eat outside. Settling themselves at the outdoor dining table, Ava sighed and sipped her wine, the smell of their lemon ricotta pasta hovering in the air.

It was a lovely evening, the cool fall breeze bringing a slight chill. While the front yard had little trees besides the forest to allow sunlight to all the flowers, the back was almost fully shaded. The landscaping contained hostas, bleeding heart, ferns and other shade-loving plants. Dogwoods grew underneath the larger shade trees, and a stone birdbath was integrated seamlessly in one of the flowerbeds, surrounded by blue hydrangeas.

Breaking the silence, Ava blurted, "Henry kissed me."

"What?" Eleanor's eyes lit up. "Already? Tell me everything."

"Well," she started as she blushed and sipped her wine. "We were in the greenhouse. And then a mouse startled me, and I ended up pressed against him..."

Eleanor paused, holding her fork in the air. "You made out in the greenhouse?"

"Yeah. He started kissing me and it got pretty hot and heavy... Then his phone rang and he had to leave."

"Nooooo. You got interrupted?"

Ava nodded, swallowing a bite of pasta. "Then he promised we would 'pick up where we left off' next time."

"That's hot." Eleanor laughed, but then paused. "Are you okay with this?"

"What do you mean?"

Eleanor's brow knitted as she chose her words with caution. "You've known him for what... a week?" Ava looked at her friend. "Do you feel like it's too fast?"

"I—uhhh." She pursed her lips. "Yes and no. I don't want a relationship... at least I don't think I do."

"You just want to have fun?"

"Yes."

Or so she thought she did. Still not quite sure what she wanted, she fidgeted under Eleanor's assessment, not wanting to worry her friend.

"Okay." Eleanor smiled again, seriousness gone from her expression. "I just wanted to make sure he didn't pressure you," she added.

"No," Ava said. "Not at all."

"Good."

She had wanted him to kiss her. Wanted the freedom to give in to her desires and stop worrying about everything. Henry had given her that opportunity and she relished it; wanted more of it. So she decided she would try to let go and just live a little. So what if she didn't really know him? She could definitely be the kind of person to just have fun with no strings attached. Right?

"And... he said something else the other day I wanted to ask you about..." Eleanor gestured for her to go on. "He said there were rumors about this property." Ava twisted a piece of hair around her finger. "About witchcraft and spell books."

Eleanor shook her head. "It doesn't surprise me. People in town gossip a lot and I know they thought Abe was kind of weird. Plus... maybe someone saw your mom doing magic back then."

"Good point."

Ava was about to suggest they go inside and look for clues when a growl erupted from Luna and she leapt from the outdoor couch, trotting around the side of the house to the front. Ears perked up and tail twitching while her fur stood on end, the cat snarled and hissed at something in the distance.

Goosebumps chilled Ava's arms as she turned to Eleanor, whose eyes had widened.

"What's wrong with Luna?" her friend asked.

"Umm. I don't know."

The two women rose and followed the animal to the veranda on the side of the house, stopping behind her. Luna stared in the direction of the forest, growling and hissing feverishly. Looking toward the woods, Ava still didn't see anything, so she tried to soothe the cat to no avail. Maybe whatever had injured Luna was out there. They continued to scan the tree line when Eleanor gasped.

Lifting her shaking arm, Eleanor pointed to the forest beyond the flower field. "There," she whispered.

Ava searched where her friend was pointing, eyes scanning back and forth, but all she saw was the dark tree line.

Looking one last time, her eyes caught on a silhouette. Beyond the moonlight ensconced in shadows, was the figure from her dream. Claws emerged from its fingertips as it remained motionless and watched them.

Waiting to strike.

6

———

"Shit," Ava whispered.

"What is that?" The panic in Eleanor's voice rose.

It was unmoving. Staring. Watching.

"I've seen it before. The other night..."

Luna backed away and growled louder, breaking them from their trance. Ava grabbed Eleanor's hand and pulled her toward the back door, glancing over her shoulder. It was gone. She faced the backyard again, backing away as she tried to locate the threat, Luna snarling next to them.

"Where is it?" she asked.

Eleanor's voice quivered. "I don't know."

There.

Standing in the middle of the flower field. Even the flowers were frozen, no breeze flowing through them. As if the creature would cut them down should they reveal themselves.

"Run," Eleanor said.

They sprinted to the backdoor, Luna at their heels. Ava slammed it shut, turning the deadbolt, then ran around the house checking all the windows and doors to make sure they were locked, Eleanor helping. Luna was pacing but not growling anymore. Hopefully, that was a good sign.

The dream-not-dream she had the other night. The one that had felt real. It was the same creature, she was sure of it. Confirming it hadn't been a dream after all.

Brave enough to check outside once more, they went to the front of the house and peered through the windows. The blustery breeze had resumed and a whip-poor-will called in the woods as if there wasn't a sinister shadow lurking among the trees.

It was gone, and Luna was calm as further proof of its disappearance.

"What the fuck was that?" Eleanor asked as they walked back to the living room.

"I have no idea," said Ava. "But I don't think you should drive home right now."

"I agree." They took their places on the couch, when Eleanor turned to her. "You said you saw it before…"

"Yeah." Ava took a deep breath, trying to slow her still racing heart. "I had a dream—well, I don't think it was actually a dream. I don't know. But I followed it outside, to the edge of the woods. It seemed like it wanted me to go…"

"Wanted you to go where?"

"The forest I guess… Remember those screams we heard before?" Ava asked. Eleanor nodded. "I'm pretty sure that's what made them…"

"How do you know that?"

"Because it screamed in my dream or whatever and sounded exactly the same," explained Ava. "I don't know what's going on," she whispered as she fidgeted with the throw blanket she had pulled into her lap.

Eleanor leaned forward and gave her an intense look. "We'll figure it out, okay? I'll help you."

"Okay," Ava replied as she attempted a smile.

"Hey, where's your bathroom?"

Ava gave her directions and settled back on the couch, still tense from the encounter. Was she safe in this house? What if that creature came back? Could it get inside?

The toilet flushed and the sink turned on then off again. A door shut and Eleanor began to walk back to the living room, but the sound of her footsteps stopped.

"Umm... Ava?" she called out.

Getting up, she met her friend in the hallway. "What is it? What's wrong?"

Looking down at the floor, Eleanor pressed one of the wooden planks with the ball of her foot. "Has this always been loose?"

Ava knelt. "I don't know. This whole house is creaky and old."

Eleanor crouched down beside her. "This seems like more than just a random loose board."

"Really?" Ava responded as they tried to remove it.

"Yeah, it sounds more hollow than the rest of the floor."

They couldn't get their hands under it, so Ava went to the kitchen and retrieved a screwdriver, handing it to Eleanor. "Try this."

Kneeling together, Eleanor pried up the board with the tool, while Ava slid her fingers under the gap and pulled. The wood ripped free with a loud snap and Ava set it aside, the women peering into the hole.

"What is that?" asked Eleanor.

Ava reached in, hoping there were no spiders hiding in the dark, and pulled out something wrapped in fabric. "I don't know."

She unwrapped the worn cloth, revealing a key. Holding it to the light, she turned it in her hand, examining the detail. It was old. Ancient. It was heavy in her hand and made of brass. The head of the key was adorned with scrollwork woven together to form a tree. Something about the design felt familiar, though she couldn't put her finger on it.

"This key... have you seen anything in the house with a matching lock?" asked Eleanor. "Any old doors?"

Ava shook her head. "No."

Before the women could get a closer look, Luna waltzed over, took the key out of Ava's hand and ran upstairs.

"Luna!" Ava shouted. "You little shit! Give that back."

They chased her upstairs, but she was too fast. Darting into one of the bedrooms, Luna stopped in front of the closet and scratched as she looked at the women, waiting for them to open the door. Looking at Eleanor, Ava shrugged and opened the closet. Key still in her mouth, Luna walked to the back of the closet and pawed at the wall.

The closet was large enough for both women to enter, so they strode to the back and looked at the wall where Luna was scratching.

"I don't see anything," said Ava. "It looks like a normal wall." She ran her hands along it and almost gave up when her fingers snagged on something. "It's a seam. There must be a door here to the attic or something. Hand me that screwdriver."

Eleanor handed the tool to Ava and she started scraping away the paint along the newfound seam. After ten minutes of work, they could see the outline of the door. A door that had been painted shut, probably for good reason. Ava hesitated, unsure if they should pursue this any further but Luna was insistent, growling and scratching at the space as if urging the women to break through.

"I'm going to grab a crowbar," Ava said as she ran downstairs, returning moments later with the new tool and a couple of flashlights.

The door was difficult to move, but after a few minutes of prying, it gave way.

They froze as it creaked open, revealing the dark dusty attic.

They had to duck to enter as the door was only about four feet high. Ava led the way, shining the flashlight to light their path. Once inside, they stood and evaluated the room, letting their eyes adjust to the dim light. Luna stayed in the closet, seemingly reluctant to enter the dark space.

If her grandfather was hiding information, surely it would be here.

"Look around to see if there's anything that looks important," said Ava.

"Okay."

Ava made her way across the floor, wooden planks creaking with each step. Dust covered every surface, and the smell of mildew permeated the air. An old piano covered in cobwebs occupied one corner, next to a stack of worn music sheets. Boxes were stacked along the walls, dotted with knickknacks in varying states of disintegration. Vintage lamps with broken shades, picture frames with cracked glass, moth eaten rugs rolled up and stacked together took up ample space in the attic.

"Anything?" Eleanor asked from the other side of the room.

"Nothing..." Ava replied. "You?"

"No. Not even sure what we're looking for."

"Uhh... witchcraft stuff?" Ava said, eliciting a soft laugh from her friend.

Ava walked by an old stack of records sitting on top of a box. As she passed, she thought she heard something. Pausing, she turned back, approached it and knelt.

Noticing her change of direction, Eleanor walked over. "What is it?"

She looked at her friend. "I thought I heard..." Ava shook her head. "Never mind," she added as she began to rise.

Before she had a chance to stand, she heard it again. A whisper. "*Ava.*"

She whipped her head toward Eleanor, still standing behind her. "Did you hear that?"

"Hear what?"

"My name. I heard someone whispering my name..." Ava tensed, hearing it again. "*Ava...*" She looked back toward the box, heart racing as she reached for it.

"You don't hear that?" she asked again as her trembling hands grabbed some records and worked to uncover the container.

Kneeling beside her, Eleanor helped, moving more records off to the side. "I don't hear anything..." she said.

"Something's in that box," said Ava as they cleared it.

She ripped the tape off the top, opened the flaps and peered inside. "*Ava!*" the voice called again, louder this time, causing her to flinch. As Ava shined her flashlight on the contents of the vessel, she gasped at what was inside.

"It's a chest. With an old lock..." she exclaimed, turning to Eleanor.

Eleanor's eyes widened. "Oh!"

Ava picked up the chest. It was heavier than it looked and made of rusted metal. "Let's open it downstairs where we can see better."

"Good idea," Eleanor replied. "It's creepy up here."

Hurrying, the women exited the attic and walked downstairs, Ava carrying the chest and Eleanor the key. She set it on the dining room table with a thud and turned on the overhead lights, Luna taking her place near Ava's feet. Eleanor stood across from her as she leaned forward and traced her fingers over the symbols. The chest was rusted, the symbols adorning it indiscernible, but they didn't look familiar from what she could tell.

"What is this?" Ava whispered before reaching her hand out. "Hand me the key."

"I don't know... I have a bad feeling. I don't think we should mess with it." Eleanor's voice was strained.

Ava looked at her, biting her lip. "I need to know."

Sighing, Eleanor handed it over. "Be careful."

Ava's trembling hand inched forward as she fit the key into the keyhole. "Ready?"

"Ready," Eleanor responded, voice barely audible.

Ava turned it and a click sounded as the latch was released inside. "Here goes nothing..." she whispered as she let go and lifted the lid.

Ava's shoulders sagged as nothing happened, though Luna appeared restless, pacing between her legs. She chirped at Ava, encouraging her to look inside.

Both women inched forward, peering into the chest.

"What is it?" Eleanor asked.

"A book."

They stared at each other in shock, remembering Henry's words about spell books.

"Open it," Eleanor urged, fear replaced by excitement.

Reaching inside, Ava lifted the tome from its hiding place. The moment her hands closed around its bindings, she felt a wave of nausea come over her and a sudden sense of falling, like she was being pulled down. The voice sounded again, louder than before. *"Ava!"*

Gasping, she dropped it onto the table and leaned forward, placing her hands on her knees. "Oh god," she said.

Eleanor rushed to her side, placing a gentle hand on Ava's back. "What? What is it? Are you okay?"

Ava took several deep breaths, allowing the nausea to ease before she stood straight again. "Yeah. I'm fine. I just... got a weird sensation." She continued to steady her breathing. "Like I was falling... and I heard that voice again." She looked at her friend. "I just realized I've heard it before. In my dreams."

Eleanor's eyes widened. "Are you serious?"

"Yeah." She turned back to the table. "Should we open it?"

"Should you really touch it again?"

"We've come this far..."

They looked at the book. It looked old. Black leather bound a large volume together with a gnarled tree embossed on the front cover.

"Eleanor..." Ava whispered as she realized what she was seeing. "The dreams I've been having... there's a tree in them. It looks like that," she finished as she pointed to the symbol.

It was the same tree that was on the key.

Eleanor was speechless.

Steeling herself, Ava reached toward it. Her fingers grazed the leather as she lifted the cover, the temperature in the room plummeting the moment it opened. Shivering, the women looked at each other. They could see their breaths in the frigid kitchen.

A chill went down Ava's spine as she looked at Eleanor, voice shaking. "What the fuck?"

Luna didn't seem upset, but jumped onto the table and sat down, staring at the book. As if saying 'well... read it.'

Unsure what to do, they remained still for a few moments, the temperature of the room rising back to normal. After the icy air had seemed to disappear, Eleanor inched closer to Ava and whispered, "I think your house is haunted."

"Ghosts aren't real," Ava responded unconvincingly, giving her a wan smile.

As they sat down at the table, she flipped through the pages but nothing else unusual happened. No chilled air, no strange sensations. Relieved for that part to be over, Ava's heart calmed down as she tried to read but the text was in an unfamiliar language. It was like nothing she had ever seen before. Flipping through more of the book, the pages revealed drawings. Archways with symbols on them with swirling black voids in the center.

"We can't read it," she said. "It's in some foreign language."

"What are those pictures?" Eleanor pointed to the archways.

Tracing her finger along the drawings, Ava said, "I don't

know. Maybe I should start to explore the property more and see if there's any more clues."

Eleanor nodded, glancing at the time on the microwave. It was past midnight. "Oh god, I didn't realize what time it was. I really should go."

"You're right," Ava said. "I need to get to sleep too."

After bidding her friend goodbye, Ava poured herself another glass of wine and sat down at the table. She knew she should go to bed, but she had to look through this book more thoroughly and didn't want to wait.

She spent almost two hours attempting to decipher each page while Luna slept at her feet but had little luck understanding the information in the tome. The language was unrecognizable.

She tried focusing on the pictures of those strange archways. She couldn't help but trace each one she came across and every time her fingers grazed the symbols lining the void, she felt that tug.

The book was another piece to the puzzle. The puzzle that still meant nothing to her. She would have to keep looking.

7

Fall was in full swing, and tonight Henry was taking Ava to Piney Hollow's annual Halloween festival. Ava had spent all day cleaning her house as a distraction from her nerves and now her house was spotless. It had helped, and the anxiety was now a low buzz as she anticipated Henry's arrival. Cleaning always helped when she was nervous.

Henry had been coming over regularly to help with farm tasks and though it had been several weeks since their greenhouse make out session, nothing further had happened. They kissed a few times, and the flirting was much more intense, but she still hadn't invited him inside.

The crunch of gravel outside announced his arrival, and she bounded down the stairs in her black jeans and cream-colored sweater. Her long waves cascaded down her back from her high ponytail, bouncing as she made her way outside.

Ava leapt down the porch stairs and Henry grabbed her hand and pulled her close. "Hello," he said, voice low, as he enveloped her in his warmth and gave her the tightest squeeze.

"Hi." She smiled back, heart fluttering.

"Are you ready to go?"

"Yes!" Ava said, trying to hide her nerves under her enthusiasm about this being their first official date.

She climbed into his vehicle and Henry grinned at her like a child excited to go to an amusement park as they pulled away. His eyes looked exceptionally blue against his black sweater, sparkling in the evening sunset as they headed down the drive toward town.

TWENTY MINUTES later they were walking through charming booths lining the barricaded streets, with ebony awnings and purple twinkling lights highlighting the wares displayed on deep violet tablecloths. Witch hats and bats were strung about, decorating each stall with a festive spirit, flowing together seamlessly as if all designed by the same person, the sellers and wares the only difference between each alcove.

Clusters of pumpkins and lit jack-o-lanterns lined the walkways, glowing in the fading daylight. Music resounded from the main stage near the town square, a local cover band playing renditions from festive popular movies such as *Halloween* and *Hocus Pocus*, adding an air of revelry to the night.

Children in costumes darted between the crowd, stopping at booths to trick-or-treat and collect their bounty of candy. Witches, goblins, cowboys and princesses dashed in front of Henry and Ava as they wound their way hand in hand through the crowd.

"This is amazing," Ava said as she looked at Henry.

His eyes lit up as he replied, "Let's get something to eat."

Ava nodded and they continued walking toward the center of town to the food stalls. The green space in the town square had been converted into a giant haunted house, the sounds of shrieking children and adults alike drifting from the entrance.

She smiled at herself at the feel of Henry's fingers interlaced with hers. The intimacy that small act created was something she'd been craving without even realizing it until he appeared on her property that fateful morning.

The food stalls were neatly positioned near the main square, also adorned with purple lights and dark fabrics, full of mouthwatering smells of pumpkin, turkey legs and apple cider.

"I'm starving," she said, inhaling the scents as her stomach growled.

"Me too."

They decided on a turkey leg to share and some cold apple cider for the time being, though Ava wanted to devour all the pastries and confections she could find, satisfying her never ending sweet tooth. They sat on a bench near the lawn, watching patrons enter and leave the haunted house with faces full of excitement.

Henry handed her the turkey leg. "Thanks for coming as my date."

Blushing, she fidgeted in her seat. "Thanks for asking," she replied, taking a bite.

"We have a spring festival too. You should set up a flower booth next year," he suggested.

"That's a great idea," said Ava. "You could help me build a display stand!"

"Only if you let me do the hammering," he said as he took a sip of cider.

She rolled her eyes and laughed.

She imagined herself in her overalls, collecting and organizing flowers and transporting them to the town square. She could see her booth, decorated with light purple fabric with bouquets for sale but also single stems for purchase. The combination of pink tulips, white hyacinths and yellow daffodils would make a lovely display as she visited with the townsfolk who purchased her goods. Maybe she would even create a 'build your own bouquet' station.

After they finished the turkey leg, Ava announced, "I need something sweet." And led Henry to the stalls with the delectable dessert options.

She opted for a deep-fried pumpkin ice cream sandwich while Henry ate a fried apple pie, and they wandered toward the artisan stands as they munched their treats.

"This is so good. Try it," she moaned as she held it up.

He took a bite. "That's delicious." Then leaning in, he whispered, "Save those sounds for later tonight." He turned and faced her, stopping in the middle of the crowd, and his eyes dipped to her lips.

Her heart skipped a beat as she looked up. "I—Um. What?"

He took a step closer as he murmured, "We never got to finish what we started in the greenhouse."

Butterflies erupted in her stomach as he turned and continued to walk, reaching around her waist and pulling her closer as they strode side by side.

Wandering through the crowd, they came upon a tent with a sign that read, *Have Your Fortune Told. $10.*

Henry noticed her looking at it. "Do you want to?"

"Sure, I guess. What's the harm?" She shrugged as they turned and headed toward it, knowing it was all a ruse anyway.

They entered the small shelter and a woman rose from her folding chair in the corner. "Welcome, welcome! Which of you would like to have a reading?"

Ava didn't recognize her from town. She was old, with cavernous wrinkles hiding her deep-set brown eyes. A turquoise floral scarf was fastened over her snow-white hair, and she wore brightly colored layers of flowing chiffon, her skirt billowing with deep purple and royal blue as she approached.

"Both of us," answered Henry.

She regarded him, scrutinizing every feature. "I'm sorry, young man. Only one person at a time. My readings can be intense, and I insist my patrons have complete privacy. It's their choice if they want their partners to know about what happens in my tent."

Henry shrugged and looked at Ava. "You can go. I don't really want mine done." He handed a ten-dollar bill to the woman and exited the tent. "I'll wait outside."

Now it was the woman's turn to inspect Ava, and inspect her she did. She recoiled at the sharp gaze as the fortune teller regarded her, as if she could read each thought swirling through Ava's mind. Though she knew this was likely a scam, the way the old woman evaluated her had her questioning the decision to come in here.

Looking her up and down, she waved her hand. "Have a seat."

Ignoring her unease, Ava sat in an old wooden chair at a small round table covered in a royal blue tablecloth sprinkled with silver moons and stars. The inside of the tent was lined with bookshelves decorated with dozens of flickering candles, casting eerie shapes against the plum-colored velvet walls. The ceiling rose, the fabric joining together at the apex with colorful glass lanterns casting a glow and contributing to the supernatural shadows.

The old woman sat across from Ava and yanked a piece of velvet off the table, revealing a crystal ball. Ava tried not to roll her eyes at the theatrics, and remained quiet, waiting for the woman to speak as she adjusted her sweater.

"You look nervous, girl," the woman spoke in a hoarse voice.

"I'm not," Ava lied.

The crone sighed and closed her eyes, gnarled hands hovering over the crystal ball. She hummed to herself for a while before opening her eyes and peering into the void. Ava saw nothing and tried not to laugh as she prepared herself for the cheesy fortune.

"You will find your true love soon," she said as she watched her prop on the table. "He will be handsome, kind and very powerful." Ava stifled a giggle. "You can trust him, and he will always keep you safe. Fate is bringing you together as we speak. He is part of your path forward." She looked at Ava, watching for a reaction.

"Oh wow!" She feigned surprise, assuming the old woman invented this after seeing her walk in with Henry. "That sounds amazing," she added as she began to rise from her seat. "Thank you for your time."

The woman grinned wildly, revealing rotten broken teeth scattered throughout her mouth and shot her hand across the table, gripping Ava's wrist firmly and forcing her to sit back down. "We're not done," her voice echoed, different now.

"I—" Ava tried to wrench her arm away.

"Be still and listen to me," the woman insisted as she opened Ava's palm with her other hand and traced the lines. "You must take this seriously, child," she hissed in her ancient voice, volume rising.

Ava looked at her, wrist throbbing under the feeble woman's grip as her heart started to race. "Let me go."

The woman held tighter as her eyes bored into Ava's. "You found the book."

"What?" Ava whispered. "How the hell do you know that?"

It wasn't possible. There was no way this random woman was an actual psychic. Ava didn't believe in psychics.

"Shhhh...listen." The woman's voice changed, molding into something deeper. Something supernatural. The candles flickered, flames guttering from an invisible force. The hair on the back of Ava's neck stood erect as the woman spoke, voice echoing nowhere and everywhere as her eyes glossed over. "You won't be able to run from the prophecy, young lady."

"Prophecy?" she whispered, as her hands shook.

"You must go back. Find your homeland," her voice croaked. "Do not trust anyone. There are deceivers."

"Stop," Ava pleaded as she tried again to free her hand.

The woman quieted, eyes closing. "The voice in your dreams," she whispered harshly. "You must find him."

Panicking, Ava yanked her arm free and rushed out of the tent leaving the old crone and her omen behind. She stood in the cool air, feeling dizzy as she took deep breaths, willing herself calm before Henry noticed her alarm.

How did the woman know about the book and the prophecy? What the hell *was* the prophecy? Other than a brief snippet in her grandfather's journal she had no idea what it could even be about. Who was the voice in her dreams? Her homeland? Ava's efforts to write off her grandfather's ramblings were crumbling with each discovery. The book, the creature in the woods and now this. Plus, there was something about Luna she still couldn't figure out. And what was this about deceivers? Uneasiness brewed inside Ava's stomach as she ruminated over what the woman said.

The one thing she was almost certain of was that she was on the cusp of finding answers. Like a small seed of truth had been planted when she was a child and was continuing to grow, now on the verge of blooming. A great and terrible bud about to burst open and upend everything.

She rubbed her temple and looked at the night sky, allowing the crisp breeze to cool her face. Nerves waning, she turned to search for Henry. She found him lingering a few booths away, eyeing the art displayed with care along the walls of the kiosk. She hoped he couldn't tell she was still rattled, and it took every effort to hide her nerves.

"How'd it go?" he asked, taking her hands in his and stepping close.

"Well." She smiled, heart still racing. "She said I would find my true love soon."

His eyes twinkled. "Is that so?"

She shrugged. "I doubt it."

Henry laughed and pulled her down the aisle and they resumed their shopping. "I guess we'll have to see about that."

THE REST of the evening had gone wonderfully, Ava and Henry giggling throughout the ridiculous haunted house. Those in charge had made sure it wasn't too scary, allowing even the youngest children to participate, causing it to be hilarious rather than terrifying.

At one point, the diner owner, Mel, had barged through a false wall bellowing, "Leave this place!" covered in spaghetti and meatballs. Ava had laughed so hard she had tears streaming down her face and Henry was right there along with her, shouting, "Beware of the spaghetti monster!" as they continued down the hallway.

Though Ava enjoyed the rest of the festival, she couldn't stop thinking about what had transpired in the tent with the fortune teller. The woman spoke about the book and the prophecy and Ava knew it couldn't be a coincidence. But she still didn't understand what any of it meant.

They pulled into the driveway, and Henry walked her to her front door.

She stopped and turned toward him. "Do you want to come in?"

The words had come out before she even had a chance to think about it. With him around, there was no chance to even process what she wanted to do. Because the only thing she wanted was him.

He crept closer and looked down at her, eyes full of need. "Yes," he rasped.

She could barely get the keys in the door as she trembled with anticipation, but she was able to get it open and tossed her purse onto the entry table as the door slammed behind them.

The moment she turned around, Henry's lips were upon hers, hands gripping her hips and pulling her closer. The kiss went on, intensifying and filling Ava with uncontrollable desire as she ran her fingers through his hair. Henry pulled away and placed light kisses down her jaw, her throat, the place where her shoulder met her neck. He continued lower, kissing below her clavicle. She moaned, needing more. He continued up the other side and met her lips again, his hand now cupping her breast over her sweater.

He reached down and pulled the sweater over her head, tossing it to the ground and she followed suit, removing his shirt and revealing his lithe muscled torso. He looked down at her black lace bra and hummed, running his fingers down the straps before grasping her breasts again.

"Upstairs," she ordered.

He briskly picked her up, hands under her thighs as she wrapped her legs around him. He carried her up the stairs attempting to steal kisses along the way as she looped her hands over his neck. They entered the bedroom and Henry laid her on the crisp sheets as he stood before her.

The next thing Ava knew, the rest of their clothes were flying across the room and Henry was upon her. His palms moved along her soft curves, the heat of his touch sending shivers over her as he explored every inch.

She relished the warmth of his hands as he dragged the tip of his nose along her jaw and then kissed her again. Ava had never known this kind of hunger. As if she was starving and would never be satiated.

Her breath caught as he moved closer and they joined, his

heaviness pressed against her body. Her longing for intimacy and pleasure overrode any semblance of practicality left and she moved with him.

Faster, harder, their mouths full of teeth and tongue, they frantically kissed as pressure began to build. She arched against him as waves of pleasure washed over her and she gasped, clinging to him in desperation as she lost herself in the fog of lust.

8

"*A*va! Ava wake up!" Someone was shaking her.

Opening her eyes, she turned and saw Henry's face. "I think you were having a nightmare," he said, concerned. "Are you okay?"

She sat up and looked around to clear her mind. She was not in the forest. She was at home, in her bed. Henry was with her. Realizing she was safe, she looked at him. "I'm fine."

"What were you dreaming about?" he asked, brushing the hair from her face.

"Just a bad dream about my mom. That happens sometimes. I'm fine," she answered.

But it had been another one of those strange dreams about running through the woods toward the glowing tree and the man calling her name. Why did she lie to him? Unsure of why she felt the need for dishonesty, she knew for some reason she didn't want to tell him about her recurring dreams. They felt too important, too personal.

It had been a couple of weeks since the Halloween festival and Henry had gotten in the habit of spending the night frequently. Their relationship was progressing rather quickly, and he had proven to be a kind and attentive boyfriend.

She wasn't initially looking for a relationship. She wanted a fling, some fun. Someone to flirt with and maybe companionship, but over the last few weeks she was feeling drawn to him. As if she couldn't stop herself from wanting to be in his presence, needing to be around him. He radiated sensuality. Underneath the handyman persona was a suave man, smooth-talking until she became a puddle of nerves.

She'd never experienced anything like it.

It came so easily for them. They never argued; never even got irritated with each other. He was always kind to her; helping her fix things around the house and providing a comforting presence. And the sex. She'd never known pleasure like that before. Every time he kissed her it was as if she lost control of herself and was pulled into a haze of desire. It was almost too easy.

He pulled her to him, and she settled onto his chest as he stroked her hair. "Are you sure you're alright? You're having nightmares a lot."

He was right. She was having them almost every night, but she didn't admit it to him. "I'm fine. They come and go."

What she didn't say was she was exhausted, barely sleeping these days. Ever since moving to the farm, these recurring dreams appeared and had been getting more frequent, as if she was getting closer to something she couldn't yet see.

She trusted Henry, and though she wasn't ready to talk about the dreams, she decided to reveal a little to him about what she found.

She tilted her head to look at him. "Remember when you said there were rumors about witches and stuff here?"

"Yes."

"I found something," she said.

He sat halfway up, looking down at her. "Really? What?"

Though she had brushed off most of the whole 'love' part of the fortune, the old woman had said she could trust him. She knew it was silly, but it brought her comfort for some reason.

Rising out of the bed, she threw on her robe and opened the top drawer of her dresser. Digging under her clothing, she retrieved the book and handed it to him, sitting back down on the bed. "This."

He carefully regarded the tome. "Wow. Is this real?"

"I think so. Okay, so… please don't think I'm crazy." She took a deep breath. "But when I touched it for the first time, it made me sick."

He looked at her, incredulous. "Really? What does that mean?"

"I don't know." She laughed quietly. "Eleanor joked that my house was haunted."

"Eleanor saw it too?"

She nodded. "We found it together. I promise I'm not crazy…"

He placed his hand on her face. "I don't think you're crazy. Why didn't you tell me sooner?"

"I didn't think you'd believe me."

"Of course I believe you. Can I look inside?" he asked as he removed his hand and looked back down at the book in his lap.

"Sure."

Henry opened the book, treating it with reverence as if he was afraid it would break.

"It's in a different language," Ava said.

"I can see that. How strange," he said as he stopped on the page with archways and symbols. "What are these?"

She shook her head. "I don't know… but they look like portals or something?"

"They do. But portals aren't real." He laughed, but there was a brief flash in his eyes. A subtle expression that almost looked like he was deep in thought. Maybe he didn't believe her; he was just humoring her to be kind.

"I never said they were," she teased. "That's just what it looks like."

"Have you found anything else?"

She pulled her robe tighter. "No. But—"

He met her eyes and took her hand. "But what?"

"I think there's something in the forest."

Henry scrunched his brow. "Like what?"

She ran her thumb over the top of his hand. "Like shadows or something. Like—" She paused. "Like there are people watching me."

He frowned. "People? Watching you?"

Exasperated, she let out a breath. "I don't know, it's just..." She tugged on her earlobe. "I feel them. And see shadows moving." She stared at him. "Oh god, you think I'm crazy."

He shook his head enthusiastically. "No no no. I believe you... but—" He hesitated. "Do you think it's the lack of sleep?"

It didn't seem like he believed her.

She sighed. "Probably."

"If it'll make you feel better, I'll install a security system for you."

"Thanks." She gave him a quick kiss. "I'll think about it."

LATER THAT EVENING, Ava was snuggled on her couch with a cup of chamomile tea to catch up on some reading. She was in the middle of an epic fantasy series about dragons and politics and war and hadn't had as much time to read in between managing the farm and spending time with Henry. She was lost in an intense battle scene, swords clanging, tension rising and one of her favorite characters was gravely injured.

Luna was nestled at her feet, fast asleep, now a constant

companion at the farmhouse. It was getting late and though she was starting to get tired, she wanted to finish a couple more chapters before going to sleep, needing to know what happened next. But Ava found herself barely able to keep her eyes open and nodded off, the book face down on her chest.

She was interrupted by frantic growling and pawing at her face. Sitting up, she saw Luna awake and staring at her. "What is it?" she asked, rubbing her eyes.

A small feminine voice replied in her head as the cat evaluated her. *Hello, Ava.*

Panicking, Ava jumped off the couch. "Did you just talk to me? How?"

I can talk to you in your dreams. But in our world, we can communicate any time, Luna replied.

"What? Our world? I'm dreaming?" Ava said shakily, staring at her feline friend.

Luna tilted her head. *Yes. You're dreaming, but this is real. I'm not an animal of this world, I come from another realm.*

"What?" Ava blanched.

Things are not as they seem. Those pictures in the book are portals. You were right.

"Portals to where?"

Anywhere. Other worlds, realms. There's one in the forest.

Ava gasped and stared at Luna. "Here? On this property? Where does it lead?"

Home.

Shaking her head, Ava replied, "This is my home."

No, it's not. You've always wondered, haven't you? Why you were different. How your mother could do magic. It's because that's where your family is from. The book you found. It's sacred. You mustn't let her attain it.

"Who?"

The demon queen.

"I don't understand," Ava pleaded, shaking.

You must find the map and go home. To Eorhan.

"Why?"

Because it was prophesied.

"What was prophesied?

I don't know all the details. Only that you must go back.

"What do I do?"

Find the map. Find the portal. You must go home.

"I... I can't."

You can and you must. I know the Elderoak calls to you. Whispers to you in your dreams. It is your destiny, Ava.

"Elderoak?"

The Elderoak is a sacred tree. Revered by your people.

"Can't I just search the property for the portal?"

No. Your grandfather made it so the portal is invisible unless you have the map.

"He could do magic too?" Ava had never seen him do it. At least, not that she could recall.

Of course he could. Most of those from our world can do magic. To find the map, you must look in the place where life is created. Only then will you find the answers you seek.

"What does that even mean? Please tell me more," she begged the cat who was still staring at her seated on the couch.

You must hurry. There isn't much time left. She's coming. Eorhan needs your help.

AVA AWOKE and scanned the living room, her eyes landing on Luna who was still asleep at her feet on the sofa.

Everything seemed normal, though the eerie feeling from her dream remained. Thoughts of talking cats and mysterious portals swirled about in her head, blurring the lines of what was real and imagined.

She tried to calm herself by denying the plausibility of

these strange occurrences. Animals couldn't speak. She knew that. It was just a weird dream. Probably because she had been reading, it was late and she was exhausted.

And yet.

Something continued to badger her, to push her to believe. To accept. *Magic.*

She stood and headed to the kitchen for a glass of water. After taking a long gulp she set the cup down harder than intended. Deep down she knew it was true; all of this meant something.

Clenching her fists she took a deep breath and closed her eyes, her body overcome with anger. Her mother died, then Grandpa and now they'd left her this disaster, keeping secrets her whole life. If this so-called prophecy was true, why didn't they tell her? Why didn't they go back to their world and face it? What were they hiding from?

Ava knew nothing about magic or what she herself was capable of. If only they had helped her, trained her, she'd be more prepared. But now here she was, alone, scrambling for answers she wasn't sure she wanted any more. She was settling into a life here with Eleanor and Henry, and now she was supposed to go help some world she had never heard of?

She opened her eyes and glared at Luna, still fast asleep.

"Fine," she said out loud. "I'll look for the fucking map."

Luna perked up and looked at her, staring as if she understood what Ava had said. She continued to scowl across the room at her cat. "Is that what I need to do? Find the map?"

Luna huffed and set her head back down and Ava rolled her eyes.

She glanced at the microwave and saw it was well past one in the morning. Finishing her water, she set the glass in the sink and trudged upstairs leaving Luna asleep on the couch. Thunder rumbled in the distance as the pitter patter of rain tapped on the bathroom windows. A cold front was arriving in preparation for the transition into winter.

She washed her face and changed into her soft sage green pajamas. The storm rolled closer, gaining momentum as the wind blew the leaves on the trees and the thunder increased its volume. Flashes of lightning illuminated the dark hallway through the windows of the bedrooms across from hers, throwing eerie shadows along the walls.

As she walked back to her bedroom, a deafening clap of thunder sounded, followed by complete darkness. Ava cursed as she stubbed her toe on the corner of her bed frame in the pitch-black room.

Using the flashlight app on her phone she looked around her room, locating the light switch on the wall. She flicked it on and off, willing the lights to return.

Nothing.

Her power was truly out.

This was the worst storm Ava could remember, concern growing as deafening thunder clapped repeatedly, barely any down time in between crashes. She made her way toward the stairs to check on Luna, phone in one hand while her other felt along the wall to orient herself. The almost constant lightning created disconcerting shadows along the walls and the floor like a sinister dance of tree branches enveloping the staircase.

About halfway down, a glimmer caught her eye. There was water glistening on the floor in the entryway. Assuming she had a leaky window, she rushed down the stairs, preparing to grab towels from the linen closet.

When she reached the water, she froze. It was sitting in individual puddles leading toward the living room, almost like... footprints. Those were footprints.

Thunder crashed again, this time causing her to jump.

The muddy footprints were leading further into her house. Scanning the hallway, the sounds of heavy rain and wind increased, and her attention was turned to the front door. It was open.

Someone was in her house.

She tried to call Henry or the police, but she had no service. Even the emergency bypass function didn't work.

Heart racing, she tiptoed to the kitchen to grab a knife, scanning everywhere in case someone jumped out. She wasn't sure where Luna was, her spot on the couch now empty, but she hoped the cat had not been harmed.

The footprints made their way toward the kitchen and living room but veered to the office and Ava sprinted the last few steps to the knife block on the counter.

She stood in the kitchen, her trembling hand gripping the knife, unsure what to do. She could sneak back outside and get in her car and drive away, but her car keys were in the office, and she didn't want to follow the footprints. Even if she managed to get her keys, the rain was coming down so heavily she was worried the road could be washed out and she would then be stuck outside in the storm with the risk of a flash flood whisking her away. She could hide upstairs until morning and hope whoever had entered would leave without issues. Maybe it was someone passing by looking for shelter from the storm.

As she stood there, frozen, a bright flash of lightning illuminated the house. In the office doorway was a shadowed figure, chillingly still.

The creature from the woods. And it was looking straight at her.

Ava could sense the power emanating from the monster as it assessed her, tilting its head like it was preparing for a hunt.

She gripped the knife harder, hoping her shaking hands didn't betray her, and backed away toward the hallway, her breaths coming in rapid bursts. She needed to get away. Now.

Another flash of lightning. It was closer, standing only

about thirty feet away. She increased her pace of retreat when the creature dashed forward, claws elongating as it closed in.

Ava turned and sprinted down the hallway, willing to take her chances outside.

She risked a glance over her shoulder. It was gaining on her with its arms outstretched, claws ready for shredding. It was still cloaked in shadow, and she couldn't see much other than its enormous height and pointed teeth.

Almost there. Just a little further. Hurry, Ava.

She pushed herself hard, pleading with her legs to go faster. She was a few feet from the threshold of the front door when she slipped in the mud. Tumbling down, she tried to regain her footing to no avail. Arms flailing, she reached out to grasp onto something but failed to keep herself upright.

She went down as if in slow motion when a sharp pain struck her forehead.

The world slipped away and there was nothing.

9

*B*right light pierced the room as Ava awoke, squinting against the intensity of the sun. Softness surrounded her, enveloping her in its warmth. Opening her eyes further, she sat up. She was in her bed in her room, and it was morning. No storm. No horrifying figure lurking about. Had it all been a dream? No, it couldn't have been. It had felt so real.

She reached up and touched her forehead, wincing. Running her fingers below her hairline, she felt something stiff... like... bandages? So, it was real. She had truly fallen and hit her head. How did she get to her bed?

The sound of footsteps turned her attention to the door, and Henry entered with a glass of water and a couple of pills.

"You're awake," he said with a smile. He sat on the edge of the bed, brushing her hair out of her face. "How are you feeling, beautiful?"

"I... my head. What happened?" She touched her forehead again. "How did I get here? When did *you* get here?"

"Here, take this." Henry handed her the glass of water and medication. "You hit your head pretty hard."

She obeyed and swallowed the pills, chasing them with a cool gulp of water, realizing how thirsty she was. Her head was pounding incessantly, forehead especially tender near the injury.

Setting the cup on the nightstand, she took a shuddering breath. "What happened?"

"I was worried about you in the storm," he explained. "When I got here, the front door was open, and you were on the floor. It looked like you had fallen and hit your head. You were unconscious so I carried you upstairs and treated your injury."

Ava looked around and then back at Henry. "Did you see anyone else? Someone in the house?"

"No, it was just you." Henry scrunched his brow. "It looked like you went outside and then when you came back in, you slipped."

No, that wasn't right. She never went outside. She was running away from the kitchen, the creature chasing her. Then she fell and everything went black.

"What about footprints? There were footprints leading from the front door all the way to the office." She fidgeted with the comforter. "Did you see them?"

"No. I saw muddy footprints from when you went outside. The rest of your house was clean and untouched."

"But I *know* I saw something." She shook her head. "Someone was in my house."

Henry pondered, obviously not believing her. "I think you hit your head so hard you don't remember exactly what happened. You were in and out of consciousness for hours."

"No, I remember it very clearly. I saw it," she insisted. "It had claws and sharp teeth and chased me!" Her voice rose, hands starting to shake.

"The power was out. You couldn't see well in the dark and between the lightning and noise of the storm, your eyes must have been playing tricks on you."

"Don't patronize me, Henry. I know what I saw," she spat, anger making an appearance at his apparent disbelief.

Henry put his hand on hers. "I'm not patronizing you. I'm just saying sometimes when we're scared, we can't trust our memories."

She sighed and pinched the bridge of her nose. He wasn't going to believe her. It wouldn't help the situation if she took her frustrations out on him.

"Have you seen Luna?" she asked, changing the subject.

She had told Henry about her companion not long ago, and while he had caught glimpses of her every so often, she seemed to remain hidden from everyone except herself and Eleanor. Though sweet and affectionate, Luna still came and went as she pleased and Ava assumed she was wary of most strangers, including Henry.

"No." He shook his head. "She wasn't here when I got here."

"I hope she's okay..." she wondered.

"I'm sure she's fine." He pushed a strand of hair behind her ear and looked at her. "She's a wild animal. They know what to do in a storm."

"I guess so," she said, looking out the window as if she could will her friend to appear in the yard.

"You need to stay in bed today," said Henry, voice soft. "I can stay with you for a little while if you'd like." Brushing his fingers over her jaw, he planted a kiss on her forehead. "I'll get ready to go make you breakfast." He rose from the bed and left the room.

She lay back down and mulled over last night. The dream where Luna spoke to her and the invader in her house. Though she was shaken by the events over the last few weeks, a small part of her wasn't surprised. There was a deep truth that had been hovering just below the surface ever since she was a child, and it was on the verge of revealing itself.

It was all connected somehow but she couldn't quite put

her finger on it. Whatever was going on seemed to be escalating and after Luna's urgent warning last night, Ava was determined to find the map.

She'd invite Eleanor over to help in a couple of days and together they'd try to figure out the clue and search the property. If there truly was a map that led to a portal on her acreage... Well, she'd figure out what to do then.

"Is there anything I can help you with?" Henry asked as he followed Ava into the house after they finished the morning chores on the farm.

"No, I think I got it," she answered.

Eleanor was coming over later tonight and Ava wanted to clean up and run to the store before she arrived. They made their way down the hallway into the kitchen and Henry reached for his keys on the counter.

"Okay, then," he said as he leaned in. "I need to get going. I have some errands to run."

He kissed her, winding his hands into her unbound hair as she returned the fervor, arms around his neck. She moaned into his mouth, pulling him closer as he deepened the kiss.

He reluctantly pulled away. "Have fun tonight and don't get into too much trouble."

"I won't." She smiled as Henry turned and headed out the door.

Ever since Ava hit her head last weekend, Henry had been excessively cautious with her. He finally believed someone was in her house and had installed a security system the next day, showing her how to view the camera feed and set the alarm.

As she walked upstairs to shower, her mind returned to the riddle from her dream. She had mulled it over daily and still couldn't make sense of it.

The place where life is created. What does that even mean?

The vague statement could mean a multitude of things and she had no clue how to interpret it. Life was created when a baby was conceived, or maybe in a laboratory... or could it be referring to animals? The riddle felt incomplete, just out of reach, as if it was taunting her.

She had scoured her house, hunting for any semblance of a clue or a map, even a hint of anything different or otherworldly.

Nothing.

She came up empty handed every time.

Finishing her shower, she threw on some athletic clothing and walked downstairs and out the front door. The trees were in their full autumn glory now. Deep scarlets, oranges and yellows embellished the forest as if they had been plucked from a painting and placed around her property. Marveling at the beauty, Ava entered her car and journeyed into town for supplies.

AVA WAS ARRANGING the charcuterie board on the kitchen island, complete with artisan meats, cheeses, berries, nuts and honey, when the doorbell rang.

"Coming!" she shouted.

She opened the door and greeted her friend, who was dressed in her usual conservative librarian garb. Jeans, a cardigan and her hair pulled half back.

"Hey." Ava smiled.

"I brought dessert," Eleanor replied as she handed her an apple pie.

"I love it when you bring me sweets," said Ava and they headed down the hallway.

After setting the pie on the kitchen island, Ava joined Eleanor on the couch and handed her a glass of wine.

Eleanor grinned at her, mischief in her eyes and whispered, "I also brought something else." She reached into her pocket and held out a baggie containing a joint.

Ava raised her eyebrows. "Weed?" She laughed. "I haven't smoked since college."

Though Ava was usually a rule follower, she had enjoyed the occasional joint when she was in school, finding it sometimes helped her sleep after a long day of studying and stress.

"Me either." Eleanor shrugged. "But maybe it'll open our minds and give us some ideas on that riddle."

Ava had called her and explained the riddle the other day and both women were still stumped about what it meant.

"Well... alright. I could use something to help me relax, honestly. Let's go outside," Ava said.

They gathered the food, wine and a bunch of blankets to stave off the November chill and nestled themselves on the outdoor sectional, charcuterie board sitting on the coffee table within reach.

Eleanor lit the joint and handed it to Ava after taking a puff.

Ava inhaled and blew out the smoke. "Mmmm... I remember now why I stopped in college. I liked it too much."

Eleanor laughed and they ate their dinner as they gossiped about Henry.

"So, he's that good in bed, huh?" Eleanor asked.

"God." She laid her head back on the couch. "So. Fucking. Good. I can't get enough."

"Damn, I'm jealous. I need to get a man."

Ava looked at her. "What about that one guy?" She sipped her wine. "The one that works with you?"

"Theodore?" Eleanor looked taken aback. "No way."

"Why not? He's cute."

Eleanor popped a grape in her mouth. "First of all, his name is Theodore. Can you imagine?"

Ava made fake moaning sounds. "Oh, Theodore. Yes! Harder!"

Eleanor let out a loud bark of laughter. "Exactly. Second of all, he's way too young."

"He's not *that* young. Like twenty-six or something, right?"

Eleanor frowned at her. "He's twenty-one!"

"Gross! Nevermind."

The women burst into laughter at the thought of Eleanor sleeping with baby Theodore.

"Okay, okay, okay." Eleanor held up her hand. "Now that we're sufficiently stoned, let's talk about the riddle."

"Look in the place where life is created," said Ava wrapping a blanket around her shoulders.

"Like a womb?"

Ava couldn't control her laughter, head floating from the weed. "Why the hell would it be a womb?"

"It's the first thing that popped into my brain!" Eleanor tossed a napkin at her.

"Okay." Ava clapped her hands together. "We're on a farm." She paused. "It grows stuff."

"Duh."

"Hush, I'm thinking out loud." She smiled. "Seeds?"

Eleanor shrugged. "That makes sense. Where are your seeds?"

"In the office," she answered as she stood and grabbed her wine.

Eleanor followed Ava inside to the cozy office, turning on the desk lamp. It was a big enough room for them to start at opposite ends of the space and they began to pull out the labeled drawers along the back wall. They checked the envelopes, picking up each one and searching for writing on the front and back, shaking the seeds and even feeling with their fingers to see if anything felt strange within the packet.

Ava felt nothing different and didn't see any notes or other strange items resembling clues.

"Anything?" she asked.

Eleanor shrugged. "Nothing that seemed off."

They headed back outside and sat down. Ava ate a bite of salami as she remained deep in thought while Eleanor munched on her own food.

"I've looked this house up and down," Ava fretted. "I have no idea where it could be."

Eleanor pondered out loud. "There must be something we're missing. What else could it—" She paused, seemingly on to something.

"What?" Ava said through a mouthful of cheese.

"The greenhouse!"

"I never saw anything strange when Henry and I cleaned it out... but it's worth a shot."

The women rose from their seats, each pulling their respective blankets around them tightly. Luna awoke from her spot on the couch, happily trotting after them. Entering the greenhouse, Ava flipped on the lights Henry had installed for her and they looked around, unsure where to start.

Ava pointed at one of the potting tables. "That's where the make out session happened," she giggled, head buzzing.

"I think I need to make out in a greenhouse too." Eleanor sighed.

"We should have brought the joint in here." Ava couldn't stop laughing. "Then it really would be a green house."

"Wow," Eleanor said. "Get a little stoned and you're suddenly spouting dad jokes."

They laughed together. "Well." Ava looked around. "I guess we need to explore."

The greenhouse was mostly empty, save for some seed starting trays, garden tools and a few random bags of soil propped against the wall. It was much cleaner since she and

Henry had discarded all the old trash and fixed the wobbly shelving.

Ava picked a spot toward the back left corner and started her search. Bending down and looking at the bottom of the wooden shelves, she ran her fingers along the seams and crevices of the wood. She got on her hands and knees and looked in between the floorboards and then stood to inspect the wall.

As she looked, she heard Eleanor humming a familiar tune. "Why are you humming the theme song from Indiana Jones?"

Eleanor looked at her from the other side of the greenhouse. "Because I feel like an archaeologist right now." She giggled.

"I hope there are no booby traps in here," she replied, hands on her hips.

"Yeah, because then Henry would be sad if your boobs got damaged." Eleanor snickered.

"Who's the king of dad jokes now?"

They continued their search but after twenty minutes, they had found nothing.

"Let's ask Luna," Eleanor announced.

"I'm high, but I'm not *that* high," answered Ava.

"I am." Eleanor shrugged and looked down at the cat. "Where's the map, Luna?" Luna tilted her head, listening while Ava suppressed a smile. Eleanor tried again, kneeling and looking directly at the feline. "Show us the map, kitty cat."

"This won't work," whispered Ava.

"Shhhh... she's thinking."

They remained quiet, the only sounds from the crickets chirping their nighttime song and the fall breeze rustling the leaves outside. Luna turned to look at Ava, tilting her head the other way. Huffing a feline sigh, she turned and walked through the open door outside.

The women followed as the cat padded around the yard to

the back of the greenhouse and stopped, pawing at the ground. Eleanor retrieved a shovel and handed it to Ava. "You're stronger than me," she said.

Ava laughed as she started to dig in the spot Luna had indicated. "Only because I've spent weeks hauling heavy bags of soil."

She was quite strong, though. Before she moved out to the farm, she had been regularly attending weightlifting classes. The barbell had been another way for her to cope with her anxiety and grief, giving her something to channel her frustrations and boost her confidence. She also loved the feeling of being physically strong. Ava had never been thin, and it didn't bother her like it used to. When she was younger, she was always too tall and too wide, towering over her peers and taking up too much space. But using her strength in the gym made her fall in love with her thick thighs and broad shoulders. Her body was one of the few things she wasn't insecure about anymore.

She dug down for almost five minutes, starting to feel defeated there was nothing there. The hole was getting deep, probably close to a foot now, and she hadn't uncovered any hint of a clue or foreign object. As she was about to take a break, the tip of her shovel hit something hard.

"I found something."

Eleanor had collected two hand spades and knelt as she handed one to Ava while Luna watched from a few feet away. The two of them ended up on their hands and knees, scooping dirt with tools and fingers, excitement hovering around them like an electric charge, anxious to unearth their find.

Finally, Ava's fingers were able to grip what felt like a tube.

"I think I can get it out of here."

She pulled it out with a groan and laid it on the ground, light from inside the greenhouse casting an eerie glow. The moment Ava pried it from its home in the earth, she was overcome with a feeling of dread. The crickets were silent and the wind stopped, as if the forest was on alert, anticipating what was to come.

Silent, she and Eleanor stared at each other, eyes wide. Even Luna had perked up, ears listening for danger.

"Let's bring it inside where there's better light," Ava suggested.

"Good idea."

Though the crickets had resumed their song, and the breeze once again whipped their hair, there was a nervous energy in the air. Eleanor pulled her blanket closer and followed Ava inside.

They sat at the kitchen table, a reminder of the night they discovered the book, and looked at each other.

"What if you get sick again?" asked Eleanor.

Luna leapt onto the table and pawed at the metal cylinder as if indicating it was safe to open. "Then I guess I get sick again?" Ava shrugged, trying to hide her nerves.

Heart racing, she ran her fingers along the sides and found the top, prying it open. As she slid out a rolled-up piece of parchment, she was relieved no supernatural sensations washed over her this time.

With shaking hands, she unrolled it, revealing a faded map of the farm.

There was the house, the flower field and forest beyond. A winding dotted line representing a path led deep into the forest from the side of the house, twisting and turning through the woods. Along the path were several landmarks. Stones or oddly shaped trees to mark the way. The path ended far into the woods, deeper than Ava had ever dared venture, opening into what looked like a clearing.

There it was. The portal.

Eleanor was looking over Ava's shoulder and gasped. "There it is."

"Yeah," Ava replied, throat dry, unable to look away.

Eleanor pointed at the picture. An archway covered in symbols with a black abyss in the center lined in blue that seemed to leap from the paper.

"It's true," Eleanor whispered. "Like in the book."

Ava set the map down and paced the room, the new information immediately sobering her. "I—I don't." She ran her shaky hands through her hair. "This can't be real." Eleanor watched her silently. "I'm just going crazy," she rambled. "I haven't been sleeping.... And—I just—I miss my mom... and this is my subconscious brain trying to make sense of things.... And—"

Eleanor cut her off as she approached. "Stop. You're not crazy. I've seen it all too, remember?" Ava looked at her and swallowed. "Your mom's magic. The creature. The book and now the map," Eleanor encouraged. "If this was some elaborate prank then kudos to whoever pulled it off."

Ava sighed, sitting down at the table and placed her head in her hands. "What now?" she whispered.

"We go check it out."

Ava's gaze snapped to her friend. "We?"

Eleanor sat down beside her. "Sure. Indiana Jones, remember? Let's explore."

"What if it's dangerous?"

"Then we plan." Eleanor grasped her hand. "This is supposedly your home, Ava. Aren't you a little curious?"

Ava bit her lip. "Well, yeah. But... we can't just go through a random portal..."

"Why not?" Eleanor asked. "I'll come over tomorrow evening and we'll plan. We'll just go through it and look around and then come right back."

"I don't know..." She closed her eyes. "What do I tell Henry?"

"Invent an excuse why you can't hang out tomorrow. We'll be back before he even realizes you're gone."

Ava narrowed her eyes at her friend. "I think this weed made you brave." She laughed softly.

"Probably... but let's do it before we chicken out."

10

Ava sat on the porch, lacing up her tennis shoes as she waited for Eleanor to arrive. She couldn't believe they were doing this. Couldn't believe it was even real. It was impossible to wrap her mind around the fact that she was from another realm. She didn't even know other realms existed until recently.

Ava wondered if her grandfather had been talking about this other realm when he told his mystical tales. Eorhan, Luna had called it. Were the fae actually real? Could they manipulate gravity and shoot lava from their fingertips like her grandfather had said?

Her mind was a whirlwind of magic and monsters. Mythical creatures and ancient kings. Princesses and orcs and goblins. She had to admit, she was just a little excited. Like she would be entering the pages of one of her many beloved fantasy books.

She was still furious at her mother and grandfather for keeping things from her. For thinking she wasn't old enough or couldn't handle the truth. She had always felt different but every time she tried to ask her mother about it, she would coo at her and say things like 'You're just special, my little bird,' or 'You're destined for great things.'

'What things?' she wanted to scream at her.

And now she was dead, and she'd never know the truth. Not unless she went through the portal.

A car door slammed and Ava rose from her seat on the porch, meeting Eleanor at the steps.

"Ava!" Eleanor shouted as she rushed toward her with fear in her eyes.

"What's wrong?" She grasped her arms, steadying her.

"He's coming—" Eleanor took a breath, frantic. "He knows about it."

"Who? What are you talking about?"

Eleanor looked around in the dark, eyes darting over the yard, then took Ava's hand and led her to the back yard. "They might be listening," she whispered.

They stopped in the back and Ava turned to her, clutching her hands. "You're scaring me. Slow down, take a deep breath." Ava tried to calm her friend, her own heart beating out of her chest. "Who's listening?"

Eleanor stopped talking for a moment as she tried to slow her breathing. "I overheard him talking on the phone," she rambled. "I don't think he knew I was there. He talked about the portal and somehow knew what we were doing tonight. He also mentioned blood. Something about using blood to open the doorway."

"Who are you talking about? Who said that?" she asked, unsure if she wanted to know.

"Henry," she whispered, eyes wide. "He said he needed your blood."

Ava let go of Eleanor's hands. "What?" she exclaimed as she stepped back shaking her head. "No. You—you must have heard someone else..."

Dizziness overwhelmed her and her mouth went dry. It

couldn't be Henry. He cared for her. He would never harm her; she was sure of it. Right?

"Ava please. We have to get out of here. He's on his way," Eleanor said, trying to approach Ava.

Another car door slammed, causing the women to jump.

"Ava! Are you out here?" Henry's voice sounded.

"It's too late, we have to run!" Eleanor whispered harshly.

"Fuck. This is crazy," Ava whispered, heart racing. She turned and shouted, "In the backyard!"

Eleanor widened her eyes at Ava. "No! Don't let him see the map!" she whispered.

Henry turned the corner and walked over to Ava, noticing she was trembling. "What's wrong? Are you alright?"

"I'm fine, I just...What are you doing here?" she asked Henry.

Looking suspiciously at Eleanor and then back to Ava, he ran his fingers through his hair. "I came to check on you," he said. "I, um... overheard Eleanor talking to someone on the phone. I don't know what's going on, but she sounded like she was going to hurt you."

"What?" she said looking at Eleanor.

"He's lying! Please, listen!" Eleanor frantically tried to explain.

Ava backed away from them, unsure what to do. She didn't believe Henry would hurt her, but she also didn't think Eleanor would make this up. Her boyfriend and her best friend. Her only friend. Fear churned in her gut as she wrestled with what to do, who to believe.

"What's going on?" she whispered, looking back and forth between them.

"Ava, you're my best friend! Stay away from him!" Eleanor shouted, getting angrier no one was listening to her.

Henry remained calm. "Ava, I think Eleanor's sick. Can't you see she isn't making sense?"

"He's a liar!" Eleanor was uncontrollable now. Ava had never seen her like this. She was usually so put together. But now her eyes were wide and darting around, seemingly paranoid.

"Eleanor," Henry said gently as he turned to her, taking two steps forward. "Calm down. Do you want to go to the hospital? We should call an ambulance and have them take you to a hospital."

Eleanor looked at Ava, defeated, as tears streamed down her face. "Ava," she whispered. "Please... Why don't you believe me? I thought you were my friend."

Ava's chest ached as her heart broke at her friend's despair. Eleanor was her best friend. She wouldn't accuse her. Needed to help her. Ava approached, preparing to comfort and calm her until they figured out what to do.

But something emerged from the woods behind Eleanor.

Ava froze.

It was the creature.

She could see it better in the moonlight as it stalked toward Eleanor, who remained oblivious to the danger behind her.

It was so tall. It had to be over seven feet.

Swirling shadows distorted most of its features, but Ava could make out long hair, glowing red eyes and sharp teeth forming a wicked smile.

Ava backed away as its claws elongated, stalking closer to Eleanor.

"Eleanor, run!" Ava shouted, continuing to retreat when she bumped into Henry.

Eleanor scanned her surroundings, confused. Spotting the creature, her eyes widened and she stilled, terrified. Too frozen to move.

As Ava was about to yell at her again to run, the creature took two steps toward her friend and she started to back away.

The figure's hand shot out before Ava realized what was happening, swiping a singular claw across her throat.

"No!" Ava screamed, lunging for her friend as Henry held her back.

A gurgle sounded as Eleanor grasped her throat and sank to her knees. Terror gripped Ava as blood seeped from between Eleanor's fingers, desperate to stop the flow. She turned toward Ava and started to crawl, one hand trying to stop the bleeding while the other propelled her forward. She inched closer, making her way across the grass as the creature took slow steps toward her.

Eleanor's voice gurgled as she tried to speak, warning Ava one last time. "Henry. Run..."

She had to get to her. Had to help her. Henry grabbed her waist and she fought against him, twisting and writhing. "Let me go!" she screamed again, tears pouring down her cheeks. "Please!" she wailed as she tried to wrench from Henry's grip, hitting and kicking him but he was too strong.

Eleanor continued to crawl, the creature stalking her, preparing for the final blow. It reached Eleanor and grabbed her hair, pulling her backward. Unable to keep her hand on her throat, blood poured like a crimson waterfall from the giant laceration, flowing down her neck and painting her white shirt with death.

The creature knelt and lowered its face toward Eleanor's throat. Opening its mouth wide, sharp teeth glinting in the moonlight, it released a triumphant scream.

Ava slammed her hands over her ears as the scream raked over her very bones, Henry's arms still wrapped around her waist. Nausea roiled in her stomach as she trembled, unable to turn from the gruesome scene. The creature began to drink, voraciously gulping as it continued to tear into Eleanor's throat. She attempted to get loose, scratching at the creature's face, flailing around for only a few moments.

Ava tried struggling against Henry again, sobbing as she watched her best friend die right in front of her. The only friend she had. And now she was gone. Killed by the creature that had been plaguing Ava's farm; that had entered her house. Would it come after her next?

Eleanor's body twitched as the figure continued to rip into her and eventually, she was still.

Henry tugged her toward the house. "Ava, we have to go! Now!" he whispered loudly.

"I'm not leaving her!" She was still hysterical as she struggled again to go to her friend. She had to help. This couldn't be happening. It wasn't real.

Refusing to take no for an answer, Henry scooped her up and took off toward the house as she cried and moaned in disbelief. The front door slammed shut and Henry set her down. She ran to the nearest bathroom in the hallway and vomited everything in her stomach. Henry's hand was rubbing her back a few seconds later, telling her she was okay, and everything was going to be alright.

After she had nothing left to purge, she stood and walked into the hallway, Henry following. Eleanor was dead. And it was all Ava's fault. She was so selfish to want to see Eorhan. She should never have involved Eleanor, should never have looked for the map.

She couldn't stop the tears as she paced, her whole body shaking, replaying Eleanor's death over and over in her mind. They needed to leave. To jump in the car and get away as fast as possible. It would kill her and Henry too if they didn't escape.

"What the fuck is that thing?" she shrieked. "We need to call the police!" She continued to pace. "Oh god. She's dead. I killed my friend!"

Henry walked over and wrapped her in his arms, rubbing her back as Ava sobbed into his chest. She could barely breathe and felt the panic overwhelming her as she tried to make sense of what she had witnessed.

She was about to demand they get in the car and leave when Henry whispered in her ear, "Give me the map, Ava."

She pulled back to look at him, a new fear stirring inside her. "What did you say?" she whispered.

He tilted his head in a feline grace, an unfamiliar expression on his face. "The map."

Ava pushed herself out of his arms and backed away, heart pounding.

He stood in the hallway facing her, hands clasped behind him and a look on his face she had never seen before. "I've been looking through your house for weeks. Never able to find anything your crazy grandfather left regarding the portal." He strolled closer to her, looking at her with eyes full of disgust. "Until you showed me that book."

"Henry..." she croaked, trying to hold back the tears that had just stopped flowing.

Eleanor was right, she thought. *I should have listened to her, and now she's dead.*

"Deidamia coming into your house was the perfect excuse to install the security system," he said as he continued stalking closer.

She shook her head. "Who?"

"You'll meet her soon enough." He paused a few feet in front of her. "All I had to do was look at your camera feed. I knew you'd find the map for me."

Continuing to back away, she started thinking of an escape route. The front door was to her right, but the creature was out there, so she started to inch her way to her left, planning on grabbing a knife from the kitchen, like when the creature had invaded her home.

"I have everything I need now," he said as he held out the book he had hidden behind his back. "Except that map." He resumed strolling in her direction, floor creaking with each step.

She decided to keep him talking, hoping to distract him as she inched further left and prepared herself to run. Tears ran down her face, heartbroken she was deceived.

"Henry, please," she begged. "I thought you cared about me."

He scoffed, continuing to creep forward. "You were so easy to manipulate. A lost little puppy with her dead mom." He was mocking her now. "You're pathetic," he spat, looking at her with hatred. "I've been stuck in this god-forsaken world for decades. We were so close a few months ago." He slipped a hand into his pocket. "But then your stupid grandfather had to go and kill himself. The blood must be fresh. Flowing from the vein to open the portal. And since he was dead, we couldn't use his."

Sniffling as she backed away further, she shook her head. "What? No... I don't understand..."

He continued waltzing toward her, slowly, like he was enjoying her fear.

Who was he? What did he mean stuck in this world? He knew about the portal and the map, which meant he must know about this other world.

She bolted to the kitchen. Henry appeared just as she made it down the hallway, blocking her escape. Before she had a chance to change course, he threw her backward against the wall. Her body slammed into the entry table, and she collapsed on all fours, gasping for breath.

"Give me the map!" he shouted, then kicked her in the ribs, a sharp pain stabbing her side as she fell further.

Pulling herself back up, she tried to crawl, ignoring his demands. She wasn't fast enough, and he was on her, lifting her by her throat as her feet barely scraped the ground. He slammed her into the wall again, holding her neck with one hand.

She tried to scratch him, tried to pry his hand off her throat. She was going to die; he was going to choke her right here. Panicking, she attempted to kick him, but her bruised ribs made it difficult to move.

Henry looked at her as he reached into his pocket with his other hand. When she saw the syringe he was holding, she flailed and tried to get away. She tried talking but nothing would come out, his hand too tight around her throat and her feet still not touching the ground.

"Give. Me. The. Map!" he shouted inches from her face.

"No," she managed to croak out in a whisper.

Then he plunged the needle into her neck.

11

Shadow surrounded her, her body was leaden. Moving was impossible.

Something soft caressed her skin. Grass?

The smell of outdoors and a damp, musty scent reached her nostrils. Pine and moss and something... old.

She couldn't lift herself, head pounding. Eyes heavy.

Muffled voices spoke near her but she couldn't make them out, as if she was in a well.

It had been minutes. Hours. Days?

She kept fading in and out but then... darkness came again, and she was lost.

IT WAS STILL dark outside when Ava came to. Her surroundings were fuzzy and she blinked, attempting to clear her vision. Trees encompassed the area, illuminated by moonlight. The smell of the earth enveloped her and grass tickled her cheek as she turned her head. Sounds of the night were still echoing through the air; the chirp of crickets; the cry of a fox; the whisper of the breeze.

Groaning, she attempted to move but couldn't, limbs still heavy from the effects of the drug, like they were weighed down with sandbags.

Something painfully pinched her wrists. Her ankles too.

Rope? Was she tied up?

Her head still throbbed, a relentless hammering within her skull.

She didn't hear the voices anymore, and she looked around, vision clearing. Turning her head was painful, the pounding unwilling to cease.

Continuing to assess her surroundings, she saw a clearing encompassed by tall pine trees. Was she in the forest? There were crumbling ruins next to her, exactly like the ones from her dream.

Her dream. Had it been a premonition? She was sure these were the same ruins, but she didn't see a glowing tree anywhere.

She was lying on her side, hands tightly bound, and feet tied together at her ankles, leaving her little room to move. Her stomach churned and heart raced as though it would beat out of her chest. She willed herself to remain calm, to develop a plan, and took a deep breath, wincing at the pain in her ribs and the bruises on her throat.

Then, she remembered. The map. Though difficult to move due to the sedative still coursing through her system, she reached into her pocket where she'd left it.

It was gone.

You can't freak out right now, she said to herself.

Glowing eyes shone from the dense woods, then a cat appeared from the shadows.

"Luna?" she whispered, barely audible.

She still didn't hear anyone else. Where was Henry?

Luna padded to her on silent paws and looked at Ava, concerned. She rubbed against her face, as if promising to help her escape.

Footsteps sounded from somewhere to her left. Unable to turn her head, she couldn't see who approached but Luna darted back into her hiding place among the shrubs. A strong hand grasped under her arm and sat her up to lean against a stone wall.

She looked up and met eyes with Henry. Though he looked the same, his eyes were different. There was no love. No warmth.

"You're finally awake."

"What do you want from me?"

He leaned down until he was inches from her face. "I already told you."

What had he said before he drugged her? Something about using her blood to open the portal. That they were stuck in this world and needed her to get back. And she had walked right into his trap. Racking her brain for information from when she took self-defense classes in college, she scrambled to figure out how to keep him talking. If she could sidetrack him, maybe she could get away.

"Why do you want to go back?" she asked.

"Humans and their questions," he said, looking annoyed. He wasn't going to answer her.

"Why is my blood so special?" she said, trying again. "Are you going to kill me?"

He raised an eyebrow. "You must think I'm a fool if you think you can distract me with your questions."

So much for that idea. She tried to ignore the dread working its way through her. The fear washing over her as she realized this was really happening. There was no more denial. No more explaining it away. Everything Luna had told her was true. Why her grandfather had been so paranoid, why they always moved around. They were hiding from whoever Henry was. Whatever Henry was.

"If this is true," she began. "If magic and portals are real? Then why can't you do magic?"

A female voice sounded from the trees. "Because magic barely works here," said the voice as she emerged.

A stunning woman with long auburn hair and bright blue eyes sauntered up to Henry and kissed him. The two of them turned to her. "Andras used the small amount of magic he could muster to seduce you. To help us find the map and then the portal."

He'd used magic to make her want him? Oh, god. It explained so much. Why she couldn't get enough, why it felt like a drug every time they kissed. How she would lose herself in lust, like she was out of control. She thought it was passion, maybe even love, but it was magic.

She was a fucking idiot.

Ava attempted to scoot away, eyes wide as she took them in. Hands shaking, she tried to wiggle them out of the rope though it was too tight. "Who are you?" she whispered, though deep down she already knew, remembering what Luna had told her in her dream state.

The demon queen.

And Henry. She had referred to him as Andras. That must be his true name. Was he a demon also?

"You know who we are," the woman answered. "You were so easy to manipulate."

Ava tried not to cry, tried to appear strong, but underneath she was a weak terrified little girl who just wanted her mother. Her mother always knew what to do.

"You can open the portal, Ava. That's why you're here with us now," Henry said. No, not Henry. Andras.

Ava looked at the two of them, standing intimately close to each other. The demon queen and her consort. This must be the Deidamia that Andras mentioned.

"I can't do magic," Ava said. They ignored her.

Andras stalked toward her and kneeled.

He then hoisted her up by her armpit, dragging her over to an arch, her feet scraping the ground as she attempted to balance herself. The doorway to nowhere was engraved with symbols just like the pictures in the book.

"What is this place?" she asked, trying to bide herself more time.

If she could somehow get out of these bindings, she would run. Escape into the woods.

Andras continued to drag her closer to the archway, disregarding her questions, as she tried to pull from his grip.

They reached the archway, and he withdrew a knife from his pocket. Ava twisted harder in his grip, trembling as he brought the knife closer to her.

"Hold still," he demanded.

She stopped squirming and looked at him. He leaned over her and as he got close enough, she head butted him, catching him by surprise, and used her bound hands to shove him down. She had hidden the fact that the rope around her ankles had come loose and wiggled free and took off running.

"You bitch!" he screamed as she hurtled into the forest.

It was difficult to see in the shadowy woods, the canopy so dense only slivers of moonlight penetrated the leaves. She tripped over a fallen branch, cursing as she scraped her hands and arose again to continue. She had to get back to the house, her car. Where was it? She had no clue which direction to go.

She barely made it twenty feet before the tall creature who had killed Eleanor was standing right in front of her, looming and primed to attack. The shadows swirled around it as it bared its teeth, grinning at her predicament.

She froze and backed away, not letting it out of her sight.

Searching for a way out, she glanced to her left, when the

creature lunged at her. She fell back over a log, sharp pain from her bruised ribs shooting through her side, and crawled away in a feeble attempt to escape. The creature stalked forward and raised its hand, full of claws. Ava closed her eyes, waiting for the killing blow.

A growling sounded from her right and something crashed through the brush. She opened her eyes as Luna leaped at the creature, claws out, piercing its leg with her canines.

Ava was on her feet in an instant and took off in the other direction, no idea where she was going. She didn't think Luna would win this fight but at least it had given her time to run. As she darted through the trees, she heard a yelp and then the sound of something large coming after her.

"Shit," she said as she tried to run faster.

She entered the clearing with the ruins once again and froze, panicking. In her fervor to get away, she had run right back into the hands of her enemy.

Andras was there in an instant, fist meeting her face so powerfully she fell to the ground. She curled over herself, eye throbbing where he had punched her, and held her face in her still bound hands.

Dazed, she could barely move.

He reached down and yanked her up by her hair, turning her to face the woods where the creature emerged. His body was hard against her back as he held her, holding her wrists down in front of her with his other hand, and tilted her head to expose her neck to the creature.

"If we didn't need you alive, you would make a wonderful meal for Deidamia. She hasn't consumed anyone with magic in their blood in decades and she's hungry," he whispered into her ear.

The creature stalked forward, taking its time. It leaned in and smelled her, breathing in slowly as if savoring her scent. Long claws caressed her throat and trailed down the rest of her body. Ava trembled as she tried to lean away but Andras was too strong. A whimper sounded from her lips as the claws caressed her throat again, like it was preparing to do to her exactly what it did to Eleanor.

In the blink of an eye, the figure shifted into the woman. Deidamia.

"I thought you said magic doesn't work here," Ava croaked.

"It doesn't work well," she said as she walked around the two of them. "Hold her still." She flicked her hand toward Andras.

Andras dragged her over to the archway, letting go of her hair as he urged her to walk forward. Reaching the archway, he held her as they faced the ancient symbols.

Deidamia followed, reaching into Andras' pocket for a knife and he wrapped his arms around Ava so she couldn't move. She tried struggling but he was too strong and too close for her to kick.

If she let them get the portal open, that meant this world called Eorhan was in danger. Her world, supposedly. She had to try to stop them. She struggled harder, fighting against Andras' grasp but he held her firm as Deidamia walked closer and grabbed Ava's left wrist, gripping it so hard she thought it would break. She tried to pull away, but they were so much stronger than she was. Deidamia sliced Ava's palm deep and she gritted her teeth against the sting of the blade. Blood blossomed from the cut as the throbbing almost overtook her, dripping onto the grass.

Taking her palm, Andras walked her closer to the archway and pressed it onto the stone. At first nothing happened, but then the throbbing turned into burning and excruciating pain spread to her wrist, her arm, then coursed through her whole body. Her muscles went rigid as the feeling intensified, making her dizzy as she stared in horror at the archway.

The voice from her dreams sounded, shouting her name to stop.

"Ava! No!"

Was that only in her head? Or could they hear it too?

She tried to pull her hand away, tried to stop the doorway from opening but Andras was still pushing her hand against the stone with immense strength as the pain continued to pulse through her.

Her vision started to hum in rhythm with the throbbing throughout her body. Fading in and out.

In and out.

It was like thousands of needles were piercing her skin, deeper and deeper.

The symbols glowed an eerie blue, bathing the clearing in a turquoise light. Brighter and brighter until the empty space within the archway filled in. Swirling blackness erupted framed by the blue glow of the symbols.

She had failed. The doorway was open.

She had brought death to an unknown realm she had never heard of.

A realm she had learned she was from. Where her parents were from.

Oh, god.

Andras pulled her back and the pain subsided as they backed away, gazing at the portal. Deidamia regarded it with reverence, triumph on her face forming into a wicked smile.

"We did it," she whispered.

Maybe Ava could still escape. Leave them to conquer whatever they wanted. She didn't know anyone in this other world, she could stay here and live her life. Leave them to handle the demons themselves. She was still human. It wasn't her responsibility to fight their battles.

She wanted no part of it. If her mother truly wanted her to

go save their world, she should have told her everything years ago.

Except now she had nothing in this world either. No Henry. No Eleanor.

"Please let me go," she pleaded, pain still coursing through her.

Deidamia smirked as Andras whispered in Ava's ear. "We still need you..." and he shoved her forward into the archway and the blackness beyond.

12

Casimir jolted awake inside his tent, his fingers instinctively wrapping around the hilt of his sword. Something ominous; something terrible had happened. It was like the whole world had awoken and cracked open, breathing a great sigh of surprise as it trembled. He pushed the flaps of his tent aside and emerged, looking for his fellow warriors.

"Did you feel that?" he asked Quinn, already outside.

"Yes," she whispered, upturned brown eyes wide with trepidation. "Something's coming." Her long black hair swished along her back, tied back in intricate braids and her olive skin glistened in the morning sun, sweat already forming along her brow.

A massive black bear ambled up to him and huffed. His shoulders reached the height of Casimir's chest and he towered over everyone when standing on his hind legs.

Something's not right, the bear's low voice said telepathically.

"*I know,*" he answered back.

Their animal companions were on edge. Quinn's black panther was pacing along the tree line as if searching for the source of their unease.

Another warrior emerged from his own tent as his large silver wolf growled from the edge of camp, both prepared for a fight. His blonde hair was bright in the sunlight. Tying back his long locks, revealing pointed ears, he asked, "What the fuck was that?"

"I don't know, Raine," he said. "Where's Jorrar?"

"Probably out for his usual morning stroll." Raine shrugged. "He must stretch his old legs lest he get stiff in the mornings," he added, winking at Quinn.

Quinn rolled her eyes and looked around for their fourth companion. They were camped in a small clearing among towering trees of white bark and moss green leaves. Small yellow flowers grew among the grass like little drops of sun, sparkling over an emerald sea.

Their tents had carefully been placed in the clearing, ensuring little damage was done to the plants thriving among the forest; respect for the native flora vital to their way of life. The sun filtered through the trees, casting a subtle light around their makeshift homes. The cry of an animal sounded in the distance as Casimir searched for Jorrar.

A low voice called from the dense trees. "Casimir!"

The three fae warriors turned in his direction as their fourth companion with ebony skin and short hair peppered with gray emerged from the forest, out of breath. He rubbed the back of his neck, silver eyes wide with concern as he stopped in front of them.

"Well, out with it," said Quinn, impatiently.

"They're back," he said in between breaths. "I can feel them."

Casimir's golden eyes widened as he took in what his friend was saying, knowing exactly who Jorrar was referring to.

"Who?" asked Raine.

"Deidamia and Andras," he answered.

Quinn shook her head in disbelief. "No."

"Fuck," said Raine as he started to pace.

After nearly one hundred years, they were back. Though Casimir had fought plenty of daemon soldiers throughout the years, their leaders were different. Almost undefeatable. Rogue groups of soldiers were nothing compared to what they would face now their queen had returned. Jorrar was the only one of them old enough to remember the old wars—Casimir had been just a child—and now their worst fears had come to fruition.

He must inform his king.

"How is that possible?" Quinn asked.

Jorrar shook his head. "I can't say for certain. But this is how it felt before."

"Looks like our scouting mission got a lot more complicated," Quinn grumbled, starting to take her tent down.

Casimir nodded to Jorrar. "Send word to the king."

Jorrar whistled as he turned to the woods. A moment later a gray and black marbled owl appeared, swooping down to land on his arm. He turned to the bird. "Send a message to Thorne. Inform him what's happened and that we will wait for his instructions." Seconds later, the owl hooted and flew off toward the towering mountains in the distance.

The rest of their companions had disappeared as well, on their own missions to gather intelligence; one of their many uses.

They had been in the Greywood Forest for a couple of months now, using this small camp as their base. Though Deidamia had been gone for decades, parts of her army remained. They didn't try to conquer completely without her, but caused plenty of trouble. Casimir and his three best warriors had been sent by their king to take care of rogue soldiers who were wreaking havoc on some of the smaller villages at the outskirts of their kingdom.

"How far are we from Oakshire?" asked Casimir.

"About two days' walk," answered Raine. "Why? Are you craving an ale, general? Maybe a romp in the sheets with a pretty bar maiden? You'd better bathe first. You stink."

Casimir raised his eyebrows at his closest friend. "There will be no *romping* this time. We need better rest, some real food and a place to wait for Thorne's instructions. Besides, we need to replenish our supplies."

"Real food? You dislike my cooking?" Jorrar scoffed at Casimir as he attached their supplies to their horse, a gray mare with a white patch on her chest named Snowheart.

"Nobody likes your cooking, old man," Quinn jabbed as she strapped on her many daggers.

Jorrar furrowed his brow.

Raine poured water over the smoldering embers of their fire. "It reminds me of the smell of Cas' feet when he takes his boots off after we've been traveling for weeks."

"It's not *that* bad," Jorrar grumbled at Casimir who was adjusting the hood of his forest green cloak.

Casimir gave Jorrar a blank look. "It's tolerable."

Jorrar huffed and finished packing their gear.

"Time to go," he announced. "We must be swift."

Casimir led his group through the woods, sun high in the sky as it beat down on them. His hand absently traced the scar that started just above his jaw line and stretched down his neck, ending at his collarbone. Long lost memories usually kept at bay now churned near the surface as he worried about what the daemon queen and her consort had in store for Eorhan. For his kingdom.

For his home.

13

*A*va fell through space and time.

Down and down.

Plummeting but floating at the same time.

She wasn't in pain. Not like when she touched the archway.

But her skin tingled as something shifted. As she flew into everything and nothing.

There was only infinite darkness. An absence of light, as if it had been devoured.

Her dream had come true, no longer a premonition. No longer an intangible thing.

The ruins, the voice, the figure chasing her through the woods. As if she would never have been able to escape her fate. The voice sounded again, calling out her name in a panic. As if he was searching for her and warning her.

It was a forceful voice; radiating power and authority as it yelled for her to stop.

But whoever it was, she had let him down.

Failed.

Hands still bound, she barreled into the earth, breath knocked out of her as she hit the ground. An identical archway stood before her with the same swirling blackness lined in blue.

Maybe she could jump back through. Maybe she could go back. Though she had no one left, she'd be safe on the farm. Away from the daemons.

As she was starting to rise, Deidamia and Andras emerged, walking through gracefully. After they arrived, the portal began to close, the black swirling abyss shrinking.

No.

She couldn't jump through now, especially with the two of them standing in between her and the doorway, and she watched her chance to escape slip away.

Just before the portal sealed shut, Luna emerged from the black abyss and dashed in the opposite direction into a group of trees before the daemons noticed her. Momentary relief poured over Ava. Luna was alive. Perhaps she could help in some way.

Andras and Deidamia beamed with triumph, gazing around them and taking it in. So elated they almost forgot about Ava. She looked around, searching for an escape route before they remembered her existence.

They had landed in a scenic meadow, peppered with trees of white bark and rounded golden leaves, quivering in the breeze. The trees were more brilliant than those back home, brightly colored and teeming with energy. The emerald grass was interspersed with patches of flowers. Orange, blue and purple blooms reached for the sun. Unlike any flowers she had ever seen, they glimmered in the light.

The weather was pleasant, and the sun peeked over the trees, radiating an orange glow as it rose overhead. It wasn't fall here, but spring? Did they even have the same seasons?

She couldn't see much beyond the groups of trees surrounding her, unsure which direction would be safest.

About to head where Luna had gone, she was interrupted when Andras lifted her roughly by her arm.

He looked different. As if the magic residing within him was now unleashed and his true form took over. His short blonde locks had grown and were now long and black, his skin porcelain but his eyes were the same bright blue.

Taller, wider and stronger, he was utterly terrifying as he looked down at her. "Welcome home, Ava."

His voice. It wasn't the same smooth timbre but more powerful, filled with deep seductive tones, echoing with a strange presence.

Trembling, she turned to look toward Deidamia who had also changed. If Andras was sensual maleficence, then she was brute terror. Slightly shorter than him, her waist length hair had changed to a ghostly white.

Her pale blue eyes bored into Ava as she smiled, revealing fangs. Holding out her hand, a fireball started to form in her palm. Not a fire of reds and oranges, but something far viler. Deep purple flames danced around themselves, whirling and writhing, ready to destroy. It was as if the fire had a mind of its own and longed to incinerate that which was around it.

"My magic." She beheld her fire.

Her voice was different too, melodic yet laced with echoes of death and destruction. She shot the fire toward a tree, and it immediately caught flame.

Nodding, as if confirming her magic still worked, she looked at Andras. "Go ahead."

Andras' eyes darkened and shadows emerged from him. Coming from nowhere and everywhere, swirling around him.

Ava started to pull away, but the shadows surrounded them and tendrils climbed their way around her body. Andras let go of her but when she tried to move, tried to run, the shadows held her in place. Black tendrils wrapped around her wrists and raised her arms above her head as Andras stood over her.

Another wisp of smoke twisted around her throat, cutting off her air.

Ava tried to get free, struggling against the darkness but the swirling smoke and shadow held her still. She couldn't breathe and panic threatened to engulf her. Andras released her, shadows disappearing as he pulled them back and she fell to the ground, coughing and clutching at her neck.

"Don't try to escape," he said. "You won't get far."

Something rustled as it emerged into the meadow through the white-bark trees, announcing the arrival of half a dozen soldiers. Large and tall, their eyes promised torture and death. Dressed in spiked armor so dark it seemed to suck the light from around them, they marched forward. The spikes were strategically placed on their knees, elbows and forearms, making them deadly in hand-to-hand combat. All they had to do was place a carefully aimed kick, or throw their elbow to gut their enemies.

The right breast displayed an insignia of horns surrounded by flames.

This was the army of Deidamia.

One soldier had a gold bar under his insignia. The leader, then. The group approached, Ava still on the ground trying to catch her breath and develop a plan to escape, though she knew it was futile. What could a human do against powerful daemons and warriors with magic?

As the leader advanced, he knelt and removed his horned helmet.

Bowing with reverence, he spoke with a deep gruff voice. "My queen. We've been waiting almost one hundred years for your return."

His cadre followed suit and knelt behind him.

"General Or'thir. Your loyalty will be rewarded," Deidamia replied in a powerful voice. "Rise and give your report."

Or'thir rose but glanced hesitantly at Ava, seemingly reluctant to reveal potentially secret information in front of a stranger.

He was massive. With broad shoulders and a heavily muscled body beneath his thick armor. His hair was long and golden, and his face was peppered with brutal scars, one of them slicing right over his left eye, changing it into a milky white while the right was a deep, haunting black.

Clearing his throat, he answered, "Should we find somewhere more private? A large camp is just a few days' away and I'm sure you'll be more comfortable there. Scouts had been monitoring this portal with the hopes you would return."

Deidamia glanced at Ava and waved her hand. "Yes. Lead the way to camp and bring her along. Keep her alive as we may need her later."

She should run now. Hurry and try to get away while her feet were still unbound.

She glanced toward the direction Luna had run off to, but she didn't see any sign of her friend. Even Luna knew she couldn't fight against them.

Ava, Luna said.

Ava almost jumped at the sound of Luna's voice in her head. She'd only spoken to her once before, and that was in a dream. Then she remembered Luna had said they could also speak in this world. It was so strange to be able to consciously communicate with an animal.

"Luna! What do I do?"

They're too strong. I'm going to try to look for help.

"Where?"

I don't know. I was very young when I followed your grandpa and mother into the human world.

"Will I be able to talk to you wherever you are?"

Not if I get too far away. I'll be back, I promise.

"Okay."

At least she had one friend in this world.

Ava stood and started to back away but a hard body behind her blocked her path. Andras. "Hold still," he said as his arms wrapped around her and his fingers dug into her forearms. She gasped at the pain, adding more bruises to her already battered body.

The general gestured to two of his men, both equally as frightening, and they produced a small wooden wagon from the trees being pulled by a massive black horse with red eyes.

Andras held her arms tightly as they removed the rope and replaced it with shackles. Ava trembled, her breaths coming in short bursts, as fear gripped her like a vice.

The wagon stopped in front of her and a soldier opened the door on the back. No. They couldn't put her in there, she wouldn't let them. Flailing, she tried to wrench away from Andras but he squeezed her arms so hard she thought her bones would break and she cried out as he shoved her into the wagon.

The side of her body hit the hard wooden floor as her head throbbed at the impact of her fall. Everything hurt as she lay there, bound and trapped, her fate sealed now that she couldn't run away.

"Please!" she begged as the door was slammed followed by the sound of keys turning in a lock.

Using her chained hands, she pushed herself up and leaned against the wagon's wall. It was mostly dark, the only light filtering in through a narrow-barred window at the top of the door. She looked around for anything she could use to assist her, but the enclosure was empty. Rough wood scratched her as she adjusted, attempting to find a comfortable position. Dark stains smelling of iron colored the floor with the promise of pain.

"What do I do?" she whispered to herself in the dark, allowing the tears to fall.

She was an idiot, digging into her grandfather's past and

seeking out the map. If she had left it alone, maybe Andras never would have figured it out and found some other way to reach their goal.

She thought she had found peace at the farm, the spirit of her mother and grandfather a quiet comfort. Her growing friendship with Eleanor and relationship with Henry had started to satisfy her need for companionship. It was the first time she had been happy in years, and it was all a ruse.

Ava had been selfish in her fervor to find out the truth; disregarding the warnings from her dreams and from Eleanor. Everything was her fault.

Now she had nothing.

She couldn't stop the vision of Eleanor's death from replaying again and again. The sound of her gurgle as she crawled for help, Deidamia's scream, the sight of Eleanor's body twitching.

Hopeless, she buried her face in her hands and wept, surrendering to a deep despair as the wagon started to move.

<h1 style="text-align:center">14</h1>

asimir sat in a dark corner of The Winking Fox. His friends were off on their own assignments in town, gathering supplies and information as needed, and their animal companions were still investigating the nearby forests.

He kept his hood up to hide his face in the dim lighting and took a sip of ale as he surveyed the bar room. Dark wood surrounded him, lit by a few candles and lamps scattered about. Drunken townsfolk reveled and danced across the stone floor, enjoying the upbeat tune being played by the bard in the corner, strumming along on his mandolin.

A multitude of races lived in Oakshire, the town closest to the border inside the earth kingdom of Monterre, and the tavern was filled with a collection of creatures. Pixies flitted about and sat at little tables attached to the wall, their iridescent wings glistening. A table full of goblins, gnomes and high fae laughed as they played a hand of cards. A brown-bearded gnome pounded the table enthusiastically then wrapped his arms around the acorns in the middle, pulling them toward him as he delighted in his win.

Monterre was the only place you could go where you would

find a high fae sharing a meal with a hobgoblin, or a pixie forging a friendship with an orc. It was what Casimir loved most about his kingdom. Most of the other kingdoms looked down upon the lesser fae creatures, separating their housing quarters from the high fae who ruled. As a result of this, the lesser fae rarely mingled even with each other, sticking to their own species. They were seen as mischievous, unintelligent and even a nuisance. But not by his king.

But Casimir wasn't here to mingle or find companionship for the night. He was here to listen. Where else could you hear all the local gossip but the most popular tavern? And he didn't want to be recognized.

He had been observing the comings and goings for about an hour, nursing his ale, but hadn't gleaned anything helpful yet.

The barmaid approached him, speaking in her gruff voice. "Can I get you anything else? Some stew perhaps?" She was an orc with olive skin and twinkling gray eyes. The owner of The Winking Fox. Her pointed ears peeked out from her brown curls, and she was broad-shouldered, wearing a white blouse tucked into her long brown skirt.

Casimir shook his head. "I'm fine. Thank you."

Before walking away, she leaned forward, speaking low so only he could hear. "If you need anything, general, I'll be here."

"Is it that obvious?" he grumbled.

She stood, chuckling, and placed her hands on her hips. "Only to me. I'd recognize your skulking anywhere. You used to do that when you were just a young one, sauntering into my tavern with your friends, ready to drink and fuck as if your lives depended on it. It drove all the ladies crazy."

Casimir's face heated under his hood. "You know me too well, Sugha. I don't do that anymore, though," he said, shaking his head.

"Yes, yes. I know. You're the general now. All noble and

honorable. No time for fun anymore." She waved her hand at him.

"I'm here on business."

"I figured. You've got the covert warrior in the corner disguise going on. Anything specific you need to know?"

He shrugged. "Just listening for now. I'll know it when I hear it."

She leaned back down, reaching into his hood and pinching his cheek like an old aunt might. "It's good to see you, Casimir."

He smiled, despite himself. "Good to see you too, Sugha."

"Tell your friends I said 'hi.' Oh, and by the way..." She paused. "That scruff on your face makes you look old."

He laughed quietly to himself as she walked away, comforted to know nothing had changed since he'd last visited this town.

Casimir waited another hour but after hearing nothing of use, he prepared to leave and seek out his group. They'd have to get their information elsewhere. As he was about to stand, a fae at the table behind him whispered to her companion.

"Did you hear what happened?" she said. "The daemon queen has returned."

"I know. It's horrible. And do you know what *I* heard?" her friend responded.

Casimir paused, ears perking up as he listened with his sharp fae hearing.

"What?" the feminine voice asked, terror in her voice at the prospect of more bad news.

"They brought a human with them," he said.

Casimir sucked in a breath. *A human? How was that possible?*

"What's a human?"

"They kind of look like a high fae, but have rounded ears and are much smaller. They're also weak and don't have any magic. They live in another realm."

"No magic?" She gasped. "What an awful existence! Why did they bring one with them?"

"No one knows. Though some say she was the one who allowed them in. That she is *working* with them to take over Eorhan," he said, keeping his companion riveted to her seat.

His friend gasped again. "Oh, how awful! What are we going to do? Will we go to war again?"

"It is likely. Very likely."

Casimir rose. He'd heard enough. He must find his friends and inform them of what he learned. It should be impossible. Though he'd heard of humans, he had never heard of one arriving in Eorhan. They lived in their own world in a faraway realm he thought was inaccessible. It was likely these were only rumors, ignited by fear of what was to come, but he must take heed, nonetheless.

He stepped out of the tavern and onto the cobblestone streets. Oakshire was a small town, shops nestled so closely together they felt almost oppressive at times. Golden lanterns lit the streets, joining the warm lights shining through the windows of the shops in town. He passed by a small bakery, a bookstore, even a brothel—something he never had much interest in, but Raine loved—as he strolled along.

As was tradition in his kingdom, the town was integrated into nature as much as possible, with trees interspersed among the wooden buildings and vines climbing along the walls. The glow of the setting sun brought a fiery orange tint to the sky, as the night prepared its arrival. All manners of fae bustled about, a flutter of activity in the cool evening. He continued to make his way down the street, looking for any signs of his companions.

As he came upon a small potions shop with a wooden sign hanging above the door that read *Arcane Elixirs*, arguing sounded from within. He grumbled and rolled his eyes, knowing what he would find as he pushed open the door.

Upon entering the crowded shop, filled with wall-to-wall shelves of tinctures, bottles and jars, he found Raine bickering with the proprietor at the front desk. Quinn was sauntering about the shop, looking at the goods stocked on every surface. Noticing Casimir, she raised her eyebrows at him and jerked her head pointedly toward Raine.

"That's not what you said earlier," Raine was saying to the short, gray-skinned goblin who was seated behind the counter upon a stool. "You said twenty coppers for the healing balm, *not* thirty."

Casimir approached the scene and lowered his hood. Raine turned to him. "Cas. Where the fuck have you been? This damn goblin is trying to swindle me over some healing balm."

"I am not!" the goblin insisted in his scratchy high-pitched voice. "I said twenty coppers for the tin of salve sitting next to the healing balm. That's the one you pointed to."

"It is not, and you know it. You switched them around when I wasn't looking." Raine waved his hands. "Twenty coppers is all I'll pay." Raine looked at Casimir with frustration, running his hand through his platinum locks. "Cas, help me out here."

Casimir turned to the proprietor of the shop. "Will you take twenty-five?"

The goblin nodded enthusiastically. "Yes, general. Thank you, general."

He turned to his friend and gestured toward the pouch hanging from his leather belt. "Pay up."

"But... twenty-five coppers?" Raine scoffed. "Oh, come on, this is outrageous."

"Just do it. We have more important things to worry about right now," replied Casimir, patience waning.

Sighing, Raine retrieved the money and set it on the counter. "Here," he said as he snatched the balm off the desk and huffed out of the shop mumbling to himself as the goblin gave a triumphant small smile.

Quinn appeared next to Casimir, holding up a bright purple vial and dropping her coppers into the goblin's hand.

"You came in here for soap?" Casimir asked.

"I'm tired of smelling like you brutes." She grinned.

He gave her a flat look and grunted.

She laughed as they walked back out into the night and joined Raine who was still huffing and puffing in the street. "You heard something?" she asked Casimir.

"Yes. We need a private location to speak."

A moment later, Jorrar appeared with a new quiver of arrows. "What did you learn?" he asked as the four of them walked down the lamp lit streets.

They found a quiet alleyway between two buildings and stopped, scanning the area for prying eyes or ears.

"There's a rumor a human woman was brought here with Deidamia," Casimir informed them.

"A human?" Quinn was incredulous. "Impossible."

"I thought so too, but we need to keep our ears open for more. Jorrar, what does this mean?" he asked his wisest warrior.

Jorrar thought for a moment as he shook his head. "To my knowledge there has never been a human in Eorhan before. I'm not sure what to make of it. Did you learn anything else? Talk to anyone?"

"The two fae who were discussing the human were scared. Afraid she was helping the daemon queen. But that's all." He paused. "Oh, and Sugha told me I looked old. She says hi." He smirked.

Raine clapped him on the back, sour mood gone. "It's the beard, Cas. Makes you look dirty. I told you; the women prefer clean shaven faces."

"Like you would know," taunted Quinn.

Casimir rubbed his jaw. "I happen to like my beard. It's..."

"Disgusting," said Quinn.

Glaring at her, he finished. "Rugged."

Jorrar chuckled along with the rest of them. "Let's find something to eat and we can discuss our next move."

As they filtered out of the alleyway, an ear-piercing scream rang out from the other side of town.

Immediately on alert, the warriors looked around before heading in the direction of the panic. They hurried down the streets, darting in between buildings and leaping over low stone walls, eager to help whoever was in trouble.

They made it to the edge of town, screams increasing in frequency and volume, when a gnome ran toward them, shouting in fear. "Creatures! Awful creatures! They're attacking the farmers." He pointed in the direction of the chaos before running off.

They took off faster, running toward the fields where crops were grown and harvested. They jumped over a wooden fence and ran in between tall rows of corn before stopping in the yard in front of a small house with a thatched roof.

The warriors froze. "What the hell are those things?" said Quinn.

On top of the roof were two black creatures with wings and long front claws lined with spikes, piercing holes in the straw and trying to get in while a third hovered in front of the door, blocking the exit. They looked like giant insects of some sort, with six dangling legs and massive pincers below their shiny compound eyes. Their buzzing echoed over the screams of the family of orcs inside.

From beside him, Raine whispered, "There are children in there."

That was all Casimir needed before he leapt over the fence and jumped into the fray, unsheathing his sword.

15

*A*va's wagon arrived at the main camp, the pounding of iron and murmur of soldiers sounding in the air. The smell of smoke, sweat and dirt snaked its way into the prison cart from the small window.

She had no idea how long they had traveled. There was no way to discern time in her dismal box and though she had tried to mark the days based off the sunlight, her fear and exhaustion had her losing count by day four. She had only been let out for brief moments to relieve herself and then shoved back into the wagon with measly scraps of food and hardly enough water to parch her dry throat.

She hadn't heard from Luna yet and hoped she was safe and still looking for help. Maybe she could try to run when they moved her to the next location. It was worth a shot.

The cart rattled to a stop and Ava waited for the guard.

The door opened and bright light almost blinded her, forcing her to shade her face with her bound hands. After days of the dark wagon, she hadn't accounted for how painful the sun would be. The guard reached in and dragged her out, setting her on her feet in the mud.

They were in an open field surrounded by hundreds of tents. Smoke from scattered fires emerged in different directions. To fight the mud, there were paths covered in straw, allowing the soldiers to walk around without sinking into the muck. She looked around subtly, learning the layout and searching for a place to run if she got the opportunity.

Scorch marks and tree stumps lined the camp, evidence of the devastation of the land, and Ava felt an ache of sadness for the flora and fauna that once was. A sense of violence and savagery floated through the air as the grunts and shouts of daemon soldiers sounded.

A sharp yank of her arm had her stumbling as they walked through camp.

"Come on," the guard said, pulling her along.

She couldn't see much beyond the massive camp but caught a glimpse of towering mountains far in the distance behind more rolling fields and clusters of trees. The moment she saw those mountains, something washed over her. Like a sense of peace remained out of reach and urged her to go there, to find something beyond those green peaks. She had to reach those mountains, though she didn't know why.

Soldiers bustled about in their daily activities, some of them sparring while others laughed around a fire. Some wore the same armor as the group surrounding her while the rest of them were in tunics and pants of browns and blacks. They passed by a blacksmith, hammering away at a giant weapon with spikes and blades, the clang ringing in Ava's ears.

The smells of sweat, roasted meat, refuse and mud stung her nostrils as she trembled while the guard led her down the center of their stronghold. Her hands were clammy as she pleaded with her tears to stay away.

As they passed through camp, the soldiers noticed their party and immediately bowed. Voices young and old sounded, revering their queen.

"You've returned, my queen."

"We've waited for you."

"It's an honor to be in your presence again."

Deidamia barely acknowledged them other than a curt nod and Andras looked at them with apathy as they led Ava and her guards to a tent in the center of camp. It was larger than the others; built for royalty. Crimson pennants embellished with their horned insignia flapped in the wind atop the tent.

Creatures occupied the space near the large tents. Terrifying demon-like animals in cages, snarling and lunging as they passed by. Giant wolves with red glowing eyes, black fur and huge paws, drool dripping from their canines as they growled. Winged creatures, bigger than men with claws and teeth, flew overhead, grinning greedily. There were giant insects, black as night with pincers buzzing about the camp and great silver serpents were chained near Deidamia's tent, hissing and snapping as they walked by, foot long fangs dripping with venom.

If she tried to flee, would they send these beasts after her?

She should have jumped out of the wagon and taken off the moment the door was opened but it was too late. Even if she was able to free herself from her guard's grip, she would barely make it a few feet before either soldiers or animals were upon her.

Or Andras' shadows.

Trembling and terrified, knowing any one of these creatures or soldiers could cut her down in one swipe and not think twice about it, she decided against running for now. She would have to wait for a more sensible opportunity.

They stopped before the large tent and Andras turned to Ava and her guards. "Put her with the other prisoners," he ordered, and they led her toward a smaller tent guarded by two soldiers.

"What do we have here?" one of them crooned as she

walked forward and grasped Ava's chin, inspecting her. She tried to jerk away but the soldier was too strong and laughed in her face as she released Ava and opened the flap of the tent to allow the party to enter.

It was dark inside, the only light from several braziers with their crackling embers providing a subtle glow. The tent was larger than it had appeared and contained several metal cages, two of them holding other captives. On the side opposite the cages, three metal poles stood, rings welded onto them where one might attach chains or manacles. The tent reeked, a mix between rot, body odor and feces and the prisoners appeared to be asleep as they entered.

They brought her to one of the poles and produced a long chain.

Panicking, she tried to break free and slammed her bound hands against the face of one of the soldiers who wasn't wearing a helmet.

He snarled as two others shoved her into a seated position on the ground.

She kicked and screamed, trying to break free, as they held her down, back against the metal pole. The soldier she had hit walked up to her and backhanded her across the cheek. Ears ringing, the world spun as they attached her wrists to the metal ring above her. Binding her ankles, they chained them to another ring at the bottom of the pole. Barely enough room to stretch her legs, but not enough to kick or attempt to escape.

They left without saying a word. Why hadn't they killed her? Why keep her here? Her cheek throbbed and head pounded as she worried about their plans for her.

Laying her head back against the pole, Ava let the tears fall once again.

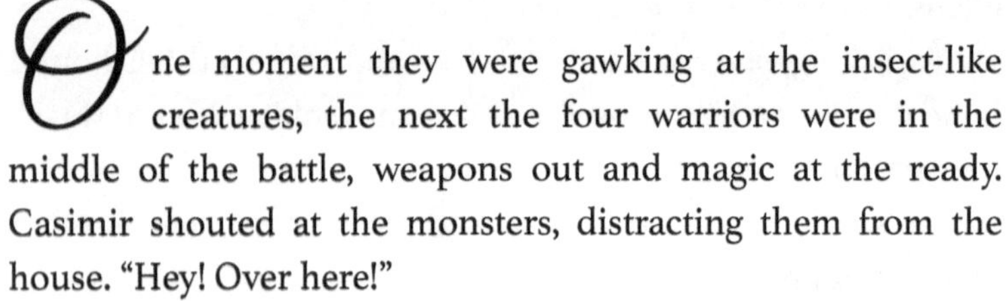

One moment they were gawking at the insect-like creatures, the next the four warriors were in the middle of the battle, weapons out and magic at the ready. Casimir shouted at the monsters, distracting them from the house. "Hey! Over here!"

Two of them took the bait and flew down toward the group with a loud buzzing sound that rang in his ears. To his left, Jorrar used his earth magic to create a golem from the mud. It was large, close to eight feet tall and punched and kicked the air as it ambled toward one of the creatures.

Bright green shoots burst from the ground as Quinn created vines along the roof, reinforcing the house and covering the holes. The tendrils snaked their way along the sides of the house as they wove together, temporarily protecting the family inside from the blood hungry insects.

Raine nocked an arrow, the best archer in the group, and prepared to provide cover as Casimir lunged at the first creature.

It was bigger than he realized, almost as large as he was, and it hovered in front of him with its pincers snapping eagerly.

He swiped at the insect with his sword, but the creature dodged it, much faster than he expected.

The beast darted in his direction, slicing the air with its dagger-like arms. Casimir ducked and rolled out of the way at the last second, barely escaping the attack. Jumping to his feet, he ran and slashed with his sword, but his attempt was skirted yet again.

Jorrar's golem was growing and punching at the other insect, but it was too quick, and it failed to land a single blow. Raine tried with his bow, loosing an arrow directly at its eye, and yet it evaded this attack as well. A couple of guards from town had joined the fight but their blows were deflected every time.

"They're too quick!" Casimir shouted at his friends as he ducked, avoiding another attack. "We need a new strategy."

"I've got an idea!" shouted Quinn. "Follow my lead."

The other three readied their magic and weapons as Quinn stalked toward one of the insects, offering herself as bait. Behind her, she was creating a makeshift cage out of roots growing from the soil. The brown roots twisted around each other, making the perfect trap. Understanding her plan, Casimir caught her eye and nodded while the other two occupied the other creature, distracting it.

Quinn stood still, arms outstretched, waiting for the insect to attack. It hovered out of reach of her weapons, buzzing with ire as it decided what to do. "It's not taking the bait, Quinn," Casimir growled.

"Let's see if you want *this*," she said as she unsheathed one of her many daggers. Slicing along her forearm, she let the blood drip onto the grass. "Hungry, you ugly bastard?"

It fell for the trick, scenting the blood, and shot directly at Quinn. Casimir positioned himself near the makeshift cage, waiting. At the last second, Quinn rolled and landed in a crouch, threw out her arms at the roots and created an opening.

The monster slammed into the root ball, now unable to escape, as she wove the trap together. Seconds later, Casimir was upon it.

He lunged, impaling its chest with his sword. Its carapace was strong, and it was harder to pierce than he expected, but it worked. It was dead and remained twitching on the ground as they turned to the remaining two.

"Good work." He nodded at his captain. She never second guessed herself in a fight. That was exactly why she was second in command to their armies.

Quinn joined Jorrar and Raine as they attempted to kill one of the creatures and Casimir directed his attention to the one still on the roof.

The screams of the children inside were rising, too frozen in fear to flee as the insect sliced the roof, creating a hole large enough to fit through. Quinn's vines hadn't lasted, the being cutting through them like butter, and while they were distracted with the other two, it had made progress in reaching its prey. He waved and yelled, trying to get its attention. He even tried Quinn's trick, slicing his arm and enticing it with his blood.

It didn't work.

As he prepared himself to climb to the roof, someone pulled on his arm.

"Those are my grandchildren!" He whipped his head around and there was Sugha, the tavern owner, eyes wide and welling with tears. "Please, Casimir. You must save them."

"Stay here," he said as he ran toward the house, a mere thirty feet away.

Quinn, Raine and Jorrar were working on the third beast and had it surrounded. Assured his friends had their fight handled, he made his way to the side of the house and searched for the easiest place to climb.

He found several barrels stacked in the back and used those

to scale the wall, heart racing as he pulled himself onto the roof. It was almost fully inside now, blood curdling screams escaping through the numerous holes in the ceiling.

He dashed forward, but as he brought down his sword, aiming for the unsuspecting insect, it shot straight into the air carrying something in its six dangling legs.

A child.

He froze, panic erupting. His palms were clammy, grip on his sword slick while sweat dripped down his brow. The young girl screamed and suddenly he was back in that place, cowering as shadows burst into his home. Soldiers outfitted in solid black armor with spikes marched into the kitchen, boots pounding the wooden floor. Screams resonated all around him as the soldiers burned down his village, killing everyone in their way. He shook violently in the cupboards as he held her tight, trying to tamp down his fear as he protected her. But a cabinet door opened, and she was ripped from his arms, her screams echoing in the house as he tried to stop them. Tried to save her. The tangy iron smell of blood hung in the air as it pooled at his feet while he watched her die...

"Casimir!" A voice pulled him out of his flashback, and he looked around, still on the roof. "Cas!" Raine shouted again. They had killed the other creature and were looking at him with concern.

He climbed off the roof, looking for the last insect and the girl. Sugha was sobbing, begging them to help as he joined his friends, ready to develop a plan. "Save her!" Sugha said in between breaths. "Oh, Mother have mercy. *Do* something!"

Jorrar took her hands in his and assured her. "We'll get her back. I promise you."

"But how?" she asked. "She's in the air!"

His three companions looked at him knowingly. "You have to do it, Cas," encouraged Raine.

Casimir shook his head. "I don't know if I can."

He loathed the magic he needed to use to save the girl. The way it felt as it erupted from him made him sick and the reminder of his past was often too much to bear. It had been decades since he'd used his 'other' magic, he called it. He preferred his earth abilities or his skills with the sword, but now wasn't the time to balk. He was the only one who could get her from above the treetops.

"You can and you must," said Quinn. "This isn't like back then. You have full control. Don't doubt yourself. Get your ass up there and save that little girl," she insisted and grasped his shoulder, looking at him with steel in her brown eyes.

Nodding, he looked around for the girl. There, high above the tree line. The creature was carrying her away as her screams faded into the night.

"Check on the others in the house," he said before running after them.

He reached the insect and stopped just under it, concentrating on its mass. Pulling, he made himself lighter, manipulating the gravity around him. It required tremendous focus not to affect everything else in the vicinity and he trembled with effort as he continued to pull on the creature. Getting the force exact, he jumped up and held his sword at the ready. Before the monstrous beast had a chance to flee, he gutted it from below, carefully avoiding the girl.

The insect fell apart in the air, innards raining down on the trees, as Casimir held the child in his arms and fell back to the ground with precision while he returned the gravity to normal. Landing with a thud, he took a deep breath and looked at the girl.

Her dark eyes were full of tears, but she was smiling at him. "You're glowing," she said as she reached out her small green hand and cradled his face.

His heart warmed. "That happens sometimes. You're safe now, little one."

Abruptly he was surrounded by his friends and onlookers, Sugha pushing her way through. He handed the girl to her and she sobbed with relief as she enfolded her grandchild into her arms.

"Oh, my sweet, sweet girl. You're safe. Everything's okay," she said to the child, then looked at Casimir. "Thank you."

He nodded and walked away, needing to be alone.

He found a fallen log in the forest near the edge of the farm and sat down, breathing deeply and waiting for his glow to fade. He hated the way that magic felt as it snaked across his skin, hated the reminder of how he had failed so many years ago. Retrieving a small carving from his pocket, one he carried everywhere he went, he exhaled and stared at it. It was a fox which he had meticulously carved himself, a hobby of his that brought him peace.

He caressed its head. "I'm sorry, Elara," he said, whispering to himself.

Casimir hadn't struggled with memories from that time in many years. But with the return of the daemon queen and that child in danger, it all came rushing back. As if the wound he thought was healed had been reopened, shame and anger pouring out.

After some time, the crunch of leaves underfoot sounded as someone approached. He placed the fox back into his pocket as Jorrar sat down next to him.

"Are you alright?" he asked.

"I froze."

"Everyone freezes now and then."

Staring straight ahead, Casimir replied, "If Raine hadn't called my name... The girl... she would have died."

"But she didn't. Thanks to you."

He sighed, placing his hands beside him on the log and stretching his legs out in front of him. "Does it get any easier?" he asked Jorrar.

"Does what get any easier?"

"Carrying the burdens of failure. The loss of loved ones. All of it," he whispered, looking at the sky through the canopy. The reminders of his past were making themselves known and he was overwhelmed with the feel of it all. "I thought I had moved past it."

Jorrar leaned forward, arms on his knees as he thought. "I don't know that we ever move past the death of those we love." He paused. "And I don't think it gets easier. You just get better at living with it."

"And how do you?" Casimir turned toward him. "Live with it."

Jorrar sat back up. "I focus on those that I love. The ones that are still here. And try to find joy in small things. The pitter patter of rain on the roof; the laughter of a child; the taste of a fresh berry tart; being with my friends."

Jorrar rose, patting Casimir on the shoulder, and began to walk back to town.

Casimir called after him. "And that's enough?"

Jorrar stopped, looking at him over his shoulder. "It has to be."

Something hard hit Ava in the face and she lifted her head from the pole as she opened her eyes. It hit her again, this time on the side of her head and she jerked to her right, searching for the source.

"Pssst." The prisoner in the cage next to her was throwing pebbles, trying to get her attention. "Good. You're awake," he said as Ava met his eyes.

"I am now. That hurt."

"Sorry," he said in a high-pitched, scratchy voice.

She looked at the prisoner. He was much shorter than most human adults, broad and stocky but the height of a child. His skin was a mossy green, peppered with bumps and warts, and his face would not be considered handsome by most standards. His teeth were crooked, eyes full of mischief and he had long pointed ears. He was thin and malnourished, with tattered clothing that didn't cover much above his waist.

"I'm Remy," he whispered. "What's your name?"

Keeping her voice quiet, she answered, "Ava. What is this place? Where are we?"

Remy regarded her intensely. "You aren't from here, are you?"

"No."

Well, technically she was. But she wasn't going to explain that to a stranger.

He regarded her intensely. "You aren't a daemon though. Nope nope nope. Not you. You're different," he said with his strange little voice.

"No, I'm not. I'm a human."

"What's a human? I've never heard of that. Are they tasty?" He smiled.

"Um... I don't think so," she said. "I'm a human. Just me." She tried to be friendly in case this creature did indeed want to eat her.

As if reading her mind, Remy said, "Don't worry. I won't eat you. You're too pretty and seem kind. I can tell. Do humans have magic?"

Ava smiled. "No, they don't. And I'm relieved to hear you don't want to eat me. Deidamia and Andras tricked me and brought me here."

Remy gasped. "They're back? Oh no. Oh no no no. This is bad. Bad bad bad." He rocked with his head in his hands.

Ava tried to get him to talk more but he kept repeating himself over and over, rocking back and forth to soothe his terror.

"Remy!" she whispered louder. "Talk to me. Why is it bad? Tell me everything."

Remy stopped rocking and looked at her with his large eyes. "They were stuck in another world. It was the only hope we had. That they couldn't come back. Their armies have been waiting. Watching. Hoping. And they hurt us. For fun. Fun fun fun. Except it's not fun."

"How did they get here in the first place?" Ava asked. "Are they from Eorhan?"

"No." Remy shook his head. "Legends say the daemon of seduction tricked a king into letting them in. A king that wanted power."

Tricked a king. Just like her grandfather's story. The one that had terrified her as a child. It was true. So far everything was turning out to be true.

"Why didn't anyone kill off the armies while Deidamia was gone?"

"I don't know. The kingdoms weren't getting along, I think. Not helping each other. Not strong enough. Nope nope nope."

"Why did they capture you?"

His voice changed, became angrier. "They killed my parents and captured me. Why? Because they could. No other reason. To show their power. Oh no. No no no." He shook his head again.

"I'm sorry about your parents, Remy. I've lost family too," she said, and Remy looked at her expectantly, so she continued. "My mom died a few years ago." And Eleanor, but she wasn't ready to talk about that yet, the guilt and shame washing over her.

Interested now, Remy asked, "How did she die?"

"Cancer."

"What's cancer?"

"Um—" Ava paused, realizing their language and terminology was likely different in this world. "It's a sickness. Sometimes you can stop it but sometimes you can't."

"Did healers help her?" Remy asked, mesmerized by Ava's story.

Ava smiled sadly. "They tried. But it didn't work. I'm sorry you lost family too."

Remy smiled back, an ally for the time being.

"Do you think we can escape?" Ava asked. "Is there somewhere safe we can go away from the army?"

"No. No safety." Remy looked scared again. "Not near here.

If we got far away... maybe. Escape is impossible. No one has ever been able to. We stay here until we are dead. Dead dead dead."

Ava sighed. "Well, I have to try..." Remy looked at her, blinking. "So, um... what are you?" she asked, hoping she didn't offend him.

Remy laughed. "What am I? You are human. I am a hob. Hobgoblin. We live in the woods all throughout Eorhan."

Ava smiled back at him. "What other beings live here? Can you tell me about this world?" she asked.

Excited to give her a history lesson, Remy settled back against his cage and looked at her, speaking quietly so the guards didn't hear.

"Eorhan is ruled by the High Fae. They are powerful magic wielders, and they rule over us all. Split into five kingdoms. Some wield ice, some lava, others can manipulate stone and rocks. Some have the power of the stars and others have powers of the earth. All creatures are ruled by them. All creatures great and small. Even hobgoblins."

If she was truly from here, did that make her fae? Was that even possible? She had not felt any different since arriving and still didn't have magical abilities. How would being born in the human world have affected her heritage? Her magic?

Deciding to keep this information to herself for the time being, she asked, "Are the fae nice?"

Remy looked at her mischievously. "It depends on what you think is nice. They are warriors. They can be ruthless. Some are benevolent and some crave power. Most have stood against Deidamia and her army, but others have allowed them into their kingdom, hoping they won't be slaughtered. Better to be ruled by daemons than wiped out, they say."

"Do you agree with that?" Ava asked.

"Oh no. No no no. I'd rather die," he whispered harshly as he stared into her eyes.

As they spoke, a prisoner in another cage stirred, groaning and turning her head. She didn't seem to be aware of what was going on around her and appeared as though she'd been brutally beaten and close to death. She opened her eyes and looked at Ava as she lay there, breath coming in short slow pants.

"What's her name?" Ava asked Remy.

"I don't know," he answered. "She was here before I arrived, and she will not speak. I think she's dying."

"What did they do to her?"

"I don't know." He shook his head. "Sometimes they take the prisoners somewhere else."

"For what?"

He shook his head again and shrugged.

Ava looked at the prisoner with compassion and fear for herself. She appeared mostly human aside from her pointed ears. Her hair was short and curly, but she was so caked in filth her skin tone or hair color were imperceptible, and her tattered clothing revealed gruesome bruises.

The flaps of the tent opened and a guard entered. He was tall, slim and muscular and had cunning green eyes, short black hair and a pock marked face. He stopped and stood in the center of the room, inspecting the prisoners with disgust, but the moment he noticed Ava, his eyes turned feral.

"What do we have here?" he said as he stalked toward her. "A new prisoner for me to play with, I presume."

He reached the spot where Ava sat chained, crouched in front of her and stroked her face with his hand.

Fight back, Luna's voice sounded.

"Get away from me," she said before spitting in his face.

He calmly stood, wiped his face and then looked down at her with barely contained rage. "You're going to regret that."

He walked over to the cage with the prisoner and unlocked the door. The girl didn't fight as she was dragged out by her hair, resigned to her fate. Remy covered his ears with his hands and backed into the corner of his cage, rocking with his eyes closed.

Ava looked at the guard. "Please don't hurt her."

He laughed as he dragged her to the ground in front of Ava and then set the fae woman down. She didn't move, breathing ragged as she opened her eyes and looked straight at Ava. Her eyes bored into Ava's as she conveyed a message. It was a silent plea; kill me.

The guard looked at Ava and knelt in front of the prisoner. "See how she's run out of usefulness? This is what will happen to you if you don't cooperate," he said as he held the woman's head between his hands.

Then the light went out of her eyes as the guard snapped her neck.

Ava screamed as nausea took over. Fighting against the bile working its way up her throat, she started to sob and tried to remind herself death was a blessing for this poor fae.

Death. So much death she had already witnessed in such a short amount of time. Eleanor and now this woman. How was she going to get out of here?

The guard kicked the body away from Ava and knelt back down in front of her. His eyes roved over her body filled with desire and the promise of pain. His hand gripped her hair and yanked her head back, baring her throat to him. He leaned forward and ran his nose along her neck, breathing in deeply.

"Your fear smells delicious," he whispered.

Ava whimpered and tears streamed down her face. The guard pulled back and gave her a cunning smile when the flaps of the tent opened and Andras stepped in.

He paused, looking at the guard. "I told you to dispose of the useless prisoner. I did not give you permission to touch the new one. Get out," he barked.

The guard rose and nodded to Andras then glanced at Ava one last time before leaving.

She looked to Remy, but he was still rocking in the corner, hiding himself from witnessing the death of his fellow captive.

"What do you want with me? Please send me back home," she begged Andras through her tears.

He towered over her, placing his hands in his pockets. "We have plans for you."

"What plans?"

He remained silent, looking at her with boredom.

"How long will I be here?" she asked.

He knelt, closing in on her. "As long as it takes, Ava dear. We'll use whatever means necessary to get what we need." He crept closer, watching her reaction. "It may take months. Until then, you'll remain with us."

No. She wouldn't allow it.

"Henry..." Ava began, thinking maybe if she used his other name, his other identity. The man she had cared for... or thought she had. Maybe she could reach him. Maybe see reason.

Andras looked down at her, as he rose.

"Do *not* call me that," he bristled.

"I know you aren't all bad, Henry," she continued. "I saw it in you when we were together. You were kind, and loving and—"

She was interrupted by a slap to the face. Adding to her previous injuries her body was becoming bruises upon bruises upon bruises. She reeled from the pain and realized there was no talking to him. No reasoning. She knew he wasn't Henry, but she had to try one last time.

"You know nothing."

He left the tent and she looked over at Remy and saw he had stopped rocking and was assessing her.

"Are you okay?" he asked, wringing his hands.

"Yeah," she lied.

"Ava?"

"Yes?" she whispered through the pain, head throbbing.

"How did you get to Eorhan?" he asked.

"Andras tricked me and used my blood to open a portal that led us here," she said.

"Your blood... The portal. You have magic?"

Sighing, she answered, not wanting to face the truth. "I don't have magic. I never have."

"But it opened the door. Yes, it did. How?" he insisted.

So she told him the rest of her story; explained it all. That her grandfather and mother escaped into the human world before her birth, but she hadn't known about any of it.

He listened intensely, eyes wide and when she finished, he said reverently, "You came back. You came back to help."

"No, Remy. I made things worse by letting them in. I don't have magic. I can't do anything." She shook her head.

Not listening, face now lit with hope, he urged her. "You need to escape and get to your homeland. Yes yes yes..." he trailed off and mumbled to himself.

"Remy, what are you talking about?" she tried asking but he was lost in his thoughts, mumbling to himself and looking around.

Wondering if he had always been this odd or if being imprisoned had damaged his mind, she knew he wouldn't answer her now.

LATER THAT EVENING, two guards entered the tent, carrying what looked like a big stew pot and some bowls.

"It's time for dinner," one of the guards said as he looked over Ava and Remy.

The body of the other prisoner must have been removed as

she slept, every trace of the captive erased. As if she didn't matter. Had never even existed. Ava hoped if there was an afterlife in this world, she was resting peacefully with her loved ones there.

One of the guards scooped what appeared to be dark oatmeal into the two wooden bowls, sounds of the thick paste plopping grotesquely, while the other unchained Ava's wrists. He put one bowl in Remy's cage, and he took it and ate voraciously as if he couldn't get it down fast enough. The guard then handed her a bowl and spoon for herself and stood over her.

"You will only be unchained for you to eat. Don't try anything." Ava looked at the slop and then back at him. "You better eat. This is the only meal you'll get each day."

Knowing she would need strength for her escape, she choked down the glue-like mush. After finishing, she handed the bowl back to the guard and he shoved a water skin into her hands and she chugged the contents, quenching her thirst.

"Um... what if I need to use the bathroom?" she asked tentatively.

She needed to learn their schedule. The meals and bathroom breaks. Times where she may not be chained so she could plan her getaway.

"Twice a day someone will bring you a bucket and unlock your chains. Anything more and you can soil yourself," he said. "No one will be in again until tomorrow so now's your only chance." He retrieved a wooden bucket reeking of unwashed urine and feces.

It seemed as if this was the bucket all the prisoners used and other than dumping it, was never washed out. Ava tried to keep her food down as she looked at the vessel on the floor beside her.

Hesitating, she looked at the guard. "Aren't you going to give me privacy? Or unlock my feet?"

He threw his head back and laughed. "What kind of fool do you think I am? The foot chains stay on. They're long enough for you to move over the bucket."

Stomach roiling Ava decided to get it over with. Humiliated she stood and positioned herself over the bucket, unbuttoned and pulled down her pants and released her bladder. She didn't even try to ask for something to wipe herself as she knew he would laugh her off again. Quickly pulling her pants back up, she sat down.

He picked it up and silently walked out of the tent.

Ava remained silent as the other guard chained her arms back above her head, gathered the dishes and left without saying a word. Ava looked at Remy, already fast asleep, and was relieved he missed her humiliating bathroom routine, though he must have done the same many times already. It was night-time now. She had caught a glimpse of the darkness and stars through the tent flap as the guards left.

How long had it been since she had left home? A week maybe?

She had failed. Utterly and truly failed.

In her selfishness to learn about her past and her anger at her mother and grandfather, she had brought her homeland's own enemies back. Back to destroy and conquer. To burn and maim and kill. Even if she escaped, then what? Was she supposed to go to those mountains? Find her ancestors if anyone was even still alive? She doubted the fae would even believe her, especially when they found out she was the reason the daemon queen had returned. They'd probably kill her on sight.

18

asimir joined Jorrar across the table from Quinn and Raine, watching them shovel breakfast into their mouths in the tavern. He reached across the table and served himself roasted pork and fried eggs, topping it with a thick brown sauce and set his plate down in front of him.

Sugha had spoiled them, ordering her cooks to make the largest breakfast feast as a thank you for saving her daughter and grandchildren. She had placed platters of meats, eggs, grits, berries and pastries in front of the four of them, insisting they eat as much as they liked. He took a sip of tea, steeped from local herbs Sugha grew herself in the garden behind her tavern, and sighed at the warmth.

He absolutely loved tea. There was a small tea house back home that had every flavor you could imagine and he missed it. Couldn't wait to get home and sample their concoctions while he watched the animals visit the stream outside the window.

Home. He was ready to be back in the city. Though he took his role as general seriously and would do anything to protect his kingdom, he often longed for the quiet of Mosshaven. A simple life. That's what he ultimately sought. Maybe after the war was over he'd find it. What he wouldn't give to sip tea by the fire while he read his favorite book without the fear of his home being destroyed. Perhaps he'd have a partner to share it with too. Someday.

But for now, he would focus on assuring the safety of his people against the daemon queen.

Casimir turned his attention back to his two captains across from him. "Do you know how disgusting the both of you look? It wouldn't hurt you to eat more... civilized."

Raine raised an eyebrow. "Like you're one to talk. You're so full of grunts, growls and body hair, I'm surprised you haven't turned into an animal by this point," he said through a mouthful of honeyed grits.

Casimir grunted as he raised his fork to his mouth and dug in.

"See?" Raine pointed at him with his spoon.

Quinn laughed, setting down her tea. "There's a reason your nickname is The Bear, Cas. And it's not because of Aro."

"It is because of the bear," he retorted, ripping into a pastry.

"Sure," Raine said.

"Any word from Thorne?" Casimir asked, changing the subject and looking at Jorrar from the corner of his eye.

He shook his head. "Not yet, but I suspect we shall hear something soon. Percy should return any day now."

"We need to come up with a plan," Raine said, taking a drink of his tea.

"We follow the king's orders," Casimir responded. "We rest here a few days longer while we wait."

"We should talk about last night," said Quinn.

"Like how Cas almost wet his pants at the sight of those creatures?" said Raine.

Casimir tilted his head with predatory grace. "Just like you almost did the first time we visited Nelida?"

Jorrar and Quinn burst out laughing as Raine looked

incredulously at Casimir. "That wood nymph is utterly terrifying! I don't care if she can see the future or whatever, she gives me the creeps. Besides, I was young then." He brushed his hair behind his shoulder.

"Sure," said Cas, taking a bite of eggs, a smirk on his face.

Quinn piped up after a moment. "What *were* those things? I've never seen anything like that before."

"I have no idea," replied Casimir. "I assume they're some sort of creatures of Deidamia's. Whether they were created or came over from her homelands, I don't know."

"They were really fucking hard to kill," said Raine.

Jorrar nodded. "Indeed, they were. And I fear it won't be the last time we see them."

"You're probably right," said Casimir. "We need to send for some extra guards to patrol the towns. Where there are three, there are likely more."

They finished breakfast and decided to take a walk through town, speaking with the guards and explaining the best strategies to use should more of those insects appear. It seemed luring them to the ground in some way and trapping them was the most efficient, though once they figured out what they were trying to do, they didn't fall for it as quickly. Not only fast, they were smart, and this concerned Casimir a great deal.

They walked through the shops and Casimir sat down on a bench next to Raine while Jorrar and Quinn went inside to talk to the fletcher about the possibility of stronger or faster arrows. Should they encounter those beings again, they'd need them. None of the others could rise into the air like him and he didn't want to have to use that magic any more than necessary.

"You saw her again last night, didn't you?" asked Raine carefully, his usual humor gone.

Casimir nodded, staying silent.

Raine placed his hand on Casimir's knee. "Her death wasn't your fault, you know. You were just a child."

Casimir turned to his best friend. "I know that. But it will never stop haunting me."

"We all have things that haunt us. Quinn deals with it by pretending she hates everyone. Jorrar deals with it by being overly nice and helping others. I deal with it by being an insufferable rogue. And you deal with it by being a brooding, grumpy asshole, and beating yourself up over every perceived misstep. By taking responsibility for everything when it's not your job."

Casimir looked at him. "I'm the general. It is my job."

Raine rolled his eyes. "We just need to get you laid. That will bring a smile to your face. When was the last time you had some beautiful thing in your bed?"

"That isn't the answer to everything, Raine. That stuff doesn't matter anymore."

"What stuff?"

"Sex. Companionship..." He paused. "It's just a distraction."

"A distraction from what?"

"From this war that's about to erupt," he insisted, eyes boring into his friend's.

"I know," Raine said. "But there's nothing wrong with having a little fun."

"Fun?" Casimir tilted his head. "Is that what that was last night when I saw *three* orcs leave your room disheveled and smiling?"

"Exactly." Raine grinned widely. "You should try it some time."

They were interrupted by a faint hooting in the distance.

Raine stood. "Looks like Percy's back."

Jorrar and Quinn stepped out of the shop in time for the owl to swoop down and land on the back of the bench next to Casimir. Percy ruffled his feathers and softly hooted at his companion. Jorrar tilted his head, listening to the information the owl had brought with him.

"He has news from Thorne," he informed them. "The rumors about the human are true. All the animals are speaking of it."

Quinn gasped. "Seriously? What does that mean for us? What does he want us to do?"

"They have the human woman. It sounds like she's their prisoner. Thorne wants us to start scouting the lands in between Monterre and their largest army camp. Not get too close but see if we can gather any intelligence from the creatures of the nearby forest."

"Well, alright then," said Raine. "I was kind of hoping he'd tell us to come home, but who's up for a little adventure?"

"Only if I get a tent to myself," grumbled Quinn. "I'm sick of listening to Raine mumble in his sleep all night."

"Oh, thank The Mother. I'll finally be free of your incessant snoring," he replied, a twinkle in his eye.

"I do *not* snore," she bit back, shoving him. "Right, Cas?"

"I'm not answering that," he remarked as he led his friends back to the tavern. "We need to gather our supplies and move out."

Quinn scoffed behind him as Raine laughed and continued to taunt her. The four warriors made their way back to their rooms above the tavern at the inn and began to pack, preparing for their next mission.

"I hope we don't run into any more of those horrid insects," said Raine. "Their black blood was impossible to wash out of my hair."

19

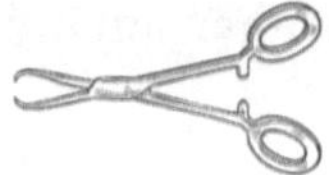

$\mathcal{A}$va's throat burned as she screamed and thrashed against the two guards carrying her to the other side of the tent. She tried to kick and flail as they laid her on a large wooden table with metal cuffs at the head and feet.

Whatever they were about to do, she was determined to fight against them. To make it as difficult as possible. Panic fueled her as she turned her head and bit one of them on the arm, tasting iron as her teeth sank into his flesh. The soldier yelped in pain and her head spun as he punched her in the jaw. Now subdued, they secured her wrists and ankles to the metal cuffs and left the tent.

Nausea gripped her as she took in a smaller table next to her, displaying jagged knives, rusty saws, forceps and other tools whose purposes she could only imagine. The instruments reflected the orange firelight as if vibrating with the thrill of promised pain and suffering. The horrors of Deidamia's war camp personified. Right there before her.

Her hands were clammy, and her throat tightened as she realized the purpose of the set up. Heart racing, she frantically looked around as if help would materialize out of thin air, eyes landing on Remy. He placed his hand over his heart and gave her a nod as if signaling he was there for her.

"What are they going to do?"

"They will try to unlock your magic. Yes. Yes. That's what I think."

"I don't have magic. I told you."

Remy shook his head. "Your blood. Magic. The daemons. They need more. More portals. For more conquering. They will try to make you have your great tribulation."

"Great tribulation?"

"Fae are born with lesser magic. But the great tribulation... that happens to the powerful ones. Those destined for more. When they go through something big. Something bad. It stresses their body, and the big magic comes out," Remy whispered.

"But—" She took a deep breath. "You're saying they're going to torture me into having a traumatic experience, so my magic comes out?"

"Yes, Ava. I'm sorry. Sorry sorry sorry." He shook his head, tears welling in his large eyes.

As Remy finished speaking, Andras entered the tent followed by Deidamia and a savage looking soldier she had not seen before. He evaluated Ava with a look of excitement and cruelty gleaming in his eyes. As if he was looking forward to her torment. His dark greasy hair was pulled back in a ponytail at the base of his skull and his mouth was full of yellowed broken teeth.

Deidamia stopped at the head of the table and looked down at Ava, gesturing to the newcomer. "This is Vazgeth. Most of the other soldiers call him The Scourge as he has the stomach for cruelty and enjoys it more than most." She trailed her nails gently down Ava's cheek, delight flickering in her icy eyes as Ava squirmed.

The pounding of her heartbeat drowned out the other

sounds of camp, her hands shaking and palms sweating. Andras stood at the foot of the table inspecting his nails as Deidamia stepped back, allowing The Scourge access to his table of instruments, then walked around to the other side of Ava, stroking her hair.

"Now Ava, dear. This is going to hurt," she explained. "We promise not to kill you. You'd be useless to us dead."

Ava's lower lip shook as her eyes blurred with tears. "Please let me go home," she said. "I promise I won't tell anyone about you. You can stay here, please!"

But Deidamia didn't even acknowledge her words. "You may begin," she said as she nodded at Vazgeth and continued to stroke Ava's hair.

The Scourge picked up a glowing red hot poker that had been sitting among the coals of one of the braziers. Ava shook uncontrollably as he crept closer and swung the poker back and forth, purposely taking his time. His lazy steps became a hollow sound in her ears as nausea rose in her throat.

The soldier stopped, a gleam in his eye as he stood over her, while Deidamia watched eagerly. Andras observed from her feet, still looking completely unbothered, arms crossed and tapping his foot almost impatiently. Deidamia lifted Ava's shirt, exposing more of her torso, and before she had a chance to prepare herself, there was hot searing pain below her rib cage.

She arched upward, screaming in a way she didn't know was possible, as the hot iron pressed on her skin. He removed it after a few seconds and she gasped, sobbing. The agony of her flesh ripping coursed through her as it stuck to the scorching metal.

Before she had a chance to recover from the first, Vazgeth pressed the poker onto her torso a second time, then a third. She screamed again through her clenched teeth as he moved to her stomach. The burns blended together as he continued his abuse, painting her skin in anguish.

She couldn't do this, wasn't strong enough.

There was no way she could withstand this torture.

How would she get out of here? She was wrong wanting to come here. Eorhan was terrifying and though she wanted to learn about her heritage, this wasn't worth it.

If only she could go home.

You are home, Luna said.

"*Where are you?*"

I'm still looking for help. The animals don't know me. I have to find one who will trust me. Just hang on.

"*Hurry.*"

Vazgeth set the poker down amongst his tools and reached for a set of rusty forceps. Already delirious from the burns, Ava didn't think she could take any more but he grabbed her pointer finger and held it still as he used the forceps to grasp her fingernail and yanked it out.

She almost passed out. The pain was so intense she didn't know where she was, as if someone had impaled her finger and the anguish snaked all the way up her arm. This was so much worse than the burns. She whimpered and cried, delirious and writhing against the restraints. If the injuries didn't kill her, the pain surely would. She tried to be strong, tried to push through but she couldn't focus.

As her torturer prepared to pull out the next nail, she heard a small "psst" from Remy's cage. Turning her head, she met his eyes and he tilted his head slightly as if saying "I'm here. I got you. Watch me. Everything is going to be okay."

So, she did. She maintained eye contact with him through her tears, vision swimming, as The Scourge yanked out another nail and this time she passed out.

AVA AWOKE HOURS LATER, lying on the ground in her usual spot though her arms were no longer above her head, a longer chain connecting to the floor instead, allowing for slightly more movement.

She was alone in the tent with Remy, no sign of her abusers. Someone had removed her clothing and replaced it with a tan sleeveless shift. There were no undergarments underneath and the wool scratched her body. Her bare feet were dirty and her hair unbound, tangled and flowing down her back.

She pushed herself up and inspected her hand first, noting the two fingers the nails had been removed from were bandaged and sore, though not as sore as she would have expected. She lifted her tunic and looked down at her torso to find bandages where she was burned. She touched them lightly and winced.

"They stopped after you passed out," Remy said, startling Ava. "The healers took care of you."

"Oh," she said, voice hoarse from her screaming. "Where are my clothes?"

"The healer asked to change you. To heal you better. Oh Ava," he said, voice rising. "That was bad. Bad bad bad."

She shuddered as her eyes caught on the table where she had been strapped. "Yes. It was. How long have I been out?"

"Two days," he said.

Two days? The healers must have given her a tonic. That explained why she felt so groggy. Remy gestured to a plate on the ground before her holding a piece of stale bread and a cup of water, she immediately consumed both, gulping earnestly to quench her unending thirst. The bucket had also been left and since she had no remaining dignity, she used it and lay back down on the dirt.

"Ava?" Remy said.

Whispering back with the last of her energy, she replied, "I don't want to talk right now, Remy." Then allowed herself to be swallowed by sleep.

HER NEW ROUTINE of torture went on for weeks. Burns, cuts with daggers, broken fingers and toes. A couple of times they even waterboarded her, like something out of a movie. It was worse than she ever could have imagined.

Sometimes she would last an hour or more, attempting to fight through the pain, swallowing her screams until they burst from her lips with no remorse, using Remy to ground her. Other times she would pass out and succumb to the torture within minutes.

But her magic never came. No changes happened that she could see or feel. This so-called great tribulation a mere myth to her.

Today's particularly gruesome torture session had nearly incapacitated her and had her begging for death. The Scourge burned her body several times, including the bottoms of her feet, and sliced her belly with jagged knives. Then she was strung between two poles and whipped, Deidamia taking over at one point, releasing her frustration that nothing seemed to be working to induce even a flicker of power.

This time Ava didn't pass out due to a tonic Deidamia forced her to consume, keeping her conscious for the whole session in hopes this would be the difference. That her magic would finally appear.

Ava didn't even have Remy to ground her this time, as they had brought her to a separate tent. Away from her only lifeline in this world.

But the torture hadn't worked and in anger the group left, leaving Ava hanging, blood dripping down her ravaged back. It was hopeless. Her plan of escape a figment of the past. She would die here. Die in this filthy tent surrounded by daemons and evil. There was no possible way she could get free.

Her head hung low as unbearable pain coursed down her back and through the rest of her body. She tried to keep her breathing even. Tried to fight through the pain, but she was overcome and woozy; her head fuzzy as she barely remained conscious. So, she let herself hang there, naked from the waist up, exposed to the world. And she didn't care anymore. Didn't care about what they did to her. She only hoped they would hurry and kill her.

She gave up.

A voice sounded. Calling her name softly.

I'm hallucinating, she thought with closed eyes, ignoring the words.

But there it was again.

"Ava," it repeated, lilting and feminine and so... familiar. "Ava, dear. Little bird."

Lifting her head, Ava opened her eyes. Before her was a woman wearing a white gown and casting a heavenly glow.

"Mom?" Ava whimpered.

Her mother smiled, face aglow with a golden light. "Yes, little bird. It's me."

Ava's heart broke as she looked closer at the apparition. Her golden hair flowed down her back as she regarded Ava with piercing green eyes. Her mother looked the same as she remembered her, except powerful magic radiated from her and her ears were pointed. Fae.

Her lip quivered and her vision blurred as she couldn't keep the tears at bay. "Why didn't you tell me?"

"I'm sorry. We wanted to wait until you were old enough. When your grandfather and I left Eorhan, our only goal was to keep you safe. We didn't know Deidamia and Andras had followed. Not until it was too late."

Ava let the tears fall. Streaks of grief washing away the dirt on her cheeks.

"I can't do this," Ava whispered, the sound barely audible.

"You must," her mother responded.

Ava shook in her chains. "Why? I didn't ask for this. I don't want to be here. I just want to go home." She broke on the last word, and she let out a loud sob.

Her mother spoke with authority, voice smooth and powerful. "This *is* your home, Ava. We don't always get to choose our path. Sometimes it's chosen for us. Eorhan needs your help."

"What if I don't want to help?" Ava asked. "What if I refuse?"

"Then you doom this whole realm. Everyone here will die or become slaves to the daemon queen. They will never stop hunting you, Ava."

Ava shook her head. "I'm not strong enough."

"My little bird," her mother interjected. "You've always thought you weren't strong enough. That you weren't good enough. But I'm going to remind you that you *are*. You are always enough."

Ava sighed, breath shaking, as she stared at her mother who remained silent and looked back at her with equal parts love and steel in her eyes.

"So, I'm truly fae? But I don't have pointed ears or any magic."

"You are," she answered. "Though I would not share that information with anyone until you're sure they can be trusted. You're different because you were not born here."

"How do I know who I can trust?"

"You'll know," she replied.

"Do Deidamia and Andras know? About me?" she asked.

"Yes."

"Where am I from? Which kingdom? Is there a way to attain

my magic?" she continued, words spilling out faster than she could keep up. She had so many questions.

"We were from Monterre, the earth kingdom."

"Okay," she whispered. Finally, a real answer. It made sense. Her mother's abilities with the plants and flowers on the farm.

"I have no one left back home. Where do I go?"

"I'm sorry about Eleanor. She was a good friend." Ava felt the sting of tears welling. "When you escape, you must get to the capital city of Monterre. You'll be safe there."

"Will the fae welcome me?" she asked.

"Not at first. They've never met a human. You must not tell them everything right away, lest they accuse you of trickery. Most of the fae there are welcoming, but they're very suspicious of outsiders. A path will be opened for you to make your way there."

"How do I get out of here?"

"Look for a friend," her mother replied. "Help will come to you when the time is right." Ava's heart crumpled. She was sick of the vague replies. She wanted more answers. Even in death her mother was keeping things from her. "Ava," her mother said.

"Yes?"

"You used to be tenacious. Determined when you were truly passionate about something. You used to argue with all your science teachers because they got information wrong about plants and animals." Her mother laughed quietly. "Where did that woman go?"

Ava's eyes welled with tears. "You—mom. You left me... and I—can't do this without you..." she was crying hard now. "You're all I had... and I don't know how to be strong anymore," she whispered, tears falling.

"Ava," her mother spoke with strength in her voice. A greater strength than Ava had ever heard from her. "Remember who you were *before* my death. You are strong. It's always been there, you just need to believe in yourself. Be the stubborn obstinate woman I know you are deep down. Be *angry*."

Ava stared at her mother, taking a deep breath. She felt that anger. Had felt it ever since Eleanor was killed, but her fear had taken over and she'd let it.

"They killed your best friend, Ava."

Her arms shook above her as Eleanor's death replayed in her head. "I know," she said through gritted teeth.

"They will keep killing. They'll kill children. Innocents. Anyone in their path without a second thought. What are you going to do about it?" Her mother was radiating power, like warm static electricity pulsing in the air. She'd never seen her like this before. This was her true fae form showing through; her magic and her authority emanating from her, even in this corporeal body.

"I'm going to get out of here," she whispered. "I'm going to go to the capital and befriend the fae that live there."

Her mother walked closer, her face inches from Ava's. "And then what?" she spat.

Ava felt it then. Her anger. Her wrath as her mother stared into her very soul. "Then I'm going to figure out how to kill Deidamia and Andras."

"Yes. Yes, you are." Her mother smiled proudly, tears in her own eyes, as she touched Ava's cheek. "Find the man you've heard in your dreams. He will help you. Teach you what you need to know."

She barely felt her mother's touch, but it was there. Like a phantom stroke of air, brushing down her face. "I miss you so much," Ava said.

"I know, little bird. But I'll always be with you." The figure began to fade, as if her time here was cut short.

"Mom," Ava said, voice breaking again. "Don't go yet. Wait."

"I love you, sweet girl. Remember what I used to tell you when you were scared." Her face was becoming more distant, body wavering. "If anyone stands in your way. Crush them. *Crush. Them.*"

20

Time was lost to Ava as the days and nights blended, rendering her completely ignorant of how long she had been imprisoned. Days? Weeks? Months?

How she had survived each session, endured the pain, she had no idea.

But she took strength from her mother's visit and those parting words. Her belief and faith in her. It had awoken something in her that had been dormant for years. Her perseverance, fervor and passion. Her wrath.

Crush them.

It became her mantra. A song in her head.

She would. At the first opportunity, she would.

The healing tonics and magic performed on her after every torture session prevented the horrific pain from lasting, erasing most of the injuries. Only leaving bruises and soreness behind that was bearable. Still painful, but manageable.

But her strength was waning, toned muscles breaking down with the minimal movement and her body was wasting away from the meager nutrition. She couldn't hold out forever. At some point her body would give out.

And she needed to be long gone before it did.

She had accepted the fact that she was fae, though she didn't look or feel like it. But for some reason, knowing that she wasn't completely human, comforted her. She had always felt so different, so abnormal, and now she knew why. There wasn't something wrong with her. She wasn't 'weird,' like the other kids called her growing up. She was just in the wrong world.

Ava would try to find this capital city her mother spoke of. With nothing left for her back on the farm, she hoped somehow she could find her place in this world. She focused on the anger that was starting to bubble up inside of her, using it to fuel her determination to get out of this camp and as far away as possible.

When she wasn't being tormented every few days, she either slept or spent time sharing stories with Remy though they always made sure to speak quietly and never in front of any guards.

She asked Remy as many questions as she thought of, begging for any information she could gather about Eorhan, learning about its peoples and cultures.

He told her about the five kingdoms which ruled and their different magics and abilities. There was her home kingdom, Monterre, where the fae communed with nature and had abilities revolving around plants and animals. Remy explained they used vines and other earth magic in battle and even made golems, creatures created from mud or stone, to use as they fought.

They were the most peaceful and welcoming kingdom, however, the general of their armies was known to be harsh. Powerful yet honorable, he would do anything to protect his people and eliminate anyone he considered a threat. He had been nicknamed The Bear due to his strength and the giant bear who often accompanied him during battle, Remy explained with an equal mix of fear and awe. He informed her the most powerful fae in the earth kingdom each had an animal companion. One they were bonded to and could communicate with telepathically, being able to utilize them in battle or for other tasks such as spying. They were one of the few who were able to stand against the daemons due to their strong armies and mountain range that surrounded most of their kingdom.

He told her about Igneothenia, the province set among valleys of active volcanoes and rivers of lava, its residents having some natural immunity to the heat. The fae there were not as welcoming, Remy said, and sadly their lava magic was not strong enough to fend off Deidamia's armies. It was currently being ruled by one of her many terrible commanders, the daemon army seemingly unbothered by the environment, and the king and queen had disappeared and gone into hiding along with as many of their citizens as possible. The other kingdom that had been taken over was Frosthaven. Set in the snowy bitter mountains, they allowed the daemons in rather eagerly, hungry for the power that was promised as the ice fae had long wanted to rule all Eorhan.

The two other territories that had successfully made a stand against Deidamia were Saxumdale, home of the stone fae, and Caelestia, where the astral fae resided. Geography helped these two kingdoms win in the wars as the astral fae lived high in the sky and clouds, a floating magical place whose residents harnessed the power of the stars. Ava thought it sounded beautiful as Remy described a floating ethereal palace ruled by beings with pale skin and various shades of golden hair. Saxumdale was secluded on rocky islands and through their powerful stone magic, they were able to raise new jagged mountains, blocking the path of the daemon armies attempting to invade.

Ava took it all in, committing it to memory should she need the information later. She told Remy all about the human world and her life and he listened with fascination. She tried to explain phones and technology to him, but he just laughed and told her he did not understand at all what she was trying to say.

THE SCREAM TORE from Ava's lips as the Scourge burned her leg for what felt like the thousandth time, another session in the books with no result save for her pain.

Andras leaned over, inches from her face. "Had enough, Ava dear? Just show us a little magic and this all goes away."

"Fuck you," she seethed through her clenched jaw.

"Oh, my dear. You already did that," he crooned as he cupped her face. "And you *loved* it." She turned her head and bit his hand as hard as she could, eliciting a furious scream from the daemon.

His fist hit her so hard along her jaw she saw stars, and everything went fuzzy. Nausea rose as her head pounded and she moaned while she lay on the table. Turning her head, she tried to look at Remy but she couldn't focus on him, could barely keep her eyes open.

Through her fog, she heard Andras and Deidamia whispering desperately across the tent, assuming she was too out of it to overhear. She allowed her eyes to close, but focused through the throbbing in her skull as she listened in on their conversation, attempting to piece together the snippets she could make out.

"We must raise the stakes and bring her closer to death," Deidamia seethed through her teeth.

"It's not working," Andras crooned smoothly. "The book must be translated first. It should inform us how to create a new portal. The torture may end up killing her. We cannot retrieve the remainder of our forces if she's dead."

"One more week," Deidamia spat. "If her magic doesn't

come by then, I'm increasing the length of her sessions. We may even need to bring in one of our creatures to terrorize her."

Their voices lowered again and faded away as they exited the tent, leaving her alone with Remy. Fear washed over her as she took in what Deidamia said. How could they extend her sessions? Surely, she would die if they went any longer. She shuddered at the thought of how they might use those creatures she had seen the day they arrived at camp. Their growls and cries often floated into the tent at night and infiltrated her dreams.

Ava lay there; thoughts still foggy as she reminded herself that she was going to escape. She'd figure it out somehow. And she would take Remy with her.

Ava, can you hear me? Luna spoke into her mind.

"*Yes. Where are you?*"

I think I found help. Hang on just a little longer.

"*They have the book, Luna.*" She had forgotten all about it until she heard them mention it.

I know. But we can't worry about that right now. You must get far away.

"*How?*"

There will be an opening for you to escape. Soon.

"*Hurry.*"

I will.

"*We need to get to the capital of the earth kingdom.*"

I know. I'll be waiting for you, Luna replied and then she was gone. Mind silent again.

Help was coming. She had to hold out a little more; endure the pain and torture and then she could get out of this living nightmare and make her way home. Not to the farm, but to her true home. Monterre.

21

The healer worked on her back, cleaning the acid from Ava's wounds. Deidamia had promised to increase their efforts and she was true to her word. The acidic powder The Scourge had rubbed into the deep lacerations along her back had burned so intensely she had wished for death. Begged for it. Cried and pleaded for the release from the pain.

Even Andras participated this time, slicing her right thigh with a jagged knife and rubbing that powder deep into her leg. "It will be a beautiful scar to remember me by, dear."

The healer moved tenderly and without speed, taking more time than necessary and attended to Ava with care. The other healers were rushed and coarse, but this one was different; compassionate.

Ava turned slightly to get a look at the healer. She wasn't brutal and terrifying, and empathy radiated from her silver eyes, black curls and dark-skinned face. Tall, with pointed ears; she was fae. Not a daemon like the others.

"I've never seen you before," Ava said, voice barely audible.

"Some healers are not here willingly."

"Have you tried to escape?" Ava asked.

Careful, she had to be so careful in case she decided to inform the guards of her questions, to protect her own hide. She had been forbidden to speak to the healers and she hadn't tried. Not until now.

"It's not time yet," she said bluntly.

"Why?" she asked.

"These are dangerous questions, Ava." The healer dabbed a healing oil into Ava's wounds and she winced. "How do you know I won't report you? Don't you know what they'll do to you if they know you're asking a healer about escaping?"

"It couldn't be any worse than it already is right now."

The healer leaned closer to Ava's ear, whispering harshly. "You have no idea how much worse it can be. You best remember that."

They both remained silent, the healer continuing to work slowly.

Out of nowhere, a roar sounded in camp, not far from their tent.

Ava tried to sit up but was still chained. "What was that?"

The healer was suddenly bustling about, packing a small bag that Ava hadn't noticed before. Commotion continued to sound outside, the shouts of soldiers and clash of swords ringing out over more roars. It sounded like absolute chaos outside.

The healer unlocked Ava from the table. "You must hurry. We don't have much time."

Ava sat up and looked around. "What's going on?"

Rushing toward her, the fae handed her a tunic, brown pants and leather boots. "Put this on. Quickly. The distraction won't last long."

Ava slipped the tunic over her head, adrenaline pushing the lingering pain away. She put on the pants and the boots then the healer handed her a belt with an ebony dagger, stolen from one of the guards. Ava's fingers fumbled as she put the belt on while the healer put a small leather satchel over her head, the strap crossing her body between her breasts.

"Take that tonic twice a day to prevent infection. There's some food and water in here as well," she said and began ushering Ava toward the back corner of the tent, near Remy's cage.

"Wait," Ava said as she looked at Remy. "What about him?"

The healer shook her head. "I shouldn't. If two prisoners are missing, they'll suspect something."

Ava grabbed the healer's arm, pulling her close. "They're going to suspect something anyway. I'm *not* leaving without him."

The healer sighed and grabbed the set of keys, kneeling to unlock the cage.

Ava bent down and placed her hands on the bars as Remy came close and grasped one of her hands, pulling it in and giving it a squeeze. "You don't have to worry about me. You need to get out of here."

"Not without my friend." She smiled, eyes watering.

Remy grinned back as the door swung open.

"You two need to hurry," said the healer, glancing frantically toward the entrance to the tent.

Standing, Ava asked the healer, "Why? Why risk yourself for me?"

The healer took Ava's hands in hers. "Because I believe hope has returned. And has come to save us all."

Ava didn't know what to say. She looked at her, noting the awe in the healer's face. "What's your name?" she asked.

"Isolde."

"Come with us," Ava insisted but Isolde shook her head.

"Not until I finish my own plans," she repeated.

Her own plans? Unsure what that meant, Ava held Isolde's

steel gaze as determination washed over her face. She wasn't going to leave yet.

Ava hugged her quickly. "Thank you."

Isolde nodded and then lifted the bottom of the tent, looking outside.

"The coast is clear," she said, backing away to make room for Ava and Remy. "Head straight ahead into the woods and don't stop until you cross a river. There you will find a small cave where you can rest tonight. Travel only by night to remain hidden but be careful of the creatures in the woods. Not all are friendly. Look for the brightest star in the sky. It will lead you to safety. If you get lost, follow the mice."

"Okay," Ava said and crouched, looking at Remy. "Are you ready?" she whispered.

He nodded, and hands tightly clasped together, they crawled under the tent and into the night.

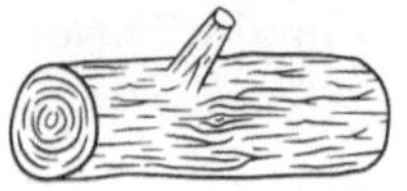

*M*ud squelched beneath her hands and knees as Ava crawled out, the stars and moon lighting her way. Rising into a crouch, she wiped the muck from her hands on the canvas of the tent, cleaning them in case she needed to use the dagger. Remy crouched next to her, breathing evenly and ready to follow her lead.

She scanned for any signs of danger. Isolde had said to head straight for the trees in front of where she emerged from the tent. Luckily, they didn't appear too far off, maybe thirty yards. They snuck in between the other tents waiting for some rogue guard to notice them and sound the alarm.

But there were no guards anywhere. No soldiers or grunts milling about.

The commotion on the other side of camp was almost deafening, the sounds of swords, growls and shouting soldiers a symphony of chaos. Curiosity got the best of her as she peeked around the corner of the tent, searching for the source of the thundering roars. It was difficult to see through the smoke and soldiers running around but she could have sworn she caught the sight of a giant black bear barreling through the tents, snarling as he bit through the daemons in his way.

As she neared the edge of the camp, subtle movement on the ground in front of the trees caught her eye. It was a group of three mice.

Follow the mice, Isolde's words echoed in Ava's thoughts as the rodents scurried toward her and then back to the forest again.

So, they did.

Pushing herself to a run, she bounded through the last open area outside the camp, Remy right behind her, before being engulfed by the forest. Chancing one last glance over her shoulder, she looked to where the bear had been. It was gone and had left a dozen bloody bodies and several crushed tents in its wake. She turned back to follow the mice, hoping they were leading her the same direction Isolde told her.

Ava ran at full speed through the dense forest, trying to put distance between her and the camp before they noticed the two of them had gone missing. Remy stayed right beside her, keeping up surprisingly well. She knew it wouldn't take the soldiers long to figure out they had escaped, and hoped Isolde didn't pay the price. Legs weak and wobbly from weeks of her captivity, she pushed on, using the adrenaline to overcome her fatigue.

She was free. Liberated from her torture, she focused on what lay before her. She must get as far away as possible and find somewhere safe. Now that she was no longer in the army camp, she could feel that thread of fate pulling her to the mountains once more. The ones she saw the day she arrived. That must be where the capital of Monterre was.

So that was where she would go.

Her energy eventually started to waver and she had to slow down, hoping they were far enough away by now. "I'm tired," Remy whispered from beside her.

"Me too," she replied. "Hopefully we'll be there soon."

She continued walking, ducking under trees and stepping over logs, breathing deeply to slow her heart rate and conserve energy. Her companion stayed next to her throughout the journey and remained silent.

The forest was mostly quiet, though an occasional screech or growl sounded in the distance. The trees were crowded, and it was difficult to make out the terrain under the dense canopy. Some had giant roots sticking out of the ground, forming little makeshift shelters for the animals of the forest.

Some time later, the forest opened and they came upon the river. Loud and raging, it wound through the landscape and looked impossible to cross, capable of sweeping them away within seconds. Like a sliver of anger cutting through the terrain, it churned and roiled its wrath.

She sat on a small boulder near the edge, resting for a moment as she assessed the best way to cross without drowning, Remy plopping down next to her. Reaching into her satchel, she found the water skin Isolde had left, and handed it to her friend.

Remy took a big drink and handed it back. "We must cross," he said, gesturing to the river.

"Do you think we can make it across that?" She pointed to a fallen tree.

"Yes. Carefully."

Thank you, she mouthed to no one as they made their way toward the makeshift bridge.

The mice had disappeared, and Ava wondered where they had gone as they crossed the river, careful not to slip off the moss slick log.

Once safe on the opposite shore, Ava turned to Remy. "Can you help me push this log into the river?"

"Why?" he asked, curiosity in his eyes.

"Hopefully it will slow them down if they come after us," she answered.

Remy nodded and they both knelt and placed their hands on the fallen tree. A small boulder sat just a couple feet from the log, so Ava pressed against it with her feet as she lowered down and pushed with all her might. Though weak and malnourished, her years of weight training paid off as she imagined she was pushing a weighted sled across the gym floor. With one last grunt, the log moved and a loud splash sounded as it fell into the river and was swept away.

They both stood and she wiped her hands on her pants and looked at her friend. "Alright," she said. "Next, we find the cave."

Illuminated by small slivers of moonlight peeking through the canopy, they began to search. Unsure where to start, they walked back and forth, starting at the shore and making their way back into the forest.

The dagger bounced at her hip with each step, reminding her of its presence should she need to use it, and the sounds of night drifted through the forest. The familiar hoot of owls comforted her, their haunting song threading through the night sky as they searched for their mate. The buzz of insects was a constant hum, different from back home, but pleasant nonetheless. If the creatures called, she knew no predators lurked about. Knew this meant the soldiers were not nearby.

They came upon a clearing in the trees at the top of a hill, providing them with a better view of the area. She scrutinized the landscape and noticed a rocky bluff with definite potential for a cave and pointed. "I think it might be over there."

"Yes. The rocky place. Let's go."

Working their way down the hill, they meandered through the trees and reached the limestone, searching for any semblance of an opening. They walked back and forth for an hour, and Ava felt more and more lost as time went on.

"I don't see anything," she said to Remy as she leaned against a tree and closed her eyes.

"It's there," he said from beside her. "Somewhere close."

At the sound of his voice, she prepared herself for more searching when a rustling sounded in the bushes behind her. She whirled around, dagger in hand, and pushed Remy behind her. The bushes moved again, and she backed away, readying herself to grab him and run if necessary.

The three mice emerged.

"Oh! You came back!" she said as she slid her dagger back into its sheath and crouched down. "Do you know where the cave is?"

Remy watched with curious eyes from beside her. The mice took off toward the hillside, running along the stone, and then disappeared into a small opening she never would have noticed on her own. As she crept closer, the opening appeared, only visible from a particular angle, and they were able to slip inside as dawn was breaking over the horizon. The entrance was an illusion, cleverly hidden among the brush and shadows. It should be impossible for Deidamia's soldiers to find them unless they knew about this cave already.

She hoped they didn't.

The entrance was narrow, eventually opening into a small room brightened with the glow of a neon blue fungus growing in the nooks along the walls.

"We're here." She smiled down at her friend.

An old bedroll lay against the wall, surrounded by several discarded weapons. A reminder this cave had been used before, but not in a long time if the dust and cobwebs were any indicator. A forgotten sanctuary for a former hunter or perhaps an adventurer looking for a place to sleep for the night. Ava inspected one of the glowing mushrooms on the wall, reaching out her finger and touching the cap gently. It quivered and glowed brighter for a few seconds before returning to its dimmer illumination.

Fascinating.

She set her pack next to a bow and quiver of arrows, relieved at the sight of the familiar weapon. A weapon she knew how to use. A small dagger had also been left behind by the previous occupant.

Settling herself on the bedroll, she unbuckled the belt and laid it next to her, within reach in case she needed the weapon, and then opened her pack and removed the packages inside.

Remy scurried about, cleaning the cave with a fully leaved tree branch he was using like a broom.

"Remy, what are you doing?" Ava asked, curious.

"A dirty cave is no place for the one who saved my life. Too much dust," he replied.

Ava smiled. "You don't have to do that. But thank you."

So, she let him clean, having something to do obviously bringing him peace. It was something she used to do as well, and she understood the comfort of having a task to focus on. Laying the contents of her bag in front of her, she took inventory of her supplies. Her food consisted of several apples, some dried meat wrapped in fabric, hard cheeses and bread. Not much, but hopefully she could make it last until she got to her destination. There were also four small vials containing the tonic Isolde had referenced.

Remy sat down next to her, finished with his cleaning. She handed him an apple and sighed. "Where's your home?"

He took a bite of the apple. "Deep in the forests of Monterre. Not close to any towns. In a giant tree with my brothers."

"I'm from the earth kingdom too," she said.

"I know."

"How do you know?" She laughed.

"The animals listen when you speak to them." He smiled.

"I suppose they do. How did you get captured?"

He looked at her with his giant eyes, long pointed ears twitching. "I went too far. I was exploring. My brothers always told me it was a bad idea. Hobgoblins are supposed to stay close to home. We don't *explore* or care much for adventure. Or we are not supposed to. But I like it. 'Tis fun. Seeing new things. Learning new things. I feel different than most other hobs."

Ava smiled as she grabbed an apple for herself. "I know what it means to feel different."

He surveyed her and tilted his head. "You say that like it's bad. It is not bad to be different. It is bad to be *same.*"

"I don't know, Remy. I've been different my whole life and people didn't like it. They thought I was weird. That I wasn't normal."

"Ha!" He laughed. "Normal? Why would you *want* to be normal? Normal is boring. Boring boring boring."

She smiled. "You're right. Normal *is* boring... So, you said you were exploring when you were captured?"

"Oh, yes. I was pretending I was an adventurer, climbing trees and watching the animals. It was much fun. But then they came. They had killed my parents, and I was too close to their camp. I didn't know!" He placed his head in his hands for a moment before lifting his head, his eyes wet with tears. "They said I was a spy. They threw me in the cage as punishment. To sit there and die. But then you came. And you saved me."

Ava smiled and reached over to grab his hand. "You saved me too. In more ways than you'll ever know." They smiled at each other before she let go and sat back. "When will you go home?" she asked.

"I must leave tomorrow. Sorry. So sorry. But I need to see my family," he answered regretfully.

"I understand," she said.

Home, she thought. Upon arriving here, something small had awakened within her. Minuscule and barely noticeable, she could feel that pull, subtly tugging her away from her old life and toward something else.

Something new.

"Where are you going?" he asked her.

Ava fidgeted with her tunic. "I guess I'm looking for the capital of Monterre."

"It's called Mosshaven. A lovely city."

"How do I get there?" she asked.

"Isolde already told you."

"The star?"

He nodded.

"Humans are smart, yes?" Remy asked.

She laughed. "Some of them are."

"You are."

Ava shrugged, looking at her friend. "I'd like to think so... but sometimes I make really bad choices."

He regarded her curiously. "That doesn't mean you are not smart. It means you have a heart. A big heart full of love. I can see it, yes I can. Yes yes yes."

"Remy," she whispered. "What do I do when I get there?"

Remy shook his head. "I don't know. The high fae there are very welcoming... but I don't think there has ever been a human here before. Nope nope nope. You must be careful. They are very protective of their kingdom."

"Okay," she said. "Thanks."

She had no proof to give them she was truly fae, only her word. And she didn't think they would take it if they were as protective as Remy suggested. She needed to be smart. Maybe she could get an audience with the king and try to explain her situation. Perhaps he would take pity on her and she could go from there.

Her stomach growled, hunger unsatisfied by the apple. She could have devoured the entire contents of her bag, but forced herself to resist, unsure when she would find her next meal.

She found the water skin hiding in the bottom of the bag and let Remy drink his fill before she finished it off, planning to refill it at the river before leaving.

Thirst quenched and hunger tampered for now, she drank a tonic, wincing at the bitter taste, and lay down upon the bedroll. Remy had already curled up on the floor and was fast asleep.

As she lay there, she mentally assessed her injuries, pain now coursing through her battered body. Adrenaline had kept her attention from it but now she was motionless, everything hurt.

The lacerations on her back were still raw and covered in bandages, nowhere close to being fully healed, and burned every time she moved. Her fingers were sore where more nails had been pulled but were thankfully on the mend, and burns, cuts and bruises adorned her body in different states of healing providing a constant ache even as she lay still. And her leg. That injury Andras had given her still hurt significantly and after running through the woods, it would not stop throbbing. Though Isolde's magic had healed it enough that it wasn't an open wound anymore, the skin was still tender and raw under the wrappings she had used to cover it.

Torture. She had been tortured. Abused for weeks at the hands of her false boyfriend and his daemon queen. She wasn't ready to look at that. It was a trauma she would shove into a box along with Eleanor's death, and lock the key, never to be examined.

She knew if she let herself go there, let herself truly ponder over what had been done to her, the reality of her predicament would overcome her.

And she would fall apart.

23

*A*va slept all day without any interruptions, stirring around sunset when her tiny rodent companions tickled her face. She turned to wake Remy, but he was already up and about, preparing for the next leg of their journey.

She was happy to see her furry companions darting around her feet. Though they hadn't been with her long, they were a small beacon of promise, providing her guidance and a little bit of entertainment with their silvery fur and tufted tails.

As she waited for the sun to continue its voyage below the horizon, she gathered her supplies and prepared for another night of travel, feeling a sense of sadness that she and her friend would be parting shortly. She wondered where Luna was, curious why she had seemed to disappear even though she said she'd be waiting. But Luna had always been that way. Coming and going as she pleased.

I guess she'll reappear when she's ready, she thought as she buckled the belt around her waist then secured the quiver of arrows on her back.

She didn't know how far she was from her destination, but assumed it would take her at least a few days, if not longer.

Ignoring the worry that she didn't have enough food, she focused on her goal. Get to Mosshaven. Get an audience with the king. And somehow find this man from her dreams, though she had no idea how she was supposed to do that.

If she encountered anything nefarious on her way, she would survive. Be angry.

Crush them.

When the sun was below the horizon and the moon had welcomed the night, she felt it was dark enough to leave her shelter. Slinging her bag across her chest, she added the new dagger to her belt and picked up the bow, ready to search for the brightest star.

"Are you ready?" she asked Remy.

"Yes yes yes," he replied as they exited the cave.

The night was cool, a breeze providing relief against the heat of the day, and Ava made her way to the top of the hill with her companion to give herself a better chance of spotting the star. Out of breath, she reached the apex and surveyed her surroundings, hands on her hips.

There.

High above the treetops blazed a shining star, much brighter than the others and even a different color. While the other stars shone with their usual golden-white glow, this one was light blue, like an aquamarine suspended in the sky.

It was beautiful.

Home. That was the way to her true home. She was still in disbelief.

She turned to Remy and pointed at the star. "That's the way I'm going."

He smiled, looking up at her, pride flickering in his eyes. "I know it is. You'll be safe there. Safe safe safe," he said. "My home is that way." He pointed in a different direction.

She got down on her knees and grasped Remy's shoulders, looking into his globe-like eyes. "Remy," she said as tears welled, blurring her vision. "Thank you for being my friend when I was in a dark place. Thank you... for everything."

Remy looked at her. "Thank you for freeing me, for saving my life. I owe you a debt."

Ava shook her head. "You don't owe me anything. Just enjoy being with your brothers."

He looked at her with affection in his eyes. "I will see you again. Someday. I know it. Yes yes yes."

She pulled Remy into a hug and his arms wrapped around her neck. "I hope so," she whispered. After a moment they pulled away and Ava removed the extra dagger from her belt, pressing it into his hand. "Be safe," she said.

Remy nodded and headed down the hill. He paused and waved enthusiastically before trodding on again. As Ava watched him go, tears flowing freely, she whispered, "Goodbye, Remy."

Her only friend in this world had left on his own journey. Safe, but not with her. She was alone again, and her heart ached with the realization. Everyone was gone. Her mother, grandfather, Eleanor and Henry. And now the one person she had connected with since arriving was gone too.

She thought she used to like solitude, the peace and quiet with no one to worry about but herself. Between the way others treated her family and her mother's death, it was safer not to let anyone else in. But these last couple of months had begun to change that. The awareness that she didn't want to be just a lost puzzle piece, trying to shove itself into the wrong spots. She wanted, no *needed*, to find where she fit.

Wiping her eyes, she took one more look at the star and sniffled.

Committing the direction to memory should she be unable to see it in the depths of the forest, she took off down the hill, climbing over low bushes and brambles, and continued to trek through the woods.

She walked for hours, large trees looming overhead as glowing insects darted among their twisting branches. The forest was dense, and she had to step over roots and fallen logs with almost every step. In between the roots of the trees, violet bioluminescent flowers bloomed and when Ava got too close, they retreated into their stalks as if hiding from the threat of being found. She'd never seen anything like it and the biologist in her wanted to stop and study each and every living creature in this forest.

But she kept on, urging herself toward her destination and fueled by the fear that the daemons would come after her if she stopped for too long.

Surrounded by the noises of the night, she occasionally hid beneath a shrub or behind a tree when she heard the larger creatures sniffing about, hunting for their dinner. Though she couldn't make out their features in the dark, she knew enough to avoid them, not risking her safety to get a closer look.

Taking a break, she found a spot on the mossy ground and leaned against a tree, anxious to rest her body and eat, feeling faint from pushing herself for so long. Her three mouse companions remained by her side, darting around her and catching small insects for their own meals.

As she was chewing on a piece of dried meat, something rustled in the shrubs in front of her. Staying silent, she slowly unsheathed her dagger and faced the direction the noise was coming from, holding completely still and hoping whatever it was would pass by in the night. If the creatures here were anything like back home, as long as you didn't pose a threat, chances were they wouldn't even spare you a second glance.

The rustling became more pronounced when something emerged from the bushes, glowing faintly. It was small, about the size of a house cat and looked like a fox with its fluffy tail and oversized ears. Except it wasn't a fox because the foxes back home didn't glow.

A golden light shone around the animal, emanating from its fur as it tilted its head and looked at her with curious eyes. Slowly approaching, it sniffed at her feet as it assessed whether she was a threat.

"Hello, there," she whispered.

It sat on its haunches and inspected her, ears moving as if it was listening and she sat silently, in awe of the magical creature before her. After a minute or so, it turned its head as if hearing something far off Ava couldn't make out and took off into the woods, the glow fading as it disappeared.

"Amazing," she said, rising to continue her trek.

She plodded on, pushing through the night and keeping an eye out for a place to sleep and hide for the day. Though she heard growls and cries in the night, she never came across any other animals and was thankful the dangerous ones seemed content to leave her alone.

THE NEXT FEW days repeated the same pattern. Walking all night, then searching for a hiding place to rest and spend her day.

She had to be getting close. Surely, she would arrive at some town or the capital soon. Weakness and starvation were starting to set in, and each day was becoming more difficult to continue. Her body ached with her injuries, and she often had to pause and rest before the dizziness overcame her. She was out of food and struggling to find a place to refill her water. She needed to get somewhere safe as quickly as possible.

Luna had appeared to her the day before, but hadn't stayed long, explaining she had to stay hidden until Ava reached the capital. That the fae wouldn't believe she had a companion.

Though she was disappointed, Ava had shrugged and bid her friend farewell and hoped it wouldn't be long before she returned. She was used to her comings and goings now and wondered if the other animal companions of Monterre did the same.

She had passed through the thick forest for most of her expedition, terrain barely changing except for the towering green mountains in the distance which were getting closer each day. Mosshaven must be somewhere near those mountains. Faithfully following the star, she pressed on, thankful she had heard no inkling of Deidamia, Andras or their terrible army.

As she walked, her mind tended to wander and tonight she couldn't stop thinking about Remy. Was he okay? Had he found his way back home? He was a strange creature, repeating words half the time, but he was tenderhearted and generous. Her very first friend in Eorhan, she hoped to see him again, unsure of what her future held.

She wouldn't let herself think too hard about Henry. Or Andras. Or whoever he was. The heartache was too raw, too deep. Unable to acknowledge she was deceived by a man, she didn't want to face it. She just needed to get to safety.

Maybe they had a library in Mosshaven where she could get lost in a new book. Would she even be able to read it? She wondered what the fae there were like, if they would be kind to her or be wary of her human appearance. Would she make friends? How would she find a place to live if she had no money? Maybe she needed to ask for a job somewhere.

Lost in thought, she continued, unaware of her surroundings.

So unaware she didn't notice she wasn't alone. Didn't hear the almost silent steps approaching until it was too late.

A low growl rumbled behind her, and she whirled, removing her dagger and gripping it tightly. She had been fortunate enough not to come across any of the dangerous creatures lurking in these woods, but it seemed her luck had run out.

The reflection of eyes stared at her from between trees and she backed away, heart in her throat, as a creature emerged from the shadows.

Its body was vaguely human, but it crept on all fours, arms and legs unnaturally long and attached to the sides of its torso. Gray skin glistened in the moonlight and glowing white eyes leered at her through its gaunt face, mouth opening wide revealing hundreds of needle-like teeth dripping with saliva. It had no nose and looked at her with a hunger in its eyes.

Realizing a dagger would do her no good, not wanting to get close enough to the being to use it, she sheathed it and reached behind her back for her bow instead. Her trembling hands grabbed an arrow and nocked it into place, slowly drawing the bow and readying to release the arrow into the creature.

It slunk toward her, and she willed her hands to stop trembling, reminding herself how to aim, hoping the skills would come back to her easily. She had been an excellent archer, but a moving creature was different than a stationary target.

As she took aim, a twig snapped under her foot, startling the creature. Its speed increased, creeping like a spider over the brush and fallen trees then crouched into a lunging position, preparing to strike.

Now. It had to be now, before it leaped for her.

She drew the bow further, aiming for its mouth, as it let out a low horrific scream. The creature leaned back on all fours and leapt into the air.

Ava released her arrow, her aim true, and clumsily scrambled out of the way as the creature crashed down where she had been standing. It twitched violently as she took her dagger and stabbed it in the head, assuring it was truly dead.

Heart still racing, she rose, backed against a tree and took deep breaths, calming her body and reminding herself she was safe. She hoped there were no more of those monsters lurking about and she closed her eyes, allowing the breeze to cool the sweat from her brow.

She had killed something. It didn't matter if it was about to attack her, she had never killed anything in her life and she began to shake at the reality of her predicament. There was no time for panic, not when there could be other monsters in the forest. She had to keep going and get out of here as fast as possible.

Ava pushed off the tree and stared at the creature she had killed as she prepared to continue through the forest when movement in the treetops caught her eye. She whipped her head up and met eyes with a large owl. Its soft feathers were marbled black and white, and it tilted its head and watched her intensely, as if it had a secret it wanted to share. Hooting softly, it spread its wings and took off silently into the night. Before she had a chance to wonder about the peculiar way the bird had been looking at her, something sharp pressed into her side, a hard body beside her.

"Move, and I'll gut you where you stand," spoke a harsh feminine voice.

24

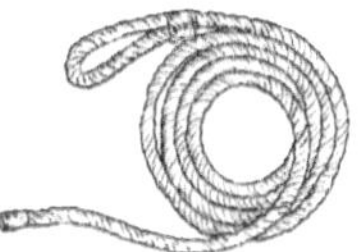

Ava froze.

They'd found her. Deidamia's army had found her. Just when she thought she was getting close. Almost to safety. The small bit of hope she had been clinging to fell away as she scrambled to come up with a plan.

Two other figures emerged from the trees, too dark in the waning crescent moon for her to see them clearly but she heard them as they discussed her fate.

"Well, this is a nice surprise," said a smooth male voice as he stalked toward Ava and her captor.

No. She wouldn't be a prisoner again. Wouldn't be laid out and tortured on The Scourge's table again. She'd rather die. There would be no missed chances of escape like when she was at the camp. She was going to fight back *now*.

Ava turned and slammed her head against the face of the woman beside her. The woman released her with a surprised gasp, and she sprinted into the woods. She barely made it ten yards before the tall man grabbed her around her waist and lifted her off the ground as if she weighed nothing.

"No!" she screamed as she tried to wrench herself from his grasp. "Let me go! Get off me!"

She managed to get her dagger and tried stabbing him, but she missed.

"Stop," he urged as she continued to kick and tried to get away.

She reached down again and thrust her dagger toward his leg, this time finding purchase in his thigh.

"Fuck!" he shouted, but still didn't let her go.

Quicker than she was able to make sense of, he adjusted his grip and had her arms pinned at her sides, carrying her as she still struggled against his hold.

"I'm not going back!" she screamed. "I'm not going back!" She repeated it over and over, screaming and snarling like a feral animal.

"Don't let her go, Raine," said the woman.

"I'm not, but she fucking stabbed me and now my pants are ripped," said Raine.

"You're fine," replied the woman.

"Bring her to the general," said an older sounding man as he approached. "See what he wants to do with her."

The general? That terrifying general Or'thir who appeared in the woods the day she arrived through the portal? Panic taking over again, she tried kicking at her captor whose name she had learned was Raine, but it was no use and he kept a tight hold of her.

She tried looking at the three soldiers, but it was still too dark in the thick woods and she couldn't see their faces. Couldn't tell who they were.

"Stop struggling," he said. "I don't want to hurt you but if you try anything again, I'm going to be pissed."

Underneath the authority in his voice, there was something else. Something... almost kind and even a little humorous. There was no aggression or malice, and it made her pause. She took a breath and stopped, the fight leaving her as exhaustion took its place. If this really was a group of daemon soldiers, she'd have to wait for a better chance to escape. They were obviously much stronger than she was. Though now she wasn't quite sure they were part of Deidamia's group.

"Get the rope, Jorrar," said the woman.

Jorrar approached as Raine held her tight, binding her wrists in front of her.

"Let me go," she insisted, trying to hide her trembling.

"Just following orders, human," said Raine who held her tightly while the other finished binding her hands.

Jorrar placed a piece of cloth in her mouth and secured it at the back of her head.

"I'm going to let go of you, but don't try anything," commanded Raine.

He let her go and held onto a long rope attached to her wrists, leading her into the woods, while the woman and Jorrar flanked her.

Their short trek ended as they came upon an open field with rolling hills and the same mountains in the distance, even closer than they were before. The sun started to peek over the horizon, and she was now able to get a look at her captors as they led her to a small camp.

A fire of mostly coals and cinders still glowed in the middle of their site, surrounded by a few small logs being used as seats. Four tents were neatly set up around the fire and they appeared to have been carefully placed so as not to disturb the terrain. As if they cared for the flora around them, not wanting to harm the grasses and flowers growing in the field.

The opposite of the brutal army camp where she had been staying before.

It wasn't the daemons.

She watched them with suspicion as Raine led her to the center of their camp. He was tall, lean and stunningly handsome, with a beautifully sculpted face and perfectly symmetrical features. His hair was so blonde it was almost white and cascaded down his back, his pointed ears peeking out, and he had cunning blue-gray eyes filled with mischief. He was dressed in leather armor thick enough to halt blades but allowing for better movement than the cumbersome metal armor the daemon army wore.

Fae. They were fae. Though they weren't part of Deidamia's army, they still might be dangerous, and she didn't know what they wanted with her. Why they grabbed her and brought her to their camp.

The woman to her left had olive skin, the same pointed ears and captivating upturned eyes of brown. Her long black hair was woven into intricate braids down her back, and she had multiple daggers strapped to her. She wore a forest green cloak over the same leather armor as her companion.

The one to her right, Jorrar, was older than the other two but just as handsome. With smooth ebony skin, peppered with a few small scars and graying hair at his temples, he donned the same armor and cloak as the woman and had the same pointed ears.

Are all the fae this good-looking? She wondered.

They reached the center of camp as the woman spoke.

"Cas, we found something interesting you might want to get a look at," she said looking over Ava with suspicion.

Ava stood, waiting, surrounded by the three warriors as the flaps of a tent opened and a large fae stepped out. His presence was imposing, lacking any semblance of kindness on his face. While his expression wasn't mean, he was stoic, giving nothing away. He wore the same armor and green cloak, and an emblem was stamped into the leather at his shoulder.

A tree.

Her eyes widened when she recognized it as the same one from the book. The book which was still in Deidamia's hands.

The Elderoak, Luna had called it. Were they from her kingdom?

They had called him the general. Realization washed over her as she recalled what Remy had said. This had to be the general of the Earth Kingdom's armies, The Bear. This was a group of fae from Monterre. Racking her brain for more information, she remembered Remy said the earth fae were welcoming but protective. She had to be careful but figure out how to win them over without telling them her secrets.

He walked toward her with the grace and brutality of a trained warrior who had seen many battles. His chestnut brown hair matched the color of his beard, and flowed below his shoulders, adorned with several small braids, his pointed ears barely peeking through. He had a scar that began near his chiseled jawline that trailed down the side of his neck and disappeared under his collar. Though he wore armor, it was obvious that he was rippling with muscle as he stopped and crossed his arms; a general assessing the threat before him. Despite the suspicion in his bright golden eyes, he was devastatingly handsome, and Ava shifted beneath his scrutiny.

"Percy found her sneaking near our camp, Casimir," said Raine, still holding the rope. "She killed the helwraith we were tracking. And fucking stabbed me."

Ava glanced at Raine's leg. Blood dripped down his thigh, though he wasn't acting like he was in much pain. She didn't feel bad about it.

Casimir's eyes widened at his companion's statement and bored into hers as she met his stare.

Ava wanted to blurt out she wasn't sneaking; she was only trying to get somewhere safe. She didn't want to be here with yet another group of people she knew nothing about. That they scared her and she fought back, thinking they were part of the enemy army.

But she remained gagged and didn't attempt to speak.

Casimir grunted and looked to the older male awaiting his assessment.

"It looks like we found the human woman," Jorrar stated.

The warrior spoke, a gruff yet smooth low voice. "Obviously."

Ava kept her face neutral and said nothing. If they wanted her to speak, they could remove the gag. Casimir walked forward and stopped a mere foot from her. Though she was tall, he still towered over her five-foot nine frame, causing her to look up to meet his eyes.

Fuck, he's huge, she thought.

"Do you have anything to say for yourself?" he asked.

She shrugged and glared at him, sick of being treated like a prisoner. She didn't want to condemn herself by giving him any information. Remembering what her mother had said in Deidamia's camp, she used her anger, channeled it. She didn't want these fae to see her as weak.

Casimir turned away and stalked back toward his tent. "Start packing. We leave in an hour. The king will know what to do with her."

Assuming the king was in the capital, they must be taking her to Mosshaven. Could she be so lucky to run into a group who wanted to take her to the place she was supposed to go? She couldn't blurt out she was some long lost fae. They'd never buy it. She would remain quiet, observe their dynamics and hope they didn't want to kill her.

Raine told her to sit down and not to move as the other three packed up camp. They had one horse with them, a stocky gray mare who was being used to carry the rolled-up tents and other supplies. Looking at the horse, she was relieved she didn't have to ride it. Her nervousness around horses was something she didn't want them to see. She sat on one of the logs next to the embers, watching the group with suspicion and a slight bit of fear.

The woman caught her staring and smirked at her. "Are you scared, darling? You should be." She winked, before turning back to the horse, securing the last of their supplies.

"Stop taunting her, Quinn," said Jorrar, who seemed to have a hint of warmth in his eyes.

She had now learned all their names. The woman was Quinn, the older one Jorrar and the brute was Casimir, their leader and the one they called The Bear, though she saw no signs of his ursine companion. Raine was the gorgeous blonde one she had stabbed in her panic to get away.

Once the packing was complete, Casimir said, "Keep her in the middle, Raine. Quinn and Jorrar you flank the sides and I'll lead. Let's get going."

Casimir led the way of their small party, heading toward the expansive green mountains in the distance, Raine walking next to him. Ava followed a few feet behind them flanked by Quinn who was still carrying her weapons and satchel, and Jorrar who had the lead for their horse.

She was still gagged and though she had dozens of questions stirring in her mind, she said nothing. At least no one was torturing her.

25

asimir could sense her presence behind him as they walked toward Mosshaven. The fear and anger emanated from her as he felt her eyes boring into his back, likely unhappy about being a prisoner yet again. But they couldn't be too careful. Not when they didn't know her.

He was surprised to come across the human they had been hearing about, assuming she was still a prisoner of the daemon army. But when Percy had spotted her close by in the woods, he'd told Jorrar and the three of them had brought her back immediately.

He tried to recall what the ancient texts had said about humans and other realms. He had hated his history lessons as a boy, much preferring the thrill of fighting and learning the art of the sword. His tutor would chastise him for getting distracted as he sword-fought with his pencil instead of completing his assignments.

Now at over one hundred years old, he barely remembered any of his lessons. All he knew was despite the lingering armies of the daemon queen and her lover, his kingdom had remained safe. Protected by the surrounding mountains, massive trees, rivers and their powerful earth magic.

He was a boy during the first wars when Deidamia had rallied her army and entered their world through the portal created by a power-hungry king. Those wars had taken his family from him, leaving him alone in the world and fighting for the freedom they had so longed for. That ancient king was long dead, but not forgotten, as Casimir's kingdom had cursed his name and warned all who lived there about the dangers of craving power, using the old king as an example to stay away from portal magic.

A dangerous, risky magic that was rare and hadn't been seen in decades.

Now some human woman had somehow led them back from wherever they had been banished to, single-handedly responsible for the potential demise of their whole world and he was furious.

He still didn't know how she fit in the picture. Her role in this war.

Perhaps she was a spy.

A part of him had wanted to kill her on the spot, if only to protect his kingdom, but not before talking to his king. He knew Thorne would want to interrogate her and seek answers on how to defeat Deidamia once and for all.

Had she opened the portal herself? Or had they somehow figured out how to do it and dragged her along? It was impossible. Humans didn't have magic. Weak, mortal beings with little strength and short lifespans, but he had to admit her presence unnerved him. Made him wary.

He looked over to Raine, walking next to him, holding the woman's rope. "What do you think about this?"

Raine whispered back quietly so the human couldn't hear. "Something doesn't feel right," he said. "I sense there is more to the story than a naive woman suddenly appearing here with Deidamia."

Casimir nodded his agreement. "Do you think she is in league with them?"

"No. I could sense her fear when she fought against me. There was no ill-intent, just terror. She kept screaming about not going back. She thought we were part of Deidamia's army."

"She stabbed you in the leg."

"It's already basically healed." Raine shrugged. "Besides, she isn't that strong. The dagger didn't go deep."

Casimir sighed. He had noticed her injuries, painful even for an immortal. The way her eyes darted around and how her hands trembled though she tried to hide it. How she regarded him with suspicion, attempting to stifle her flinch at his approach. Her limp and the bruises on her body.

They continued their trek throughout the day, briefly stopping for food and water which Casimir allowed Jorrar to give their prisoner. Even though his benevolence often frustrated Casimir, he respected and even loved him for it. Raine was also that way; always laughing and up for new friendships. It was up to Casimir to remain wary and watch the woman, though something in him whispered that she wouldn't hurt them. That his world was about to be transformed by her sudden arrival.

THEY HAD FINALLY STOPPED to make camp and Ava's legs were heavy from trying to keep pace with the fae warriors. Not even pretending to slow for her sake, she had to jog at times to avoid falling from the tug of the rope. They'd told her they still had several days left in their journey and she was unsure if her legs would even make it.

"Sit down," Casimir said gruffly as he pointed to a tree next to camp.

She obeyed, relieved to be allowed to rest, and leaned her back against the tree. He took the rope from Jorrar and tied it to the tree with a complicated knot she knew she'd never be able to undo. There was enough slack for her to put her hands in her lap but not much more, wrists bound together so tightly the rope was starting to chafe. Her body ached and exhaustion made itself known from days of hiking through the forest.

"I'll remove your gag but don't think I won't immediately put it back should I deem it necessary," Casimir stated, standing over her. "Understood?" She nodded and he leaned down to untie the fabric. Standing up again, he asked, "Where did you get that dagger? The one you stabbed my captain with."

"Someone gave it to me."

"That's a daemon weapon." He looked at her accusingly.

"Okay." She shrugged. "Like I said, someone gave it to me. They probably stole it from one of the soldiers or something."

"Don't cause trouble again. You're lucky you stabbed the nice one."

"You call kidnapping me nice?" she retorted, irritation flaring.

He knelt again, face to face with her. "You wouldn't have liked what would have happened had I been the one you stabbed."

Asshole, she thought.

Turning on his heel, Casimir walked over to Raine and Quinn, having a hushed conversation as they set up the tents. They had chosen a small clearing for their camp, surrounded by towering trees with vivid green leaves and bark that was mottled black and gray. A number of the plants and animals in Eorhan looked similar to some of those back home, yet they were more vibrant and teemed with magic that Ava could sense, even in her human body. The clearing was full of soft grasses interspersed with minuscule white flowers, like tiny brilliant pearls.

Ava had been paying close attention to the warriors all day, noting each of their behaviors and the hierarchy of the group. The other three looked up to Casimir and he was a focused leader, almost never cracking a smile and always alert for danger.

Jorrar was the most generous, offering her water and food when they rested. According to Casimir, Raine was nice as well. Though she had yet to see it.

"Those are some painful looking injuries," Jorrar said as he approached and sat down on the ground across from her.

She didn't respond.

"Who did that to you?" he asked.

"Who do you think?"

"What's your name?"

She realized no one had asked her yet and didn't see the point in lying. They didn't know who she was anyway. "Ava."

"What a beautiful name. Well, Ava," he said. "Why were you lurking in the woods near our camp? Did you really kill that helwraith?"

She sighed, trying to decide how much to reveal. "I wasn't lurking. I was trying to find somewhere safe. I was told to follow the bright blue star. I didn't know there was anyone around. And yes... I killed that creature. That helwraith. What was it?"

Jorrar frowned when she mentioned the star. "Someone told you the star would lead you to safety?"

"Yes."

He assessed her for a long time before speaking again. "It's risky to be in those woods at night time. A lot of foul creatures live there, as you noticed. Helwraiths were brought over with Deidamia from her world. They're her assassins. And I have reason to believe it was stalking you," he said.

So they'd been hunting her after all.

"Why were you being tortured by Deidamia?" he asked.

Dangerous. This felt like a dangerous question. One she shouldn't answer. Not yet.

"I never said I was tortured," she said instead of answering.

"We recognize the signs. Your injuries, the small limp you try to hide. Your fear when you were found. We can sense it; can tell you're afraid you will be hurt again."

She quietly looked at him, then nodded.

"Why didn't they kill you? How long were you there?"

"I don't know," she said.

She could tell he didn't believe her, but he didn't push.

"Very well," he said, and rose to help the others prepare dinner.

As he was about to walk away, she asked, "What are you going to do with me?"

"That depends on you," Jorrar said, turning to look down at her. "The king will have many questions and if you are deemed a threat, possibly execution." His eyes briefly softened before he turned back and joined his friends.

Execution?

The panic set back in. Of course she wasn't a threat. She couldn't fight, wasn't strong and had no idea where she was. But what if the king had her killed for opening the portal? She was a liability if she could open more and if Deidamia found her again, it would put their whole world in even more danger.

She leaned against the tree, watching the group as Jorrar cooked over the fire. It smelled amazing, and her stomach growled in response. She hadn't had anything but apples, dried meat, bread and cheese in days and no real food in weeks. The other three sat and watched him quietly, always making sure one of them had an eye on her.

When dinner was done cooking, Jorrar brought her a wooden bowl and spoon filled with a hearty stew. She thanked him and ate as best she could while her hands were still bound together.

Closing her eyes, she almost moaned as she took the first bite. Nothing had ever tasted this good in her life. At last, something with flavor and substance, filled with foraged vegetables and the meat of some game they had likely killed during their travel. The meat melted in her mouth, and she sipped on the warm broth contentedly. There had always been something about soups and stews that comforted her, as if wrapping her in a warm hug.

"Did they even feed you at all?" Quinn asked, noting Ava's pleasure at the stew. "I've never seen anyone react to Jorrar's shitty cooking in such a way."

Jorrar made a face as if he was used to Quinn's comments. Casimir watched the three of them with a flicker of amusement but said nothing as he ate his dinner.

They seemed easy around each other. Used to the antics and jokes.

She glared at Quinn, irritation rising before she had a chance to realize it. "Anything tastes amazing after you've been living off stale bread and old meat for weeks. Even Jorrar's *shitty cooking*."

Quinn gave her a flat look as Raine snorted at Ava's comment.

Raine pointed at her with his spoon. "I like you. Even though you stabbed me." He paused and smiled wider. "Actually, that makes me like you even more."

"You're an idiot," lamented Quinn.

Ava allowed herself a small smile. At least one of them liked her. They finished their meal in silence, and she supposed the silence here was preferable to the awful screams and sounds back at the army camp.

After dinner, Quinn approached her and untied the rope from the tree.

"What are you doing?" Ava asked with trepidation.

"The general assigned me to take you to the creek. You stink." She glanced at her as she grasped the rope. "Come on."

Ava stood and followed Quinn into the woods where they stopped before a clear stream illuminated by the moonlight, snaking its way through the trees. Quinn untied Ava's wrists, watching her closely.

"If you run, I'll shoot you in the leg with an arrow," she said as she dropped the rope and pulled a bow off her back. "Throw your clothes onto the shore."

Ava walked to the stream, and though she wasn't keen about being naked in front of a stranger, she was so caked with dirt and grime the temptation of feeling even a little bit cleaner overrode her remaining modesty. After tossing her clothing onto the ground, she lowered herself into the stream and sighed. The water was waist high and surprisingly warm, soothing her aching muscles.

"Why isn't the water cold?" she asked.

Quinn was leaning against a tree, arrow nocked into place and aimed directly at her. "Hot springs."

Ava settled lower into the stream, allowing it to reach her neck and closed her eyes, pretending there wasn't a fae warrior poised to shoot her at any second. "It's lovely."

"They sure did a number on you, didn't they?"

Ava opened her eyes again and looked at Quinn, suddenly aware of how bruised and battered her body looked. "Yes."

Quinn's icy demeanor faded momentarily as she set down her bow and reached into her pocket, pulling out a vial full of purple liquid. "Here," she said as she tossed it to Ava.

She caught it and inspected the vial. "What is it?"

"Soap." Quinn left the bow on the ground and crossed her arms, not taking her eyes off Ava. "I bought it for myself. But you smell much worse than I do," she said.

"Wow... um. Thanks."

She uncorked the vial and poured the viscous material into

her hand and began to lather her body. It smelled of lavender and lemon, instantly relaxing Ava as she breathed it in.

"Sorry, I snapped at you," Ava said as she washed her arms. "I'm—I'm exhausted and was starving and... I don't know."

Quinn shrugged. "At least you have a backbone."

"Normally, I don't." She tilted her head back to rinse her hair. "I just couldn't help it. Honestly... the stew wasn't even that good," she explained. "I was just so hungry."

Quinn let out a small chuckle and Ava looked at her. "Don't tell Jorrar. I don't want to hurt his feelings," Ava added.

"As long as you don't tell the guys I gave you my soap. I'll never hear the end of it."

"Deal." Ava gave her a small smile and the corner of Quinn's lips lifted, just barely.

Ava lowered back into the creek and spent the next several minutes scrubbing the rest of the dirt off herself the best she could, never wanting to leave the warmth of the stream.

AVA WATCHED Casimir as he sat by the fire, taking first watch. She was back in her previous spot, wrists bound and tied to the tree she was leaning against. Quinn had given her some clean clothing; a pair of brown trousers and a tan tunic. She wore the same boots Isolde had given her and though cleaner, she still felt dirt and grime on her skin. What she wouldn't give to sit in a bathtub for hours and scrub every inch of her body until her skin was raw. As if she could wash away all the horrific memories of the recent weeks along with it.

Alone with The Bear, she was unable to take her eyes off him as he sat on a fallen log. Relaxed and staring into the flames, his sun-kissed skin was aglow from the light. Curiosity getting the best of her, she broke the silence. "Is it true you have a giant pet bear?"

He turned toward her, irritation flickering in his eyes. "Where did you hear that?"

She shrugged. "Some prisoner at the camp told me."

He watched her, as if he was trying to decide if he should answer and said, "Aro is not a *pet*," the last word coming out harshly. "Most pets aren't able to gut you in one swipe of their paws."

"So... where is Aro? I haven't seen him yet."

"Elsewhere."

"Do the others have animals?" she dared to ask, wishing for the hundredth time that Luna was still with her.

He was silent as he turned to stare back into the flames.

"Can you do magic?" She couldn't help her questions. She was nervous, yes, but she knew she needed to get to know these fae. Maybe earn some trust.

"Yes."

"Will you show me?"

"No."

"Do you always reply with one-word answers?" she asked.

"No."

"You literally just did," she said.

He slowly turned his head back toward her, eyes narrowing. "Do you always ask annoying questions?"

"Only when I realize it irritates a fae general," she bit back. Why did she say that? Just like when she snapped at Quinn, her stupid mouth didn't know when to shut up. Something about being around this group was tearing down her defenses.

"Do you have a death wish?"

She stared at him. "Are you threatening to kill me for asking you questions?"

He shook his head. "I'm just saying your mouth will get you in trouble if you don't learn when to keep it shut."

"You know—" she said. "You're kind of mean."

"I'm not mean, I'm cautious," he retorted.

"Whatever."

"Go to sleep."

She sighed, wondering if Casimir ever smiled. She didn't know why she said that. She knew she shouldn't antagonize the general, but for some reason she couldn't help it.

Careful Ava. Don't poke the bear, she thought. Her heart ached as she realized the joke reminded her of Eleanor. When they had gotten stoned and told horrible dad jokes as they searched for the map to the portal. The map that had upended everything and gotten her killed. Stifling the tears, she closed her eyes and leaned her head against the tree, trying to think about something else.

26

hey walked for two more days and camped out at night, resting and filling their bellies. The gag remained off but Ava didn't speak much, unsure of what to say and nervous she'd condemn herself in some way or she'd accidentally snap at one of them again.

The starvation, torture and exhaustion had caught up with her and it was almost impossible to filter her words. She just wanted to get to the capital, bathe again and sleep for days. And devour every single piece of food she could find.

She felt safer with this group than with Deidamia's army but still didn't trust them and feared her potential execution. Would the supposed kind king actually kill her? The protectiveness Remy had told her about made her nervous as she tried to imagine what the capital would be like.

As they got closer to Mosshaven, the terrain began to change. The trees were larger, older and had patches of lichen on their massive trunks. The leaves were an energetic chartreuse and the shrubs at their base a deep forest green. The ground was soft and mossy interspersed with rocks, blue and purple flowers, emerald ferns and little red capped mush-

207

rooms. They were at the base of the mountains now, peaks towering over them with their snow-capped tips and dense forests.

As they settled in for the third night, Ava mustered up the courage to speak again. They were in a grove of moss-covered trees, the glow of the moon casting shadows along the edges of camp. Smaller trees grew beneath the larger canopy, packed with rose pink blooms that had opened just as the sun set. White moths flocked to the flowers, stopping at each bloom as they drank their fill of nectar.

As they ate their dinner, she saw the four of them were deep in conversation, whispering to each other. Too quiet for her to hear.

Ava cleared her throat, trying to get their attention but they continued their discussion, ignoring her. She tried again and still nothing. With a big sigh, she was about to try a third time when Casimir snapped and looked at her.

"If you have something to say, just say it. We can hear you over there grunting like a fool," he said.

"I was just going to ask if we were getting close to our destination," she said.

"We should arrive in Mosshaven the day after tomorrow." He continued to watch her. "Anything else?"

She shook her head. "No. That's all."

That was soon.

She closed her eyes and tried contacting Luna yet again.

Luna? Where are you? Can you even hear me? Luna!

Nothing.

The evening went on without incident and everyone retired besides Jorrar, who took first watch while Ava dozed against the tree under a blanket.

Rustling noises from the trees behind her jarred her awake. Something was coming.

Jorrar leapt to his feet and whistled to his companions. The other three burst from their tents, armed to the teeth with weapons. Before she realized what was happening, Jorrar cut her restraints and told her to stay low and silent as something emerged from the trees.

It was massive, the size of a large wolf with leathery dark gray skin and hollow black eyes. Saliva dripped from its fangs as it stalked forward on all fours, long claws digging into the ground with each step. Where there should have been a nose, there was a flat spot with two slits and its bat-like ears tilted as it listened to its surroundings. It was not a helwraith, it was something different, something worse; a bloodthirsty beast sent straight from Deidamia's war camp.

Ava sat as still as possible, watching the creature prowl toward the warriors. It hadn't noticed her yet and she hoped it wouldn't. She had no idea how to fight against one of these things, especially without any weapons.

"Why is it here?" Quinn growled as the warriors took their positions.

The others didn't answer, backs to each other and weapons at the ready. The creature continued to stalk forward, unafraid of the warriors. Three more monsters emerged from the woods. The four fae were now surrounded, preparing for a fight.

The first monster jumped at Quinn, and the warriors burst into motion. They were so quick, faster than Ava could even keep track of. Their fae blades squelched as they met the flesh of the monsters.

As she watched them fight, a fifth being emerged from her right, eyes locked on her. She jumped to her feet, looking around for a weapon but her eyes found none. The warriors were distracted with the other four and didn't notice the new threat creeping toward Ava.

Weaponless and vulnerable, she took off and ran into the woods as fast as she could, hoping she could escape. She had gained some strength over the last few days thanks to the hearty meals and sleep, and she pushed herself hard, flying through the woods.

As she got further away from camp, the sounds of battle faded, and she kept running as the creature crashed through the brush behind her. Growls sounded as sticks snapped under its heavy paws and she increased her speed. Why did she leave camp? In her panic to get away she wasn't thinking, and her terror had taken over. Now she was alone with the monster with no way to fight it.

She should go back because they knew how to fight, and it was her only chance. Maybe she could outrun it and lead it back to camp to be killed by the warriors. She started to change direction, looping back to lead the creature to the camp when she tripped and fell.

Scrambling for purchase she tried to rise but excruciating pain exploded in her calf and ran up her leg as the daemon hound's teeth sank into her flesh and muscle. She screamed as it dragged her deeper into the woods.

Her leg was on fire. Unimaginable pain crawled up her calf, spreading through her whole body. Poison? It was just her luck they would have poison in their fangs.

She clawed at the ground, trying and failing to grip onto something. It was taking her somewhere. Maybe somewhere else to savor devouring her bite by bite. She tried everything, hitting it with her fists, scratching at its eyes. Nothing worked. It barely even flinched.

She was going to die out here.

As her hope faded, something leapt out from the woods and crashed into the creature, throwing it into a tree. She scrambled away, dragging her injured leg and hid behind a boulder, peering over the top to watch the fight.

It was a bear, midnight black and larger than a grizzly, it roared at the daemon and charged as the creature rose onto its haunches after being thrown. Though the monster was huge, the bear was bigger and within a few seconds, it had the creature's head in its mouth, snapping its neck with ease and leaving it to crumple to the ground.

She'd seen this bear before. It was the one causing chaos at camp. The ursine giant lumbered toward her, curiosity in its eyes. This must be Aro. Why was he at the camp when she escaped? Had he helped her somehow? Did Casimir know?

Though the creature was dead, Aro very well may kill her too. She sat still, looking into his yellow eyes as he stopped and stared at her, mere feet from where she was sitting.

"Thank you for saving me." Her voice quaked, but she didn't shy away.

He walked closer, stopping with his nose inches away. She closed her eyes, waiting for a blow. She could smell the dirt in his fur and feel his warm breath upon her. Then, something wet trailed down her face.

Opening her eyes, puzzled, she looked at the bear. Did he just lick her? Aro lowered his head and nudged her hand as if asking her to pet him. So, she did, scratching behind his ears and laughing.

"You are so sweet," she said, rubbing Aro's muzzle and scratching his head with both hands as a low happy growl rumbled in the back of his throat.

Aro walked around the boulder and nudged her back, attempting to get her to stand up. She tried and was able to stand on her uninjured leg but the moment she tried to put weight on the other, she gasped in pain and almost collapsed, holding on to the nearest tree.

"I can't walk," she said, looking at Aro whose height on all fours reached the level of her shoulders.

Gosh, he is huge.

Aro lowered himself down and looked at her expectantly.

"Um…. You want me to ride on your back?"

He chuffed as if saying, "Duh."

Aro watched her every move as she nervously hobbled to him, swung her leg over and gripped his fur, hoping she didn't hurt or upset him. He rose and ambled toward camp, carrying her as if she weighed nothing. Her leg throbbed with every step.

She was riding a bear. She was in a magical realm, with a group of fae warriors and she was riding the bear of the general, Ava realized with disbelief.

They had only been walking a couple of minutes when Casimir burst from among the trees, breathing heavily. Was he coming to help her? As soon as he caught sight of her on his bear, he froze, eyes wide. His eyes took in the scene as he inspected her, then moved down to her bleeding leg.

"He saved me," she said hesitantly.

He narrowed his eyes at Ava and then looked at Aro. "Let's go." He turned around and headed back toward camp, the bear following with Ava.

Aro made a chuffing sound resembling laughter as he followed his friend back to the others. Casimir's shoulders looked more tense than before, silently brooding as they walked back.

She remained quiet as they made their way through the woods, running her fingers through Aro's rough fur and scratching his ears during their trek. Aro made happy growls the whole time and Casimir glanced back at one point, seemingly curious about his bear's quick acceptance of her.

They emerged from the trees into camp, the remains of the other creatures the fae had killed lying on the ground, one whose head had been severed clean.

"How the fuck is she riding Aro?" exclaimed Raine, looking from her to Casimir.

Jorrar was holding back a smile and Quinn raised her eyebrows and crossed her arms, looking at Ava and the bear.

"The fluffy moron apparently has a soft spot for human

fools." Casimir shook his head as he dragged one of the bodies away to dispose of it.

Raine laughed as he walked up to her and glanced at her leg. "That's two pairs of my pants you've now ruined."

"I—shit. What? These were yours?" Her face turned red.

"They were. But it's fine. I'll get more," he said and held out his hand for her to hold onto.

Ava carefully climbed off Aro and collapsed to the ground. Raine returned to aid the others in cleaning up camp and she leaned back against the tree she had been tied to as Jorrar approached.

"I can't even walk, so tying me up is pointless," she said.

He nodded his agreement and inspected her injuries, asking her what happened. She explained one of the creatures had grabbed her leg and was dragging her away when Aro showed up and killed it.

"Dragging you away?" he said as he ripped open the leg of her pants to better access the bites. "It didn't kill you on the spot?"

"Obviously not," she said. "I figured it was taking me somewhere else to eat me or something."

He opened a small satchel and removed a vial of brown liquid.

"This will hurt," he warned, before pouring two drops on her wounds.

She gritted her teeth, holding back a scream as tears formed in her eyes. Aro walked closer and lay down next to her, plopping his giant head in her lap, comforting her through the pain. She stroked his head and he purred with contentment.

"I'm sorry. I know it hurts but those daemon hounds have poison in their fangs. This is leeching the poison from your wounds and it's quite painful," he explained as he continued to pour the liquid over the remaining punctures. Then he looked at Aro. "I've never seen him act this way before."

"Who? Casimir? Or the bear?"

He chuckled. "The bear. Casimir is often grumpy, that's nothing new. Aro likes you. The only person he's ever let touch him or ride him is Cas. I've known them both since they were barely able to walk and Aro hardly tolerates my presence."

"I've always been good with animals." She shrugged. "There was this cat... Anyway, she was injured, and I helped her. From then on, she became sort of a friend to me."

Jorrar listened quietly as he bandaged her leg. "Animals are precious to those of us from Monterre. It is our sacred duty to care for them and keep them safe. That cat sounds like she was special to you."

"She was. I miss her," she said.

Jorrar finished treating her wounds and made his way back to the fire as Casimir approached and stood over her, arms crossed, taking in Aro's head in her lap. She smiled sheepishly. "Jorrar said Aro likes me."

Casimir ignored her comment. "Why was the daemon hound taking you away? Why didn't it kill you?"

"I don't know."

"Those hounds were sent from Deidamia," he said. "They were hunting you. Why? What do they want from you?"

"I told you. I don't know."

He knelt, closer to eye level, and quietly said, "You're lying."

She held his gaze but said nothing. She wasn't ready to tell them her story, still not sure how much she trusted them. It made more sense to wait and meet the king. Then she could go from there.

Casimir stood and walked away, joining the others by the fire. "We will get the truth eventually, Ava."

27

Casimir reluctantly allowed Ava to ride on Aro the next day. Raine had walked next to her most of the time, keeping her entertained with stories of debauchery from his younger years. The others had rolled their eyes when he told her about the time he got caught with the daughter of one of the lords of a local village. Raine had frantically pulled his pants back up as he fled into the woods, the girl's father shouting obscenities behind him.

"That was before I was named a captain though," he'd said as he winked at her.

"Like your rank has stopped your ridiculous behavior," Quinn had called out from in front of them.

Ava had decided then, that she liked Raine. He seemed to have forgiven her for stabbing him and was funny, considerate and appeared to want to be her friend. She hoped his kindness wasn't a ruse.

Tonight, they'd allowed her to join them for dinner, and she watched them curiously. Clearing her throat, she dared to ask a question. "So... um. What's it like in Mosshaven?"

She'd remained mostly quiet after the first night where

she'd bit back at both Quinn and Casimir and the four warriors looked at her, surprised she had broken the silence.

Jorrar answered, "It's beautiful. More beautiful than anything you could ever imagine." He spoke of it with a reverence so great, it moved her. "The city was built into nature itself. There are trees and flowers and plants everywhere you look. Our kingdom specializes in farming, and we provide a large portion of crops to trade with the other kingdoms. Our farmers are proud and incredibly talented. The food there is so good, it will make you cry."

"Better than your stew?" she asked, attempting a joke.

The four warriors were silent, taken aback by her jab. She froze and blushed, worried she had offended them. But Raine started laughing, soon joined by Jorrar. Even Casimir was wearing a small smirk, shaking his head. Quinn tried to suppress a smile, glancing at Ava.

"Yes," Jorrar responded. "*Much* better than my stew."

Raine tilted his head and asked in his smooth voice, "Do you like sweets, Ava?"

She smiled. A genuine smile for the first time in what felt like forever. "Yes," she said. "They're my absolute favorite."

"Well, we have every pastry, tart, cake, pie, cookie you could imagine. Things that you could only invent in your wildest dreams. One bite and its pure ecstasy," Raine explained, eyes twinkling.

"Ew, are you turned on?" said Quinn.

"Wouldn't you like to know?"

She glared at him. "Gross."

Ava laughed quietly, quickly clamping her hand over her mouth. "Sorry," she said, stifling herself.

"Don't be sorry," said Jorrar. "The two of them are always like that."

"Insufferable is what they are," mumbled Casimir.

"Can it, you big lout," said Raine. "You'd be bored out of your mind without our entertainment."

Casimir shrugged.

This felt good. Sitting with people around the fire, laughing and enjoying their fellowship together. Ava had never truly had this. The ease of the way they were with one another. These fae were bonded deeply, loyal to the end. She could see beneath the jabs and laughter that they truly cared for each other, would give their lives for each other, and she longed for it. Craved it.

Ava listened to their banter as she ate her bowl of dinner quietly, smiling to herself and surprised she was finding joy in this. Even if she was still technically their prisoner.

Braving another question, she asked, "So... are any of you... you know... together?"

Choking on a mouthful of stew, Casimir blanched. "Together? Us?" He shook his head and made a disgusted face. He pointed to himself. "Me?" Then looked at the others. "With them? Never."

Quinn was smiling broadly, the first time Ava had seen genuine joy on her face, and Jorrar grinned. Raine looked put out and scoffed at Casimir. "Is imagining yourself with us so bad?"

Casimir looked at his friends. "You're old enough to be my grandfather," he said pointing at Jorrar. "You're a downright jerk most of the time," he said to Quinn, who grinned even wider. "And you..." he gestured to Raine. "You're just...you."

Raine waved his hands. "What the fuck is that supposed to mean, you grumpy asshole?"

Ava tried to hide her smile as she watched the taunting unfold.

Casimir continued. "You're a vain, preening man who can barely stand to get his precious hair dirty."

The other two laughed at Raine's expense and his thunderstruck expression.

"It's true," Quinn said. "You were just complaining the other day about how muddy your boots were."

"They're fine fae leather," he retorted. "I wanted them to last." He lifted his foot and inspected his boot in the firelight.

"See?" said Casimir. "Vain."

"Well, it's your loss," said Raine, looking at his friends. "I've been told I'm quite the lover."

"That's probably because you'll bed anyone who looks your way," said Quinn.

"I welcome all."

Casimir shook his head as the teasing died down.

"So, what about you?" Raine turned to Ava. "Do you have someone back home waiting for you? A lost love or something like that?"

Ava's heart leapt in her throat as she thought about Henry. "I..." she wasn't sure what to say, or if she even wanted to say anything. "Not anymore."

Jorrar leaned forward and asked softly, "What happened?"

Ava shook her head. "He wasn't who I thought he was. But I don't want to talk about it."

They nodded their understanding, and didn't bring it up again.

"Well, Ava," Raine said. "How about I show you around Mosshaven and we have a tasting tour of all the sugar we can handle? My sister owns a bakery, and she's very talented."

Ava smiled. "I'd like that."

Casimir turned serious. "Raine... we can't be promising tours for her. She's technically our prisoner."

Raine rolled his eyes. "Yes yes, but I'm sure we can find time for fun."

Eventually, most of them retired to their tents, leaving her alone with Casimir, who was taking first watch as he so frequently did.

She sat in silence, staring at the fire and listened to the symphony of the forest. The breeze rustled the leaves of the trees, providing a soothing sound occasionally interrupted by the faint call of an owl, while the crackle of the flames whispered as they devoured the wood.

She looked up and caught Casimir watching her, seated on the log to her right.

She met his stare. "What?"

His golden eyes reflected the fire before them as he answered, "You're not like I thought you'd be."

She narrowed her eyes at him. "What does that mean?"

"You're just... different."

"Is that a good or a bad thing?"

He raised an eyebrow at her as he leaned his elbows on his knees and continued to stare. "I haven't decided yet."

They sat in silence for a moment unable to break eye contact.

"Does it bother you that Aro likes me?" she asked.

"Yes."

"Why?"

"I don't know." He kept looking at her. "Because you're hiding things from us." She stared at him, silent. "Tell me what you're hiding," he tried again, eyes boring into hers.

"Not yet," she said, fidgeting with a loose thread on her pants.

"Why not?"

"Would you?" she asked.

"Would I what?"

She sighed, looking toward the fire. "If you were thrown into a world you never knew. Filled with beings you didn't even know existed, tortured, and then captured by a group of warriors..." She looked back at him. "Would you trust them?"

His eyes softened, almost imperceptibly. "I suppose not."

"Exactly," she said. After a few moments of silence, she added, "He was there. At the army camp."

"What? Who?"

"Aro," she said, and his eyes widened.

"What do you mean, he was there?"

"When I escaped. I heard growling and I saw him. I think he was creating a distraction..." she explained. "To help me."

Casimir looked confused as he shook his head. "Why would he do that?"

"I don't know. Ask him," she said. "You *can* talk to him, right?"

"Of course I can talk to him."

"Then ask him." She pushed herself up, putting all her weight on her good leg. "I should get some sleep. I need to be well rested in case I have an execution to look forward to tomorrow."

He stared at her with bewilderment but didn't reply, handing her the large tree branch Raine had found for her to use as a makeshift crutch. Using it for assistance, she hobbled over to her bedroll, now placed in between two of their tents for more protection.

Before she had a chance to make her way to the ground, Casimir interrupted her. "Take my tent."

She turned to him. "What?"

"Use my tent," he repeated.

"Why?"

"You'll feel safer with walls around you."

"I'm not scared," she whispered.

Casimir raised an eyebrow. "You're not a very good liar, you know."

She glared at him.

He nodded and gestured toward his tent. "Sleep well."

"Thank you," she said as she lifted the flaps and crawled into the small tent.

There wasn't much inside the brown canvas quarters. A bedroll topped with a soft fur beckoned her from the corner. She hobbled over and lay down, pulling a thin blanket over her that smelled of dirt and the hint of cedar and sage. She had barely closed her eyes before she was dragged into a deep slumber, embraced by the comforting scent and feeling safe for the first time in weeks.

WITH AVA ASLEEP in his tent, Casimir stared at the fire and thought about what had transpired the last several days. He no longer thought she should be executed, it was obvious she wanted nothing to do with Deidamia and Andras, but he was unsure what the next steps were. They needed whatever information she had, and though he understood why she was reluctant to trust them, not having answers irritated him. It was his responsibility to ensure the safety of his kingdom and she was making it difficult to accomplish this.

Her behavior had surprised him. He was expecting a terrified, whimpering girl who cowered at the sight of the warriors. Instead, he found a sassy woman who tried to hold her ground even though she was nervous and lost in a world strange to her. Who had killed a helwraith with a bow and arrow in a single shot. Who stabbed Raine, one of his captains and his best friend.

She had noticed him watching her at the fire. His eyes caught on her fair delicate face dusted with freckles, her piercing green eyes framed by long lashes that matched her strawberry blonde locks, flowing over her rounded ears. She was much taller than he expected a human to be and could tell she had ample curves if she hadn't been so starved in Deidamia's camp.

While she was still dirty and bruised, he admitted she was beautiful. She exasperated him and yet he was equal parts intrigued. Then there was Aro, who had never let anyone even touch him besides Casimir, and he hadn't even hesitated to save her life and let her ride on him. And was he really at the camp when she escaped? When he had asked him about it, Aro just replied 'Ava is special,' and wouldn't say anything else.

Damn animals and their secrets.

28

$\mathcal{A}$va was awoken by the sounds of shuffling around the tent and the camp being packed up. Rubbing her eyes, she looked around and remembered where she was. Inside an army general's tent in the middle of a forest in a magical world.

The flaps opened and Casimir's head peeked through. "Get up. It's time to go."

She threw off the blanket and put on her boots, flinching as the leather rubbed her injured leg. Crawling out of the tent, she found the makeshift crutch and stood outside, watching the fae tear down their camp.

Jorrar handed her some bread. "We're eating breakfast on the road." Then turned to dismantle Casimir's tent and pack the last of their supplies.

"Do humans always sleep that late?" Quinn asked as she helped Jorrar.

Looking around at the bustling warriors she felt a twinge of guilt. "I didn't... I'm sorry... I didn't mean to sleep that long."

"Ignore her," said Raine, readying the horse. "Cas told us to let you sleep. She's just giving you shit."

She glanced over at Casimir who nodded. She gave him a

223

tentative smile and turned away, waiting for them to finish packing their supplies.

As she took a bite of bread, she realized with a lump in her throat they would arrive today in the capital city of the Earth Kingdom. Her kingdom. It made so much sense why she had always been good with animals and plants, and explained the connection she had with Luna and why her mother had been able to use magic on plants in the garden. Though reluctant to meet the king and learn of her fate, she admitted to herself she was excited, curious to see where her mother grew up.

Ava rode on Aro, still unable to walk, while Casimir and Quinn walked ahead. Casimir appeared to be slightly less grumpy this morning which gave her some relief.

Raine walked next to her, willingly answering some of her questions.

"So does everyone have an animal companion?" she asked.

"No," he said. "It's usually the most skilled or powerful. The best healers, warriors, blacksmiths and the like. It's an honor to be chosen by an animal and it usually happens in childhood. The animals can sense your potential and they choose to bond with you."

"What kind of animal is yours?" she asked.

He looked at her and paused. Then turned his head and whistled between two fingers. After a moment he jerked his head toward their right and a large silver wolf appeared next to him, eyeing Ava warily.

"Her name is Sabriel." He scratched between her ears. "She likes ear scratches too," he added.

Ava smiled at him as she looked at the regal creature.

"She's lovely," she said, and Sabriel happily yipped in response and wagged her tail as she disappeared back into the woods.

"Interesting..." Raine muttered as he stared at Ava, taken aback by Sabriel's friendly reaction.

She asked him what animals belonged to Jorrar and Quinn, but he told her they would reveal them when they were ready.

After a while, she turned back to him, fidgeting with Aro's fur who didn't seem to mind. "Will I be tortured again?"

He started and looked at her with slight compassion before regaining his swagger. "I'm still in disbelief you were able to endure that."

"Me too," she said quietly as she looked forward.

Raine was silent, tension thick as they all listened to Ava's words.

"These torture sessions. What did they do?" he asked after a moment.

She sighed. "The Scourge did most of the torturing while Deidamia and Andras watched," she answered, noticing Casimir tense in front of her at the mention of The Scourge. "Deidamia gave him free reign to do what he wanted. I'm sure you can use your imagination."

Raine tilted his head and looked at her reverently. "Yet you got through it."

She turned and looked at him, sitting up straighter. "Yes."

"How?"

"I thought about home," she said, not telling them her true home.

They looked at each other for a moment before Raine grinned. "Impressive."

Ava smiled back.

"Speaking of home," Jorrar interrupted from behind them. "We're here."

They had walked over fields and through copses of trees until they were stopped at the base of the mountains. They were so tall, it hurt Ava's neck as she tried to find their peaks. Covered in the greenery of a dense forest, their very tops reached to the sky and were sprinkled with a light snow at the highest altitude. The jagged stone wall before her was shrouded by thick vines, woven together so tightly you could barely see the rock they covered.

Facing the wall, Casimir walked forward with his hands extended and placed them against the vines, mumbling something inaudible. Light flared from him, and the vines began snaking through themselves. When they finished their movement, a tunnel was revealed.

A tunnel leading through the mountain.

Ava inhaled a sharp breath at the magic; the enchanting way Casimir controlled the vines as they parted wide enough to allow their party through. She looked at Raine and he winked at her, amused by her awe.

They continued into the tunnel illuminated by glowing fungus along the rough stone walls and ceiling, like the cave she had stayed on her first night of freedom. The vines closed behind them, concealing the entrance and they continued on, walking along the stone walkway leading to the capital city.

The tunnel stretched on for miles, their party silent except for the clopping of the horse's hooves echoing behind her. The passage was otherworldly, covered in moss with glowing insects and butterflies flitting around them, providing even more light. Smaller channels branched out at different angles. It was a road system under the mountains. A way to keep the center of their kingdom safe from their enemies.

They emerged from the tunnel into a town, surrounded by immense mountains all around as if it was protected by the tree-covered giants. The city was built into and around the terrain, blending in with the trees, rocks and moss seamlessly. Homes were built into the enormous tree trunks with bridges connecting them above and below. A sense of peace radiated throughout the city, the citizens going about their daily business without a care in the world.

She marveled at the beauty as Raine leaned in. "Welcome

to Mosshaven, Ava." She smiled, despite herself, and took in the city around her.

Casimir led their party through cobblestone streets, surrounded by businesses built among towering and moss-covered trees. They passed by a potions shop, a bookstore and a tailor. The other side of the street housed a charming looking teahouse, the smells of herbs escaping as patrons entered and exited. Slivers of sunlight filtered through the dense canopy hundreds of feet above them, protecting the city from watchful eyes in the sky. The city would be too dark were it not for the lights and oil lanterns strung along the roads and through the town, lit by small flames and casting a warm glow.

Ava was captivated as diverse creatures milled about. Small fairies flew by with iridescent shimmery wings, and short goblin-like creatures reminding her of Remy wandered in and out of the vine covered shops. Bright yellow and blue flowers grew among the grass that lined the streets, framing the buildings with their blooms.

It wasn't long before citizens spotted them in the streets and shouted their praise, cheering with joy. They appeared to revere Casimir and were excited he had returned after what she assumed had been a lengthy journey, whispering among themselves. "He's back. The Bear is back!"

Then, they began to notice her. "Who is that woman?" "She isn't fae." "Look at that. Who is that?"

Ava fidgeted under their scrutiny, wishing she was more presentable than her current appearance as they continued along the main road. Their party wove in and out of shops and bypassed side streets that led to small neighborhoods built into the giant trees.

They stopped in front of a vast castle made of white stone covered in moss and vines. The tops of the towers were rounded, and bridges connected the different wings, suspended above crystal clear brooks and streams. Animals were everywhere. Birds flew among the trees, their feathers full of bright pinks, purples and greens. Several of those glowing foxes she had seen in the woods were darting along one of the streams, chasing each other like they were in a game of tag.

Everything in this town, including the castle, seemed to be built with the utmost of respect to the landscape, using the trees and rocks when they could and disturbing as little as possible. Flowers and plants grew on almost every surface, vines climbed buildings and trees provided the shade.

She couldn't help the tears welling in her eyes as she took in the beauty. Prisoner or not, she had never seen anything so moving in her entire life and she could feel it. Feel the sense of belonging the moment she entered the city. It was as if the seed that had been planted upon her arrival at the farm was now being watered and ached to bloom.

She leaned in toward Raine. "Do you have any advice?"

He tilted his head. "Thorne is a fair ruler. I doubt he will order your execution." She exhaled at his statement. "He's going to want information. My advice would be to trade something for it."

"What do you mean?"

"Tell him what he wants to know, but only if he agrees to do something for you. Ask for food or a healer or something you need first. It will earn some respect from him too if you state your needs."

"Thank you."

They passed under a towering archway built from tall willow trees woven together. Golden lanterns hung from the arch with bright blue butterflies hovering among the willow leaves. Casimir stopped their party and looked back at her, nodding.

"Get ready to meet the king," he said.

29

The castle was radiant in the mid-afternoon light. Beams of sun glimmered through arched glassless windows, as the breeze wound its way through the hallways keeping the space at a balmy temperature. The sounds of running water and the laughter of citizens wafted inside, a pleasant and comforting noise.

As their party continued through the castle, Ava found herself wondering about how the fae in Eorhan lived their lives without the modern amenities she was used to back home in the human world. Was the weather always this pleasant or did they have to worry about seasonal changes? Did they have plumbing or running water? What were those strange glowing lights in all the lanterns they used in place of electricity?

She knew if she asked Raine, he would smirk and say something about magic.

So, she kept quiet, preparing herself to meet the king, trying to muster the courage to face what would come next. What her fate would be and if her life would be spared.

She scratched Aro's head as he ambled through the castle,

allowing her reprieve from her leg as it throbbed incessantly. She hoped the healers here could help with the pain.

They wound through the extensive hallways, iron lanterns hanging from the stone ceilings to illuminate the way. The walls were composed of a pale golden stone glowing with a soft light. Lush rugs of greens and browns were laid along the paths, framed by artwork on the walls depicting motifs of animals. A small rabbit asleep by a stream, a pack of wolves howling, a glimmering lizard basking on a rock. Where there wasn't artwork, there were plants and flowers surrounding them. Hanging from every window and even along the walls and ceiling were green vines of every shade. Flowers of bright pinks, blues and purples brought a fairy-like feel to the space, attracting dragonflies and fast little birds reminding her of hummingbirds.

"We're here," Casimir said from in front of Ava, pulling her from her observations.

They had stopped in front of a large set of double oak doors, displaying a tree carved into the wood. The Elderoak. Trying to keep her shaking hands still, she took a deep breath and looked at Raine standing to her right.

"Remember what I told you." He smiled warmly.

She nodded as the party moved forward yet again, heavy doors swinging open.

They entered a massive throne room, ceilings even higher than the halls, concealed by lush greenery and more flowers. Walls to the left and right were dotted with more of the glass-less windows, providing the same cool breeze throughout the rest of the castle. Hundreds of colorful lanterns of different shapes and sizes brightened the space, illuminating a large wooden throne with the Elderoak carved into the back.

Seated upon the throne was the king. Thorne Everwood, Raine had told her.

Though seated, she could tell he was tall and muscular, as

most other high fae men seemed to be. Dressed in a tunic of forest green lined with gold, dark brown pants and boots, he emanated a sense of restrained power, inspecting her with a scrutiny that seemed to know her every thought; a frankness that made her heart race. Like he was watching for her to do something rash, ready to defend his kingdom at a moment's notice. It unnerved her.

Appearing to be in his mid-forties, but likely much older, a golden crown of vines sat upon his scarlet red hair, tiny emeralds adorning each leaf and glistening in the sunlight.

Turning his piercing green eyes to the rest of her party, he smiled as he greeted his friends. Though he appeared warm and friendly to the others, he regarded Ava with scrutiny and distrust.

"Tell me... who is this strange woman sitting on Aro, General?" He looked pointedly at Ava, his low voice smooth and powerful.

"We found her near our camp a few days ago," he replied.

The King's eyes paused on her calf. "Your leg is injured. Can you stand?"

"I'll try."

Raine walked closer and held out his hand to help her down. As Aro knelt, Ava swung her leg over, wincing as she landed on the floor and placed all her weight on her good leg. Leaning against Raine, who had offered his arm for her to cling to, she straightened herself up and feigned confidence.

Aro turned and lumbered out the still open doors, guards giving him a wide berth as he disappeared down the hallway.

"What is your name, human?"

"Ava," she responded.

His eyes flashed briefly, but he collected himself, leaning back on his throne before continuing, regarding her even more intensely than before.

"Your Majesty," Quinn asked. "Are you alright?"

"I'm fine," he assured his friends and then turned back to Ava, preternaturally still on his throne. "Tell me, *Ava*." He emphasized her name. "How did you arrive in Eorhan?"

Hesitating and remembering what Raine told her she answered carefully. "I..." she cleared her throat. "I was tricked."

He looked at her expectantly, waiting for her to add more details. "Go on," he urged.

"First, I'd like to make a request," she said, gripping Raine's arm tightly.

Casimir coughed as the group looked her way.

The King raised a brow. "A request? From a human woman? Why would I grant such a thing?"

She remained silent, mulling over what to say next.

Sighing, he waved his hand again. "What is your request?"

"I'm exhausted, starved and hurt. I would like to see a healer, get some rest, have a real bath and eat some food *before* I answer your questions."

Despite her brief bath in the stream, her hair was still filthy, her shirt was covered in dirt, and she had blood stains on her ripped pants from the attack on her leg. Suddenly self-conscious, she forced herself to meet his stare and did not look away.

"Why not answer my questions now and then receive those things you've requested?" Thorne asked as the rest of the group silently observed their interaction.

"Because I don't know you. Therefore, I don't trust you. You might change your mind and throw me in the dungeons after I tell you what you want to know."

He stood up and strolled down the steps, his hands clasped behind him, and stopped before her. His eyes bored into hers. "I could throw you in the dungeons right now for your refusal to answer my questions."

"Try it and see what happens," she seethed, a flare of her temper showing. She would not be a prisoner again after what she'd gone through. Refused. They would have to kill her before she'd let herself be locked away.

"What are you doing?" Raine whispered.

Thorne stepped closer with a feline grace. "Are you threatening me?"

Ava gripped Raine's arm as her voice trembled. "No. That's not what I meant."

"Explain," he said, anger sizzling in his eyes.

"I was already a prisoner at Deidamia's camp for weeks," she stated. "I want to help you. But I won't be locked away again."

Thorne backed up and looked her up and down. "You stabbed one of my captains."

"I—" she tried to explain but he held up his hand.

"Do not interrupt me." He paused, waiting for her to comply. She remained silent. "You stabbed one of my captains and rumors say you brought the daemon queen back to Eorhan. But—" he looked at her pointedly. "I will grant your request."

"Thank you," she said, shoulders relaxing.

"I've spent many years building up this kingdom to its true potential. Though we occasionally capture prisoners, I'm not in the business of putting a helpless woman in the depths of our dungeons."

Ava scowled at the word 'helpless' but remained silent, letting Thorne finish.

"Ava," he said, piercing eyes meeting hers. "I will give you quarters to stay in while you recover. It will be heavily guarded, and you are not to leave your rooms without an escort. I will allow you to rest and provide you with the comforts you need. We will reconvene in three days' time when you *will* tell us everything."

"Thank you." She bowed her head.

He took one step closer to her and added, "But do not speak to me like that again. I may not be so generous next time."

"Understood." She nodded, shivering at the unspoken threat in his voice.

"Casimir," Thorne said, looking at the general. "I'm putting her in the empty suite adjacent to yours. Please take her there now and send for a healer."

"Yes, Your Majesty. I'll make sure she's watched closely." He turned toward Ava. "Can you walk?" She nodded. Though she didn't know how she'd make it, she was determined not to show weakness in front of them. Casimir turned, not waiting to see if she would follow and made his way toward the doors. "Let's go."

30

*A*va and Casimir arrived in front of a wooden door. They had walked through countless hallways decorated in congruence with the rest of the castle; plants, flowers and trees adorning each space. She was relieved to be at the end of this painful trek. Her leg was throbbing, and she could barely put any weight on it.

"We're here," Casimir said as he turned around. The first words he'd spoken since leaving the throne room.

The door was protected by two guards, one on either side, dressed in thick brown leather armor like Casimir's. The oak tree insignia was imprinted on their shoulder, and they were armed to the teeth with swords and daggers. One guard was a fair-skinned fae woman with violet eyes and blue hair in one long braid over her shoulder. The other was an orc with green skin, dark brown eyes, and black hair shaved on one side of his head. They both watched her curiously.

Casimir spoke to the guards with a voice full of authority as he opened the door. "She is not to leave this room unless she is accompanied by me, Raine, Quinn, Jorrar or The King. If you find her a threat, do not hesitate to throw her in the dungeons. Understood?"

"Yes, general," the guards replied.

"Pax, will you send for Kai?"

The orc nodded and disappeared down the hall as Casimir led Ava into a large living room and gestured toward the plush forest green couch. "Sit. I want to look at your leg."

Sighing, she plopped down, relieved to be off her feet at last. "Why? You're not a healer."

"Because I've been bitten by one of those before. Just want a closer look."

The living room was large yet cozy and a roaring fireplace took center stage in front of where she was perched on the sofa. Plush rugs and chairs dotted the seating area, providing enough room for at least half a dozen people. This room continued the castle's theme of integrating nature into its essence. Everything was decorated with warm greens and browns, vines hanging from the ceiling among the same lanterns she had seen throughout the castle.

A dining table sat at the other end of the room, surrounded by six wooden chairs, all intricately carved with designs of leaves and vines. Another corner housed a bookshelf and a desk.

One wall was made of open archways, leading to a balcony overlooking an elaborate garden. The balcony was shaded by a massive tree and plants grew all along the carved stone railing.

"This castle is beautiful," she said quietly.

Casimir nodded as he sat on the other end of the couch and carefully lifted her leg, placing her foot in his lap as he inspected her injuries. Removing her boot, he set it on the ground and slowly pulled up her pants leg. She winced as he touched the punctures, now red and inflamed from walking. Sweat dripped from her brow as she gritted her teeth.

He looked up at her, golden eyes flaring with a tinge of guilt. "You're in a lot of pain."

She glared at him as he held her ankle on his leg, his hand warm despite the rough calluses. "Making me walk down these long halls sure didn't help. So, how did you get bitten?"

He sat back and removed his hand from her ankle, putting his arm on the back of the couch. "One of the many battles I've fought in to keep the army away from Monterre. I was younger and got distracted."

"Why wasn't their army killed off while they were gone?" she asked.

"Well," Casimir said, crossing an ankle over his knee. "We don't have enough forces. All we've been able to do is keep them at bay. We lost too many during the battles and retreated long ago."

"Won't the other kingdoms help?" she asked.

"It's a long story. And I'm not answering any more of your questions until you've answered ours." He gave her a small smirk, the first time he'd even attempted to smile at her.

"Fine."

He looked at her, silent for a moment. "That was really stupid you know."

"What was?"

"What you said back in the throne room."

"I wasn't threatening him."

"It sure sounded like it." He looked at the fireplace and then back at her again. "Let me give you some advice." She stared at him, waiting. "Don't threaten a king the moment you meet him. You're lucky Thorne is kindhearted. There are other kings in Eorhan who would have immediately had you beheaded for your disrespect."

"Fine." She sighed. "I'll be more careful." She didn't care at the moment, her pain so great it was clouding her judgment and she wanted to bathe and sleep for a month.

"Alright," he said. "I presume Kai will arrive soon. Can you walk to your room, or do you need to be carried?" he asked with reluctance.

"I'll walk, thank you." She was not letting the brute carry her, no matter how badly her leg hurt.

He stood and offered his hand. She grasped it, and he pulled her up, offering his arm to lean on. Reluctantly, she gripped it and leaned into him as they walked to the other end of the large living space. She caught a whiff of his scent as she unintentionally leaned closer. It was like a mix between cedar trees and sage, and for some reason it relaxed her, comforted her. She didn't know what that meant.

He cleared his throat, indicating they had stopped before her door. She quickly pulled her arm away from him and put her hand against the wall for support, meeting his curious gaze.

"Your bedroom and bathroom are beyond this door. Mine is this way." He pointed to another door on his right.

"So..." she hesitated. "We're sharing a living room?"

Raising his eyebrow, Casimir looked down at her. "Is that a problem?"

"No. No. Just asking," she replied as she turned the brass doorknob.

"Um... where do I get food? What do I do for three days while I'm not sleeping?" she asked, realizing she might be stuck in this suite with him. Maybe there was a library she could explore.

"Food will be brought to you. As will clothing. The attendant to this suite will help you bathe and dress. As for what you will do to keep yourself occupied. I don't care. Raine seems taken with you. You can take him up on his offer of a tour," he answered. "Anything else?"

"No, that's all. Thank you."

"Your room attendant will be here shortly as will the healer.

They'll knock when they arrive," he said before crossing the living room again and exiting into the hallway.

"Well, okay then," she muttered as she entered her bedroom and closed the door behind her.

If the living room was beautiful, the bedroom was stunning. A small balcony sat on her left, the breeze bringing in the floral scents of the garden below. Dark green curtains framed the windows and Ava paused, running her hand along the velvet fabric. The bed sat in the corner, up on a small, raised platform and was surrounded by draped fabrics and floral vines.

A small desk perched in another corner with a matching chair and a lantern dangling above. Limping to an open doorway, she passed by a reading chair next to yet another window and walked into the bathroom.

Nature had entered here too, the sunken stone tub facing open windows draped in dark green vines with vivid orange flowers. Brightly colored bottles of soaps, shampoos and oils were carefully placed along the tub's edge and soft towels hung on the bars along the wall. A robe and sage green slippers had been left for her and she sighed as she imagined herself getting clean. Though she desired to snuggle in her cozy bed, she needed to wash the remaining grime off first.

She wandered back to the bedroom and sat in the reading chair, leaning her head back, and allowed herself to doze as she waited for the healer.

31

Casimir ventured down the hallways, through twists and turns in the brightly lit pale stone castle, buzzing birds and insects flying among the flowers along the walls. He reached the royal suite, a large wing at the other side of the castle. Nodding to the guards outside the double doors, he entered.

Following the sound of laughter, he walked through the living quarters and entered the large private dining room through a doorway on the right. Seated at a table with enough room for a dozen or so people, were Thorne and the rest of his friends.

The dining room was decorated in congruence with the rest of the castle and a fireplace roared at the back of the room. The smells of roasted meats, herbs and yeast permeated the air as he joined his friends.

"Ah, Cas! You finally deigned to join us!" said Raine, lifting his wine goblet.

Casimir took a seat next to Raine and looked at him. "Drunk already?"

His friend laughed. "There are no finer wines than those made in Mosshaven. How I've missed this during our travels."

Casimir smiled and held up his empty goblet.

Raine grabbed the golden pitcher and filled his goblet to the brim, while Thorne asked from the head of the table, "I presume our guest is situated?"

Casimir took a sip. "She is. Though I don't see why you had to put her in *my* suite."

"It's because you're the scariest one out of us," said Raine. "Makes her much less likely to pull any human shenanigans."

"Human shenanigans?" Thorne asked, humor in his voice. "And what, pray tell, are those?"

Raine waved his hand. "No idea," he said, laughing.

Casimir leaned forward and started loading his plate with food. Roasted quail, meat pies, cakes, pastries, breads and bowls of steaming vegetables covered in herbed sauces sat at the center of the table.

As he continued piling on his fares, he said, "You should have put her with Quinn. She is *much* scarier."

"Well, if she sees your eating habits, she'll be terrified. Do you think you could fit *any* more food on that plate?" Quinn said.

Biting into a drumstick, he said through a mouth full of food, "Leave me alone. I'm starving."

Thorne laughed. "Welcome home. I bet you're all glad to be free of Jorrar's cooking."

"Well, I'm the only one who even tries when we travel. You lot should be thankful of my effort."

"I'm certain they are," said Thorne. "By the way, Casimir. What is that horrid thing on your face?"

Casimir paused his eating, raising his eyebrows. "My beard?"

"Oh, is *that* what that's called?"

"I just decided not to shave one day, and it grew on me."

"Literally," Raine muttered.

Casimir ignored Raine and looked back at his king. "So, *that* was interesting back in the throne room."

"Ava threatening Thorne?" blurted Raine. "I thought we were about to have a brawl."

"I could use a good brawl," uttered Quinn.

"And *I* could use a good fu—"

Casimir clapped Raine on the back, interrupting him. "Then get on with it and free us from your perverted mind."

"But bathe first because you reek," said Quinn.

"We all do," said Jorrar.

Thorne shook his head and huffed a small laugh, then responded to Casimir's earlier comment. "Ava's tenacity surprised me. I'm curious to see if she learns her lesson."

"Doubtful," murmured Casimir.

She didn't know the first thing about etiquette and their fae ways. He wouldn't be surprised if it wasn't the last time she stumbled and got herself into trouble.

"Now that we're all here," Jorrar began as he looked at Thorne. "May I ask what that was earlier, back in the throne room?"

"To what are you referring?" Thorne asked.

"When you learned her name... I noticed... a reaction."

Thorne sat back in his chair, tapping his thumb and index finger together, a nervous habit Casimir had noticed ever since they were young. Thorne was an incredible ruler, always concerned with the happiness and safety of his subjects. The opposite of his father and their former king, Vardan Everwood. But with the reintroduction of the very enemies that killed Vardan, Thorne was likely stressed as he carried the fears of each citizen. Fears that Monterre would be next.

Thorne heaved a sigh. "Since you all have been gone the last few months, I've been having these dreams." He rubbed his temples briefly before continuing. "Dreams where I'm running through a forest, trying to stop someone from something."

"Alright," said Jorrar. "And?"

"It always ends with me calling out someone's name…"

"What was the name?" Raine whispered.

"Ava."

Everyone stilled.

"What does that mean?" Quinn inquired.

"I'm uncertain." He turned to look at Raine. "What's your take on this?"

They had seers in their world, ancient beings who could see the past and parts of the future. While Raine wasn't a seer, he could often sense things others could not and had proven an asset in making decisions within the kingdom. His intuition was invaluable.

Thorne watched closely, appearing to hang on Raine's every word. "I can't feel much regarding this situation. Regarding Ava," said Raine.

"It's probably a coincidence," said Quinn. "What reason would there be for you to be dreaming of a human?"

"I don't think it's a coincidence." Raine shook his head. "Perhaps you were trying to stop her from opening the portal?"

"But what's the connection?" Thorne replied.

"This is supposed to happen. She's supposed to be here. As much as it terrifies me to know Deidamia and Andras are back in Eorhan, it feels like this is fate. We need to figure out where to go from here," Raine continued. "Besides, I like Ava."

"I do too," said Jorrar.

Casimir and Quinn remained silent as Thorne looked at both of them.

"She's okay," Quinn muttered as she crossed her arms. "I don't trust her yet though. What if she means us harm? Means *you* harm?" She looked at Thorne, concerned.

Thorne and Quinn had a long history. Their on again, off

again relationship had caused them to be protective over each other, almost to a fault.

"Cas?" Thorne raised a brow.

"She's hiding things from us," he answered. "Until we learn what she knows, I won't trust her."

"I don't think she'll hurt us," interjected Raine.

"Says the one she stabbed," Quinn replied.

"She thought we were Deidamia's soldiers taking her back to camp," said Raine. "You would have fought back too. You and Cas have sticks so far up your asses, you think everyone is a threat. Even a weak dainty human."

Jorrar interrupted, "Thorne... I think we should bring her to Nelida."

Nelida was their kingdom's greatest seer. She was a terrifying wood nymph who lived deep in the Whispering Bog. The creatures that lived in those woods weren't always friendly and it was not an easy trip, winding through treacherous mists that tried to trick travelers into getting lost.

"That's one way to scare the shit out of her," Raine remarked.

"He's right," Thorne said. "We risk the trip and take her there. This is too big to sit and do nothing."

"I agree," said Quinn.

Casimir stroked his beard. "How are we making this journey with her in tow? There are foul things in that swamp I imagine will want to taste human flesh for the first time."

"There are five of us. I think we can manage. I'll make sure to have Skye on stand-by should something truly terrible happen. She can fly us out if needed," Thorne answered.

Casimir nodded. Skye was Thorne's companion. A giant golden eagle with the ability to carry several of them at a time, who often came in handy if they had to make a quick escape.

"Great," Raine mumbled. "Am I the only one that doesn't want to see that creepy wood nymph ever again?"

"Yes," the rest of them said in unison.

"You don't have to come if you're scared," Quinn purred at Raine.

"Of course I'm coming," Raine retorted. "You'd be bored out of your minds without me to entertain you all."

"Then it's decided," Thorne stated. "After the three days of rest I promised her is up, we'll meet and prepare for our venture to the bog."

32

A knock sounded from Ava's bedroom door, startling her out of her doze on the chair.

"Come in," she said, voice scratchy as she rubbed her eyes.

The door opened and a striking older fae man with light brown skin and curly chocolate brown hair entered, carrying a wooden apothecary box with a handle on top. He wore cream-colored robes, a brown fabric sash around his waist, and his yellow eyes twinkled as he smiled at her. Small horns peered out from his mop of curls as he leaned over to set down the box near her bed.

"Hello, Ava. My name is Kai," he said, voice warm and melodic. Gesturing behind him, he added, "and this is Ivy."

An angelic doe with a cinnamon coat and white spots, looked at her with bright green eyes as it emerged from behind Kai.

"Hello," she answered, looking back at Kai. "It's nice to meet you... and Ivy."

The deer trotted over to Ava and placed her head in her lap, immediately at ease. Smiling, Ava stroked her soft fur as she looked back up at Kai. "She's lovely."

"Yes, she is. She comes everywhere with me and relishes her job as she provides comfort for my patients. I'm the head healer here in Mosshaven. I heard you injured your leg. May I look?"

Ava nodded and Kai sat on the ottoman of her chair and gingerly picked up her leg, placing it in his lap. He pulled back the shredded fabric of her pants and felt around the punctures, assessing their depth and severity.

She winced as he worked, attempting to distract herself by petting Ivy who was still nestled in her lap. "So, the head healer?" she asked. "You didn't have to come all the way to see me. You could have sent someone else. I'm sure you have more important patients."

"Nonsense," he replied. "This is important. Besides, Jorrar sent me a note about you, and I must admit, I was a little curious to attend to a human," he added with a sheepish smile.

Ava looked at him. "You know Jorrar?"

Kai smiled back, eyes twinkling again. "He's my husband."

"Oh!" she responded. "That's lovely. I like him. He was the first one who was kind to me."

"He's like that," he said, still smiling as he finished his examination. "This bite is bad. I was told he applied some ointment and was able to withdraw most of the poison, which helped, but it seems there is a little still lingering, hence the pain. It won't heal until I can extract every drop."

"Will it hurt?"

"Very much. I'm sorry. This is challenging because I don't know how our magic and medicines will affect human bodies. I need to be careful what I use, and our numbing agents might be too strong for you."

"Okay," she replied, hands slightly shaking as she continued to pet Ivy. "I guess just get it over with."

Kai hesitated, choosing his next words carefully. "I heard you may have other injuries as well... from The Scourge..."

She went still, memories of her torture at Deidamia's hands days ago still raw. "Yes."

"May I look at those? I promise to be gentle."

She nodded, gut twisting with apprehension as she looked toward the balcony, trying to hold back the tears. Her other injuries covered her body and though she wasn't keen on undressing for anyone after what she had gone through, she immediately felt safe with Kai.

Kai took one of her hands in his. "Ava, I promise not to harm you. I know you must have been through a lot these past few weeks and my sole purpose here is to help you and heal you. I am always professional."

She turned toward him as a single tear fell down her cheek, his warm hand bringing her solace. "Okay, I trust you."

A knock at the door sounded and Kai rose. "Just in time," he said as he opened the door and an older fae woman walked in, followed by a couple of other staff wheeling in a portable bed. They locked the wheels into place in the center of the room and left as Kai turned to Ava. "This is Cirilla, your attendant. She will bring your food, help you bathe and dress and get anything else you need."

Cirilla was shorter than most other fae. She had shoulder length golden brown hair peppered with gray, pinned back on the sides, and deep brown eyes.

"It's nice to meet you," Ava said.

"You as well," Cirilla answered curtly, as if she was unsure about waiting on a human. "Is there anything I can get you right now?"

"Umm... I don't think so," she answered. "I am a little hungry, though."

"There's already food being prepared. I'll bring it to your room when it's ready."

Kai turned to Cirilla. "Can you help her bathe while I set up my workstation? We also need tea with honey, cinder bark and mountain flower."

Cirilla nodded as Kai turned to his apothecary box and opened it.

"Come," she instructed as she disappeared into the bathroom and began to fill the tub.

She limped after her attendant and slowly undressed. Cirilla walked over to help her, and Ava paused.

"Nudity isn't taboo here, girl. I don't even notice bodies; I just do my job."

"Okay..." answered Ava, reluctantly. It had been easier in the dark forest with Quinn. But for some reason her insecurities were now making themselves known as she prepared to undress in front of yet another stranger.

She helped Ava pull the tunic and pants off, careful as the material brushed her leg. She then turned toward the tub and poured some oil into the water. She pointed to the collection of bottles along the tub's edge and explained their uses. "Hair. Body. I'll return with your tea soon."

"Thank you," she replied.

Cirilla left the room and Ava made her way to the sunken tub. She walked down the couple of steps and sighed at the instant relief as the hot water caressed her skin. The smell of oranges and rosemary hit her nostrils and she inhaled deeply as she settled into the water, humming to herself.

She scrubbed her scalp, enjoying the feel of the shampoo as her muddy hair turned from stained brown back to its light strawberry blonde. After washing her body, she climbed out of the tub, dried off, and wrapped the robe around her. A comb had been left on the counter near the sink and she thoroughly brushed through all the tangles, her scalp sore after minutes of pulling.

Ava padded back to the bedroom. Kai had pulled over the small desk to sit next to the bed, creating a makeshift table to host his tools as he worked. The apothecary box atop it was wide open, revealing a set of drawers and shelves stuffed with balms, tinctures and herbs. The bed had been lowered and Kai was leaning over and adjusting the back, allowing Ava to sit up.

"So, how does healing work here?" Ava asked, breaking the silence. "Do you use magic or medicines like those?"

"Both. Not many earth fae can use healing magic on others. Those who can, are trained to utilize both. The combination of magic and natural herbs is a powerful one. Especially here in this kingdom where we rely on plants so heavily."

"Is it different in other kingdoms?" she asked.

"A little. Some kingdoms trade with us for healing balms and other supplies. Others have their own magic or abilities. The fae of Caelestia have powerful healing magic and do not use other methods," he explained. "Do you think you can manage getting up onto this bed with your leg?"

"Yes," she replied.

"I'm so sorry, but you'll need to disrobe. There are blankets here you can use to cover yourself. I will only uncover the part of your body I am working on, is that okay?"

"Yes."

Kai headed to the door to the living room. "I'll wait out here for a little bit. Take your time."

Alone in the room, she limped over to the bed and removed her robe, tossing it onto the chair, and lifted the blankets before sitting down.

The bed was comfortable, with a soft cushioned mattress that smelled like chamomile and cradled her aching muscles. She slowly swung her legs up and covered herself, awaiting Kai's return.

CASIMIR WALKED THE HALLS, heading back to his suite after the long meal with his friends. Jorrar walked beside him, visibly eager to see his husband. Both men remained quiet, pondering over the plan that had been finalized regarding their venture to the Whispering Bog.

Kai was seated on one of the couches when they entered the suite, quietly watching the fire. The moment he noticed Jorrar, his eyes lit up and he leapt to embrace his husband, tears in both of their eyes.

Jorrar leaned back and wiped away Kai's tears before kissing him deeply, pulling him close as Kai's arms wrapped around his neck, deepening the kiss further.

Jorrar ended the kiss, looking at his husband with adoration as he brushed a stray curl from Kai's face. "I missed you."

"I missed you too." Kai smiled, meeting his stare.

Casimir shifted on his feet, question on his lips but reluctant to interrupt his friends' reunion. He'd always admired the gentle way Jorrar and Kai were, how they loved and honored one another and always took care of each other. He had to admit, he was a tad jealous. Though he often denied it, deep down he wanted what they had. A love so deep and passionate that nothing could topple it. They would go to the ends of the earth for each other, and Casimir longed for that.

Kai let go of Jorrar and held his hand instead, turning toward Casimir. "Hey, Cas."

Casimir smiled. "Nice to see you, Kai."

"I assume you both want to know how Ava is faring?"

Casimir nodded.

"Not much to tell yet," said Kai. "Her leg is bad, but I can heal it. I haven't had the chance to assess her other injuries. I'm about to do that now."

Jorrar looked disappointed and turned to Kai. "I guess that means you won't be home any time soon."

"I'm sorry, dear. I'll return home as soon as I'm finished. It may be a few hours."

"It's alright. A healer's work is never done. I need to bathe anyway." Kissing Kai on the forehead, he added, "I'll see you at home later." Then walked out the door as he waved a quick farewell to Casimir.

Casimir turned to Kai. "I need to clean up as well. I'll leave you to your work."

"ARE YOU READY?" Kai asked through the door as he cracked it wider.

"Yes."

Opening the door fully, he walked back into the room and closed it softly behind him, then headed to the desk full of supplies.

Back turned, he said, "I'd like to work on your leg first, then we can assess the other injuries. Does that sound good?"

"Fine," Ava replied. Barely able to get words out, she quivered slightly, losing grip on her ability to tamp down the trauma.

Having someone inspect her body, truly assess her injuries, was more difficult than she thought it would be. The healers at camp had been quick and most of the time she had been unconscious. But for Kai to spend what she expected to be a significant amount of time treating her wounds had her shaking involuntarily. The last time people touched her, it wasn't out of kindness.

Kai turned around, noticing her trembling and leaned down to gently grab her hand. "You're okay, Ava. You are safe here. No one will hurt you."

She gave him a wan smile.

Kai let go of her hand and reached under the table to crank

it back to the working height, then released a contraption to elevate her leg.

A light knock sounded, and Ava looked up, facing the door. Kai cracked the door open, assuring Ava's privacy. She heard Cirilla's voice and then Kai carried a tray of hot tea into her bedroom, setting it on the desk next to his supplies.

Handing her a teacup, he said, "Drink this. It has a light sedative effect and will help you relax. It won't do a lot for the pain, but it will keep you warm and less anxious."

"Thank you," she replied as she grasped the white porcelain in her still shaky hands.

The tea smelled amazing. It had a floral scent reminiscent of roses and jasmine, with a touch of honey. It tasted even better and Ava sighed as it warmed her body immediately, muscles relaxing and her stomach calming down.

"Ava, I'm about to begin. I will walk you through each step along the way. First, I'm going to clean your wounds to prevent infection," he said, reaching for a bottle with a blue liquid and a large cotton ball.

Deciding to distract herself with conversation, she asked, "Do you have any tips for winning the group over?"

Kai poured the liquid onto the cotton ball and dabbed each puncture, vigorously cleaning them out and causing Ava to wince.

"Getting them to like you?"

"Yeah." She flinched again, gritting her teeth. "I want them to like me."

As the words left her lips, she realized she truly did. She wanted them to like her. And not just because she was lonely and lost, but because she liked them. For some strange reason, she felt comfortable around the group, as if her soul was awakening upon arrival to Mosshaven. Was her heritage recognizing its homeland and its people?

"Sorry, that was a deep one," he said before continuing.

"Jorrar and Raine are easy. They both like you already, I'm sure. Though maybe don't stab anyone again."

She grimaced. "I didn't know who they were. I was scared."

"I know. We heal quickly so Raine was fine. Just don't expect him to forget it. It will be added to his repertoire of things to tease you about."

"Great."

"Quinn and Casimir act cold but they really aren't. Quinn's very protective and wary."

"And what about Casimir?"

Kai laughed quietly. "He's loyal to a fault. He'll do anything to protect those he loves, even put himself in danger." Kai cleaned out another wound. "He can be gruff sometimes though."

"You don't say." She smiled. "And the king?"

"He has a big heart, though he comes off as harsh. Protecting Monterre is his top priority. Just be yourself," he said. "And maybe don't threaten him again. He doesn't tolerate that well."

"You heard about that?"

Kai laughed. "Word travels fast."

"Wonderful," she huffed.

Keeping the conversation going, Kai asked, "How did you get to Eorhan?"

"I'm not ready to talk about it," she said, gazing off toward the balcony as her mind went to Eleanor. She tried focusing on the little birds buzzing about each flower to ground herself and stave off the anxiety. A trick her mother taught her whenever her fears attempted to take over.

"Pick an object in the room, Little Bird," she'd say. *"Focus on what it looks like. Focus on the rest of your senses too. What do you smell? What do you hear?"*

So Ava did. Watching the hummingbirds and listening to the buzz of insects searching for their meal among the flowers helped her refocus and calm her beating heart. She inhaled the floral notes of the tea as she tasted its honey-like flavor.

Ivy still dozed on the floor, an ever-calming presence in the room, as Kai finished cleaning the last wound. "You don't have to talk about anything you don't want to," he replied. "Just know I'm willing to listen, should you need an ear. Not all healing is physical. Eventually, you'll have to talk about the things you've been through."

She remained silent as she mulled over his words. Like with her mother's death, she knew she was shoving down the events of the last few weeks. Her betrayal, her torture. Being lost in a city with people she didn't know. Eleanor's death. But she wasn't ready yet; needed more time before she processed. She'd never been any good at talking about her traumas, leaning more toward withdrawal and silence. When her mother died, she'd just thrown herself deeper into work, trying not to think about the giant hole in her heart.

"Now, I need to extract the poison. This is the part that will hurt. A lot," he said, placing his hands on her leg. "Take another sip of tea before we begin."

Ava gulped more tea before setting the cup down on the table within arm's reach. Taking a deep breath, she grasped the blankets. "I'm ready."

Kai closed his eyes and Ava nearly passed out from the pain, a scream leaving her lips, her ability to silence herself gone.

Casimir lounged in his bathtub with his eyes closed, done washing but relishing in the warmth as it soothed his aching muscles. His body was littered with scars from years of battles and training, but it didn't bother him. They felt like badges of courage, as if he had proven to himself he was not a coward.

It was now quiet after several minutes of Ava's screams resounding throughout the suite. He knew how painful the poison extraction was. He could barely suppress his own scream when he was bitten and couldn't begin to imagine how painful it must be for a human.

He rose from the tub, water dripping down his muscled body, grabbed a towel and dried off before heading to the wardrobe in his bedroom. His bedroom mirrored Ava's, but while hers was clean and free of dust, his was a disaster. It wasn't technically dirty, the housekeeping staff cleaned, dusted and made his bed daily, but it was messy. Books and papers were strewn about, covering the surface of his desk and there was a large worktable in the corner where he whittled his wooden figurines. Wood shavings littered the table and every tool imaginable sat in piles, while his creations decorated his room. Birds, deer, rabbits, and other creatures of the forest added a whimsical touch to the space.

He donned a casual pair of brown trousers and a white tunic, leaving his feet bare. After combing his damp hair, he went into the living room in search of a book. It was getting late and, exhausted, he planned on reading for the rest of the evening until he decided to go to bed.

The door to the suite opened and Cirilla entered with a tray of food. She was flustered, hurrying through the suite.

"What's wrong?" he asked.

Cirilla had been his attendant for years and while she was amiable, she had a no-nonsense way about her he admired. It reminded him a little of his mother.

"I'm sorry general, but I've been requested to help in another suite. It seems one of the attendants is *sick*," she replied, irritated.

"I'll take it. You go help them."

She handed him the tray, bowed her head and left, grumbling about lazy staff and their unwillingness to work when they felt the least bit tired.

Balancing the tray on one arm, he opened the door and walked into Ava's room. He made it not even four steps in before he froze, locking eyes with her. She was lying on her stomach, completely nude save for the blanket covering her from the waist down, and her sea glass green eyes were filled with tears. His eyes moved to her pale back, where he saw countless wounds that looked as though she had been whipped and her ribcage was more visible than it should have been, evident she had been starved during her imprisonment.

"I... uh... sorry," he stammered, making eye contact again.

Kai looked up. "Hey, Cas. You can put the tray over there." And nodded to the side table next to Ava's bed.

"Oh, yes," he replied and quickly walked over and set it down. Walking back to the door, he looked at Ava's back one last time. "Is that what they did to you?" he whispered, unable to stop the question.

She sniffled as she responded, "Yes... and then some."

He clenched his fists and replied, "I'm sorry." Not knowing what else to say. He turned on his heel and left.

Dammit, Cas. He chastised himself.

Locating the book he wanted, he grabbed it off the shelf and walked back into his room, running his fingers through his hair. He wasn't thinking when he barged in there. Forgot she was lying there, vulnerable on the table, in a world she didn't know. Seeing those wounds covering her body had infuriated him. Though he didn't even know her, something deep and carnal awoke and he wanted to hunt down The Scourge and listen to his screams as he cut him up slowly.

Piece by piece.

Ava's heart raced as she lay on the table. Casimir had barged in, mumbled something about food, asked about her injuries, and awkwardly left.

"What was that about?" she asked Kai.

"I have no idea."

But it wasn't just that Casimir was speechless. His demeanor had changed when she confirmed her injuries were a result of her torture. His face had filled with rage and he had clenched his fists as he walked out. As if he was bothered by someone hurting her.

"I'm finished," Kai interrupted her thoughts.

Kai walked back over to his table and packed up his supplies. "You did well. I'm leaving two things here for you to speed up the rest of the healing process. One is an oil; place four drops in your bathwater every day and stay in the bathtub for at least ten minutes. Afterward, rub this salve all over your body."

"Thank you so much." She looked at him. "You've made me feel safe here."

"You're so welcome," he said, squeezing her shoulder. He picked up his wooden box, Ivy following him after stopping to let Ava pet her one last time and opened her door. Pausing, he turned to her. "If you need anything else, send for me or find me in the medical wing. And remember, we've all been through horrors due to this never-ending war," he added, eyes sad. "If you ever need to talk about yours, we will listen. It was nice to meet you, Ava."

"You too," she whispered.

Alone now, she climbed off the healing bed. Though she still had quite a limp, her leg was already feeling better as were the rest of her injuries. A light ivory nightgown had been placed on her bed, and she pulled it on over her head. It had thin straps and reached to just above her knees. She caressed the delicate fabric, glad to be in something clean for the first time in weeks.

She was about to settle into her bed and devour the whole tray of food sitting on her side table, when something sprang into her room from the balcony.

"Luna!" she cried, hobbling toward the cat. Her companion had remained hidden for the last few days. "Where have you been? I missed you."

Luna jumped onto Ava's bed, regarding her with her lilac purple eyes. *I've stayed close but I can't be seen yet. Not until they know who you are.*

"Okay. I understand. Will you at least visit when you can?" Ava asked, realizing how truly lonely she felt. Luna was the only piece of home she still had with her, which was ironic since she wasn't even supposed to be there.

I'll stay the nights with you.

"Okay." Ava smiled and climbed into bed, rubbing the cat's soft head and put some pillows behind her back to prop herself up.

She leaned over, grabbing the tray of food, and set it before her, legs crossed as she sat on her bed. Her stomach growled as she inspected her meal. It looked delicious. Roasted quail, root vegetables with an herbed sauce, potatoes covered in butter and spices, a fluffy roll and a small fruit-filled pastry were piled upon the plate. There was also a goblet of wine, and she took a sip, savoring the tannins.

When her stomach felt like she couldn't handle any more, she placed the tray back on her table and settled under the covers. Luna was already asleep at the foot of her bed, a comfort she didn't realize she needed.

The blankets wrapped her in their warmth, and she laid her head on the pillow, relaxing. The soft sounds of nocturnal insects and birds floated through the windows as a light breeze rustled the vines hanging around the room, lulling her quickly to sleep as Luna snoozed at her feet.

33

*A*va slept off and on for almost two days. She would awake for brief moments to see to her needs, take a bath and apply the balm Kai had left, and wolf down the tray of food that was always left for her. Then she'd crawl back under the covers and lose herself to exhaustion once more. Luna kept her company whenever she could but was now hiding as Ava emerged from her bathroom, Cirilla waiting to help her dress. Raine was taking her on the tour this morning.

"Off with your robe, girl." She waved her hands.

"Okay."

She walked to the bed where Cirilla had laid out her clothing and took off her robe. The attendant handed her a cotton shift she pulled over her head and helped her don the rest of her outfit. She wore an ivory shirt with long sleeves that puffed near her forearm before the cuffs cinched around her wrists. The shirt had a leather tie below her collar bone, the small gap showing a hint of cleavage, something she was pleased to realize had not completely disappeared despite her starvation, and there were green leaves embroidered around the hem of the sleeves.

Cirilla helped her slip on an ankle length mahogany skirt that flared slightly at the base and was embroidered with matching leaves along the hem. She cinched Ava's waist with a wide leather belt and then asked her to sit on the bed and handed her woolen stockings and brown boots that Ava donned quickly.

She gestured to a stool seated in front of the full-length mirror. "Sit. I shall do your hair."

Standing back up, she walked over to the stool and sat down, Cirilla behind her. She brushed Ava's hair as she spoke. "Did you get enough rest?"

"I think so. I feel much better."

"Kai is very talented," her attendant replied.

Ava regarded herself in the mirror, touching her fingers to the fading bruise on her cheek. It seemed Kai's balms and magic had erased most of her bruising, leaving faint remnants of her injuries which should disappear in a couple more days.

"So... do you like it here?" Ava asked. "Do you enjoy your job?" She felt awkward having someone wait on her and didn't know how she was supposed to act.

"It's an honor to be a staff member here. We're paid well and treated even better," Cirilla explained.

Ava relaxed at her answer. She didn't like the idea of poorly treated servants waiting on her hand and foot.

Cirilla finished her hair and left the room. Ava rose and stood in front of the mirror, evaluating her attire. It was strange dressing like someone out of a history book, but she admitted she looked pretty, and the clothing and shoes were more comfortable than she had expected. Still, she noticed the weight loss she had experienced over the last couple of months. Her collarbone was too prominent and waist too small. She was happy to eat real meals and was looking forward to regaining her old body, missing the strength she felt with her athletic thighs and curvier figure.

Turning from the mirror, she walked into the living area and ran right into Raine.

"Whoa there," he said as he steadied her, gripping her shoulders. "Are you in such a hurry to see me, dear? I was just on my way to knock on your door."

She laughed. "Sorry, I wasn't paying attention."

Raine took a step back and turned to Casimir who was standing near the fireplace, dressed in a similar fashion to when she saw him the other night, except his hair was pulled back and he had his boots and weapons on as if he was headed somewhere. He nodded at her, and she smiled reluctantly back before returning her attention to Raine.

"My dear little human, you clean up well," Raine crooned. "Look at you. You look beautiful. Doesn't she look fantastic, Cas?"

Meeting her eyes, Casimir answered. "You look nice."

"Thanks," she said awkwardly.

"Well, if you need anything," Casimir said, turning to Raine. "I'll be in the training ring."

Raine walked toward the dining table covered in food while Ava followed. "You're kidding, Cas. We've only been back a couple of days and you're already training? You're allowed to take breaks, you know."

"Deidamia doesn't take breaks," he said as he left the suite and closed the door.

Raine pulled a chair out for Ava. "Please, sit. I swear he would train himself to death were it possible."

Ava sat down. "I take it he's kind of an overachiever?"

"You have no idea."

Ava looked at the fares arranged on the table before her. There were mounds of eggs smothered in a cream sauce, bacon, sausages, and small round yellow and orange fruits she had never seen before. There was also a large platter of fruit-filled pastries dusted with powdered sugar. A rainbow of flavors, the sights and smells had her stomach growling, and she couldn't wait to dig in.

"Help yourself. I heard you've been asleep for almost two days. I'm sure you must be starving," said Raine as he loaded his plate.

Ava smiled and piled a heaping scoop of eggs, followed by bacon and fruit on her own plate. "This looks amazing. Thank you."

"Don't thank me, I'm not the chef. However, those pastries are from my sister, Fanya's, shop. We'll swing by and introduce you."

He poured her a cup of tea and she sipped it, humming with pleasure as the floral notes danced over her taste buds. Birds chirped as they darted among the flowers on the open balcony and the sound of running water trickled outside.

"How do you like it here?" Raine asked, interrupting her thoughts.

Ava smiled. "This city is stunning."

"It truly is. Do you have people waiting for you back home?"

Her smile faded. "Not anymore," she whispered.

A tear fell and she wiped it away quickly. If he noticed, he didn't comment on it. She took a bite of a pastry. Flaky and sweet, it was filled with delicious red fruit that melted in her mouth.

Raine regarded her before softly responding. "What does that mean?"

Her heart lurched, unsure if she wanted to say anything. She took another sip of tea and set down her cup, looking off toward the balcony.

"I have no one left." She sighed. "No family. The only person I had was my friend, Eleanor."

"What happened to Eleanor?"

"She killed her." She didn't try to stop the tears this time. Let them fall, the release she needed.

"Who?"

Meeting his eyes again she replied, "Deidamia."

Raine's eyes widened. The air in the room shifted and the vines writhed, fury radiating off him at the mention of her name. "I started to fall for a man I met. And it turned out to be Andras." Raine frowned, waiting for her to finish. "They were in my world somehow." She shook her head. "I didn't know. He was in disguise and tricked me. I got my friend killed, then was captured and tortured for weeks. And now I'm here. With all of you."

She wasn't ready to reveal the rest. She would wait for the meeting tomorrow to tell them about her heritage and family, still afraid they wouldn't believe her.

Raine was speechless but had regained control and sipped his tea. "I'm sorry. That you went through all of that. That you were tricked. I would never wish Andras or Deidamia on anyone," he said as he handed her an extra napkin to wipe her eyes.

"Thank you," she replied as she wiped her face and took a breath. "You've been kind from the beginning. You and Kai and Jorrar. Thanks to all of you."

He nodded. "Thanks for telling me. I won't say anything until the meeting, I promise." He stopped and looked at her. "Just one question." He tilted his head. "Rumors say it was you who opened the portal. How?"

"They cut my hand and used my blood..." she whispered.

Raine shook his head. "That's not possible. Humans can't do that."

She remained silent.

"Look," Raine continued. "I understand the desire for secrecy. You don't trust us; we don't trust you." He tucked a strand of hair behind his ear. "After what happened to your friend, I get why you're reluctant to talk."

Ava sighed. "Yes."

"Just know while Jorrar and I are more understanding, the others don't take kindly to untruths."

"I'm not lying," she said. "I just haven't told you everything yet."

He huffed a laugh. "Well, some would consider that lying by omission."

"I'm sorry, I—"

Interrupting, Raine replied, "It's okay. Let's drop it for now. We'll know everything soon enough anyway. Now that I've made you spill your guts, let's go have fun. I want to show you the castle and the city."

She smiled with relief at the subject change. "That sounds nice."

THEY SPENT an hour wandering through the bright stone castle, Raine pointing out highlights throughout. He showed her the staff wing, the kitchens, the grand dining hall which served as the ballroom for events, medical wing, cellars for storage of food, and the library. Ava took it all in, in awe of the size of the castle despite its cozy feel. Almost every room and hallway had those open glassless windows with the flowers and vines she had seen throughout the rest of the castle. The temperature was perfect; she never noticed a room too hot or too cold. Each staff member, guard or other individual they passed were respectful, nodding at them as they strode by.

Her favorite room by far was the library. It was spacious and dark, massive shade trees blocking the sun from the open windows to prevent the books from fading. Three stories high, oil lamps flickered between the wall-to-wall bookshelves, providing a comfortable glow to read by. Alcoves were filled with plush settees and chairs, desks and tables, the perfect place to get lost in a book or conduct research. She couldn't wait to spend time in here, hoping she could find something she could actually read.

As they finished their tour of the castle, they exited out a different entrance than when they first arrived and walked down stone steps into a large garden. The garden was filled with herbs of every kind, some familiar and others she had never seen before.

"This is where the healers grow and harvest ingredients for their balms and tinctures," Raine explained.

"It's lovely." She sighed as she ran her hand along the rosemary, releasing its sharp scent.

They walked through the gardens onto a winding path opening into a large clearing. A waist high stone wall dotted with trees surrounded an open field where there were dozens of circular areas of dirt. "This is where we train." Raine gestured as they approached. "Let's go see if anyone is still out here making fools of themselves."

Smiling, Ava walked next to him as they ambled along the path on the outside of the stone wall. After a couple of minutes, they stopped before a dirt ring close to the wall where two warriors were facing off, Casimir and Jorrar.

"Be easy on the old man, Cas!" Raine jested.

Ava leaned over, resting on her elbows on the smooth stone and watched with a mix of fascination and fear. Casimir and Jorrar each had a sword and were squaring off in the center of the ring. Both men were drenched in sweat, tunics clinging to their bodies as they danced around each other.

Jorrar advanced and lunged at Casimir, swiping toward him. Casimir parried the blow and pivoted to Jorrar's side so quickly, Ava could barely register the move. But Jorrar had prepared for it, sweeping his leg at Casimir's own, throwing him flat on his back.

"I may be older, but I can still best the general." Jorrar smiled as he walked around the ring at his victory.

Casimir jumped up with a predatory gleam in his eye. He removed his shirt and tossed it aside before picking back up his sword. Ava watched as he swung it around, taunting Jorrar as if he was stalking his quarry.

"I'm not done yet," he challenged, a grin on his face.

Jorrar laughed and lunged back at Casimir who blocked his blow. They danced for a few seconds, swords ringing as they continued to swipe and parry, each blow deflected with swift precision.

She couldn't keep her eyes off the two powerful warriors, mesmerized by their strength and speed. She had forgotten how tall and broad Casimir was until she saw him next to Jorrar who was not short by any means.

Sweat dripped down his muscled back as he continued to land blow after blow, trying to enact his revenge. He turned, and Jorrar now lay on his back while Casimir looked down at him triumphantly. Some of his hair had come loose from the leather strip binding it together and was hanging in his face, framing his golden eyes. Ava's eyes crept down his chest that was dusted with hair, snagging on the scars painting his sun-kissed skin. Her gaze paused on the deep lines of muscles disappearing below his pants.

Next to her, Raine cleared his throat, breaking her from her trance and she looked up, making eye contact with Casimir, who smirked. Her cheeks burned as she looked away and up at Raine.

He was beaming down at her, delight on his face. "Like what you see, huh?"

"I... um..." she stammered, her face turning an even deeper shade as she rubbed the back of her neck.

She glanced back at the ring as Casimir approached. A gleam in his eye, he paused in front of them and crossed his arms. His rippling, perfectly toned arms. "How's your tour going?"

Raine answered, humor in his voice. "Oh, it's going fantastic, Cas. I thought Ava's favorite part of the tour was our lovely library but now I think I may be mistaken."

Ava subtly kicked Raine's shin from behind the wall. "Ouch!" he hissed as he reached down and rubbed his leg, glancing at her.

Casimir chuckled. "Well, I hope you two have a fun rest of your day," he replied, glancing down at Ava, suppressing a small grin.

She smiled back awkwardly and looped her arm through Raine's. "We sure will and it's time we get on with it," she said, dragging him away.

"Bye, Cas. Thanks for the show!" he called, as he waggled his eyebrows at Casimir.

"Oh god," she said quietly.

Raine patted her hand resting on his arm. "I'm sorry, dear. Did I embarrass you?"

They walked along the path taking them around the side of the castle and out to the front, following along a small brook sparkling as it reflected the sunlight peeking through the trees.

Ava looked at him and rolled her eyes. "You're insufferable," she said, releasing his arm now they were away from the training area.

"Cas tells me that too." He beamed. "Seems you two have something in common."

"Oh, you like to embarrass him also?" she jabbed as they strolled along.

He laughed. "I just enjoy pointing out the obvious." He glanced down at her. "Like when I notice someone eye-fucking my best friend."

"Oh my god, I was *not* eye-fucking him." She blushed again.

"Mm hm," he replied. "I mean, I don't blame you one bit. Cas is quite fuckable. With those rippling pecs and rock-hard abs. And if you even knew how big his co—"

Ava stopped and turned toward him, poking her finger into his chest. "No. There will be no fucking of any kind."

Raine grabbed her finger, lowering her hand from him and pouted. "Well, that's no fun." He placed his hands on his hips. "There's nothing a good romp in the sheets can't cure. You could use that. You're too uptight."

She froze, looking up at him, suddenly self-conscious. "Uhhh... are you—I—what?"

He laughed. "Are you asking if I want to take you to bed?"

She backed away a step. "No." She shook her head. "I just—you said—"

Raine shook his head. "You're very beautiful, but you're not my type." He resumed his walk toward town, and she turned to keep up with him. "I'm sorry. You're just too easy to fluster. Fun to embarrass." He paused. "Actually, you and Cas have that in common too."

"Great, thanks."

Changing the subject, she huffed. "Where are we going?"

"Shopping."

"How about this one?" Raine held up a forest green and brown dress, the bodice lined with lace while the skirts had layers upon layers of fabric with embroidered flowers along the hemline.

"When would I even wear that?" Ava replied.

They had been going from clothing store to clothing store for the last two hours, Raine insisting she needed a better wardrobe, and the dresses were all blurring together at this point.

"Out," he said.

"Out? Like to a party?" She fingered the fabric.

"Yes," he replied, holding out another dress. "This one?"

"They look the same." She frowned.

"They're completely different." He laughed as he set the latter back on the rack and draped the first dress over his arm and continued meandering through the store.

The shop was small and cozy. Lanterns hung from the warm wood ceiling in clusters and the walls were covered with racks of clothing. Sounds of the streets entered every time the door opened, the tinkling bell alerting the owner of a new patron.

"Are you sure this is okay?" Ava asked as they continued to look through the clothing. "I told you I don't have any money."

"And *I* told *you* I have plenty. Thorne pays us well." He picked up an ivory-colored cloak with green thread lining the edges and draped it over his arm. "Besides, if you're staying you need clothing. You don't have anything. And I needed some new pants anyway." He raised his brows at her as he grabbed a pair of boots and handed them to her. "Try these on."

Her face heated as they sat down across from each other on two leather armchairs, and she removed the boots she was currently wearing.

He watched her and then asked, "You *are* staying, right?"

"I don't have anywhere else to go," she said, pulling on one of the boots. "So, yeah. I guess I am."

He nodded. "Good."

She stood up and walked back and forth, testing the fit, and then sat back down. As she removed them and replaced them with her previous pair, she asked, "Am I still a prisoner?"

Raine narrowed his eyes. "Kind of," he lamented.

"What does that mean?"

"It means you're allowed to explore if you have an escort." He reached out for the boots she handed him. "That we don't think you'll harm anyone, but we still don't completely trust you."

"So, I'm on probation."

Raine stood up and frowned at her. "I don't know that word. Is it a human term?"

She followed him to the front of the store, stopping at the counter. "Oh. It means it's like a trial run. Like I get privileges but if I screw up, then it's back to the dungeons or whatever."

"Then yes. Kind of like that," he said as he handed the fae manning the desk their purchases. "Have these sent to the castle, beautiful." He winked at her roguishly, causing her to blush.

"Yes, Captain," she replied in her mellifluous voice, flustered.

"You're ridiculous," whispered Ava as they walked away.

"I'm friendly."

They exited the store and walked through the street, boughs of leaves rustling overhead from the afternoon breeze. Birds chirped as they darted in between their nests high above and the sounds of citizens permeated the air. Orcs, fae, goblins and other creatures Ava didn't recognize bustled about on their daily business, occasionally glancing at her with curiosity.

"So," Ava broke the silence. "If you don't know the word 'probation,' how do we understand each other?"

"Well, that's how portal magic works. When you pass through, you gain the ability to communicate in the main language of where you land."

"Are there other languages in Eorhan?"

Raine led them through a crowd of townsfolk, clustered around food stalls in a large town square. Smells of roasted meats and spices filled the air and the shouts of vendors selling their wares cut through the sounds of the city.

"Yes, but most everyone can speak High Fae which is what we're speaking now."

"That's so—" She glanced up at him. "Weird."

He laughed. "It's amazing. But there will still be some words we won't know. Like pro—pra—"

"Probation." She laughed. "That is not a difficult word."

"Maybe not for you," he teased. "Are you hungry?"

"Starving."

He led them to a stall where a hobgoblin who reminded her of Remy was selling a variety of foods. Heart aching at the reminder of her friend, she smiled at him as Raine approached and ordered something she had never heard of and couldn't pronounce. The hob handed Raine two of the concoctions and two ales and she followed him to a small iron table next to the fountain in the center of the square.

"This is called Laïbyêk," he said as he handed her the paper wrapped treat, setting their drinks down. "It's a specialty in Mosshaven."

"Thank you," she said as she unwrapped it, taking a bite. "Oh, that's so good," she moaned.

It was a savory pastry filled with tomatoes, herbs and some type of cheese. The flavors were familiar, but she tasted spices she had never experienced before, complimenting the acidity of the tomatoes and mild cheese perfectly.

"It's my favorite," Raine replied in between bites.

"So..." Ava glanced at him. "Why are you doing this?"

"What do you mean?"

"Taking me on a tour, buying me clothes... being so nice to me..."

He tilted his head and scrutinized her. "Because I can sense things."

"Like you can see into the future?"

He shook his head. "No, not like that. I just know things, or feel them. Not always, but in certain instances."

"And you sense something about me?" She paused her eating.

"Yes." His gaze was intense.

"Like what?"

"I don't know yet. But I sense you're important to us in some way. That there is a connection we haven't uncovered yet."

She shifted in her seat as he spoke.

"Besides, you've been through so much the last few weeks... I think you deserve some kindness. And I'm nice to everyone. It's what makes me so irresistible," he added.

They finished their food and drinks and Raine stood, gesturing for her to follow. "Now, it's time for dessert."

They pushed through the crowds to the other side of the square, stopping before a quaint shop. A wooden sign hung from the front, carved with a picture of a loaf of bread. They entered the bakery and Ava was immediately hit with the smells of yeast, sugar and fruit.

Like the other shops they had explored, it was homey, decorated in warm browns with windows letting in the sunlight. Baked goods were carefully arranged behind the large counter. Cookies and cakes sat among muffins, danishes and other concoctions she could only dream of. Loaves of bread were displayed next to large fruit pies and rolls while the shelves on the walls held baking ingredients for purchase.

Someone was humming in the back and Raine shouted, "Fanya!"

The humming ceased and a stunning fae woman appeared through a door behind the counter. "Brother!" she exclaimed as she set down the tray of pastries she was carrying and rushed to hug him.

They looked so much alike, they could have been twins. She had the same platinum hair though hers was curly, Raine's blue-gray eyes and even their nose shape was identical. Her green apron was covered in flour and a bushy-tailed black squirrel with bright blue eyes sat on her shoulder, chattering as Fanya greeted them.

Pulling away she chastised him in a sing-song voice and thumped him on the nose. "I heard you've been back for almost three days, and you just now deign to visit your big sister?"

He smiled sheepishly. "Sorry. We've had things to attend to."

"More important than your family?" She placed her hands on her hips as her animal companion leapt from her shoulder and ran over to a window and perched, tail twitching.

He sighed. "No." Turning toward Ava, he added. "Ava, I'd like you to meet my *older* sister."

Fanya huffed. "Older by just a couple of years. But I'm also wiser and much more mature." She walked to Ava and pulled her into a hug. "It's nice to meet you."

Ava smiled as Fanya released her. "You too."

"So," she said, dusting her hands on her apron. "I finally get to meet the human woman everyone has been talking about."

Ava shifted on her feet. "Everyone?"

"Oh yes," said Raine from beside her. "The whole city knows. That's the problem with being in Mosshaven. The animals are terrible gossips."

"Wonderful," said Ava.

The three of them spent the afternoon chatting in between customers and Ava learned their father was a farmer and had a plot of land on the edge of town, growing most of the ingredients Fanya used in her concoctions. Ava liked Fanya immediately. She was warm and bubbly and welcomed her to Mosshaven without any reservations.

Her companion's name was Coco and she had quickly climbed up Ava's arm and chattered excitedly within minutes of them taking their seats. Raine and Fanya had been stunned by Coco's friendliness. It seemed it wasn't common for companions to warm to strangers quickly and now Aro, Sabriel and

Coco had all accepted Ava. She wondered what the fae thought about the unusual behavior of their animals, but Raine and Fanya didn't say much more about it, though Raine scrutinized her even closer than before.

As they chatted, Fanya kept feeding the two of them samples of new confections she was creating, listening intently to their feedback. By the time they left—Raine demanding his sister stop feeding them before they became sick—they had tried dozens of treats.

Fanya even insisted on sending more to Ava's room, noting her pleasure at the sweets. Ava didn't decline the gesture.

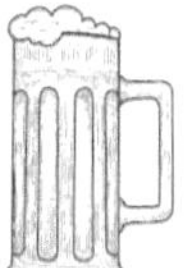

34

*A*va dragged her feet through the streets as the sun painted the town in an orange glow, turning day to night. They had been out all day, and she longed for a place to sit and something to drink. Thanks to Kai, she was feeling much better, but the exhaustion was hitting after being on her feet for hours.

She was about to suggest to Raine they find a place to relax, when he tilted his head, appearing to hear something communicated to him through his wolf companion.

He grinned at her. "Everyone's meeting at the pub. Let's go."

He picked up speed as he walked down one of the side streets and she almost had to jog to keep up with his pace. "Slow down, I'm not as fast as you."

"Sorry," he said as he slowed his stride. "I forgot you have short little legs."

She furrowed her brow. "Actually, I'm tall for a human woman. You guys are just giants."

"There are women shorter than you?"

"A lot." She rolled her eyes. "I usually towered over most of my friends. Even some men were shorter than me."

"That's…" He glanced at her as they walked. "Strange. You look dainty to me."

"I'm *not dainty.*"

"To us you are."

They turned onto another street, this one less crowded than the rest of town. Crickets sung in the shrubs and the call of a nocturnal bird pierced the night as they continued under the canopy of trees.

"So, you said everyone's going to be at the pub?"

"Yes, everyone." Raine's eyes twinkled as he looked down at her. "Even Cas."

"I don't care if he's there," she replied, looking away.

"Oh really?" he asked. "Did I imagine you lusting after him this morning?"

"I wasn't—I mean. He—" She clenched her fists as she walked next to him. "Fine. He's good looking. I can appreciate a good-looking man. It's not a big deal."

"Mmm hmm," Raine murmured, amused. "The pub's just around this corner."

"But I don't want anything. With anyone," she continued.

"Why not?"

"Maybe because the last man I fell for turned out to be a demon in disguise," she replied bitterly.

"Good point. But you'll probably change your mind eventually," he said.

Ava huffed in frustration and picked up her speed, boots sounding on the cobblestones, leaving Raine behind. She turned the corner and immediately crashed into someone.

A low voice sounded as strong hands gripped her arms. "Whoa."

It was Casimir. Arriving at the same time as them, from a different direction. And he looked devastatingly handsome in a dark tunic and pants, his unbound hair adorned with braids. Despite her insistence to Raine that she wanted nothing, her traitorous heart skipped a beat at the feeling of Casimir's hands on her arms and the way the corner of his lips tilted as he looked knowingly down at her.

"Shit," Ava backed up as Casimir let go. "Sorry, I wasn't paying attention."

"That's the second time you've done that today." Raine said from beside her, having easily caught up with her haste to get away.

"It happens a lot," she admitted.

Casimir turned to head into the pub. "See you two in there," he said, then disappeared into the building.

Ava took a deep breath and grabbed the handle of the door as Raine whispered, "Need I remind you fae have excellent hearing."

She stopped and turned toward him. "Did he hear us?"

"Probably." He shrugged and gave her a sly smile.

"I can't go in there now."

"Sure, you can," he said as he reached over her and opened the door. "Cas will pretend like he didn't hear anything. He's almost as awkward as you are." He turned her around and pushed her forward slightly. "Now let's go."

The pub was full of high fae and lesser fae creatures. There were goblins laughing and drinking with a group of orcs, while pixies darted above Ava's head. Giant golden chandeliers hung from the warm wood ceiling covered in candles, illuminating the dark space. Several bar maidens waltzed around with trays of snacks and pints, serving the full tables with a smile. There was an air of cheer about the place; everyone was laughing or dancing as they enjoyed a relaxed evening after a long day.

One wall was completely open to the outside, leading to a fenced in seating area under the trees. Glowing orbs were suspended among the branches, providing light for the area. Raine came up next to her and pointed toward the outdoor tables. "They're over there."

He led her through the crowds and outside to a long table where everyone was already seated with a drink in hand.

"Ava!" shouted Jorrar as he held up his pint, his arm around Kai. "I'm glad you're here."

"He's already drunk," whispered Raine as she sat down in an empty seat next to Kai, Raine sitting on the other side of her. "Slow down, old man," Raine said, leaning over Ava and Kai. "You gotta let me catch up."

Jorrar chuckled, taking another sip. On the other side of the table sat Thorne, Quinn, Fanya and Casimir. She was surprised to see Thorne out casually with the group, wondering if this was typical for him.

"It's nice to see you again, Ava," said Fanya enthusiastically from across the table.

Ava smiled. "You too."

Thorne scrutinized her over his mug of ale and she fidgeted at his intense assessment. "You look well rested. How are you feeling?"

"Much better, thanks to Kai." She turned to him and smiled. "Thanks again."

He squeezed her arm gently and nodded.

A barmaid arrived with two pints, setting them in front of Ava and Raine and as she was about to take a sip, a tall brooding Orc winked at Raine.

Raine leaned in. "See him?" Ava nodded. "That's who I'm going home with tonight."

She stifled a laugh and whispered harshly. "We haven't even been here five minutes and you're already lusting after a stranger and yet you gave me shit about this morning."

"What happened this morning?" Quinn asked.

"Oh," Raine answered. "Well, Ava and I were—"

Ava pinched his leg under the table. "Nothing. Nothing happened."

"You're violent." Raine rubbed his leg.

Quinn started laughing and Ava gave her a half smile. Turning away she met eyes with Casimir who was looking at her with almost no expression save for a hint of amusement in his eyes. He knew exactly what they were talking about.

Ava looked away and took a sip of her drink, almost choking immediately. "What is this?" She gasped, looking at Raine.

"It's ale, dear."

She shook her head as she noticed the others laughing at her. "That's *not* ale."

"It's made right here," explained Thorne across from her. "It's the owner's specialty."

"It's a tad dark," said Fanya apologetically. "And a bit strong."

"I'll say," Ava replied. She took another sip, wincing, but swallowed it. She didn't want to offend the owner.

Kai leaned in. "You don't have to drink that."

"Are you sure?" she whispered. "I don't want to upset anyone."

Kai nodded and then waved to the closest bar maiden. She approached, and he whispered something in her ear before she disappeared. The woman returned within minutes and set down a new pint of drink in front of Ava, smiling brightly as she disappeared before Ava even had a chance to thank her.

"I'll take that." Raine grabbed her first pint, sloshing it on the table, and took a swig, somehow already finished with his own.

Ava tried a sip of the new drink and smiled as she swallowed the sweet taste. "What is that?" she asked Kai.

"Honeyed mead," he replied. "I don't like that other stuff either."

"Thanks, it's delicious."

She sat quietly, sipping her drink as she watched the group laugh with each other. As when they were traveling in the wilderness, there was an easiness in their interactions. A closeness. They teased each other, smiled warmly and truly seemed to care. Exactly like a family, though only two of them were blood related. Though she knew they still watched her closely, not completely trusting her, she was shocked at their hospitality and quick acceptance of her into their close-knit group. Something she had always longed for.

"So..." She leaned to Raine. "How do you all know each other? Like did you grow up together, or...?"

He clapped his hands together. "Well, let's see if I can explain this long story quickly."

Hearing Raine's loud voice, the rest of the table quieted and looked at him, waiting for the story. "Jorrar and Kai have been around for... a thousand years or whatever." He waved his hand.

"We are *not* that old, Raine," countered Jorrar, playing with Kai's curls next to him.

"Yes, yes," Raine continued. "A lot of us lost at least one parent in the war. Fanya and I lost our mother when we were very young."

"I'm sorry," Ava said.

"Thank you," he replied. "Casimir lost his too and had nowhere to go. So, our father took him in and raised the three of us together."

She glanced at Casimir who was watching Raine with intensity.

"Then Quinn showed up when we were adolescents, so we all became close then. Thorne was a young king, having lost both his parents, and Jorrar was advising him as he came of age." He took a sip of ale. "It just kind of happened that way. And that's that. Our band of misfits was created."

Ava smiled at his story. Admired their devotion to each other. "My parents are dead too," she said. "I'm sorry you all had to experience that."

Everyone was watching her now and she fidgeted under their scrutinizing eyes. "What happened to your parents?" Thorne asked her.

She sighed. Maybe it was the alcohol or maybe it was the mood of the evening, but she decided to open up. "I never knew my father. The only thing my mother told me was he died before I was born. Then a few years ago, my mother died from a disease that couldn't be cured."

Raine tensed beside her and she looked at him. He was looking down at her and a realization passed over his face as if he had figured out her secret.

"Ava," he said quietly as the others watched. "Where are your parents from?"

She closed her eyes and took a deep breath, then turned toward the group. "Here."

The fae around the table were completely silent as they all regarded her with surprise.

"I knew you weren't completely human," he said, running his fingers through his hair. "I could sense it. What were their names?"

"I don't know my father's name. My mother's name was Sarah," she answered, hands shaking as she waited for their reaction.

Raine exhaled, seemingly disappointed.

"We don't know anyone by that name," said Jorrar. "It's not a fae name."

After a few moments of silence, Thorne spoke. "This is significant, Ava. We must—"

He was cut off by a scream outside the fence of the tavern.

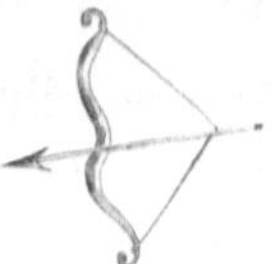

35

The group was up and out of their chairs before Ava could discern what was going on.

Raine yanked her up by her arm. "Stay close."

More screams sounded, panic ringing in the night air. Other patrons jumped from their seats and ran inside, seeking safety as they left the warriors to face whatever threat had infiltrated their quiet capital city.

A hissing sound floated toward them as the group took their positions. Jorrar stepped in front of Kai, fierceness on his face as he prepared to protect his husband. Fanya had joined her brother behind the table, standing near Ava. The four warriors and their king had drawn their swords, scanning the darkness for the source of the sounds.

Something slithered over the stone wall, glistening in the moonlight and Ava's heart picked up its pace. She'd seen this creature before.

"Raine," she whispered. "I saw those at Deidamia's camp."

It was a giant snake, silver scales luminous in the light of the moon. Casimir cursed in front of her as they watched the silver serpent slither closer, footlong fangs dripping with venom. It rose and hissed at the group while Casimir lifted his sword, bringing it down to sever its head when its tail lashed out and knocked him over.

Two more serpents crawled over the wall, racing toward the group. Quinn and Thorne lunged toward them but were thrown aside with their tails as the first snake rose and began to speak.

"We have a message," it said with a voice that sent shivers down Ava's spine.

The three warriors had gotten up and joined the rest of the group behind the table, waiting for instructions from Casimir.

"Hold steady," he said quietly.

The three serpents were now swaying and spoke in unison, their voices different. "Ava, darling." It was Andras' voice. She trembled behind Raine as Casimir and Thorne appeared, flanking her and carefully watching the serpents. "I know you can hear me, dear. Come back to us and your new friends will be spared," he crooned, his voice mixed with the hissing of the serpents. "We miss you. *I* miss you. I long to hear your screams again as The Scourge plays with his toy."

They had found her. Heart beating frantically, her hands shook as she started to back away, but Casimir put a hand on her shoulder. "We won't let them take you," he whispered with certainty.

"You're harboring a fugitive, King." The snakes now spoke to Thorne. "Release her to us and your people will be spared."

"I do not make deals with daemons, Andras," Thorne asserted. Then, turning toward Quinn whispered, "Now."

Quinn, Raine, and Thorne had been tunneling into their power while the serpents spoke. On Thorne's command, sharp vines burst through the ground, impaling the snakes through their bodies. As the monsters tried to retreat, a giant golden eagle swooped down and grabbed one of the creatures, carrying it away. Then, Raine's wolf and a black panther leaped over the wall and tore into the other two while Raine and Quinn jumped into action and severed their heads.

The snakes were gone but more screams sounded from inside the pub behind them. They all turned to the sudden chaos and one of the bar maidens ran up to Casimir and shouted, "Daemon soldiers in the tavern!"

Casimir launched into action and barked commands at the group, immediately assuming the role of fae general she had heard so much about.

"Get a team of soldiers here *now*," he said to Quinn who nodded and ran over to her panther, communicating through the animals. He then turned to Ava. "Stay behind us," he ordered.

She did as he instructed, joined by Fanya and Kai who were not trained fighters. Patrons of the tavern were screaming and running, trying to find a way out as they congregated along the back fence. Ava looked inside of the pub and froze as she met eyes with one of the daemons. He had short black hair, green eyes and a pock-marked face. It was the one who had killed that prisoner in front of her. The one whose face Ava had spit in. And when he saw the terror and recognition on her face, he sneered.

Fuck.

Ava backed up as the warriors launched into action. The daemon soldiers were outside now, and the clanging of swords reverberated as the fae faced their enemies. It was pure chaos and Ava didn't know where to look.

Raine raised green vines from the ground that wrapped around the legs of one of the daemons just as his wolf, Sabriel, jumped and clamped down on the soldier's neck, black blood painting her silver fur. Quinn unsheathed a dagger and whipped it toward another, her weapon finding purchase in his throat. Jorrar was engaged in a swordfight with a large daemon as Thorne came up behind the unsuspecting soldier and beheaded him with his sword in one smooth swipe. Though the warriors were cutting through the daemons quickly, more continued to come through the doors of the tavern.

"Hold the line!" shouted Casimir as he ducked under the sword of an advancing soldier, Aro coming up from behind and slicing the soldier with his giant paw. "Where are the rest of our forces?" he barked at Quinn.

"Almost here!"

Citizens continued to scream and tried to escape the fighting, but several were cut down by the enemy force as they pushed their way further into the fight.

"Mother have mercy," Fanya whispered beside Ava.

Ava reached down and gripped Fanya's hand as she looked at the fleeing patrons, trying to comfort her new friend. The fence around the establishment was too high, blocking their escape. Panic unfolded as she worried they'd be sitting ducks if Casimir and the rest of them couldn't control the advancing unit.

Several daemon soldiers pushed their way through and one of them closed in on a small hobgoblin, gutting him with his sword before moving on to his next victim. Ava immediately thought of Remy and without hesitation she rushed over and pressed her hands on his open wound, kneeling next to him.

"Ava!" Fanya yelled, but she didn't listen.

She couldn't just stand there and do nothing while innocent civilians were brutally murdered. Technically, she was still behind the warriors just like Casimir had instructed.

"What's your name?" she whispered as the goblin took a shuddering breath and looked at her.

"Tash," he barely got out as his whole body trembled.

"Okay, Tash. I'm here. You're going to be okay," she said. "Kai!" she shouted as she turned to where he was standing with Fanya. "Help him!"

Kai ran over, shaking his head and kneeling. "His injury's

too severe. I don't have any supplies and my magic isn't strong enough to heal him."

Ava felt the prickle of tears forming. "Please," she begged. "You can't do *anything*?"

"I can take away his pain," he said.

She nodded, sniffling as she held Tash's hand. The noise of battle sounded, shouts and screams plaguing her ears, but she tuned it out and focused on comforting the hobgoblin

"Shhhh," she said as she brushed his black hair from his face. "Focus on me. You're okay now."

Kai placed his hands on Tash and murmured under his breath. Tash's breaths slowed as his face relaxed, now free from pain. He smiled as he stared off into the distance.

"Mom?" he whispered, looking at something that Ava couldn't see.

Ava let out a sob as his breathing stilled and his eyes went glassy. She gently closed them with her fingers as Kai said a prayer to The Mother. He was gone.

Ava met eyes with Kai before searching for more injured to help. The warriors were still fighting but struggling to maintain control when a scream sounded to Ava's right and she whipped her head to the source. Fanya.

The pock-marked faced soldier had Fanya backed into a corner and was swinging his sword in his hand, taunting her. Spotting a dead daemon, Ava jumped up and grabbed the ebony dagger from his belt and bolted to her friend, ignoring Kai's warnings.

Finding an opening between his armor, she raised the dagger over her head and slammed it into his shoulder as hard as she could. He yelped and whipped around as Fanya ran to safety. When he saw who had stabbed him, he leered and yanked Ava by the hair.

"I was wondering when I'd get to play with you," he said as he pulled her toward a dark corner beneath a tree.

Ava looked around for help but there was so much chaos, she could barely discern who was who. She tried to scream but among the snarls of the animals, shouts and clanging weapons, her voice was lost in the noise.

Still holding onto her hair, he shoved her against a tree. She tried to kick him, but he dodged her attempts and put his other hand on her throat, beginning to squeeze.

"Too bad I'm not allowed to kill you," he said, leaning in close. "But Andras never said I couldn't have a little fun before I brought you back."

She screamed and clawed at his hand as his other gripped her waist, nails digging in through the fabric of her skirt. They wouldn't be able to hear her. No one would know her fate and she'd be brought back to Andras and Deidamia to be tortured all over again. He leaned in and inhaled, groaning as he continued to press her against the tree and tightened his grip; enough to hurt but not enough to completely cut off her air.

"The smell of your fear is divine," he whispered into her ear. He leaned back again and grabbed a dagger from his belt, holding it up in front of her face. "How should I play first?" he asked. "Maybe—"

His words were abruptly cut off as an arrow pierced through his throat sideways. His eyes widened and a gurgle sounded, panic painted on his face. He stumbled back, choking on his own black blood and crumpled to the ground as he clutched his wound. After a few gasps, he stilled.

Ava looked to her right and her eyes landed on Raine, bow drawn and breathing heavily with fury in his eyes. The lively humor usually on his face had been replaced by pure rage. He'd saved her life. And he barely knew her.

"Are you hurt?" he asked.

She shook her head, speechless and still shaking.

The remainder of their forces had arrived with a group of

healers and were finishing off the last of the daemon soldiers while the healers tended to the wounded.

"Come on," Raine said and led her back to where the rest of them were evaluating the aftermath. "Thanks for saving my sister," he said.

Still in shock, Ava gave him a silent nod and he joined the rest of the soldiers who were cleaning up.

The battle was over, the sounds of weapons and shouts replaced by orders being given and moans of the injured. Dead daemon soldiers lay everywhere, along with half a dozen tavern customers who hadn't been able to escape or fight back. Healers in robes walked through the aftermath, checking on each victim and assessing their wounds.

Ava's chest tightened as she took in the scene, vision fading in and out. She tried to take deep breaths, but she couldn't, as if there was a vice around her lungs and it kept squeezing. Sweat dripped down her brow as dizziness almost overcame her, causing her to sway on her feet. She was going to pass out.

"You're having a panic attack," said Kai, appearing beside her. "Sit down." He pulled a chair out. "Put your head between your knees and try to slow your breathing."

She did as he instructed. Voices sounded faintly around her, the murmurs and gasps of citizens reacting to the battle. Someone was giving orders on securing the city and disposing of the daemons' bodies. But she couldn't hear it clearly, like she was in a tunnel as she continued to try and take deep breaths.

They knew where she was and had sent creatures and soldiers after her. She thought she was safe in this city, but she was wrong. She wasn't safe anywhere. And now her presence put their lives in danger as well.

Minutes later, breathing under control she sat up, wiping away her tears. Kai was squatting beside her with a cup of tea and handed it to her.

"Here. This will calm your nerves."

"Thanks," she said, her voice quiet as she took the tea with still shaking hands.

The bodies were being dragged off by soldiers and Thorne was speaking in hushed tones to Casimir, Quinn and Jorrar. She took a sip of tea and watched the group.

Thorne walked up to her, covered in black blood. "Are you alright?"

"I—I think so." She looked up at him. "Are you?"

"I'm fine. None of us are injured."

She sighed with relief.

"We're meeting in the morning," he reminded her.

"I know."

"No more secrets, Ava," he said, voice stern. "You must tell us everything."

"I will," she promised, looking at him.

"Casimir will escort you back to the castle. Get some rest." He left and joined the others.

She wanted to apologize. To beg for forgiveness for putting this whole city in danger. For bringing back their enemies and re-opening this war. Though she'd only been with the fae over a week and in Mosshaven a couple of days, she was already falling in love with its people. With the way they accepted her without question, with how they cared for their city and each other. She wanted to say she was sorry, but her shame was too great, and the words wouldn't come.

Casimir walked over to her. "Let's go."

She rose and followed him through the pub into the street, the others not acknowledging her departure as they busied themselves with cleaning up the mess. They walked silently next to each other, Casimir on alert for any more potential danger.

She shivered and crossed her arms over herself as they walked, the night breeze blowing hair loose from her long braid. Casimir's boots echoed, and a small waterfall trickled in the distance. The streets were almost empty, most of the citizens holed up safely in their houses.

Casimir glanced at her several times before breaking the silence. "Are you okay?"

"Not really," she responded, looking ahead.

He hummed in acknowledgment but didn't speak further as they reached the castle at last. She thought she could feel anger coming from him and knew he was likely furious the daemons were able to infiltrate the city under his watch. What she wasn't expecting was anger directed at her.

They entered the suite and Casimir immediately ordered her to sit. She plopped on the couch and looked at him, hands in her lap as he paced in front of her.

He stopped and turned to her. "How long have you known?"

"Known what?"

"That you were fae."

"Not long. I had suspicions but confirmed it when I was at the camp."

"So..." He rubbed the back of his neck. "When we found you, you knew?"

"Yes."

"Why didn't you say anything?" he asked, voice sharp.

She laughed. "You're joking, right?"

He narrowed his eyes as he stepped closer to her. "I don't joke."

"Ha," she scoffed. "Sure. Whatever. You never would have believed me."

He was silent.

She slowly stood and faced him. "See? You wouldn't have."

"I don't like secrets," he said, towering over her.

She held his stare, willing herself not to look away. "I don't plan on keeping any more. I'm going to tell all of you everything in the morning."

"You have to, Ava. Lives are at stake," he said, furious. "What happened just now at the tavern. That is just a *taste* of what this war will bring."

"I know," she whispered.

"But you don't know," he continued. "You have no idea because you've never been in a war. You know nothing."

She tried to keep her face neutral as Casimir chastised her. She knew he was likely reacting to the horrors they had just escaped and was taking it out on her.

"I'm sorry, Casimir. I—"

"Get some sleep," he interrupted as he turned and disappeared into his room.

Ava ran her hand over her face as she slumped onto the couch and tried to comprehend the reality of what transpired that night. How quickly the evening had gone from laughter around the table to screams and death.

Casimir was right. She knew nothing of the horrors of war.

36

*A*va was dressed in an outfit of sepia pants, a matching long-sleeve top with embroidery along the high collar, and tall brown boots. She wore a leather belt with a small pouch and a sheath for a dagger. After tightly but intricately braiding Ava's hair down her back, Cirilla had helped her into a forest green cloak with a hood like the ones the fae wore when she had first encountered them.

Ava had barely slept last night, mind racing with all that had happened at the tavern. She couldn't stop seeing the hobgoblin die, the fear on Fanya's face, the soldier collapsing as Raine killed him. Luna had crawled close and nestled next to her, trying to provide comfort but even her dreams were full of horrors.

Ava reached for the door to the living room and took a deep breath before opening it, hoping Casimir wasn't still angry with her.

"Morning," Casimir said flatly when Ava exited her bedroom. "Let's go."

He turned on his heel and led Ava to the door exiting the suite.

"Morning to you too," she mumbled as she followed him out the door. "Not even time for breakfast, it seems."

He paused in the hallway and turned toward her. "Did you say something?"

She looked at him and shook her head. "Nothing."

Normally, Ava was a morning person. She enjoyed waking up early and sipping her coffee on the porch before she got started with her day. But she was exhausted and desperately wanted to sleep in, not realizing they would be convening so early.

Now they were off to the meeting, where she was about to tell them everything that had happened. Trying to tame her racing heart, she was equal parts hopeful and terrified. Would they judge her for being manipulated so easily? Would they blame her for their re-ignited war? Would she finally figure out who her parents were?

Casimir strode down the halls and she jogged to keep up with him. She noted his leather armor and matching cloak. "Why are we dressed this way? Are we going into battle or something?" she asked as she glanced at the sword attached at his hip.

"Or something," he replied, not slowing down.

He remained silent as they made their way through the hallways, headed toward the dining hall where they often held their meetings. Where was the swagger when she caught him training? Or his awkward stammering when he had accidentally walked in on her healing session? One moment he was charming, funny even, the next he was cold as if he couldn't stand to be in her presence. It baffled her. Frustrated her.

They reached the doors to the dining hall, the guards opening them as they entered. Everyone else was already seated at the table. Thorne at the head with Jorrar and Raine to his right, an empty seat between them, and Quinn to his left.

The dining hall was just as large as the throne room. A long table took up the center of the space, lit by dozens of candles hanging from an iron chandelier shaped like gnarled branches. Vines climbed the open-air windows as a hint of pink painted the sky while the sun prepared its greeting. Neon green hummingbirds with long tails were already zipping through the yellow flowers along the windowsills, filling their bellies full of nectar.

Ava gave Raine an awkward smile and took the empty seat next to him. There was an air of anticipation hovering in the room, and she bit her lip as she fidgeted with her hands in her lap.

"You're late," said Thorne as Casimir took his seat directly across from Ava.

"She took too long getting ready." Casimir nodded toward Ava.

She opened her mouth to argue, but Jorrar put his hand on her shoulder and shook his head, so she sat back and silenced herself, heart racing.

Thorne cleared his throat before speaking. "Ava," he said as he turned to her. "After last night, we must know everything. Start at the beginning and do not leave anything out."

"Alright," she said.

She told them about moving to the farm after inheriting it from her grandfather. About how she and her mother had moved around as a child, seemingly running from something. She described her mother's magic and how they kept everything from her. Then she explained the strange things occurring including the figures, the journal and the book. She also told them about her dreams of the tree and someone calling her name. They all tensed when she said this and she stopped, looking at them. "What?"

"I was having dreams as well," said Thorne. "Dreams of running after someone. Then I would shout her name, calling after her."

She went still, looking into his eyes. "What was her name?" she whispered.

"Ava."

She shook her head. "Are you sure?"

It was him. The voice from her dreams her mother urged her to find. It had been the king this whole time.

"I'm positive," he spoke as he looked around the table. "Please, continue. How did you end up in Eorhan?"

She readied herself to tell them the part she dreaded most. "When I was living on the farm, I met a man..." she glanced at Raine for support, and he nodded, encouraging her to continue. "His name was Henry... at least that's what he told me... and he... I don't know, I started to fall for him..."

"We don't care about your love life," Quinn interrupted. "Get on with it."

Raine bit back at his friend. "Let her finish."

The rest of them tensed, watching Raine with surprise as Quinn glanced at him with irritation before looking back at Ava.

Ava fidgeted with her cloak and stared at the table, unable to look at them as she spoke. "Like I said... I was falling for him, and then he... He wasn't Henry anymore. He was Andras."

Ava paused, glancing around the table. She could feel the tension at the mention of Andras' name. "He had tricked me. There was a portal on my property, and he had tricked me into leading him there. Into finding the book and the map. And someone else was there with him..." She took several breaths, tamping down her panic before continuing. "Deidamia."

"Shit," someone muttered.

"They kidnapped me, cut my hand open, and used it to open the portal. Then they shoved me through and held me prisoner. Eventually I escaped and then ran into you all."

The table was silent, no one sure what to say or how to

react. "I'm sorry," she added. "So sorry. I didn't know who they were. I didn't know..." she whispered.

Quietly, Casimir whispered from across the table, "Bullshit."

She looked up at him. "What did you say?"

"I said that's bullshit. You're sorry? You're responsible for leading our enemies to our gates and you're *sorry*?" he seethed.

"Cas..." Raine attempted to interject.

"I was tricked."

Cas leaned forward. "Tricked? You were blinded by your lust. By your own pride."

"I was *tortured*. For weeks! You think I wanted that? Accuse me all you want, tell me I'm stupid and naïve, that you loathe me, but there is nothing you can say to me I haven't already said to myself."

"Oh please," Casimir continued. "You want us to feel sorry for you? The poor woman that got mixed up in that which she doesn't understand and may be responsible for thousands of deaths?" He narrowed his eyes. "Those daemons came for you last night. They endangered the whole city."

"Enough," Thorne's voice boomed through the dining hall. "Arguing will get us nowhere. Blaming Ava doesn't change anything," he said as he looked at the group. "You all know as well as I do the armies were already encroaching on our land. We haven't been living in peace for over a hundred years."

Ava leaned back and crossed her arms, holding back tears. She wasn't going to let Casimir's words make her cry in front of everyone. Raine reached under the table and squeezed her knee in support.

Thorne sighed. "We must learn who your parents were. Can you tell us more?"

"All I know is my grandfather and mother fled to the human world while she was pregnant with me," she answered. "And I have an animal companion."

"You do?" Quinn looked at her with confusion.

"Yes. A small cat-like creature."

"Luna? I think it's safe to come out."

Okay.

Luna leaped from a window where she had been hiding on the balcony and padded over to Ava. Ava scooted back her chair as Luna climbed into her lap and scanned the table.

The group looked at her with surprise. "So, you truly are fae," said Thorne. "It's hard to believe when you look so—"

"Human," Casimir finished.

She glared at him but didn't respond.

"What's her name? How did she get to your world?" Raine asked.

"Luna. All she told me was that she chose me before I was born and followed us there. She'd basically been in hiding until I made it back to the farm."

Luna chirruped in confirmation.

The group was silent as they watched Thorne, waiting for him to say something. She looked back at Raine, seeking support, when his eyes widened as he grabbed her face between his hands.

"What?" she said.

"It's not possible," he whispered.

"What?" she asked, louder.

Standing up, he announced to the group, "You lot are idiots. I know who her parents are. I'll be right back." Then he disappeared from the room.

She turned to the rest of the table, feeling all eyes on her. "What's going on?" she asked Jorrar.

He smiled at her. "Raine has a subtle ability to sense things. He isn't a seer but sometimes things click for him while the rest of us are left in the dark."

Right. She had forgotten about that though he had told her just yesterday.

Moments later, he returned carrying a large, framed piece of art he had turned around, its back facing the group. Luna jumped from Ava's lap and sat down on the ground, watching curiously.

He walked up to Ava, scrutinizing her, and then flipped it around. "Do you recognize this person?"

It was a portrait of a woman. She had pointed ears and piercing green eyes. She was dressed in a regal gown and had a crown sitting atop her long golden hair. Ava reached out and touched the painting, tracing the lines of her face, as her eyes welled with tears.

She nodded. Her voice was barely audible as she answered, "That's my mother."

Several curses sounded from the table.

He set the portrait down and paced. "I knew it. It makes so much sense. No one ever found her body... it's possible she was pregnant... that she escaped with her father..." He was rambling now.

Ava looked at the rest of the table. They were all watching her with surprise and disbelief on their faces. "What? Someone tell me who that is."

Raine sat back down in his seat. "Look at Thorne," he said.

She turned and realized Thorne had gotten out of his seat and was standing before her.

"Do you see any resemblance?" Raine asked.

Thorne grabbed her hand and knelt in front of her with a mix of awe and surprise in his eyes.

"I—" she looked at him. Truly looked. "Our eyes—" she sputtered. "They're the same."

Thorne nodded. "The woman in that portrait is Queen Aurelia."

"Queen?" Ava asked. "Does that mean—" She couldn't look away from Thorne, his eyes boring into hers.

She knew she was about to be hit with the answers she had

been looking for all this time. Her whole life she wanted to know who she was, why her mother had magic, why all the secrets. Here she was, on the precipice of the answers, heart racing as she waited for someone to speak. For someone to tell her what she so desperately needed to know, what that great truth that had been blooming inside of her was.

He nodded as his eyes filled with tears. Letting go of her hands, he gently cupped her face. "That you're a princess," he whispered. "And my sister."

37

Sister? Thorne was her brother? The King of Monterre was her brother.

She reeled, glancing around the table. Quinn was looking at her with surprise, Jorrar and Raine were beaming, and Casimir was shaking his head as if he couldn't believe it.

Before she had a chance to speak, Thorne pulled her up from her chair into a hug, accepting her immediately.

"I've always longed for a sister," he whispered as he pulled back and looked at her again.

She smiled, looking at him. Truly looking. They looked so much alike. How had she not seen it before? Though different shades, they both had red hair and the exact same eyes. Even their facial features were similar though he wasn't as fair skinned as she and had no freckles.

"She told me to find you," Ava whispered as they looked at each other.

"Who?"

"Mom," she said as a tear rolled down her cheek. "She said to find the man from my dreams. That he would help me."

Thorne pulled her tight again. Family. She had family. Alive. As the realization washed over her, she leaned into him again as he hugged her. The room was silent as the two siblings held each other and cried. For their grief, the pain of thinking they were truly alone. For the lost years they could have had, and for the future, they cried.

Though they didn't even know each other, Ava could feel the bond deep within her. Could feel the truth being revealed as she held her brother. Her *brother*.

They released each other, wiping their tears.

"We still have unanswered questions," Thorne said and gestured for her to sit back down. With everyone seated at the table, he began. "Why are you still in your human form even though you're here? Why don't you have magic?"

Ava shook her head. "I don't know. My—our—grandfather's journal briefly mentioned a prophecy. But it didn't say anything else."

"A prophecy?" asked Raine. "We've never heard anything about a prophecy."

"Alright," replied Thorne. "Do you know why Deidamia was torturing you? Was it for information?"

"No," she said. "They were trying to induce my great tribulation or whatever it's called."

"That's horrific. I'm so sorry." Anger flashed in his eyes. "But I don't think that would have worked. Since you're technically still human..." He tapped his fingers on the table. "Anything else?"

"They wanted my blood to open more portals. To bring in more of their army but I think I needed more magic to do that."

"You wouldn't be strong enough yet to create new portals," said Jorrar. "Only activate established ones."

"Are there any more other than the one I came through?" she asked.

"None that we're aware of," said Thorne.

"So... what now?" asked Ava.

"Now we go visit Nelida," he replied.

"Who's Nelida?" she asked.

Raine groaned beside her. "She's a terrifying wood nymph in a terrifying swamp and we get to go talk to her."

"Um... is that why everyone's dressed for battle?" she asked, attempting a joke.

"Precisely," said Thorne. "Nelida is a seer. And while she is odd..." He glanced at Raine. "She isn't that bad, and she'll provide us with the answers we seek."

Pulling herself together, Ava responded, "Okay, then. When do we leave?"

"Immediately," replied Thorne.

"But what about breakfast?" asked Raine and Quinn in unison.

"Food has been packed for us. We must leave now to get there and back before dark."

"THIS IS A GOOD PLACE TO REST," said Casimir as the group walked through the woods, gesturing to a couple of fallen logs. Surrounded by trees, Ava looked around at the dense forest, birds chirping merrily in the early morning sunlight as the sound of a small stream babbled nearby.

They had been walking through the forests of the kingdom for about an hour. Before leaving, the staff outfitted them all with small satchels containing food and water and Ava was starving as she sat on a lichen covered log and opened a package from her bag containing bread, cured meats and cheeses.

Raine plopped down next to her. "Finally, breakfast," he said as he opened his own food.

They ate silently for a few moments before she asked the group, "So where exactly, does this wood nymph live?"

"The Whispering Bog," said Thorne. "We're still an hour away."

"Wow, that's not an ominous name at all," she mumbled, taking a bite of bread.

"You have no idea," said Raine.

She looked at him. "So, I take it you're scared of her?"

He scoffed. "I'm not scared. I just... she gives me the creeps."

Quinn laughed from the log she was seated upon next to Thorne. "You're a liar."

Ava looked between all of them, waiting for an explanation.

Thorne spoke up. "The first time we ventured into The Whispering Bog, we were young. There were rumors about the wood nymph who could tell you your future and, feeling brave, we desired to see what it was like."

"I told them it was a terrible idea," said Jorrar before taking a sip of water.

Thorne nodded. "He did. But we snuck out and went anyway, against everyone's wishes. We made it to the swamp, to her tree, but the moment she emerged Raine turned and ran all the way back to Mosshaven."

Casimir chuckled. "He had nightmares for months after that."

Raine shrugged. "Like I said, she's creepy."

"Don't worry," Ava said to Raine. "I'll protect you from the mean old swamp witch."

Raine smiled. "Why thank you, dainty human."

Quinn looked at her. "Can you fight? Do you even know how to use a dagger?"

Ava's shoulders slumped. "No. I took some classes to learn how to defend myself when I was younger, but they don't teach you how to use weapons."

"That's useless," said Quinn.

"I'm pretty good with a bow and arrow though," she added. "I was on an archery team when I was in my twenties and won a lot of competitions."

"See?" said Raine as he playfully patted Ava's head. "She'll come in handy after all. Besides, she killed that helwraith."

"True," Quinn admitted, then looked between Ava and Raine. "What's up with you two? Are you suddenly friends or something?"

"Yes," they replied at the same time.

Raine put his arm around her and yanked her close.

Thorne pointed at Casimir and Quinn. "You two should take a page out of Raine's book. Learn to relax and have a little fun once and a while."

"Says the king who never relaxes," quipped Quinn.

Thorne glared at her while Casimir remained silent, expression unreadable.

"Fine." Quinn sighed. "I hate to admit it... but—" she gave Ava a reluctant smile. "It'll be nice to have some feminine energy around here. It's exhausting being the only one among this group of assholes."

Ava smiled back. Had Quinn just accepted her?

"Ha!" Raine looked at her. "I knew you'd come around eventually."

"Oh, fuck off pretty boy."

CASIMIR WALKED at the front of the party next to his king. Jorrar and Quinn were behind them and Raine took up the rear with Ava. They were getting closer to the swamp filled with the treacherous mists and hungry beings who resided there.

"We need to stop soon and prepare everyone for what we may face in there," Casimir whispered.

"I know."

They continued walking through dense woods, the landscape slowly changing as they neared the territory of the wood nymph. The trees were more gnarled with few leaves, mostly draped in gray and green mosses and the ground was becoming soggier as they closed in on the watery terrain. Birds had stopped their chirping and the only sounds they heard were faint cries of the swamp creatures, calling to each other as they hunted.

He stopped and turned to the group. "We need to discuss our plan before we enter the swamp. There are beings in there that will try to trick you. They will try to lure you into the surrounding pools. They will use voices of those you love, whispers of souls long deceased." He looked around and his eyes met Ava's. She looked terrified and he felt a small pang of guilt for dragging her along into another perilous situation. "We remain in pairs and watch each other. Do not follow the voices. Stick together. The mists will try to confuse and separate us. And whatever you do, do not go into the water."

Thorne added, "Skye is on standby should something go wrong. But the swamp is not friendly to the other animals, so they had to remain behind." He turned to Ava. "Ava, you're with Casimir. Quinn, you're with me and Raine and Jorrar will stay together."

Casimir tensed as he looked to his king. "What?" he said at the same time as Ava.

"You're the strongest fighter and she's still human. You'll be able to protect her best. Stay in the center. Quinn and I will lead," he answered. He then grabbed his bow and quiver full of arrows off his back and walked to Ava, handing it to her. "Something familiar should you need it."

"Thank you," she said.

The party rearranged themselves and Thorne spoke from the front. "Let's go."

Casimir walked quietly next to Ava as they began their trek

into the swamp. The trees were completely different now, twisting together with no greenery at all and there was a pale mist snaking its way through them, getting denser the further along they went. The wet ground squelched beneath their feet as they made sure to avoid the deep pools of water scattered around them.

Thorne had tasked him to protect their princess. *Princess.* He was still in disbelief of the new revelation from earlier this morning. The human woman they had found lost in the woods, snarling and terrified like a feral animal. Bruised and beaten. This whole time she had been Thorne's sister. Deidamia had been torturing their princess and it infuriated him.

Last night he had felt some strange pull to protect her when the silver serpents showed up. Even though she exasperated him, riled him, he'd gone to her side without consideration. When she'd been cornered by that soldier, Aro had told him she was in danger. Unable to disengage from the fight he was in, he'd sent Raine to get her. Though he was still furious she had brought their enemies to their doorstep, he would guard her. Keep her safe.

The mist grew heavier, completely blotting out the sun, and made it difficult to see even a few feet in front of them.

"Stay close," he whispered to Ava.

All was eerily quiet as they continued. Too quiet. The group remained together as the mist closed in, but it was too dense and Casimir lost visual on Thorne and Quinn in front of them. When he turned, he could no longer see Raine or Jorrar either.

"Shit," he whispered.

"What?" Ava asked.

"We lost the others. Thorne? Raine?" he tried calling quietly to see if they could hear him, but no answer came through the mist.

He could smell Ava's fear as she inched closer to him,

seeking safety in his presence. He let her and they stopped, looking around for the others.

"What do we do?" she asked.

Before he could answer, a splash sounded from a pool next to them.

"What is that?" she whispered.

"I don't know but do exactly as I say. Keep your back to mine. Draw your bow and be ready to shoot, if necessary," he instructed as he drew his sword.

Her back was flush against his, muscles moving as she nocked the arrow and drew her bow. The splash sounded again, and they remained back-to-back, looking around for the source of the noise. To his left, something growled and came slithering in their direction.

It was scaly and gray, with eight legs and a long wide mouth revealing hundreds of teeth. They both turned to the creature as it scurried toward them, tail whipping as it closed in.

Casimir lunged, slicing with his sword, cutting off one of its legs but it wasn't deterred. One of Ava's arrows shot through the air, but the creature moved at the last minute and dodged it swiftly. The creature lunged again, but this time he was ready. He waited as its mouth opened and then shoved his sword into the top of its head through the open jaws. The creature collapsed, and Casimir turned back to Ava.

"We need to find the others," he said as he looked off into the mist, hoping to catch a glimpse of his friends.

He turned back to Ava. She had her bow drawn again, eyes wide and aiming at something behind him. Before he had a chance to turn around, she released the arrow, and he heard the sound hit its mark. He whipped around to see another creature like the one he had killed, only slightly smaller, lying on the ground twitching with an arrow through its eye. He raised his sword and severed its head to ensure its death.

He turned, a thank you on his lips, only to find she was gone.

Ava, the voice whispered from the mist. *Ava, honey. It's me, little bird.*

"Mom?" She followed the voice. "Mom, where are you?"

She couldn't see anything but swirling mist and vague shadows of trees. How did she get separated from Casimir? He had been right there in front of her and then he'd disappeared. Her mother's voice had sounded, and she couldn't help but follow, couldn't control her legs as they walked toward the sound, as if her body wouldn't listen.

Ava. Please, dear. Help! I need your help.

"Mom, I'm coming. Where are you?" she pleaded.

I'm over here. Hurry! They're coming. They're going to hurt me.

Panicking, she picked up her pace. "Mom! Mom, I'm coming!"

Here I am, said the voice from behind her.

She stopped and turned around, unable to discern the direction it was coming from. The voice surrounded her now, whispering from everywhere at once.

Ava! It floated around her in the breeze.

"Mom. I can't find you. Where are you?"

I'm here. I'm here!

Another voice sounded. This one younger.

Ava. What did you do? You killed me!

"Eleanor?" she whispered, heart racing.

It's your fault I'm dead! It's all your fault! The voice screamed.

"I'm sorry," she sobbed. "I know it was my fault."

The two voices continued to yell at her. One begging for help, the other screaming at her in anger. Her eyes blurred with tears as she searched the thick mist.

Lost and confused she had no idea where she was. Why was there so much fog? What was this place? She started to run, trying to get away. She just had to keep going. Had to get out of here. The voices screamed at her even louder, when she tripped and plunged into a deep abyss.

Ice cold, she couldn't breathe. Was she in water? She tried to swim to the surface, but she didn't know which way was up. She couldn't see anything in the black pool, as if the light had been devoured.

Something grabbed her ankle and pulled.

Down down down, she went.

The water pressed in on her, pressure increasing as something continued to pull her to the bottom, pulling her to nowhere.

She tried yanking away, tried to swim, tried to kick whatever it was holding her, but it was too strong. More hands grabbed her, pulling at her arms and hair and waist. She was going to die down here. Drown a horrible death and then the creatures of the swamp would devour her remains.

She couldn't hold her breath much longer. Her head felt light and body heavy. She was running out of time and exhaustion was setting in. Energy spent; she couldn't fight any more as the corners of her vision faded.

A faint splash sounded in the distance and then a soft glowing light appeared, approaching closer and closer. As the light brightened, the creatures let go, seemingly scared of this ethereal glow. Strong arms wrapped around her waist and pulled her up and up, faster and faster to the surface.

A light breeze brushed her face. Air. She could breathe. She coughed and wretched, spitting out water onto the ground as someone pulled her to the shore. Gasping, she tried to catch her breath as she lay on her back.

But she was still so tired.

"Ava. Ava, can you hear me?" a voice spoke from far away.

"Mom?" she asked, barely able to keep her eyes open.

"No, it's me. Casimir. Your mother isn't here," he said from above.

"What?" she whispered as her eyes tried to close. She wanted to sleep. She'd never been so tired in her life.

A rough hand patted her face. "Eyes on me, Ava."

"I—" She squinted but everything was still blurry. "I'm so tired," she whispered. Her body was still heavy. "I just need to take a nap."

If she could just close her eyes and sleep, she'd feel better. She just needed to rest. Her eyes became almost impossible to open and she let them close, surrendering to the fatigue.

Casimir cursed and lifted her head. "I'm sorry," he whispered as something bitter was poured into her mouth. She thrashed as it burned her throat. "You have to swallow this," he insisted, grasping her face and keeping her mouth closed. She met his eyes. He looked terrified as his voice rose. "Dammit, Ava. Swallow it. Now."

She did. The burning sensation coursed through her body. Nausea overwhelmed her as Casimir turned her on her side and she vomited. Over and over, she threw up until she didn't think she had anything left in her.

She rolled onto her back and took a deep breath, vision clearing, Casimir was still leaning over her, worry in his eyes. He brushed the hair from her face as he evaluated her for injuries.

"Are you alright? Are you hurt?"

She shook her head. "I'm fine," she said before coughing some more, trying to expel the rest of the water she had inhaled.

She looked up at him, still hovering closely above her, arms braced on either side of her body. Relief showed on his face as he realized she was alright and they maintained eye contact for a few moments, silent in the murky swamp. He searched her face and his eyes flared as if he realized something before the expression disappeared just as quickly as it had come. She reached out and touched his face, noticing he was faintly glowing.

"Are you an angel?" she asked, still slightly delirious.

He smiled and shook his head. "Not sure what that is, but no. Can you stand?"

He sat back as she slowly pushed herself up to a seated position and looked at him, taking a deep breath.

"I think so," she replied.

He got up then grasped her hand, pulling her to her feet. "Are you sure you're okay?"

"Yes," she rasped. "I heard voices. I didn't know what was going on." She looked around and wrapped her arms around herself, trembling. "What did you give me?"

"Something to make you throw up," he said. "You swallowed too much water. The swamp was still trying to take you." He looked at her. "You're shivering."

Leaning over, he grabbed his dry cloak from the ground. "Take yours off."

Fingers numb and shaking, she did as he said and let it fall to the ground. He approached her and wrapped his larger cloak around her, hugging it tightly. She looked up at him as he attached the clasp. "You saved my life."

He shrugged, as the corner of his lips lifted. "You saved mine first."

"I take it you aren't mad at me anymore?" she teased.

He crossed his arms and regarded her. "For the time being, no."

"Great." She pursed her lips, pulling the cloak tighter. "What was that a few moments ago?"

"What was what?"

"You had a strange look on your face."

He looked away, searching the mist for their party. "No, I didn't."

They were interrupted by voices approaching from the mist. Raine and the others appeared, out of breath, and halted as they saw the two of them, standing there drenched.

"Why are you guys wet?" Raine asked, the three others standing behind him.

"I decided to go for a swim," Ava answered sarcastically. "Then Casimir was jealous, so he decided to join me."

Casimir laughed quietly beside her and shook his head. Raine looked at the two of them like they had grown an extra head. "I don't get you two. This morning you were about to attack each other across the table and now you're laughing at what I assume was a recent brush with death?"

"Don't worry," she said. "I'm sure he'll piss me off again and we'll be back to fighting."

Raine shook his head as Thorne spoke. "I believe we're close to Nelida's burrow. Let's get moving.

Thorne led the way and the rest of the team followed behind him, Ava still walking next to Casimir. The group remained silent as they continued their journey through the swamp, fortunately not experiencing any more incidents along the way.

After another half hour of walking, they stopped in front of a large dead tree, bigger than all the others, with a hole in the root ball appearing to go down into the earth. Its branches twisted and curled around each other, covered in dark gray bark and the hole swallowed the light as the entrance disappeared into nothing.

"Are we going in there?" Ava whispered as she felt the sense of something powerful within the tree, as if the earth was vibrating beneath her feet.

"No," Casimir replied. "She'll come out."

Still shivering, she pulled the cloak tighter and stood in

between Casimir and Thorne while the other three stood behind them. The group stood silently, as if waiting for something to happen. No one spoke as the sounds of the swamp buzzed around them. Then, from deep in the hole, a voice sounded. It was deep and high-pitched at the same time, and it slithered across Ava's skin, leaving goosebumps in its wake.

"It seems someone is here for answers," the voice echoed.

38

A massive hand covered in gray bark emerged from the pit beneath the roots. The tree nymph climbed her way out and tilted her head back and forth, inspecting the group. She pulled her lithe body from the hole and walked toward them, earth trembling with each step of her long legs. Close to eight feet tall with bark growing from her limbs, she straightened out, snapping sounds echoing as her joints popped. Her eyes glowed green and tiny phosphorescent flies buzzed around her as she scanned the group of fae before her.

More gray bark covered her human-like face and every so often, a black beetle would dart out of her flat nostril and run to burrow back into her ear. She stepped toward the group with jerky movements, stopping feet away when her gaze snapped to Thorne who was standing at the front of the group.

"Hello King," she crooned in a voice both young and old. Male and female.

Ava backed up, bumping into Raine who steadied her and placed his hands on her shoulders in solidarity. She glanced up at him and gave him a look that said, 'I understand why you had nightmares.'

Thorne took a step forward. "Nelida. We've come to—"

"I know the purpose of your visit," she hissed as her eyes roved over Ava. "You wish to know about the prophecy."

"Yes," Thorne replied.

Nelida remained quiet, scanning the group again when her eyes landed on Raine. She smiled menacingly, her blunted yellow teeth bright against her gray skin. "I'm surprised to see you back. After what happened last time."

He remained silent, though Ava felt his hands tighten slightly on her shoulders.

Nelida stepped forward again, looking between Thorne and Ava. "You have figured out you are siblings, yes?"

"Yes." Thorne nodded.

"Your grandfather visited me over one hundred years ago, knowing he was the last living fae with portal magic in his blood." She paused, glancing at the rest of the group before continuing. "He wished to know how to defeat Deidamia. If he even could."

"But it was told Pellas was supposed to send Deidamia back. That he abandoned us."

"He did not abandon you," Nelida explained. "I told him it would not be him who could send Deidamia back to her realm and seal the portal shut forever, destroying it. He wasn't strong enough." She paused, then her eyes snapped to Ava's. "But there would be someone who was."

"Me?" Ava whispered, her worst fears confirmed.

Nelida nodded. "Aurelia didn't even know she was with child when he visited. I told Pellas and he made the decision to take your mother somewhere safe to raise you until you were ready."

Thorne looked at Nelida. "Ava still looks human. Has no magic. Is there a way to access it?"

"Yes," Nelida replied as she walked closer to Ava, wet soil squelching under her steps. Ava tensed. Nelida's rotten breath was warm as she stood over her. "But it is dangerous, especially for a human."

"How?"

"She must make the journey to the Elderoak Tree. Something that was done thousands of years ago for the fae of Monterre to be blessed with their magic." Growls sounded in the distance as Nelida continued. "It is a perilous journey that some fae did not survive."

"We've never heard of this," said Thorne. "Why?"

"That, I do not know. Past kings were not invested in the history of our kingdom. I assume there are ancient texts somewhere." She stepped back and looked at Thorne.

"What will she face on this journey?"

"I cannot tell you the details, for I do not know all of it." The snarling grew closer. "The journey is perilous, and different for each fae. No one knows exactly what happens in those woods surrounding the sacred tree." Her eyes bored into Ava's as she continued. "You will face your deepest darkest fears and secrets. Only then are you deemed worthy to be blessed by the Elderoak."

The sounds of the beasts were growing ever closer as the mist thickened and swirled around them, preparing itself to close in again to prevent their escape.

"The swamp creatures are getting restless. While I may not harm you, I cannot deny them a meal," Nelida said.

"Why are the creatures behaving this way?" asked Thorne.

Nelida backed up and spoke. "They do not want to see Ava succeed. They are glad the daemon queen is back. If she wins, they will be free to roam and devour as they please."

"Do you wish Deidamia to win?" he asked.

Nelida seemed to ponder on his question, then replied, "No... I do not wish to see my land destroyed."

Something screamed from behind them, and Ava jumped, the group circling around her, protecting their princess.

"Call your eagle, King. For it is time you leave before the beasts can fill their bellies. And they've never tasted human before." Nelida slinked back in her tree, leaving the group of fae alone in the swamp, surrounded by growls and snarls, screams and cries. Mist swirling feet away from them.

"Protect Ava," Thorne directed the group. "Skye's on her way."

Ava drew her bow and aimed in between the warriors, her shaking hands making it difficult to aim.

"Put your bow down," Casimir ordered from in front of her. "You're too scared, you'll only end up shooting one of us."

"No," she answered. "I'm going to help if I can."

"Quit being so stubborn—" He was cut off by a creature lunging at the group through the mist. The same kind she and Casimir had fought earlier, only much larger.

It jumped straight at Quinn, who was in front of Ava on her right, but she dodged it with a roll, landing in a crouch with her hands extended, aiming her magic. Roots came up from the ground, grasping the creature's legs to slow it down.

The monster struggled, but broke free as it noticed the opening left in front of Ava and charged directly for her. She screamed and released an arrow, but Casimir was right. She was trembling too hard, and her aim was off. The arrow landed feet away from the creature, almost hitting Quinn.

"You're going to get us killed!" Quinn yelled at her as Casimir shoved her behind him and she fell. Quinn had wrapped her roots around it again and the moment it was still, Casimir lunged and impaled it through the top of its head.

The creature was dead, but growls echoed as the monsters closed in. Shadows emerged from the mist surrounding them, more of the creatures taking shape as they crept closer.

"Where's Skye?" Raine shouted, raising green vines from the ground to build a temporary wall around them.

"Close!" Thorne yelled back.

"She'd better hurry," said Jorrar.

Ava was still on the ground, trembling and frozen in fear. Casimir turned toward her. "Get up," he growled.

She shook her head as she marveled at the creatures around them, tearing through the vines, ravenous eyes seeking their dinner. A cry sounded from above and Skye appeared, hovering above the group.

"She can't hold all six of us at once!" Casimir shouted.

"She can take three," said Thorne. "She'll drop us to safety and come back for the rest. Hold them off for a few minutes longer."

Casimir leaned down and grabbed Ava under her arm, lifting her up, then looked at Thorne. "You and Raine go with Ava. We'll wait for Skye to return."

"But—" Thorne tried to argue but was cut off.

"You're our king. You go with the first group!" Casimir shouted at him.

They widened their circle slightly, allowing Skye to land. Thorne quickly climbed on her back, and she rose into the air, grasping Ava and Raine around their waists with each of her taloned feet.

Ava screamed as they ascended, watching the remaining three fae get smaller the higher they flew. Bile rose in her throat as the eagle carried them over the swamp to safety. Minutes later, Skye was landing in a clearing in the woods, dropping both Ava and Raine. Thorne jumped from her back before she flew off, heading to rescue the remaining members of their party.

Ava was hunched over on her hands and knees, nausea rising as she felt someone's hand on her back. "Are you okay?" Raine asked.

"No," she whispered, breathing through the nausea and dizziness that followed.

She gathered her bearings, sat up and crossed her legs, rubbing her temples.

"Not much for flying, huh?" Raine quipped.

"Well, I've never been carried by a giant eagle before, so there's that."

Ava looked up at Thorne who was standing before her, obviously still reeling from the news. Reaching his hand down, he pulled her to standing.

"Are the others okay?" she asked.

He nodded. "Skye just arrived. They'll be here shortly."

She breathed a sigh of relief, shoulders slumping.

"Umm... guys..." Raine urged from behind them.

They turned around and looked at him. "Yes?" Thorne asked.

"Did you summon these animals?"

"What animals?" asked Ava, fearing there were more creatures they had to escape.

Raine gestured toward the woods. "Look," he whispered.

From between the trees and under the brush, creatures great and small emerged. Familiar small glowing foxes crept out from under the shrubs. Deer slowly inched their way into the clearing from between the trees while colorful birds flitted about. Butterflies appeared and danced around Ava, landing on her and then taking off again and again.

The remainder of their group landed with a thump as Skye remained on the ground beside them.

"What's going on?" Quinn asked.

"Shhh..." Thorne whispered, in awe of what was unfolding.

More and more animals came. Bears and snakes and even small insects surrounded Ava, as if paying homage to her. She watched in fascination and held out her hand as a butterfly landed on her outstretched finger.

Luna appeared, bounding through the crowd of creatures toward Ava and jumped into her open arms, licking her face.

The rest of the companions joined the animals; Casimir's bear Aro, Raine's wolf Sabriel, a gray marbled owl and Quinn's midnight black panther.

"They've come to honor their princess," Thorne whispered.

Ava stood still, holding Luna with tears in her eyes, fae warriors standing around her. They were surrounded by animals who had come for miles. Had come to see the princess who was lost. The one they've been waiting for to save their world.

She smiled at the creatures, heart warm at the affection they showed. Aro ambled close and bumped his head against her hip, saying hello with a low growl. She knelt and set Luna on the ground to scratch behind Aro's ears, kissing him on the head.

She looked around, surrounded by the animals and met eyes with the members of her party. They all regarded her with fascination as they took in the significance of the moment. News had spread quickly through the animals, and they had gathered, waiting for the opportunity to see her.

Aro continued to nudge her hand and she turned to Casimir who was looking at her like she was a puzzle he didn't know how to solve. Luna padded over to Casimir and rubbed against him, purring and chirping. He leaned down, scratched her head and she purred with contentment. He looked back at Ava, a sense of wonder on his face as he tried to make sense of what was happening. She held his gaze while Aro nudged her hand yet again.

The animals filtered away through the woods, leaving the way they came, until the group was left with their companions sitting around them.

Everyone looked at her, as if waiting for her to say something. "Well, that was.... weird." She smiled awkwardly.

39

They were back in the dining hall for dinner, sitting at the table with a feast in front of them. Ava had quickly bathed and changed, washing the swamp from her skin as she thought about what had been revealed. Cirilla had helped her don a simple white cotton dress with a floral pattern embroidered on the chest and the hemline, a wide leather belt accentuating her waist.

A part of her was excited and curious. What would it be like to be fae? To be a princess? The other part was terrified. She was the one who had to banish the daemon queen forever. No one else could do it. How in the world was she going to accomplish that?

Most of the others had changed as well, wearing simple tunics and pants after they had cleaned up. Everyone appeared exhausted and ravenous, the sounds of them eating and chatting filling the hall.

Ava sat to the right of her brother, across from Casimir once more. Raine was on her other side while Jorrar and Quinn had placed themselves next to Casimir. She glanced across the table

323

and saw he was stoic yet again, back to the cold general it seemed.

"Ava," Thorne spoke. "You're the only one who can banish Deidamia."

Her heart sped up as she sipped her wine. "I don't know how."

"We will teach you. And help you to do so," he replied.

Jorrar cleared his throat. "We don't know how to create new portals."

"Our library is old. Surely we can find information there," Thorne answered.

Ava looked at her brother. "Wait. If we're related. Why can't you do it?"

"Portal magic is curious. It is a rare magic that often skips generations. Our mother didn't have those abilities. Neither do I."

She pursed her lips. "Oh." After a moment, she asked, "Can someone explain how Deidamia and Andras got here in the first place? They aren't from Eorhan, right?"

"There was an old king who craved power," began Jorrar. "He was messing around with portals and accidentally summoned Andras. Andras promised him power if he allowed his queen and her armies into Eorhan."

Ava nodded. It was the same story her grandfather used to tell her.

"But Andras had tricked him and the moment he entered Eorhan, killed the king. The war went on for decades as they conquered both Igneothenia and Frosthaven before disappearing in pursuit of you it seems," he finished.

"So they knew I'd be the one who could send her back?" she asked.

Jorrar shook his head. "We don't know for sure, but it appears that way. They knew you were important at least. Important enough to pause their war and pursue you instead.

A lot of the history surrounding the early years of the war has been lost. Burned or destroyed."

"Why?"

"We don't know," Thorne answered. "My father... *our* father, wasn't invested in the history of our kingdom. In the years before he died on the battlefield, he went a bit mad. Firing librarians and destroying texts, seemingly for no reason."

Strange. Why would her father destroy books that could possibly help them defeat Deidamia? After thinking for a moment, she added, "The book at Grandpa's farm..."

"What about it?" Thorne replied.

"I think it has instructions on how to create and open portals. And Deidamia has it." She looked around at the table and caught Casimir narrowing his eyes at her.

"How do you know this? You informed us you couldn't read it," asked Thorne as he swirled the wine in his goblet.

She shook her head. "I don't know for sure, but there were pictures in it. Of portals and archways and symbols. That has to be why Grandpa hid it. To keep it out of their hands."

"And now they have it," Casimir said pointedly at her.

"I know that," Ava bit back, irritated with Casimir's moodiness.

"Maybe there's another copy," said Jorrar. "It wouldn't hurt to look."

"We should send you back to get it," said Casimir, still glaring at her from across the table. "Since you're the one who gave it to them in the first place."

Ava tensed, heart racing at the thought of getting anywhere close to that camp.

"No," said Thorne. "Their camp is too dangerous to infil-trate right now. We must find another way."

"What if there is no other way?" Casimir said, arms crossed as he glowered at her.

"Then we'll figure something else out." Thorne took a sip of wine, then clenched his jaw, obviously frustrated at Casimir's response. "Right now, entering that camp is off the table."

Ava couldn't take it anymore. The hot and cold. The glares across the table. She looked directly at Casimir. "What the fuck is your problem?"

The others tensed as he leaned forward. "You willingly showed the book to Andras. Now our ability to defeat our enemies is in their very hands."

"I. Didn't. Know," she seethed.

"Here we go again," Raine whispered from beside her.

"You've been giving us half-truths since the day we found you in the forest."

Ava steadied herself, taking a deep breath. "I've already apologized. To all of you. What more do you want?" Her voice rose. "I'm here now. And I'm going to help."

Thorne placed his hand on her arm. "That's enough you two," he said with irritation in his voice.

She huffed and crossed her arms, leaning back in her chair and looked at her brother.

Quinn whispered, "Well, she definitely has the Everwood temper."

Thorne turned to her. "I do *not* have a temper."

"It seems everyone here has a temper," Ava mumbled, glancing at Casimir.

"I don't," Raine blurted and Quinn stifled a laugh.

"Alright, stop," Jorrar intervened. "Arguing will get us nowhere. Ava will learn how to open and create portals... but first she must get her magic."

Thorne nodded, appearing cool and collected once more, though his fingers drummed on the table. "Yes. She must begin preparations for the journey."

"And how do you suggest she do that?" Raine asked. "Since we don't even know what it entails."

"We'll need to dig into the archives and see if we can find any information about the Elderoak," Thorne explained. "I'll have the scribes in the library start looking while Ava begins her training."

"Training?" Ava asked.

"We won't allow you to go without proper training." Thorne turned to her. "We'll assure you're ready."

"And who is going to do the training?" Raine asked.

"Casimir will."

"What?" Both Ava and Casimir said at the same time.

"I can't train with him." She looked at her brother. "He hates me."

Casimir scoffed. "She'll never learn." He turned toward Ava. "You almost shot Quinn earlier today because you refused to listen to me."

"I was scared," she shot back.

"This is war. You have no time to be scared, *princess*."

"Well, I've never been in a war before, *general*." She clenched her fists in her lap. "I don't—"

"Enough." Thorne stood up and leaned over the table, temper on full display. "That is exactly why you two are training together," he said, voice rising as he pointed at Casimir. "If you can't get along, our plan is doomed. So, *figure it out* and stop behaving like squabbling children. Training begins tomorrow. You're all dismissed."

"Fine," Ava said as she rose and turned on her heel.

As she was about to exit the room, she overheard Thorne say quietly to Raine, "Follow them and make sure they don't kill each other, please."

"Got it."

She strode down the hallway, steps echoing in the corridors, eager to get away from everyone and take time to think. Casimir stomped behind her and she called out to him as she walked. "Stop following me."

"I'm not following you. I'm going to my room which just happens to be next to yours, unfortunately," he bit back.

She groaned and kept walking, reaching the suite. The guards regarded her warily but opened the door and let her pass. She trudged through the living room and reached for her door when Casimir appeared in front of her.

"Move," she said.

"No." He crossed his arms.

"Cas, let her by," Raine said from behind them.

"You stay out of this," Casimir replied. "I'm not moving until you tell me why you're so angry," he said, staring down at her.

"You're joking right?" she replied. "Why *I'm* angry? Because I'm sick of you being nice one minute and the next acting like you hate me. Why don't you tell me why *you* are so angry?"

He glared at her as he kept his arms crossed. "You appeared out of nowhere and brought back our enemies. You let yourself get tricked and allowed them back. You can understand if I'm a little pissed off."

"You seem to be forgetting that I didn't even know of the existence of Eorhan or daemons or fae or any of this until just a couple months ago. How am I supposed to prevent myself from getting tricked by a daemon if I didn't even believe they were real?" She stepped closer, anger overriding logic as she got in the general's face. "Don't blame me for something that isn't in my control. You have no *idea* what I've been through," she said as she poked him in the chest with her finger. "Now let. Me. By."

He didn't move and continued looking at her, regarding her so intensely it took every ounce of will she had not to look away.

"Be ready at dawn tomorrow."

"Fine." She crossed her arms and tapped her foot.

Finally, he moved out of her way. She opened the door and slammed it closed, Raine's sigh the last thing she heard before she flung herself onto her bed and shouted into her pillow.

"Cas," Raine said after Ava slammed the door in his face. "Come sit, let's talk."

Casimir walked to the table and sat down, leaning back in his chair. Raine peeked his head out the door to ask the guards to get Cirilla and then walked back in and sat down across from him.

He looked at his best friend, waiting to be lectured.

"What's going on?" Raine asked him.

Casimir shook his head, drumming his fingers on the table. "I don't know."

"Look, I know you have a temper sometimes, but I've never seen you act like this. Are you alright?"

"I have no idea," he replied. "I just can't stop thinking about Elara," he whispered as he pulled out the fox figurine he kept in his pocket. He set it on the table and looked at Raine. Ava's appearance was reopening old wounds that he didn't want to examine again.

"It's not your fault, Cas. You must stop blaming yourself. And you can't blame Ava. She had nothing to do with what happened in the past. She wasn't even born yet," he answered.

The door opened and Cirilla entered. "You asked for me?"

"Yes. Could you bring us some wine?" Raine asked.

"Of course," she nodded and left the room.

Waiting for Cirilla to leave, Casimir answered, "I know. I'm not blaming her. I'm just... so angry."

"That Deidamia is back?" he asked.

"Yes."

Raine leaned back, crossing his ankle over his knee. "So am I. We all are."

"And you don't think Ava played a part in that?"

"Of course she did," Raine said, interrupted by Cirilla returning and setting down two goblets and a pitcher of wine. Raine thanked her, poured the two of them their drinks and sipped his, thinking for a moment. "Yes, she played a part in their return, but I don't blame her for it."

"How can you not? If she'd never found the portal or let herself get tricked, they never would have come back in the first place. We could have remained living in peace."

"Have we truly been living in peace, Cas? Her armies have been here ever since she departed. Sure, they haven't been able to conquer completely without her, but they've done plenty of damage. Ava arriving here with Deidamia and Andras in tow was fate. The only way we can truly be rid of them forever."

"How is it fate?" Casimir asked.

Raine shrugged. "You think it's a coincidence the one person who could banish Deidamia forever arrived with them? And the fact that she's our princess? This is big."

Casimir grunted as he sipped his wine and thought, unsure how to respond.

Raine leaned forward. "I know it's strange, but she's Thorne's sister. It makes so much sense. No one ever found Queen Aurelia's body and Ava looks exactly like her, and like Thorne. Lord Pellas had the ability to open portals, and everyone knows he opened one and fled, they just didn't know where to. Or that Aurelia was with him."

Casimir sighed and looked at his friend, picking up the wooden fox and placing it back in his pocket. "You truly like her, don't you?"

Raine smiled. "I do. A lot."

"Why?"

"She's funny and kind and cares about others. She's determined and stubborn. Fanya told me she ran to an injured hobgoblin last night and held his hand while he died. That she didn't even hesitate. And then when that soldier had Fanya cornered, Ava stabbed him and distracted him, saving her life."

"She really did those things?" Casimir asked, surprised. He'd been so caught up in battle, he hadn't known what else happened until Aro told him she was cornered.

Raine gave him a knowing smile.

"Why are you looking at me like that?"

"Because I know you don't actually hate her." Raine's smile widened. "I'm not an idiot."

Casimir grimaced. "Fine. I don't hate her."

"And?"

"And what?"

Raine began laughing. "I've known you for nearly eighty years, Cas."

"So?"

"Women don't usually fluster you," he said. "And Ava *flusters* you."

Casimir shook his head. "That doesn't mean anything."

"You pretend to hate her because you're scared," said Raine.

"No," said Casimir. "I don't even know her well enough to care one way or the other."

"Sure," said Raine. "You keep telling yourself that."

Casimir glared at him.

"Oh, this is going to be so much fun," said his friend. "And now, the two of you have to train together."

"You're relentless." Casimir rose and began to walk to his room.

"You think I'm relentless now?" Raine loudly said. "You haven't seen anything yet."

"Goodnight, Raine." Casimir entered his quarters and shut the door, the sound of Raine's laughter echoing in the living room.

Pacing in front of his fireplace, he realized Raine was right. Ava did fluster him. There was something about her that both irritated and intrigued him. For someone who was so nervous all the time, she sure knew how to stand up for herself when it came to him. She had no problem yelling back or arguing with him, though most others wouldn't dream of going toe to toe with the general.

For some reason, he liked it.

And the fact that she had jumped into action and helped during the battle? He'd assumed she was cowering under a table, not helping the injured or stabbing a daemon soldier.

Then there was the moment she disappeared in the swamp. He'd never felt panic like that before and had frantically searched until he found her being dragged under the water. He didn't even hesitate to rescue her and when he pulled her out, something in him had clicked.

Something he would ignore and not look at yet because they had a war to fight. And he had to get her ready.

40

$\mathcal{A}$va sat on the balcony of her bedroom, Luna curled up on the floor by her feet. Birds darted above her and chattered to each other as they landed in a nearby tree. She closed her eyes and tried to relax, listening to the sound of running water from the small brook below when a knock on her door sounded.

"Go away," she called, assuming it was Casimir.

"It's Raine," the voice answered. "May I come in?"

"Fine."

The door opened and Raine strode to the balcony and took a seat on the chair next to her. He handed her a goblet of wine and leaned back in his seat, looking at her.

"What?" she asked as she avoided his stare and remained facing forward, taking a sip of wine.

"I just wanted to check on you."

"Why do you care?" He remained silent but she could feel his eyes on her. She sighed. "Sorry, I—" She paused and pinched the bridge of her nose. "I'm just... I don't know..." she trailed off.

They sat quietly, sipping their wine before Raine spoke again.

"All of this is a lot to take in, I imagine."

The relief she felt at the acknowledgment of her situation was immense. "Yes." He waited for her to continue. "I'm just so fucking angry."

"What are you angry about?" he asked.

She turned and met his eyes. "Everything. But I think I'm mostly angry at my mother and that makes me feel horrible."

"Why?"

"Because she never told me any of this," she exclaimed, words now spilling out. "Not once did she tell me who I was. Who she was. She never explained her magic. Never told me *anything*." The reality of her circumstances weighed on her heavily as she continued to vent. "I was a normal, boring human just a couple of months ago. And now? In a matter of weeks everything changed. *Everything*. I'm some long-lost princess fated to save a whole realm. It's insane."

Raine nodded. "You're right. It is."

She couldn't stop as she continued her rant. "And now I have to train with the general who hates me. I don't even know how to fight. I'm not strong. I'm going to embarrass myself in front of all of you." She turned toward him. "I don't think I can do this."

"Listen," he responded, voice serious. "First of all, Cas doesn't hate you. He lost his whole family in the war and he's just being an asshole right now. Second, you aren't doing this alone. We'll help you. And we know you don't know how to fight. We're going to teach you everything you need to know." He turned in his chair and leaned forward, gaze intense. "You can do this."

"I'm scared," she whispered.

"Good," he answered. "Use that fear and channel it into determination." He scrutinized her face and paused, seeming to consider whether he should continue. "You know I can sense things."

She nodded.

"I can already sense your power," he said quietly. "And you aren't even fully fae yet."

"What does that mean?"

"It means that you're going to be strong," he replied.

She broke his stare and leaned her head back, closing her eyes. "That's terrifying."

He laughed. "I guess so. But it's also amazing."

She glanced at him. "You know... you're kind of scary when you're serious."

He laughed harder. "So I've been told. Don't worry, it doesn't happen often, dainty human."

"Dainty human?"

"It's your nickname." He shrugged.

Ava rolled her eyes. "Why?"

He smiled widely, humor in his eyes. "Because it irritates you and it's funny."

"Well, you won't be able to call me that forever."

"I'll think of something even better when you're fae."

"Great." She laughed quietly.

Raine rose from his seat. "I must be going. Duty calls and all that."

"Raine?" Ava asked. He paused and looked down at her. "Thank you."

He gave her a broad smile and ruffled her hair.

"Any time," he said as he left her bedroom.

Ava remained on the balcony for the remainder of the evening, pondering over what Raine had said. She felt bad for exploding at Casimir, knowing he must have been through horrors she couldn't even dream of in the war. She hadn't been able to control herself when she caught him glaring at her with so much ire. She was so angry.

But anger's real name was grief.

Though she had the answers she was looking for, who she was and where she came from, it had all come at a cost. Trauma that she refused to unpack, didn't want to examine. Couldn't face her friend's death or her own imprisonment. The violence she had already experienced and witnessed. So she tucked it away. Secured it in a little box in the back of her mind and locked it tight like she always did. It would be a distraction anyway. She needed to focus on what was to come, not the past.

As Luna continued to snore quietly on the balcony, Ava realized she loved it here. Sure, the swamp adventure and battle at the tavern were terrifying, but this new revelation and her brother, made her want to know more. She was making friends quicker than she ever had in her life.

She adored Raine. They seemed to click, and she felt a deep connection with him. Like she could tell him anything and he wouldn't judge her. She had never had a friend like him before.

Kai and Jorrar also seemed to accept her quickly without any qualms. Fanya had immediately warmed to Ava, her bubbly enthusiasm contagious. Even Thorne appeared elated she was here, and she longed to get to know him. Wanted to learn all about their parents and what he was like as a child. To explore what they may have in common. Two lost siblings reunited.

Quinn had started to warm up and if she and Casimir ever stopped arguing, she supposed she could see them becoming friends too. She admitted to herself she was attracted to him. That was another reason she was reluctant to train with him. It would be much easier with one of the others without the distraction of Casimir's amber eyes that always seemed to be watching her, or the way the corner of his mouth tipped when he smirked. Or the way he smelled.

But after Henry, she wanted nothing. She didn't know if she could ever open her heart to someone else again. It had always ended in disaster and she didn't think she could handle the devastation of heartbreak once more. Besides, she needed to focus on training and preparing for the journey to the Elderoak. Crushing on the general would be a distraction and chances were, he wouldn't want her anyway.

Overall, the fae in Monterre were friendly and she felt her soul awaken as she discovered she was accepted and fit in. As if the song she had been singing matched the tune of those around her. No longer out of sync.

It was what she always wanted, what she had longed for when she moved onto her grandfather's farm several months ago, seeking peace and healing. The tug she had been feeling was leading her here this whole time. Leading her back home.

So, she would stay. She would learn what it meant to be a princess, to be fae. She would train and complete the journey to access her magic.

And she would help her kingdom win the war and banish Deidamia forever.

EPILOGUE

"She escaped under *your* watch!" Deidamia screamed as she paced the floor. "Three of my silver serpents were murdered and our soldiers defeated!"

Andras bowed and kept his voice smooth. "My queen, the fae of Monterre have already become quite protective of her. We still have the book."

Deidamia whirled toward him. "The book is useless without her to wield it, you fool. You've failed me yet again. First, you let Pellas slip out of your fingers and now Ava has escaped. How could you let yourself be bested by a human?"

Andras remained calm, hiding his anger at the way she spoke to him. "I won't let it happen again."

"No." She approached him and grasped his face, nails digging into his cheeks. Warm blood trickled down his neck as she leaned close. "You won't. You will develop a new plan to recapture her."

"I will," he assured her and she let him go.

Mosshaven had been difficult to infiltrate, the silver serpents barely able to sneak into the capital with their small force. Andras had the power to speak through them and even see through their eyes. What he had witnessed at the pub had concerned him. Not only had the fae there welcomed her, The Bear seemed especially protective and had immediately stood at her side the moment Andras began speaking.

He wondered if they had figured out who she was. That she was King Thorne's sister and the only one with enough power to stop them. Deidamia and Andras had known the whole time. Had known who it was they followed into the human world one hundred years ago with the initial intent to kill Pellas and Aurelia, who was carrying the child prophesied to stop them.

Their plan had gone wrong and the portal into the human lands had dropped them somewhere far away. It had taken thirty years to find them and when they had gotten close to using Pellas' blood to make their way back to Eorhan, he took his own life.

Finding Ava had been easy and seducing her even easier. He barely had to use any of his magic to get her to trust him and everything had gone to plan until she escaped.

"Andras," his Queen said as she paced. "Find the girl and bring her back. If you are unable to capture her, kill her."

"We still need her to bring in the remainder of our forces, My Queen," he implored as he waltzed closer to her.

"Everything is going *wrong*," she seethed as her temper rose. "You promised me."

Andras stepped in front of her and caressed her face, attempting to soothe her. Her volatile temper would ruin everything if she couldn't control it. "I keep my promises, My Queen. You will have all the power you desire. You'll have your own world to rule, without the burden of your sisters."

She looked into his icy blue eyes and softened slightly. He leaned forward, his lips barely brushing hers. "We will rule together, you and I." He leaned in and kissed her deeply and she pressed into him, a small moan leaving her lips. He pulled back, brushed her hair from her face and said, "I will handle it."

She nodded, then turned on her heel and exited the tent.

They could possibly still win the war without bringing more of the army from Tarterius, the realm where Deidamia had to share power with her horrid sisters. Sisters who had beaten her and scoffed when she tried to rule alongside them. She wanted her own realm, far away from her corrupt family. She wanted Eorhan and he would ensure she had it.

Now that he and Deidamia had returned, they could continue their experiments on the creatures of Eorhan. Using their magic, they had been able to combine the blood of existing monsters and make them more powerful, more dangerous. They had even found a way to create beings with venom that nullified the fae's magic which would be vital in their success.

This should be enough to conquer the three remaining kingdoms, though it wouldn't be easy. Having Ava would ensure their success.

And so, Andras turned on his heel and exited the tent, preparing himself to plan the next step in their quest to rule. He would do whatever it took to get Ava back and kill anyone in his way.

AFTERWORD

Thank you for reading my debut novel, Whispers of the Elderoak. It means the world to me that you took a chance on a new indie author.

I thought I'd give just a little insight into how this book came to be and where the series is going.

Whispers started with a vague idea that bombarded me when I was obsessively playing Stardew Valley. I kept thinking "I want to write a romance book where a woman inherits a farm... but what if I make it fantasy?" That's how the Daughter of the Earth trilogy was born.

After months of planning, world-building, giant charts on dry erase boards, writing and rewriting again and again, Whispers finally came together.

I wanted something different than I've seen within the fantasy romance genre. I wanted older characters. I wanted a main character who struggles with her fears but is also capable of strength when she needs to be. I wanted a main male character who was honorable, kind and not morally gray. And I wanted a combination of deep emotional moments, action, and cozy scenes. I feel like I accomplished my goal with this book and I couldn't be prouder.

If you enjoyed Whispers, stay tuned for Journey to the Elderoak which will be releasing fall of 2025. If you're craving more romance, this is the book for you. Full of pining, tender moments, and relationship growth, it focuses on Ava's preparation to access her powers and her developing friendships and romance.

ACKNOWLEDGMENTS

Where do I even begin? To my very early beta readers: Mary, Kayla, Christine and Megan. The four of you literally transformed this book. You helped me take it from a floundering second draft to what it is today and I am so incredibly thankful for your willingness to help in this journey. A special thanks to Christine, my very first beta reader who went from stranger on Reddit to internet bestie, I couldn't have done it without you. Thank you for being honest, laughing with me and giving me the hard truths even if I didn't want to hear it. You will forever be my top writing partner. Don't worry, I saved that awful sentence to hang on my wall in commemoration of this book being published. Thank you to Matt, my late in the game writing buddy who helped me really dive into the emotions of this book and pushed me to dig even deeper. Your help has been vital in helping me become a better writer.

I want to thank my lovely editor, Laë, who not only carefully helped me edit my book to precision, but has been a cheerleader of this story from day one. Your passion and enthusiasm is contagious and I am so grateful for your support.

Thank you to my cover artist, H.M. Mast. Your creativity astonishes me. It's as if you plucked the cover from my brain and made it come alive. I will forever be amazed at your talent.

Thank you to all of my friends and family who humored me when I wanted to talk about my books, or who asked questions and supported me throughout this whole journey. You all immediately cheered me on from day one and didn't even balk at the notion that I wanted to write a book.

I want to thank Dalton, my husband, and my heart. You didn't even bat an eye the day I announced I wanted to write. You helped me brainstorm, listened to my wild ideas and even helped me with plot holes (sorry, I'm still not killing off that character). Thank you for your love, support and excitement and for going on this journey along with me.

Last but not least, I want to thank my readers. This literally could not have happened without you. Thank you for taking a chance on a brand new author and I hope you will continue to support my journey as you get to know the rest of Ava's story.

ABOUT THE AUTHOR

Katie is an author residing in Tulsa, OK with her husband, son and three troublesome cats. As a life-long bird and animal nerd (yes, she's the friend who everyone sends bird pics to asking what species it is), a lot of her books contain wildlife, animal companions and details of the natural world.

She writes stories full of friendship, romance, banter, and deep conversations all set within a fantasy setting.

When she's not writing, she's reading, hiking, gardening, birding, or daydreaming about even more story ideas.

www.km-gordon.com